JULIAN STOCKWIN

A SEA OF GOLD

HODDER

First published in Great Britain in 2018 by Hodder & Stoughton
An Hachette UK company

This paperback edition published in 2019

1

Copyright © Julian Stockwin 2018

The right of Julian Stockwin to be identified as the
Author of the Work has been asserted by him in accordance
with the Copyright, Designs and Patents Act 1988.

A CIP catalogue record for this title is available from the British Library

Paperback ISBN 978 1 473 64109 9

Typeset in Garamond MT by
Palimpsest Book Production Ltd, Falkirk, Stirlingshire

Printed and bound in Great Britain by Clays Ltd, Elcograf S.p.A.

Hodder & Stoughton policy is to use papers that are natural, renewable
and recyclable products and made from wood grown in sustainable forests.
The logging and manufacturing processes are expected to conform to
the environmental regulations of the country of origin.

Hodder & Stoughton Ltd
Carmelite House
50 Victoria Embankment
London EC4Y 0DZ

www.hodder.co.uk

'In quest of Fortune on the faithless Main /
Where Life's whole Comfort is the hope of Gain . . .'

Anon. NAVAL CHRONICLE 1801

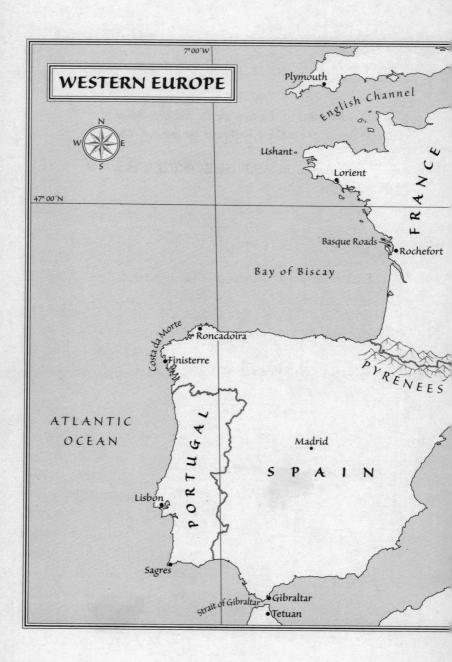

WESTERN EUROPE

7° 00′W

Plymouth

English Channel

Ushant

Lorient

47° 00′N

FRANCE

Basque Roads

Rochefort

Bay of Biscay

Costa da Morte

Roncadoira

PYRENEES

Finisterre

ATLANTIC
OCEAN

PORTUGAL

Madrid

SPAIN

Lisbon

Sagres

Strait of Gibraltar

Gibraltar

Tetuan

• Antwerp

Fondúco House;
Collingwood HQ

Cala
Figuera

4° 19′11″E

39° 53′N

Lazaretto
Island

MINORCA

Castilo de San Felipe

0   0.5
nautical miles

Saint Charles Point

• Leghorn

Port Vendres
• Cape Creux
Rosas

CORSICA

• Barcelona

MINORCA
• Port Mahon

M E D I T E R R A N E A N   S E A

0   100   200
nautical miles

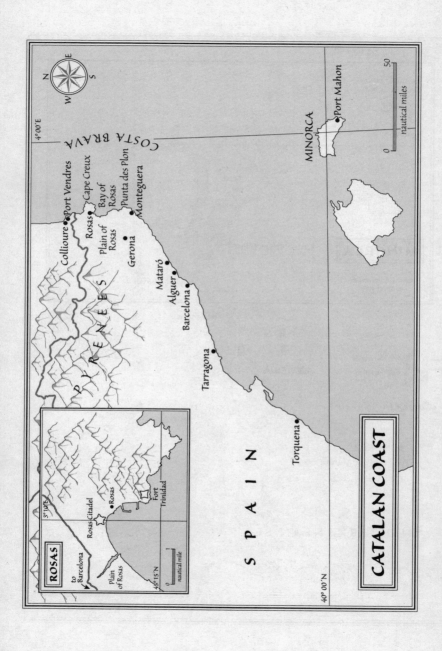

CATALAN COAST

N

COSTA BRAVA

4°00'E

Collioure
Port Vendres
Cape Creux
Rosas
Bay of Rosas
Plain of Rosas
Punta des Plon
Monteguera
Gerona
Mataró
Alguer
Barcelona

PYRENEES

Tarragona

Torquena

SPAIN

40°00'N

MINORCA

Port Mahon

50
0
nautical miles

ROSAS

3°10'E

to Barcelona

Rosas Citadel
Rosas
Fort Trinidad
Plain of Rosas

45°15'N

0
nautical mile

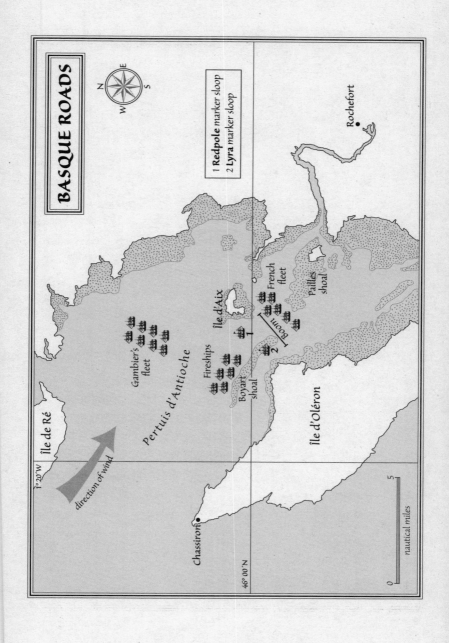

BASQUE ROADS

1 **Redpole** marker sloop
2 **Lyra** marker sloop

N E S W

1°20'W

Île de Ré

direction of wind

Chassiron

Pertuis d'Antioche

Gambier's fleet

Fireships

Boyart shoal

Île d'Aix

Boom

French fleet

Pailles shoal

Île d'Oléron

46°00'N

Rochefort

nautical miles

0   5

Dramatis Personae

indicates fictitious character

*Sir Thomas Kydd, captain of HMS *Tyger*, a.k.a. Tom Cutlass
*Nicholas Renzi, Earl of Farndon, friend and former confidential secretary

Tyger, ship's company
*Bowden	second lieutenant
*Bray	first lieutenant
*Brice	third lieutenant
*Clinton	captain, Royal Marines
*Darby	gunner
*Dillon	Kydd's confidential secretary
*Doud	petty officer
*Gilpin	midshipman
*Halgren	Kydd's coxswain
*Herne	boatswain
*Joyce	sailing master
*Lecky	able seaman
*Leech	temporary sailing master

*Maynard	master's mate
*Pinto	quartermaster's mate
*Poulden	petty officer
*Rowan	midshipman
*Scrope	surgeon
*Stirk	gunner's mate
*Tysoe	Kydd's manservant

Others

Allemand	French admiral based in Toulon
*Ashley	broker
*Bazely	captain of brig-sloop *Lynx*
Bennet	captain of brig-sloop *Fame*
*Bridgman	lieutenant colonel
Canning	secretary of state for foreign affairs
Castlereagh	secretary of state for war
*Cecilia	Kydd's sister and Countess of Farndon
Charles	archduke of Austria
Cochrane-Johnstone	Cochrane's uncle and share broker
Cochrane	captain of frigate *Imperieuse*
Collingwood	commander-in-chief Mediterranean
*Congalton	Foreign Office
Duhesme	French garrison commander, Barcelona
*Finkelstein	finance director, Thiers Oder merchant bank, Basel
*Fookes	MP, a.k.a. Prinker
*Friedrich	Markgraf of Skalvia, House of Haart
Gambier	commander-in-chief, Channel Fleet
Ganteaume	French admiral in Brest
Hammond	permanent under secretary of state for foreign affairs
*Harrison	treasury agent

Chapter 1

London, spring 1809

'My dears! So amiable in you to grace us with your presence,' purred Lucinda Matcham, eyeing Lady Kydd's sheer muslin dress, exquisitely ruched with silver ribbon. She turned to Sir Thomas Kydd, the impeccably attired naval captain in Town for the Season. 'And to have you attend, sir, a sea hero of the age – as shall have them all talking for a month, I do declare!'

It was no small coup to have been invited by the noted society hostess and Kydd bowed with a smile, quite aware of the picture he and Persephone made.

'You are acquainted with my particular friend, Lord Farndon, Mrs Matcham?' He gestured to the tall gentleman standing nearby with his wife, her handsome dark looks drawing admiring glances, too. Lady Farndon was Kydd's sister, Cecilia. He and Persephone were staying with them at their Mayfair town house.

The two men's friendship had sprung from their time before the mast together, many years before.

'Not as well as I should like,' Lucinda said, raising her quizzing glass, 'as it must be admitted he's too retiring in society for his own good. We sometimes don't see him for months on end, he rusticating on his estate as he's wont to do. You really should get him out more, Cecilia dear.'

The exquisitely furnished drawing room, with its gold mirrors and ornaments in the finest porcelain, resounded to a well-bred hum of polite conversation.

'I make it my purpose to bring together those at a similar *éclat* in society – I find it answers well in the article of social intercourse,' Lucinda continued.

Meaning those lately in the public eye, Kydd mused. Others would be mercilessly cut as their usefulness receded.

'Ah, here is Colonel Bridgman, late of Corunna,' she said, with suitable awe. 'He is reviving still from his experience, poor lamb! Have you met Sir Thomas, at all?'

'Dear lady.' The aristocratic officer bowed. 'Well I know this sea gentleman. He stood upon the quarterdeck of the last ship to leave upon granting deliverance to we still alive in that species of Purgatory.'

Their hostess watched in satisfaction as they shook hands in quiet remembrance.

Bridgman turned politely to Persephone. 'Have you ever been to Spain, Lady Kydd? With its mountains and deserts, not a prospect for a gentlewoman, I'm persuaded.'

'Rather more of Portugal, sir.'

'Oh?'

'As being promised a passage back to England upon Lisbon being taken by the French, a faithless brute left me to journey overland on foot to Oporto, an adventure I vow sets me beside those on the road to Corunna.'

'Goodness me. Did you ever think of confronting the wretch on your return?'

'I did so, Colonel – and as a measure of retribution I married him. And now he must do as he's bade.'

Others about the room glanced towards the burst of laughter resulting.

Lucinda put her hand on Kydd's arm. 'We always have a lively admiration for your Jack Tar, Sir Thomas. This night there's more than a few at my little gathering, you'll notice.' She swept across the room and ushered over a bemused gentleman. 'And here's one – I'm sure you've much to talk about!'

Kydd bowed politely to Mulgrave, first lord of the Admiralty. But what small-talk could he conjure to engage the attention of the brightest star in the firmament of the Royal Navy's administration?

Persephone came to his rescue. 'Sir, you've no conception how delightful it's been to have my husband to myself since he returned from Iberia.' Her dazzling smile was irresistible.

'Why, madam, it is the god of war who disposes such things, not my own humble self,' he answered smoothly.

Kydd had escorted the Corunna convoy with its cargo of suffering back to Plymouth and since then had been awaiting orders. The Admiralty, in turn, was looking to the government of the day to decide what the future held – a complete evacuation of the Iberian peninsula to cut losses or a forlorn seaborne support for Lisbon to keep Wellesley in his token toehold on the continent.

Before Mulgrave could go on they were interrupted by their hostess tinkling a silver bell above the noise of the gathering. 'Supper! Supper, children . . .'

The servants began refreshing glasses and the dice players from the rooms above processed down the stairs.

'Oh! I wonder who that is,' Persephone whispered, in a curious tone, to Kydd, who wheeled about to see a figure of striking patrician bearing. Inches taller than six feet, the man had unrestrained red hair and a lean but well-muscled body. His eyes darted about the room as if to search out a hidden enemy. Of the same age as Kydd, he was undeniably a handsome creature and held Persephone's attention.

'I've no idea,' Kydd answered gruffly, put out that his wife should make notice of another man.

'Er, do excuse me,' Mulgrave said, and joined the gentleman. Glances were thrown in Kydd's direction, then the first lord brought him over.

'A distinct pleasure, if not honour, to be the one to make introduction of you both,' Mulgrave said smugly. 'As it sets me to the blush who might first be introduced to whom.'

'Fire away, sir,' the red-haired gentleman said airily. 'As I've a notion while we've never met we do know of each other.'

'Very well. Lord Cochrane – of *Speedy* as was – do meet Sir Thomas Kydd of *Tyger*.'

So this was the Wolf of the Seas, as Napoleon was calling him, the officer famed for taking his tiny brig-sloop against a Spanish *xebec* frigate boldly to make boarding with every man he had, except the surgeon left on the wheel – and prevailing. Kydd had heard of the fellow but their wakes had never crossed.

He acknowledged the recognition with a bow. 'The honour quite mine, my lord.'

'The vanquisher of three frigates at once off Prussia? I must dispute your judgement, sir.' There was no change in the cool expression.

'Your cruise in *Pallas* has been well remarked, sir,' Persephone put in demurely.

Cochrane's spectacular career on the Spanish coast, with its rich haul of prizes, had taken place while Kydd was striving

4

to get his first frigate command manned and ready for sea, to take part in the climactic Trafalgar battle.

'I rather fancy *Imperieuse* is outshining even her, dear lady. Although what I shall do now the Spanish are no longer rightful prey I have no idea. What are you up to these days, Kydd?'

'Since the Cádiz Inshore Squadron is no more, I fear I'm wasting my days in idleness.'

'Which cannot in any wise be countenanced,' Mulgrave put in unexpectedly.

'Sir?'

'As you will be so informed in the very near future, gentlemen. The cabinet has decided that our reversal of fortune at Corunna should not be seen as anything more than a temporary check to our aspirations on the Continent. They desire to assume an offensive posture before the world and what better than to dispatch our two most distinguished frigate captains to the enemy shore to wreak havoc together? Gentlemen, your orders are being prepared, as I speak, for you to join Admiral Collingwood in Minorca for this very purpose.'

As they stared at him, he continued, 'And may I wish you both the greatest of good fortune in your endeavours?'

He took his leave and was lost in the throng.

'So – the Med again,' Cochrane said, with relish. 'To lay the French by the tail as is the duty of all red-blooded Englishmen.'

Persephone said nothing but her grip on Kydd's arm tightened.

'You're ready for the fray, Kydd?'

'*Tyger* and I both. You?'

'*Imperieuse* down to a split yarn to sail.'

'In Plymouth?'

'Aye.'

'And *Tyger*.'

'Then why do we wait?' Cochrane said imperiously. 'I've a crack frigate wants to smell salt water and rather fancy my pick of the berths in Mahon. As arriving first, that is.'

'I rather think not,' Kydd came back. '*Tyger*'s accounted a flyer in anything of a fresh gale, which is your Biscay and Atlantic both this time of year.'

'Oh? Then do recollect that *Imperieuse* knows the way, dear fellow.'

'And is Spanish-built and light in the scantlings, a sad liability in serious weather.'

Cochrane paused and narrowed his eyes. 'Why, this sounds very like a challenge, sir.'

'The first to make Port Mahon?'

'Hook touches bottom, stand down sea watches? I've ten guineas that it's *Imperieuse*.'

'And double that says it'll be *Tyger*,' Kydd found himself saying. Beside him came a sharp intake of breath from Persephone.

'My, and you're a chancer, Kydd. And I like that in a frigate man – you're on!'

Chapter 2

'It'll cost ye, cully!' the old man cried, leading a nervous piebald gelding into the dark stableyard, then backing it into the shafts of a gig. It was past midnight and Kydd had thought he'd never get away from the designing Lucinda Matcham. What had made him wager such a sum against a thorough-going seaman like Cochrane he had no idea but, be damned to it, he'd see it through – and every minute counted.

A sleepy-eyed ostler appeared and completed the rig, stepping back as they clambered aboard.

Kydd's plan was to cheat the hideous traffic of the day by a speedy trot through the near-deserted pre-dawn streets to reach the outer edge of the capital and its transport to the west. There, he'd hire a fast post-chaise and have the jump by half a night on Cochrane.

The old man lit the candles of the twin riding lanterns, then held out his hand meaningfully. He'd been gulled before by harum-scarum dandy prats of the fancy taking his beauties for a night-time dash of high bobbery. While these two didn't seem the sort, he wasn't taking chances.

Kydd found his price and was handed a whip. The horse was jibbing, snorting, and took some coaxing to bring out through the gates on to the highway, but Kydd was having none of it and tooled the gig around for the run to the bridge and away.

It was harder than he'd imagined: only some of the streets had any kind of lighting, and but for a sulky moon, he would have been forced to a walk. He brought the beast up to a trot and when the bridge loomed it was thankfully ablaze with pillared lights, but there was a marked thickening of traffic that had him weaving through perilously.

He glanced at Persephone next to him, bundled under a rug the ostler had provided. She smiled back at him happily and his heart went out to her. If there was any kind of adventure to be had with him, she'd do anything not to miss it.

The traffic gave out on the other side but so did the lights. Undismayed, Kydd cracked on, making good speed, the clatter of hoofs echoing back from darkened buildings with an occasional white flash of a staring face.

On one corner he misjudged the angle and the vehicle swayed and skidded, the horse whinnying in terror. Persephone leaned over gently and took the reins. 'Let me give you a rest, my darling,' she said, addressing herself to the terrified beast. It quietened at her touch and they stepped lively onward.

As they arrived the post-house was waking, and a hire was arranged in a remarkably business-like manner, which puzzled Kydd. After they'd started out at a smart clip Persephone, clutching his arm with sparkling eyes, laughed, 'Silly billy – he thinks we're eloping!'

They slept through the first stage snuggled under Kydd's boat cloak, then enjoyed the early spring English countryside slipping by until suddenly it was Exeter and the Plymouth road. They changed horses at Ivybridge for the last stage – Persephone was not going to leave him until she had to.

As they ground off, Kydd roused himself to consider his next move. *Tyger* was moored in Plymouth Sound, conveniently close to the Lambhay victualling yard. They'd arrive in the late afternoon, and if he was quick, he could get his warrants in for a quick storing foreign, and at the same time be at his watering. He'd long ago replenished powder and shot, which was the most time-consuming, and Bray, his first lieutenant, could be relied upon to have the ship in fine trim for a rapid departure.

Say, two, three days?

Kydd held his impatience as they wound down the last hill before he could get a good view of the sprawl of shipping. He sought out *Tyger*, serene and graceful, and gave a sigh as he always did when returning to her. And *Imperieuse* would be somewhere on this side of the harbour.

Leaving Persephone to ransack the shops for his cabin stores – and some warmer clothing for herself – he took a wherry out to his command, leaping up the side-steps in his eagerness. When he appeared unannounced, there was only a surprised Brice, officer-of-the-day, to meet him.

'Where's *Imperieuse* lie?' Kydd demanded.

Wordlessly Brice pointed with his telescope.

Kydd knew the ship but had never paid her much attention until now. An eighteen-pounder fifth-rate, like themselves, a rather high beakhead and more ornamentation than he favoured – but otherwise as near as possible a precise equal.

'Is her captain on board?'

'Um, no, sir. In London upon business, I believe.' It was the job of every officer-of-the-day in harbour to acquaint

9

himself with the ebb and flow of captains in case a senior officer was needed for some duty or other.

Kydd beamed. He'd done it! 'I'm to be told the moment he's back aboard.'

'Aye aye, sir.'

'Ship is under sailing orders, Mr Brice.'

This was a serious matter: every man now had the duty to be at his post when required to sail, his liberty curtailed, the Blue Peter at the masthead for all to see. Yet another of His Majesty's Ships upon some grave occasion of war.

The store demands went in, and Lambhay was used to ships in a hurry. An offer of extra hands from *Tyger* to expedite matters was duly accepted, and in the morning storing ship was put in train. And still no Cochrane!

Drake's Leat provided their water and the boatswain's requisites were delivered promptly before noon, gunner's spares and sailmaker's extras following soon after.

Persephone returned on board with Tysoe carrying parcels and set about Kydd's cabin, an affecting and enduring feminine touch for him in her absence.

'Sir?' The watch messenger stood in the doorway. 'Mr Brice's respects an' the captain of *Imperieuse* has just gone on board.'

Kydd hurried up to the quarterdeck to see Cochrane and others quickly going below. Minutes later her Blue Peter soared up. Kydd looked at his watch. Fourteen hours behind. A half-day at ten knots – that put *Tyger* ahead, something like twice the distance from Cádiz to Gibraltar!

The Tygers worked hard: it seemed their ship had been chosen for some desperate mission and they weren't about to let her down.

Not until the afternoon were victuallers seen around *Imperieuse* – Cochrane obviously hadn't been able to prime

Lambhay in time. Kydd almost felt sorry for him: he himself could look to putting to sea on the evening tide on the morrow and be somewhere south of Brest before his rival could even consider setting sail.

Chapter 3

The next day dawned. Kydd was gratified at the zeal the men were showing in turning to, and Bray's report that there were no stragglers adrift from liberty added to his good mood. At this rate he'd soon need to indicate he was ready to take on the Mediterranean station mail and—

'Sir. *Imperieuse* is getting under weigh,' Brice informed him, lowering his telescope.

'What? Let me have that!' Kydd gasped, snatching the glass. There was no doubt about it: the fo'c'slemen were winning their anchor and others stood ready at the masts to lay out and loose sail.

Her ensign and Blue Peter whipped down in perfect synchrony and sail blossomed fore and aft.

'She's anchors aweigh,' Brice said unnecessarily.

In stately progress *Imperieuse* was outward bound for her war station, a noble and inspiring picture.

'Damn it! What the . . . How's he managing that?' Kydd spluttered. Was the devil taking the chance to put out without a proper storing, forcing his men on short canny when it ran out?

'Er, what's that, sir?'

'Gets to sea, the next day he makes it to here! No victual-ling foreign, watering – he can't do it!'

'Captain Cochrane? Why, it's no mystery, sir.' Blinking in confusion at Kydd's sudden show of temper, Brice stammered, 'I was in the telegraph office at the time and understand he sent word to his first lieutenant to ready the ship for sea for when he arrived and—'

'The slivey toad!' Kydd ground out. A neat trick that turned the whole thing on its head. Cochrane was perfectly entitled to make use of the system for an impeccably valid purpose – but why hadn't he thought of it first?

'Sir?' Brice gasped.

'Ah, it's not as if to say . . . You'll keep this to yourself, but there's a wager between us as to which ship will down anchor in Port Mahon first. That is where we're headed, to join Admiral Collingwood's flag.'

'Oh, I see, sir.'

It was all around the ship in an hour. And while Kydd paced up and down the deck, men got out of his way, feeling for their captain.

In the hours after *Imperieuse* had disappeared around Rame Head on her way to the Mediterranean, a procession of well-wishers approached the quarterdeck.

Master's mate Maynard swore that he and a pair of quartermasters could be trusted to re-stow the hold to set *Tyger* half a foot deeper by the bows, which would increase the bite of the forefoot when beating to windward.

The sailmaker produced a set of topsails he'd been saving for when the current ones wore out. New sails didn't 'bag': taut and flat, they took the wind more powerfully.

But the knowing old sailing master came up with the best

trick. 'We catches the earlier tide. It'd be night but in this freshening nor'-easterly we'd be fair for Ushant in one board.' Unsaid was the prospect of threading through the mass of shipping at anchor, a delicate enough matter in daylight but in the dark a hair-raising undertaking.

Kydd bade farewell to his wife by the light of the conn, too distracted to do more than wave at the indistinct figure in the wherry pulling away, guiltily hearing her faint cry borne to him on the night breeze.

Having previously taken the bearings of the nearer vessels, he made a cast to larboard with headsails spread and, in the crepuscular gloom, gathered way for the open sea. An unlit merchantman was laid to starboard before *Tyger* luffed up to scrape past a larger Indiaman, bringing cries of alarm from her deck.

Most ships were wind-rode at their cables, in this respectable breeze nuzzling into the wind and all facing in the same direction. But an odd-looking jackass barque with, contrarily, two anchors out, was fouling their track. Falling under its stern, Kydd lost his picture of the relative positions of the others, which, from the deck of *Tyger*, resembled overlapping blocks of shadow. Now it was all up to the lookouts, who could give warning only of minutes.

He had men in the foretop and on the fore-deck, as well as a pair lying on the beakhead gratings under the bowsprit looking up and forward to catch the looming black silhouette of rigging against the sky. All on the upper deck peered fearfully ahead.

It was over quite suddenly, with the glimmer of open water before them and the comforting sight of the Eddystone Light well out to welcome them to the deep sea.

Cochrane had the best part of a day start now. What would he do with it?

The wind was fair for the south, both would benefit, but there was one move Kydd could make. As far as he knew, Cochrane had never seen service in the Brest blockade. The frightful tangle of reefs and skerries off the Goulet was foreign to him and he'd no doubt take the passage that virtually all mariners used – around the lonely outlying island of Ushant.

Kydd would instead pass inside, braving the formidable chain of granite isles centred around the Île-Molène that reached to the mainland. This was dead foul for his course, but for those with the nerve – and the light of day – it meant a possible halving of the distance to the Goulet.

Dawn brought a strengthening of the wind, now a blustering north-easterly and a piercing touch of winter still about it. With the angling swell it was a trial for those on deck, but Kydd wasn't in the mood to indulge their comfort. All sail conformable to the conditions was set, with not a reef furled anywhere, the canvas hard and taut, the rigging humming at a high pitch. An exhilarating but unnerving rush.

Tyger's bow was shouldering aside the surging combers with contempt, her deep pitch and roll in satisfying harmony with the ocean. *Imperieuse* with her finer entrance at the bow would not be so comfortable with this weather, but Cochrane knew her well and would be husbanding his efforts for the transit of Biscay. All the time, then, it was possible *Tyger* was hauling her in.

Towards the middle of the forenoon the sprawling, over-lapping low islands were raised inside the distant soft hues of storm-battered Ushant. Startlingly pale beaches, light-grey sea-washed rocks turning dark and brooding above the tide-line – but with the wind fair there was no hanging back.

For the cost of an hour or two's intense navigation they were through. Not much further on they had the satisfaction of surprising a brig-sloop of the Brest Inshore Squadron taken aback by the appearance of a frigate from where no cautious captain would go.

There was now little scope for other trickery, simply a hard beat across Biscay to the tip of Spain before rounding it for the passage south to Gibraltar.

The north-easterly, however, had other ideas. Point by point it veered until the ill-tempered bluster was abeam. The Atlantic swell directly in its teeth spent its white crests in streamers of spindrift thrown backwards while losing nothing of its spite. But *Tyger* was well able to stand against it, even if the drenching spume from larboard and the deep swell remorselessly from starboard held her to a never-ceasing roll that was stiff and wrenching.

As the day wore on the wind shifted further, and before they were halfway across the notorious bay, they were headed. Now more of a southerly veering westerly, they could never keep to a direct course for Finisterre no matter how close they clawed to the wind.

It was decision time. Most masters would wear about and head to sea on the larboard tack, as far out as they thought it was safe, then go about on the other tack to reach for the south. This prudence, though, had a penalty. It would be dead-reckoning all the way with no sight of the sun through the grey scud, and they'd be giving the deadly Costa da Morte seaboard a particularly wide margin to leeward before they moved.

Kydd had been in these waters in the same kind of blow and knew Finisterre – the 'end of the earth' – well. And there was one more trick up his sleeve. He knew his men, he knew *Tyger*. Instead of a long board out to sea, he'd make a much better approximation of their course by several tacks through the wind and deliberately heading for the iron-bound coast.

It would be fraught with peril but the saving of miles under the keel could pay off.

Going about in such conditions needed furious hauling and split-second timing.

Through salt-sore red eyes *Tyger*'s company raised the northern coast of Spain, barely visible through the wind-torn spume and fret. And, as he'd known, it was visible for miles out to sea in daylight, due to the betraying band of white at the base of the crags as the furious Atlantic waves exploded against land. It was a sight that had stayed with him since *Tyger*'s terrible escape the previous year, chasing an enemy frigate in a storm and becoming entrapped on this coast.

'Close with the coast, Mr Joyce,' he told his sailing master. 'I mean to know where we are.'

It turned out to be just to the east of Roncadoira, its weathered and knobbled heights distinct and clear. Estaca de Bares, a dangerous headland flung well out in their path, lay not so very far on. But that was part of his plan.

'Hands to 'bout ship,' he ordered. Knowing where he was and confident just how close to the wind that *Tyger* could do – five and a half points in the best conditions – he was going to make a triangle out to sea of just the right length to raise Finisterre on the return leg, cutting to a bare minimum their distance over the ground.

In the late afternoon they'd made it, but clear of the infamous cape they caught the full blast of the south-westerly, which they fought like heroes.

Not for Kydd the long reach seawards to give a safe offing, he was doing it the hard way, tack by tack southwards and in sight of land. As darkness drew in the frigate reluctantly stretched out for sea-room. He was not going to risk complex sail handling aloft where a missed handhold could send a man into the sea for a lonely death in the wastes of the night.

No doubt Cochrane would rely on hard-driving sail handling and meticulous trimming to wring every knot from *Imperieuse* but this could only make a difference on long uninterrupted boards well out to sea at the cost of miles further to sail.

Chapter 4

The morning saw *Tyger* lay Cabo da Roca to larboard – and an outlying frigate of the Lisbon squadron that could give them no news of *Imperieuse*. Was this because they'd passed her during their fight south? Or was it that, for any one of a number of reasons, that frigate had not sighted her?

With the wind shifting ever more to the west as they shaped course for Gibraltar around Henry the Navigator's Sagres, they could now stretch out close-hauled on one board.

Kydd would have given much to know where Cochrane was. He'd tried everything but nearly a day to make up was asking a lot. The likelihood was that by now *Imperieuse* was anything up to two hundred miles or more ahead through the Gibraltar strait, on her way to Minorca and victory.

But it was not over yet!

The south-westerly eased the further they converged on Gibraltar until the balmy influence that seemed to emanate from the Mediterranean enfolded them. At thirty-six degrees of latitude precisely, the old Moorish harbour and privateer nest of Tarifa firmed out of the haze ahead and they shaped course towards the Rock.

The evening was coming on when the winds dropped away even more. They entered the strait in a warm breath from the south-west, fair for the entrance to the inland sea, and before long the great leonine shape of Gibraltar loomed to larboard. Kydd had no intention of calling on the port admiral there and kept well clear, putting *Tyger* closer to the African shore.

Then from the main topmast head came an unbelieving shout and in a trice the deck dissolved into a chaos of cheers.

'What the blazes—'

'*Imperieuse* – she's been sighted, the shabs!'

With an African dusk settling they saw the frigate near becalmed in the lee of Ceuta, directly opposite Gibraltar. It took little guessing to work out what had happened.

They had indeed hauled in the crack frigate. Cochrane had thought to save himself an hour or two in Plymouth by taking in minimum water but the gale had extended his time at sea. He was paying for it now, obliged to water at Tetuan, the usual fleet supply near Ceuta – and in the spell of a counter-current to the constant inward-flowing waters of the strait. With a working wind he could escape its clutches but, as Kydd had experienced himself, if the gods decreed otherwise *Imperieuse* would go nowhere.

Cochrane was doing his best. He had all his boats out towing, desperate to reach the main channel and its eastward current but *Tyger* had both the ghosting breeze and the current in her favour.

As a violet dusk closed in, *Tyger* left them to their labours and slipped deeper into the Mediterranean night.

But they lost all wind during the dark hours and in the morning a glassy expanse of water and motionless hanging sails mocked them and their pretensions as a sea creature. The calm would not last for ever: such a state was often local to an area. Others in the distance might catch a breeze while they lay unmoving.

Imperieuse appeared above the horizon, an impossibly beautiful sight, caught and bathed by the dawning light, but maddeningly with some wafting zephyr bringing her up on *Tyger*. Dismayed, the Tygers watched as their rival, some five miles off, stood on while they remained in impotent stillness.

Hours later, with Cochrane hull down ahead, a puff and flurry set lines rattling and sails waking in fretful billows. *Tyger* was away once more – and the race was back on.

'All canvas the barky can spread,' Kydd roared.

It took half the morning to drape *Tyger* with 'sail' in every conceivable place in the rigging and a chuckle at her forefoot was their reward. But light-weather sailing in no way suited *Tyger* and *Imperieuse* drew ahead even further.

As the day progressed the breeze strengthened – now a Levanter from the east. That meant bringing in all their improvised sail, which had been set for a following wind. By early afternoon they were bowling along, *Imperieuse* still in sight, and in the morning *Tyger* had the satisfaction of seeing the frigate not a mile ahead.

It was becoming as close a race as was possible: two evenly matched ships of the breed with prime crews brought to the pinnacle of perfection. There could not be a soul with a drop of salt-water in his veins who would not be moved by the spectacle, and the decks of both were lined with excited seamen.

Tyger drew nearer, and as the noon meal was piped, she came abeam – but not one of her company wanted to go below.

Then, Minorca a day's sail away, the wind dropped and the exhilaration of the rush with it.

And over on the northern horizon a sail intruded into the

perfectly even line. It could be an innocent trader, a friendly patrol vessel or, conceivably, the enemy. In all cases their duty was plain: to run it down and challenge.

Imperieuse was closer, but if she broke off to go, the race would be *Tyger*'s. Would Cochrane do it or ignore the intrusion?

The answer came in a hoist of flags.

'Sir, "Investigate strange sail".' It didn't need Maynard's shocked report to tell Kydd that Cochrane had trumped him. With seniority of a bare eighteen months he had every right to order *Tyger* to perform the task – and lose the race.

Disbelieving cries rose from the seamen on deck. It was the end of the contest: who knew how long the business would take?

Kydd fought down mutinous thoughts. He could claim a foul, but a shrewd opponent, like Cochrane, would undoubtedly say that in a chase of this practical nature, anything and everything that a frigate would encounter in the usual run of its service would be a valid occurrence, and this must count as any other.

'We go,' he choked, and obstinately looked away from the other ship.

They'd hardly put down the helm when there was a yell of disbelief, which made Kydd wheel about in surprise.

Aboard *Imperieuse* they were bracing yards around – the ship was heaving to! In a gesture of sportsmanship Cochrane was throwing away his advantage and waiting for Kydd to finish his mission before resuming the race.

Chapter 5

As it turned out the vessel was a harmless brig-trader from Malta. When *Tyger* returned, her rival was waiting and, spreading their wings, the race was on again.

Minorca firmed out of the haze as the two ships stretched out but the breeze was dying, and as they converged at the eastern end of the island to find entry, it was impossible to choose between them.

Frustratingly, as they moved slowly forward together towards the distant outline of the ruins of Castilo de San Felipe at the narrow entrance to the grand harbour, the bane of all mariners chose to make its appearance: fog, tenuous at first, then swallowing everything to a blank soft white in every direction. It had the chill of trepidation, of unseen disaster, about it.

Beads of condensation formed on lines and rails, and the only sound was the quiet ripple of their small way through the water.

The usual course was to anchor until it dissipated – with scant steerage way, there was little to be done to avoid a collision. Kydd gave orders to prepare to anchor and saw in the ghostly grey the silhouette of *Imperieuse*, Cochrane about to do the same before they disappeared into the thickening bank.

But for some reason his thoughts turned to when, as a young lieutenant, he'd served in the old *Tenacious* in this part of the world, and an idea sprang into life that quickly brought a grin and a deep chuckle.

Port Mahon harbour used warping to bring ships through the few-hundred-yards wide entrance into the spacious but landlocked port. This obviously was not possible in the fog and they must wait for it to lift before they could pick up the warping lines and enter. Who knew what kind of confrontation might then erupt as each vied to be first?

But he'd noticed something. The very slight wafting breeze with the fog was from the south-east – directly up harbour, which he remembered was, unusually, a straight line on a bearing precisely north-west.

Why not sail in? Hazardous to say the least but it was only a mile and he could anchor past Lazaretto Island, which was always left clear: there'd be no others on the move in this fog. And to safeguard his progress he'd have boats out ahead on either bow with a messenger line that could signal 'bear off', if they strayed too near the cliff-like shore.

Yes!

The master turned grave when he heard of the plan but grudgingly fell in with it as it would be a capital exploit to include among his other salty yarns.

The boats' crews tumbled into their craft in roaring good spirits but were soon quieted. Kydd needed silence to hear of any danger and also to avoid unwelcome discovery by an officious port authority.

All he had to do was leave the southerly coastline to larboard, and as soon as they made Saint Charles Point, stand off a couple of cables and follow his compass. Thankfully the coast was steep to and the boats had no difficulty in leading *Tyger* onward to the sea-mark.

Tendrils of mist brushed across him as they glided on at a slow walking pace, sounds of the land on the air, carrying far in the fog.

It was working!

Almost as an anticlimax the starboard cutter signalled the finality of Lazaretto Island and Kydd could come aside to bring *Tyger* to her anchor.

Not only had they stolen a march on *Imperieuse* but he'd demonstrated that he was the equal in daring to the legendary Cochrane. All he had to do now was stand down his men from sea watches and wait for the fog to lift to allow his rival to sail into Port Mahon.

It lasted until nearly midday when a whisper of breeze ruffled the waters, the whiteness thinned – and vanished.

And there on their beam, as bold as could be, lay His Majesty's Frigate *Imperieuse* peacefully at anchor.

Kydd gave a tight smile. The same trick! And, with no possibility of ever telling which was first in Port Mahon, the honours had to be shared between them.

Chapter 6

Fondúco, Minorca

Cochrane and Kydd, about to make their number to the commander-in-chief, waited in a reception room of the pleasant, spacious house Collingwood had taken as his centre of operations and quarters ashore.

'So, sir. Have you ever been here before?' Cochrane said, easing the stock of his full-dress uniform. 'Used to be ours in the old war.' He flicked idly at a chair tassel with the tip of his sword scabbard.

'As a l'tenant after the Nile in Duckworth's Minorca invasion fleet,' Kydd responded. Perhaps it wasn't appropriate to bring forward that his undercover initiatives ashore had been decisive in the successful outcome.

'Hmm.'

Cochrane didn't appear particularly interested in his experiences, so he asked politely, 'And you?'

'Ah, well. I took in as prize a French 74 here to Mahon and they saw fit to give me my step to commander and *Speedy*, so I suppose it has its memories.'

'And I honour you for them, my lord,' Kydd said sincerely. 'As with your cruise in *Pallas*. I've heard your ship's company will sail with you through the gates of perdition after that first commission.'

'Oh, a fine set of fellows, I'll grant you,' he said distantly, now fiddling with his sword knot.

It was difficult to make out what was going on: why was this legendary fighting captain all but ignoring him? Did their rivalry in the race conceal a deeper motive? Was it jealousy of Kydd's reputation? Whatever was behind this, it was making it damned awkward – and they had to work out a professional relationship, Cochrane being just the senior.

Kydd's thoughts were interrupted by Collingwood's flag captain appearing at the door. 'He'll see you now,' he said apologetically. 'Not so spry as he was and you arriving without so much warning . . .'

They entered together, bowing respectfully as the admiral got heavily to his feet. 'I bid you both a good day, gentlemen,' he said, wheezing a little but with a broad smile of welcome. An equerry hovered by his elbow. 'I do confess that while you were expected per my requiring I was much taken by the manner of your arriving, magicked out of the clouds, as it were, and when the mists cleared there you lay in perfect innocence.'

'Sir,' Kydd responded, picking up on 'requiring' – Cochrane merely murmured something indistinct.

'And a mort quicker than I've a right to expect,' Collingwood added, with a dry chuckle.

'You sent for *Imperieuse*, sir?'

'I requested you both, my lord.'

Cochrane raised an eyebrow but said nothing.

'As your last cruise in these waters leads me to suspect that I might expect double the enemy's confusion should I unleash two wolves on the fold, so to speak.'

Kydd watched Cochrane's expression: there was no change in the studied polite concentration. Why had he mentioned his own ship only?

'A damned important business, I've to tell you both,' Collingwood said, with a slight frown, looking from one to the other. 'My lords of the Admiralty desire that we move actively against the enemy as token that we're not abandoning the Spanish people. The navy is, as always, best placed for this sort of thing.'

'*Tyger* will do her duty right willingly,' Kydd responded.

'As will *Imperieuse*, of course,' Cochrane added, with an irritatingly languid air.

'Then I shall give you the widest latitude in my orders to act as you will in the matter,' Collingwood responded. 'Do you care to work as a pair, French style, or more independently?'

'To work as a team seems to me the most effective in a situation like this,' Kydd said, glancing enquiringly at Cochrane.

'As you will,' was the reply, after a brief pause. 'Provided always we're not discommoded in our several endeavours.'

To Kydd it went without saying that not only was two a force multiplier but there would be many occasions when a second on the scene could form an invaluable watch-guard, deterrent and seaward defence while the other set about his task with impunity.

'Then so shall it be.' Collingwood regarded them speculatively for a moment, then went on, 'You're under my direct orders and have no purpose other than the ruination of the enemy's coastal trade and their means of protecting it, together with the severing of all possible forms of communication employed by the French.'

He gave a quick smile, and continued drily, 'Which is to say that, in addition, any Spanish offering annoyance to the

French deserves your wholehearted support, of course. Do take a few days to fettle your ships and I'll have your orders prepared in accordance.

'Oh, Captain Kydd, you'd oblige me much in the little matter of a transport of sorts. If you'd be so good as to return in an hour?'

Chapter 7

Outside, Cochrane hesitated, then turned and strolled into the well-kept garden through a side gate. Kydd followed.

At this height the harbour in its full four-mile length was an impressive sight, a brilliant emerald rather than the blue-grey of the outer seas.

Close in to the left was where the British fleet moored; Kydd remembered it as Cala Figuera, or 'English Cove', named for the numbers of sailors on liberty there and its use as a watering place. The dockyard and arsenal were out of sight along the opposite, northern, shore, including the odd eight-sided Illa Pinto careening wharf.

Kydd stood beside Cochrane as he surveyed the scene. Then, without warning, he turned to Kydd. 'I don't believe I've yet given expression to my admiration for the manner in which you disposed of that coxcomb Rowley,' he said, with feeling. 'A repulsive weasel, the villain.'

'You heard?'

'I did. Though I was in the Med, it didn't prevent me hearing the gossip. What's the rogue doing now?'

'Retired on grounds of ill health, I'm told,' Kydd said.

'These chuckle-headed loons, wished on us by working of interest or influence, are a curse on the service, don't you agree?'

'As those giving the interest should take care to favour the character who can best reflect back talent for their preferment. It worked for Nelson.'

Cochrane looked at him with an unreadable expression. 'You stood for Parliament in the Tory cause not so long ago, did you not?'

'Tory as the lesser of several evils.'

'You know I'm member for Westminster as a Radical?'

Kydd did: there were tales of Cochrane's hot-headed rebukes of the highest in the land, which he'd got away with for being a people's hero but which had made him enemies, among them the influential Earl St Vincent. Service gossip had it that, even after the outrageously improbable victory of the brig-sloop *Speedy* over a full-blooded frigate, he'd managed to offend the Admiralty sufficiently to be denied either promotion or another ship, staying on the beach in idleness through some of England's darkest hours.

'Then you'll accept how I take so against all forms of jobbery and influence-peddling, those utterly corrupt practices of plying the state's servants with Mammon to grease the wheels. Hallowed by the generations but nothing good ever comes of it.'

On the face of it a noble and principled stand – but Cochrane was a lord, a hereditary aristocrat who owed his position in life to the very practice of placement he was condemning. And in his youthful absence he'd been kept on the books of ships commanded by his relatives – false muster – until he finally went to sea as midshipman at eighteen, making lieutenant indecently fast by those very same corrupt practices.

In Kydd's eyes it was hypocrisy. 'Then, for instance, when a worthy but unconnected man of talent is brought forward by an act of influence it should be morally condemned?' he challenged. In his case it had been Nelson himself who had seen Kydd promoted post captain into a frigate but he wasn't about to flaunt it.

'You mean a foremast jack who finds himself on the quarterdeck? I've heard of such but they're a sad lot. I pity 'em,' Cochrane said dismissively. 'Tarpaulins to a man, show their breeding whatever they do, and will never amount to much.'

'Oh?'

'Your lower orders – it's not their fault they're ground down, need strong discipline and so forth. It's the world's doing with its wicked ways. Without they have the same chances as the nobs, then their views and habits are unformed, graceless, ignorant who'll never find a place among the *politesse de coeur*. They're victims of our fashion of living no less.'

Kydd bit back an angry reply but for the moment allowed that the man held his views sincerely and would have no experience of the level of society in which Kydd had his origins. That he took a Radical stand against injustices high and low was to his credit, if ill-timed and ingenuous. 'My lord, I thank you for opening your mind to me. I feel we understand each other the greater.' At the right point he'd reveal something of his own background, but not yet.

'And now we move against the French,' Cochrane murmured. 'A return to the lists for me, but you?'

'A modicum of entertainment on the northern coasts, Bilbao, Santander.'

'Um. A good start, then. *Imperieuse* will open play by paying a visit to some old haunts to see if there's been changes.'

Kydd waited. Was that an invitation to accompany?

Cochrane continued to survey the harbour vista calmly, his

hand on the hilt of his sword, unconsciously in the pose of a warrior.

'Er, should we pair up for the cruise, do you think?' Kydd said carefully. There could be no doubt who would be in charge, even though it was a loose enough arrangement that the formality of written orders would not be required, but it did need spelling out.

'You?' Cochrane said, in mild surprise. 'I can't see why. The Catalonian shore is where the action's to be. I'm heading north to the border. Why don't you sail south to Mataró, or similar, see if the Dons are up to anything?'

'And a rendezvous in a week or so.'

'Why?'

Kydd held his temper. 'As we'll both have knowledge of what's about, we'll have a chance to choose a strike where best to fluster the enemy, singly or together.'

'If you wish it.' The tone was offhand.

Was this resentment at sharing the glory or a more personal dislike? Or was he just waiting until he felt he could trust Kydd? At the very least, it seemed Cochrane was going to act the lone wolf for the moment. Kydd would fall in with it now and do what he could on his own.

'You'll want to head back to His Nobs, will you not?' Cochrane said dismissively. 'Your delivery job?'

Chapter 8

'Ah, yes,' Collingwood said, wiping his forehead wearily. 'I can't pretend other than that your arriving at this time is anything less than opportune, Captain. One of these irksome tasks that come my way has to be attended to without delay.'

'Sir?'

'I desire you shall convey a sum in specie to our treasury agent in Tarragona. As you know, it is usual to transport bullion in a frigate and I have none in Minorca at the moment. If you'd be so obliging . . .'

'Aye aye, sir.'

'In subvention to the Spanish Catalonian Army, but this will not concern you. Delivery to the treasury agent in the port is all that's required. You've shipped bullion before?'

'Yes, sir.'

'Then you'll know the procedure. A day's sail only, and return.'

Collingwood's 'without delay' meant that Kydd's return to *Tyger* did not result in liberty to both watches but a shift to an alongside berth at the dockyard. He told Lieutenant

Bowden to attend to the details for, apart from the drain on his time, if he took charge in person it would draw attention to what was afoot.

The actual lading of specie was in several long wooden cases, mysteriously black-lettered in Prussian script, encircled by three Treasury seals. They'd been brought ashore earlier from *Argus*, a 64, and had been under guard since, awaiting a frigate. The captain of marines charged with this was out of sorts, having been led to expect nothing much more than an overnight watch of the pirate's ransom and was only too happy to be relieved of it under signature.

With the cargo struck down below in the cable tiers and four sentries on watch and watch, *Tyger* put to sea for the short passage to Tarragona.

Kydd *had* shipped bullion before but that had not been genuine, merely a blind for the real article. This was unquestionably actual specie, coin of the realm in all its quarter-ton presence. Just what did it look like? Pieces of eight in a silver avalanche? Neat rows of King George crowns? Discreet rolls of gold guineas? The cases didn't betray movement within of any kind – could this mean they were packed with brightly gleaming bars of gold?

His was not to question, only to make sure that it got into the hands of the Treasury agent for its ultimate purpose. Subvention was aid to a foreign power, but Kydd knew that this was another word for bribery – payment to do the fighting for Britain in return for hard specie.

How much was he carrying? He'd signed under the bald statement that he was to freight under seal a Treasury shipment numbered as per margin in accordance with regulations and instructions in force at this time for the conveying of same. No mention of its value.

In a way it was a mundane, uninteresting task for no privateer or pirate would be insane enough to attack a frigate, and if a ship-of-the-line or other made to take him regulations were clear: he had to shun any form of engagement and simply run.

An easy overnight passage, into a wistful sunset and a darkling sea, then night, moonless but a startlingly bright star-field overhead that seemed low enough to touch. And treasure aboard that probably amounted to more by far than the lifetime's pay of every officer on his ship . . .

The Catalonian coast was in sight with the dawn and, under easy sail, *Tyger* ran down the latitude of Tarragona and raised the settlement mid-morning. It was a nondescript, sprawling township where the rumpled hills met the sea and a vast inland plain. The port was a simple facility: no bay but a single long wharf set upon a mole with buildings along its length.

Kydd hove to a respectable distance away. Common prudence dictated that he did not secure alongside until the situation there was known.

'Mr Bowden, step ashore and find this gentleman, er, a Mr Samuel Harrison.' He handed over a paper he'd prepared. 'You're to satisfy yourself that this is the man concerned, that he answers your questions with the right responses and is in a suitable position to receive our freighting. Then signify to *Tyger* that this be so and the shipment will be released to you.'

Chapter 9

Wasn't it always thus with the navy? thought Bowden, cynically, as the pinnace stroked for the mole. A frightful responsibility, in this case an inconceivable fortune passing hands, and in the end it all came down to one officer. In a strange port he'd never been to before, he had to find this Harrison, wherever he might be, then satisfy himself by means of a few questions that he actually was the man, and with no further ado hand over the whole glittering prize.

He had Dillon and his Spanish, but not a single armed escort: this could not be allowed in visiting a foreign country.

He told the boat to come in to a decrepit landing stage at the end of the mole and wait for him. Hauling himself up to the wharf level, he waited for Dillon, then stepped over to a pair of idle labourers watching them.

'We are looking for an Englishman. His name is . . .' He tailed off at the torrent of Spanish and waving arms. There must be a consul, an authority who knew where to find him. 'Ask them where the English consul resides,' he told Dillon.

They had no idea, and in ill humour Bowden set out down the long mole for the town, a good half-mile distant.

Passing a small coaster discharging cargo they reached a gap in the buildings. There were two carts, some sad-looking horses morosely in the shafts, and a detachment of Spanish soldiers lounging about. As they moved past, one got to his feet and hurried over.

Dillon heard what he had to say. 'Asks that we wait for his officer. It's important.'

One of the others was sent scurrying away. He brought back a middle-aged man in a uniform recognisably English, if rather odd in its details. 'Ah. You're from the ship with our specie?'

At last!

'Mr Harrison?'

'No. Captain Parrell. Why?'

'My orders are to make delivery only to the person of Mr Harrison.'

'I've never heard of the beggar, sir.'

'Treasury agent.'

'He may be the Great Panjandrum himself but I cannot help you.'

'Sir. You have knowledge of our shipment. May I ask how you came by this?'

'Simple. It's destined for us, the Spanish Catalonian Army, of which I'm a humble servant in the character of British quartermaster liaison officer. I'll have you know we've been waiting an unconscionable long time for this pelf.'

'Without Mr Harrison, I fear it will take longer, Captain.'

'You haven't it with you?'

'It remains in the ship until I signal satisfaction with Mr Harrison.'

Parrell took off his green cocked hat and thwacked it at his side, his face a study in frustration.

'Could I suggest you send out runners to find him?' Bowden said.

'Where?'

'You're a better judge than I of that, sir.'

Parrell barked orders and several soldiers left hastily. 'If you knew how damnably crucial this all is to the war against Boney in this part of the world,' he said bitterly, 'you'd sympathise more with my lot.'

'Oh?'

'Can't you see?' He sighed. 'No, you're a saucy sailor. Let me enlighten you. Let's say you're a general with an army of twenty-five thousands. Your head is filled with notions of how to fall upon the enemy or escape a mortal trap. You're not to be vexed with matters of domestics – how to feed, clothe, pay and shelter your brave men. Artillery and munitions are your conceiving of the necessaries of supply. You must take the field not for a day or a month but a year or more, so, I ask you, just three meals a day for your twenty-five thousands is going to require a hill of bread, meat and common salt. Where's this to come from?

'The British Army has its field train of victuals and stores in the army's wake, the Spanish has none such. It must acquire some locally. It cannot plunder or its sources will flee, so it must pay for all, for meals near fifty, seventy thousand pounds – a day. Marching soldiers wear out boots and shoes by the month. Without, the army cannot march, cannot chase, cannot run. Another thirty thousand a week. Cloth for uniform, I reckon on a hundred thousand ells of broadcloth, sixty thousand ells of facings, linen and other – say one hundred thousand pounds a month. Without leather cartridge pouches and sword-belts, this army will not be able to stand against the foe, and to keep them under repair—'

'I see, Captain. A shocking sum in all.'

'Without which our army dissolves, fades away into the countryside for I haven't made mention of its pay, that which buys your Spaniard's loyalty. At seven *reales* for your meanest private, some hundred, two hundred thousand *reales* to find – a day. Add to that expenses and contingences in doleful quantity and—'

'You do convince me, sir, truly. Then – how much coin do you expect to find in our shipment?'

There was a lop-sided grin and Parrell answered slowly, 'As it has been some time since last we took receipt it would be a grave business should it amount to less than a hundred thousand with the remainder sent on by another route.'

'P-pounds?'

'In Spanish dollars, of course.'

Bowden stared into the distance, grappling with what it meant. Near a tenth of a million – this was the pay of an able seaman for some five, ten thousand years! 'Um, yes. Purely out of curiosity, how does it come to you?'

Parrell looked at him sharply. 'Close-packed coin in kegs and casks, never your Treasury bills. Where from, I have no idea.'

'Don't you fear a descent on you and your escort with this treasure?'

'I've taken delivery of new muskets weekly. This will appear to be more of the same and does not signify. Besides which, there's a squadron of cavalry waiting for us off this mole, the first part of escort to the interior. Now, sir, you have your knowledge of our need, when shall we receive our due?'

'I can only remind you, sir, that—'

'Mr Bowden, sir!'

The hail came from the boat coxswain. 'Sir, I has a gent here says he's been waiting for you.' Beside him was a rather stout, cross-looking individual, with a satchel under his arm.

'Says as how he was only taking the shade and you missed him.'

'Mr Harrison?'

'The same, sir. Now we are met, might we conclude our business?'

Back aboard *Tyger*, Bowden mused to Kydd, 'It was all so . . . ordinary, routine. A blinding fortune handed over, sent on its way. It's war all right, but not as we'd understand it . . .'

Chapter 10

Three days later the two frigates, *Tyger* and *Imperieuse,* slipped out of Port Mahon.

Kydd had first taken the precaution of finding out what he could of the general situation ashore. The formidable barrier of the Pyrenees that separated France and Spain stood squarely against Bonaparte's armies flooding into Spain. It was a near insuperable obstacle for a field train of baggage, artillery and the necessary impedimenta of tens of thousands on the march.

If this were to be accomplished in weeks rather than months, there was only one practical way it could be done: follow the more level coastal route where it threaded around the rocky finality of the Pyrenees to meet the Mediterranean at Cape Creux. At the same time, they'd need to be accompanied by inshore hoys, victuallers and store-ships to sustain the march. Once through at Rosas they would reach a coastal plain and could surge south to Mataró, then on to the region's capital, Barcelona.

To achieve anything against Napoleon's juggernaut this was where to strike.

Collingwood's strategic objective was, as always, the close blockade of Toulon, where Ganteaume and Allemand lay, like tigers, in their lair. Given this, he had no ships of significance to spare so Kydd and Cochrane had the coast to themselves.

As Cochrane wanted to be north of Rosas, Kydd decided he would go further south, where presumably the French were consolidating. Why not Mataró as suggested – up the coast between there and the Rosas plain?

Sea charts gave only a sketchy hint of what lay inland but there was marked a continuous range of jagged mountains with occasional valleys and streams from the interior ending in tiny ports. There had to be good reason for the name given to this region: the Wild Coast, the Costa Brava.

But small coasters creeping along close inshore from the north could land supplies for Bonaparte's army inland for onward transmission by mule train up the valley. The question was, which ports? The French would guard and fortify any they used and therefore there could be no question of assistance from the shore.

Tyger raised the coast at dawn, as planned. It was as the chart was at pains to point out, a jagged and inhospitable series of mountains down to the water's edge interspersed with beaches of a startling paleness. The dark brooding of the coast, however, was relieved by a sparkling Mediterranean emerald sea in place of the dismal grey wastes at the north of Spain.

Almost immediately there came a hail from the masthead. '*Sail hooo! No, I see two sail in wi' the land!*'

'Keep 'em under eye, there!' Kydd bellowed back.

Two, close together, brig-rigged. Typical humble haulers of goods in this part of the world – but from the north and showing every sign of not desiring further acquaintance.

They put about almost simultaneously and, close to the

wind, beat desperately away. But they had no chance against a full-blooded frigate. Before long *Tyger* was on their heels and the distance relentlessly lessened.

'We'll take 'em both before the next headland – I'll have two boats away,' Kydd said, with relish. With the mountains close the coast was steep to – there was no escaping into shallow waters.

Yet their prey pressed on and disappeared beyond the next headland.

'They've found a bolt-hole.' Bray's baffled growl was echoed down the deck.

When *Tyger* reached the serrated promontory, Kydd saw into the bay beyond, a small port in a cliff-faced bowl with a mole extending from one side enclosing a harbour. And inside the upper sails of their chase were being doused.

A quick glance at the chart gave its name as Montellanaura.

'We're cutting the bastards out, o' course,' Bray rumbled.

Kydd raised his glass and sighted, then lowered it almost at once and handed it to Bray. 'Not as if it'll give pause. Look at the seaward end of the mole.'

Bray took the small telescope reluctantly and squinted. 'Ah. A fort o' the round sort. Carriage gun o' size, any number of smaller.'

'As no boat meaning to enter can live through that.'

'Sir, I see masts, sails drying. There's more of 'em inside,' said his second lieutenant.

'Thank you, Mr Bowden,' Kydd said heavily.

But while these two had escaped capture they were going nowhere, and therefore Bonaparte's army was not receiving rations.

Tyger's cruising up and down was paralysing coastal traffic. They'd accomplished their mission – the French knew now that there was a new frigate on the coast to watch for.

'Still an' all, a prize or two would be prime,' Joyce, *Tyger*'s sailing master, said wistfully.

'It's not our duty to be thinking of prizes!' Kydd cut in frostily. 'We've a job to do and . . .'

Insinuating itself into his consciousness came an idea. Long ago, in *Seaflower* cutter, they'd managed a similar feat against a sugar drogher – why not now?

'Bear away, lay us three miles out,' he snapped, pocketing his glass.

He chose to ignore the rumbles of discontent as *Tyger* made her way seaward, balked of her prey. But there was good reason for his move and towards evening it bore fruit.

Again from the north there was sail. Yet another brig, a little smaller and thinking to make a desperate dash to Montellanaura. It was unfortunate for it that news of another cruiser on the coast hadn't yet reached its departure port.

Under their lee, it was a small matter for *Tyger* to intercept and bring it to. It was laden with potatoes, greens and dried fish for the armies of France. A lowly craft, the most humble to be found, but exactly what Kydd had in mind for his little expedition. 'Mr Bray. You've a taking after the prizes we left in Montellanura?'

'Sir?'

'Now's your opportunity. I want you to seize a few to show *Impérieuse* the way it's done in *Tyger*.'

As evening drew in, a dramatic scene unfolded before any watcher ashore who cared to cast eyes out to sea. It was a piteous sight: one of the innocent craft bringing life's nourishment for beleaguered Frenchmen was flying south and it was being slowly overhauled by a wicked frigate. It was a near thing but if it could only make it within gun range of the fort on the mole it would be safe.

Mile by mile the frigate closed but at the last minute it

became clear that the gallant little coaster was indeed going to make it. Under full sail, careering towards the mole and its welcoming harbour it shot past the mole. Then came a massive thud and coil of gun-smoke – the fort was opening fire! But it was at the infernal frigate to signify to it that the poor creature was now under the protection of their guns.

Tyger rounded to and watched as the coaster slipped thankfully into its haven but, like a wolf prowling outside a sheep's fold, it remained there, a frustrated spectator.

The gathering shadows made it difficult to see what was happening but after first one, then another musket-flash it was time to move in. As soon as the coaster came inside the mole to berth with the others, dozens of cutlass-wielding British seamen had burst from its hold to fling themselves at the hapless brigs.

Closing quickly, *Tyger* loosed off her first gun. Charged with grape it blasted the fort with fury. It did little damage, but after the second gun, it was plain to the occupants that any attempt to break out into the open and come to the aid of the brigs would be suicidal.

Tyger's guns spoke again. And one by one the brigs were taken, their crews abandoning them in terror. The first and then the second appeared – and behind them, unexpectedly, a third.

Three prizes – humble enough but a worthy start to any cruise!

Chapter 11

Tight-lipped, Kydd paced the quarterdeck. The rendezvous with Cochrane had been set for three days ago at Punta des Plon, with its neat conical mount the most conspicuous point south of the Rosas plain.

Word had obviously got about of a lurking British cruiser. Prey had vanished from the seas, and for a week now he'd been without a single sighting; it was becoming tedious. The weather had been good, no driving gale or winds foul from the south – so where in Hades had Cochrane got to?

In idleness while waiting, Kydd's frustration with the man grew. He was ready to extend his respect and indeed admiration to the gifted seaman but, vexingly, his behaviour was unpredictable and unreliable.

In the late afternoon *Imperieuse* was spotted away in the south. Somehow Cochrane had worked his way around *Tyger* to come up on her from the opposite direction expected. What the devil was he doing on that part of the coast?

Kydd took boat as soon as they lay together and boarded in barely concealed annoyance.

He was met by the first lieutenant, who gestured mutely forward. On the fore-deck there was a massive tangle of fine canvas and lines, several carrying down from far aloft. Seamen fought to bring some kind of order to the gear, not recognisable in any way to what Kydd was used to aboard *Tyger*.

Cochrane appeared from under the tangle, apologetically hurrying aft. 'Ah. Kydd – glad you're here. I need your help.'

'You're three days late for the rendezvous.'

'Am I? Well, I'm here now and I'd take it kindly if you'd lend a hand in this matter.'

Kydd swallowed his irritation and answered stiffly, 'As it must bear on our task in hand.'

'It does, it does!' he replied crossly. 'Now, do hear me.'

Cochrane had taken it upon himself to devise a new method of accelerating the speed of a full-rigged ship before the wind. This consisted of an immense kite made of the lightest possible fabric hoisted to the fore masthead and let fly with three try-lines to control it and transmit the forward draw to the ship itself.

'I've near perfected it and need to make trial against another.'

'God damn it!' Kydd burst out. 'And we've a war to fight!'

Cochrane's features hardened. 'As well I know it, sir! I've hardly been idle – eight prizes in the last two weeks and a sloop-of-war put down. And you?' He didn't wait for a reply but went on, in rising excitement, 'My invention adds knots to a ship running large, and if you can't see how that can affect the odds in a chase, I pity you, sir!'

It was not the time or place for an argument and if they were to work together it were better to get it over with. 'A day,' Kydd said, with some effort. 'No more.'

'Splendid! Shall we begin?'

* * *

The wind was brisk and more in the north-west but it didn't help. The kite was huge and unwieldy and took hours to set to satisfaction. With *Tyger* under all sail to stunsails, and in *Imperieuse* the kite aloft and drawing, the best improvement logged amounted only to a knot and one quarter.

'I think a little more in the gore,' Cochrane said defensively, when Kydd stepped aboard. 'Don't you?' Those on the quarterdeck withdrew, leaving them alone.

'The cruise is half done,' Kydd said meaningfully. 'Shall we not join in an enterprise against the enemy?'

'Very well, if that is your wish. What do you have in mind?'

'My lord, I'm a stranger on the coast. Should not this be your proposing?' So much for Collingwood's hopes that they'd be setting Catalonia ablaze.

'Well, I know of a country port before Mataró as was a-building. Shall we see what they've done and conceivably undo it?'

Set as a near-perfect semi-circular amphitheatre, Alguer was not a large town but it had an enclosing quay and a road that led tortuously away inland. On the heights opposite a fortification pierced for guns dominated the harbour and next to it two long buildings – barracks.

'As I thought,' Cochrane said smugly. 'Since last I was here and cut out four prizes under their noses they've taken steps to make it hot for me. I've a notion to return the compliment.'

'*We*, you mean.'

'Naturally. It cannot possibly be entertained without I have *Tyger* at my side.'

Cochrane's plan, when it came at the last moment, was simple but effective. *Tyger* would make a pass towards the quay, drawing fire. *Imperieuse* would be taking advantage of the guns' elevation to sail in under them and open up at close range on the barracks, levelling them. Without accommodation or stores the local garrison would be destitute and the harbour defences unmanned until they were rebuilt.

The two frigates got under way. The wind was fair for entering, necessarily requiring a beat close-hauled on withdrawing, and *Tyger*'s part was not going to be easy.

Kydd headed for the centre of the bay and as the fort began its cannonade, hauled her wind and lay over, presenting her width rather than length to the gunners and a diminishing target. The balls came nowhere near the frigate, no doubt down to a parsimonious practice allowance in this out-of-the-way place.

Kydd had time to note that there were no ships of size inside the harbour before looking back and seeing *Imperieuse* go into action.

It was impressive. Cochrane had schooled his gunners in rolling broadsides, a disciplined firing one by one from forward instead of the ringing crash of a simultaneous cannonade. This had its advantages, Kydd was obliged to admit. Apart from less strain being thrown on the ship's timbers the gun captains had a chance to see the fall of shot of their gun and make better correction. And a seemingly never-ending torrent of shot smashing in would certainly affect morale ashore.

As he watched, Cochrane's guns continued their punishment. Their target was plainly the barracks. Shot-strikes sent black fragments high into the air, and before they settled, another slammed in, a continual smashing and battering that was fast demolishing the long buildings. The fort was powerless to intervene as its guns were intended to reach and destroy those attacking the quay and Cochrane, in deep water close to the steep cliffs, was effectively sailing below the guns.

Mercilessly he went about and on the return pass gave

them the benefit of his other side of guns. Not until the buildings were near razed to the ground did he lift his bombardment and join *Tyger* on guard to seaward.

The man was a natural aggressor. He'd turned what amounted to a throwaway gesture to mollify Kydd into a decisive action that had left the enemy in some embarrassment. The dispatch to the Admiralty would show Cochrane's daring stroke – sailing deep into an enclosed bay foul for his exit and leaving the enemy standing in a pile of ruins for no hurt to his ship or loss of men. It would add to his glory while *Tyger* would be held to a very minor role.

Kydd vowed that in future he'd make sure *Tyger* had a more forward one.

Imperieuse and *Tyger* cruised south together.

'I've a good man aboard with the Spanish lingo,' Kydd said casually, to Cochrane, the next time they spoke. 'I've a mind to set him ashore to discover what he may.'

'Do let me know.'

Cochrane was interested but anything discovered would be in Kydd's gift.

Dillon was landed one evening at a fishing village that could have no value to the French and therefore was safe. He was picked up before midnight with interesting news.

Not so far distant the old castle of Mongat was set on a bluff overlooking the sea and was now occupied by a French garrison. It controlled the main route into Barcelona and was long coveted by the Spanish Patriots who swarmed in the hills and mountains around it. Dillon had let it be known that he was from the two powerful warships off their coast who wanted to assist the partisans in their ambition. As a token of his good faith, his frigate would approach the land, hoist the Spanish flag at the fore and fire a salute to their new-found friendship and alliance.

They'd quickly taken up the offer and, with eight hundred *guerilleros* under arms, it promised to be an excellent start.

As dawn slowly brightened the seascape *Tyger* glided inshore and, opposite the gnarled point Dillon indicated, hove to, the red and yellow of the Spanish nation mounted to the mast-head. The thud of a full salute echoed back from the frowning ridges.

A boat put off and Kydd welcomed a fierce band on board. As he'd expected, without waiting for invitation Cochrane was with them without delay.

Introductions were made and all went below to the great cabin.

'Shall we hear of the enemy situation?' Kydd began.

Dillon translated, faultlessly loyal in his attention only to his captain. 'The castle contains upward of a battalion, five, six hundreds. It commands the road north and south. It is near impregnable, old and thick-walled, and has above it, distant a quarter-mile, a substantial outpost discouraging attack from landward.'

'A joint attack?'

'He said—'

'Ha!' Cochrane spluttered. 'These are mere irregulars, Kydd. Not expected to know the arts of war to any degree.'

'I believe we should hear—'

'As I do not.' Cochrane glowered. 'If we're to pull together, Kydd, I'd be obliged if you'd leave these matters to me.'

Was this a blatant grab for ascendancy or plain distrust? Kydd held his tongue. Whatever the reason, it was becoming increasingly impossible to work with the man.

'Sir, they grow impatient,' Dillon said calmly, addressing

Kydd. 'They propose to attack the higher outpost if we bombard the castle with our big guns to prevent relief from same. Then it will be possible to devote all to the reduction of the castle.'

'A good plan, I would have thought,' Kydd said.

'Possibly. Yet there's a detail that's escaped them,' Cochrane came in.

'Which being?'

'Reinforcements. Mongat Castle is served by a first-class road in both directions and it would be strange if there were not dragoons, artillery and the like a-horse within a very short time to dispute with us.'

Without pause, Kydd replied, 'And we will deny them the road – a charge laid above as will bring down a rock-fall they cannot pass.'

'On both sides.'

'Naturally.'

'Very well. Then I will deal with the road, you bombard the castle,' Cochrane said, taking charge. 'Tell our unwashed friends they are to descend on the higher outpost when they hear the powder charges blow.'

He stood, his lofty red-haired presence seeming to fill the cabin. 'At daybreak tomorrow then. They're to be ready to move directly – my charges will be laid during the night, *Tyger* will stand in to commence firing immediately to take attention away from the charges.'

Kydd rose, too. Why wasn't he surprised that Cochrane was again taking the dramatic front stage?

Chapter 12

In the early morning *Tyger* stood in, the castle taking the sun's early light in rose-tinted glory, the lower reaches still throwing off the gloom of night – a perfectly limned target.

Without delay her guns began their punishment on the face of the ancient fortification, built before the coming of cannon. Shot-strike leaped from its stonework with the terrible, shattering impact of balls squarely on the old walls.

In the still morning air the French flag hung inert as the castle's guns came into play. Kydd noted that these were no more than eight- or twelve-pounders: the fabric of the case-mates was probably too weak to take more.

Out in the bay they had a balmy breeze. They could keep it up for as long as it—

A flash and heavy thump happened almost simultaneously at either side of the castle leaving a roil of dust and smoke rising skywards. After a small interval another, further back. Cochrane was taking no chances.

The outpost could just be made out above. Within minutes gun-smoke eddied all about it, rapidly increasing in volume. Shortly afterwards the thud of heavier guns was heard and the space between began choking in smoke – the castle was fighting both sides.

Without warning the facing work of a corner turret gave way, dropping in an avalanche of dust. When it cleared there was a dark void down its length. It was the end for the old citadel.

Kydd kept *Tyger*'s guns on it but he didn't have long to wait. The tricolour jerked down and in its place rose a white flag.

'I believe I'll take his surrender,' Kydd said, to no one in particular. He called away a boat and a party of marines.

Oddly, the sounds of battle hadn't ceased. Furious firing continued along the battlements and the oarsmen slowed in dismay. But it wasn't at Kydd that the rage was directed. The Spanish had overcome the outpost and were racing down the slopes, intent on bringing ruin to the castle.

The boat hissed into the little beach below and Kydd stepped out apprehensively. Above him the firing, if anything, redoubled – how was he to get across the open ground to the gates, and how could the French emerge in submission?

On all sides *guerilleros* darted, shooting, howling insults, completely ignoring them.

Kydd jerked in reflex as a bullet whanged past him and the others ducked low. Should he walk away and leave them to it, the object achieved? What were the honours of war where a raging band of murderous Patriots was concerned?

Beside him a figure appeared – Cochrane. He'd landed with two boats of marines, their red uniforms and white crossbelts stark against the scrubby hillside. 'You've not taken the surrender yet?' he asked, rocking back on his sword scabbard. 'Sergeant.'

'Sah!'

'Your men fall in behind me.'

'Forward, the marines!' He stepped out into the open and, with not a moment's hesitation, marched up the slope towards the castle.

The sheer effrontery hit Kydd as much as the courage needed, but it had its desired effect. The firing died away as the little party made its way to the gates, which creaked open. Cochrane had known that the red coats would be recognised by both sides but to step out in full view took cold-blooded nerve.

Very soon the gates opened again and the marines emerged to make a guarded lane, down which the French moved nervously. Some almost ran in their anxiety to make the boats, knowing their fate if they fell into the hands of the Patriots, who shouted and threatened, a number coming to blows with the redcoats.

'Will you do the honours or will I?' Cochrane said airily, standing back to watch.

'Yours,' Kydd said flatly.

The hapless commandant was deftly relieved of his sword, and Cochrane swung round on his marines, crisply giving the orders that saw the old castle prepared for razing.

In a series of muffled thuds the walls fractured and split and slid to ruin in an untidy pile about the foreshore. The Spanish colours went up on the stump of the flagstaff and the Patriots were left in riotous celebration of their victory.

Chapter 13

Port Mahon

As *Tyger* cast her anchor in the long, enfolding harbour, Kydd glanced about the anchorage. Apart from a handful of ships-of-the-line moored together, there were few other naval vessels. Over towards the dockyard were two he didn't recognise: brig-sloops . . . and was that a sleek cutter beyond? They must be new arrived from the outside world.

They were only in for a day or so to replenish shot and powder before returning to their cruise but it was welcome for all that.

'Hoist the blood flag,' he ordered, the red-flag request for powder hoys and a warning to other vessels to keep a wide berth while it was flying. 'I'll be below.' Bray could be relied on to enforce all the usual precautions while they stowed powder, and now he had time for a hurried finish to his letter home.

Damn it, the man's a caution to us all with his fathom of energy and red hair, stalking into peril as he does, but not so easy to work with, he began, scratching away crossly. *As if he's the only one taking the war to the enemy.*

He sucked the end of the quill, marshalling his thoughts. It was not easy to put into words how he felt about the man – probably the most famous frigate captain of their time but one who flourished as a lone wolf.

Holds strong opinions and must let those about him know of them but swears that the world's against him. A fine seaman and looks after his men – you can tell, you know. But for some mad reason is in deep with the Radical interest. Rails on about jobbery and the nation swept to perdition on a tide of preferment and interest.

It really was a mystery, why a first-class sea warrior like Cochrane should be gulled by the ranting of those like Cobbett.

Pity me, my love, for tomorrow I'm to go to war with the grig and—

There was a murmur of voices outside his cabin and then bursting in, full of life, was one who, above all others, he'd most like to clap eyes on at this time.

'Bazely! Do come in, old friend. You're right welcome. Tysoe!'

But his manservant had the tray of drinks ready even before Bazely had found an armchair and stretched out with exaggerated self-indulgence. 'Ah, what's this tipple I see, Sir T?' he said critically, eyeing the blue-tinted liquor.

'Xoriguer gin, since you ask it, my heathen friend. Now why—'

'No mystery, Kydd. After I lost *Fenella* to the Ruskies, m' lords enquired of me my pleasure concernin' a new command. I told 'em main swiftly as I didn't care a fig so long as ice or snow didn't figure in it. So it's the Med, sunny shores and the good ship *Lynx*. Or should that be brig-sloop?'

What Bazely was not saying, Kydd could guess: a return to England as a shipwrecked captain, even if of heroic circumstances, the petitioning and soul-destroying waiting for a ship in the Captain's Room at the Admiralty in the company of far too many fellow commanders, then the unbelievable, heart-thumping news of a command that lifted him from bleak idleness to unmatchable eminence as captain of a man-o'-war.

'My heartiest sentiments, old fellow!' he cried, and lifted his glass. 'To *Lynx*, and that there's still enough jollification abroad as will keep us all tolerably entertained.'

It was then necessary to crowd to the stern-lights to peer across the anchorage to the trim sixteen-gun sloop, a little old-fashioned to Kydd's eye but that meant there was a proper figurehead in place of the more austere scrowl to be seen on newer craft. And a sight more ornamentation – the glint of gold leaf showed that Bazely was not sparing in his affection for his new-found love.

'Can't stay long, old fellow. Got an invitation from y'r gallant Cochrane to sup with him tonight. Have t' square away first.'

'So have I, and right glad to see you there, cuffin.'

Chapter 14

The great cabin, HMS Imperieuse

Kydd had been nominated vice-president for the night and sat at the opposite end of the polished mahogany table to Cochrane. The other five guests, all commanders, took their places along each side.

'I can well believe it.' Cochrane's high voice cut effortlessly across the companionable talk. 'The prize money I've been cheated of would fill a Chinaman's fattest tea chest.'

Kydd had never been subject to the kind of peculations many of his fellow captains had seen but sympathised. It was odd to hear Cochrane complain, though – he was so much in the public eye that surely it would be a bold and shameless swindler who made practice on a toast of the town.

The talk turned to families ashore.

'Heard tell you've had troubles at home,' Moffatt of *Culdrose* was asked.

'Aye, we did. M' father owns a stocking mill an' got a visit from Ned Ludd, the villains.' Unrest in the north was not unusual but lately it seemed machine-breaking was increasing fast. 'The damage they cause, it's animal. Agin their own interests, mind.'

'They've reason enough, some of 'em,' another muttered. 'Artisans with years o' learning before they're master of their trade, then an engine working o' steam throws 'em on the street.'

'That's not the root of it,' Cochrane cut in. 'It's that they've no chance for learning, for advancement – society denies them this while granting favour and interest to the undeserving on high. I've always said that—'

'So you'd tear down what's served England well for centuries and give it over to those in a quarrel with progress?' Kydd couldn't help asking.

'I'm saying nothing of the sort.' Cochrane snorted. 'If you'd been following what I've been about then you'd hoist aboard that, left to themselves without discipline and leadership of the right sort, they're going to riot and revolt and then you've got another French Revolution.'

Kydd was about to make hot reply when he saw Bazely down the table give him a slow wink. It was a polite reminder that politics was never a meet and proper subject in a King's Ship and he should know better. He couldn't let it go, however. 'In your reckoning then, a poor wight from the lower orders is damned at birth?'

'He must be – no education, none to make the way smooth, his means slender. How can it be other?'

'So he should be used to it and make his obedience to all the world?'

'It would be happier for him if he did.'

If this was the Radical philosophy Kydd wanted no part of it, although he had a strong suspicion this was Cochrane's individual conceiving of it.

In any case it was getting late, and with Cochrane in

dominating form, it was not the relaxed mess gathering he was used to. 'Well, and I believe I must get back aboard,' he said stiffly, 'if we're to sail tomorrow.'

He paid compliments on the meal and bade farewell. Four of the others rose as well, leaving Cochrane looking bemused at Bazely, calmly drawing on his cigar.

'Did I say something I shouldn't?'

Bazely saw that the man was genuinely puzzled. 'You don't really know Kydd of *Tyger*, do you?'

'A fine seaman and cool head in action. Intelligent – more than your usual sort. And—'

'As I thought. You don't know him.'

'And you do?'

'He's the most square-sailing, true north cove I've ever come athwart. And for learning o' where it's at, he's hard to beat.'

'I grant you that.'

'And smack opposite to what you're sayin' as gives the lie to all of it.'

'What do you mean?' Cochrane growled.

'You won't know that our Sir T is from humble origins, very humble. Starts as a tradesman, pressed into the navy, fights and wins his way to the quarterdeck. Refuses to take the easy path as would see him a tarpaulin, sets his sights on being a gentleman.'

'Yes, but—'

'Learns the graces, politeness, lingo, and marries damn well, Brooks's his club and can call the Prince of Wales shipmate. How's that for one without y'r education an' discipline?'

'Ah. I do confess I'd no idea he—'

'And y' know what I reckon prime?'

'Go on.'

'He's got society and a future at his feet – but he casts it away as he knows he's one o' Neptune's gentlemen and cares more what a common sailor says of him than all your Parlyment assembled.'

Cochrane's face was set.

'I knew him as a raw commander, first ship and in a mort o' pother shoreside. He did the right thing then – and I'm to tell you he's the same man.'

He didn't wait for a reply but stood and said gruffly, 'Well, as I've a ship to go to as well, I'll be away, and thank 'ee for a fine evening.'

The pinnace was waiting and Bazely sat in its sternsheets, his cloak around him against the coolness of the night breeze.

'Return to *Lynx*, sir?'

After a moment's pause he said, 'No – *Tyger* frigate, if you please.'

Kydd looked up in surprise. 'Why, dear fellow, no place of your own to lay your head?'

'As our host is so near wi' his brandy, I knew you'd see me right in the article of a warmer.'

'Of course.'

Bazely fiddled with his glass, then looked up with a slow, ironic grin. 'Ye're both born to it – a frigate captain, that is. An' you couldn't be more different. And on quite another tack as sees you across each other's hawse half the time.'

'He's born to the nobility, expects all around him to bow down to his views, his opinions.'

'Not quite, cully.'

'How would you know?'

'As a new-minted l'tenant, I shared a wardroom with him. There's no secrets in a man-o'-war at sea, as ye know, and for some reason he was straight with me. Tells me things as

63

opens m' eyes.' He hesitated as though debating whether to go further. 'He comes from a noble family well enough – he's to be the tenth Earl o' Dundonald when his pa passes on. What y' doesn't know is that his father's a spendthrift wastrel, not gambling an' such, I have t' tell ye, but spends his time an' means on strange inventions, which he not being a man o' business must leave his family scraping and begging. This is to say that the man is too busy to see to his son, who grows up without needful direction.'

Kydd held silent, remembering his own quiet, firm father on occasion checking him for thoughtless acts of youth.

'Come to himself at sea, as so many on us have, and quite the genius of war – but all ahoo when he has t' mix it with the common world. Glory be, but to see him lay into the Admiralty because he thinks they're agin him, stands up in Parlyment and flays the government o' the day for some trifle, goes out of his way to pick up enemies like others find friends.'

'He's a Member of Parliament.'

'The people love him as he goes for the big nobs, but being in the Radical tribe he'll not win a place anywhere in government. He's got family, scads of 'em. Not all as you'd like to meet – brother made a hill of spoils out o' knaggy India victualling, quantities of uncles on the hookum snivey and he's a rare enough time of it thinking who he amounts to be.'

'Why are you telling me this, Bazely? That he's to be forgiven all because he's a wry set o' scoundrels for a family?'

'Not as who should say,' he replied, wounded. 'Just that a helping of understanding goes a ways in dealing with the devil.'

Chapter 15

Aboard Imperieuse

'Come in, old fellow.' Cochrane stood to greet Kydd, but there was nothing to be read from his expression.

Before they sailed Kydd had been summoned to plan their cruise but he had no great expectation of high strategy from this impulsive and unpredictable man.

Charts of Cochrane's chosen northerly area were spread out, however, which was surprising.

Kydd sat in one of the chairs at the table and glanced down at them: France – the border region and the lush plains of Languedoc. 'Ah, what is it you have in mind, then?' Kydd said carefully.

Cochrane took the chair opposite and regarded him seriously. 'Kydd, dear chap,' he started, then hesitated. 'It's . . . Well, I'd rather feel it hard on me should I not clear my yardarms. With you, that is.'

'Um, why so?'

'At the dinner. I may have been a trifle out of station, must we say, on matters bearing on yourself.'

65

'I don't recollect—'

'Your origins, I had no idea. You conduct yourself as a true gentleman.'

'If I am so, it must put your Radical theories to the blush, I believe.'

'Oh? Not at all,' Cochrane said, coming back strongly. 'No. You're an exception to the breed, is all.'

Kydd allowed a dry smile. 'I'm at a stand as to whether I'm to be flattered or insulted. Surely the deed maketh the man.'

Cochrane shifted uncomfortably. 'If that were true, why do we both stand where we are? I flatter myself my service in *Speedy* is not to be scouted but where was my promotion, my post captaincy? I must needs wait in idleness while others basked in favours. Even you – bullion freight money at half of one per cent right from under my nose. And in the matter of prize money and honours I must wait still. You have your knightly baubles but for I, nothing. After the *Pallas* cruise all the world applauds but for me . . .'

His features hardened and he went on bleakly, 'All I can conclude is that there's a conspiracy afoot to deny me laurels and advancement – which I lay at the feet of their precious lordships of the Admiralty.'

The truth then dawned on Kydd. The man had been trapped in a gilded cage not of his making. Allowed to run wild in his youth, he'd then come up against the hard reality of the outer world and hit back at it, the way he saw it. The trouble for him was his noble birth: in deference to his rank there was none who could tell him to his face that he'd got it wrong. And with his eccentric, not to say colourful, family, he'd find no steer there. Such a gifted seaman and fighter – but out of his element he was lost.

'So this is what you think?' Kydd said.

Cochrane stiffened. 'Are you to be numbered with those fractious beggars, then?'

'Do you value truth above soft words?'

'What are you saying, Kydd?'

'I came aft through the hawse and you may believe in that time I chalked up in my log a gallows deal that's been denied you.'

'It could be so,' Cochrane said defensively.

'Then hear me when I say I can lay hands on who's by some leagues your worst enemy.'

'Who? Tell me!'

'You are yourself, cuffin.'

'How dare you?'

'I dare because I thought you'd take stiff words above the comfortable. Can you?'

'If you must,' Cochrane said awkwardly.

'Then it is this. You wonder why the world's against you, why so many set their faces against you. I'm here to say it's your doing – take a sight of yourself. Ten feet tall, red hair and a sharp tongue. Is it to be wondered at that others go to quarters to defend themselves or withdraw? You treat 'em like enemies and they'll oblige you.'

'Go on.'

'Do you make mellow your speech, your graces, allow them their failings, I shouldn't wonder they'll rate you friend instead.'

Cochrane held rigid, his face shadowed, and Kydd thought he'd gone too far.

'No one's ever spoken to me like that. Never,' he said slowly. 'But I do allow there could be some truth in what you say. I'll think on it.'

'And now our war.'

'Ah, yes,' Cochrane agreed vigorously, after a short pause.

'So Boney's sending his supply into Spain by what he hopes is the short way – around the end of the Pyrenees,' Kydd opened, glancing at the charts again.

'I've taken any number of coasters there but the wretches are getting wise to us. They've a string of bolt-holes now, small ports with fortifications. Their practice is to flutter from one to the next, lie under its guns while a British cruiser is abroad.'

'Shall we not discourage them, if not put a stop to it?'

'A capital idea. A sizeable one of its kind – say Port-Vendres. A battery north of the small harbour, another to its south. Both cunningly sited for protection from sea bombardment.'

'Land a force of marines to take it and spike its guns,' Kydd suggested.

'Ah. Not so easy – the rascals have a strong cavalry force in the centre. An attack on either one brings it at the gallop in aid.'

Kydd nodded – this was more like it: two minds joining as one, no casual dismissing by the man of any but his own opinions.

'Perhaps we'll take a closer look,' Cochrane said.

Chapter 16

Port-Vendres was a tiny harbour, its entrance just hundreds of yards across, heavily guarded by several batteries. Yet it was tying up enemy resources of men and guns that should have been heading south into the ferment of uprising in Spain. And it was only one of so many along the coast.

The two frigates brazenly cruised past, and Kydd realised that the French cavalry, quartered in town, could take the inland road around the port and be more or less concealed as they did so. Any landing party it caught would be cut to pieces well before they could be taken off.

A mile out to sea the two frigates lay together and made their plans. Shortly afterwards boats were seen putting off for the shore. Packed into them was a fearsome sight: the red coats of the Royal Marines in a powerful landing party, heading straight for the northern redoubt.

The frigates got under way, their objective the southern battery on the other side of the entrance. They opened up furiously but the redoubt was well protected, sunk deeply into the rocky shoreline, and returned fire with spirit.

There was no doubt in the French commander's mind of what he had to do. The cavalry were called out and, in the fiery charge for which they were famed across all of Europe, galloped wildly around to meet the landings in the north.

It was what the frigates wanted. As soon as the cavalry was out of sight, boats appeared from behind the two ships, now close in. While the guns thundered over their heads they headed inshore as fast as stout hands at the oars could speed them.

At the northern redoubt the cavalry reined in, snorting in triumph. They were in time, placing themselves between the approaching invasion craft and the gun battery. The British, though, seemed strangely reluctant to join battle, the boats easing their onrush and laying on their oars.

Suddenly suspicious, the colonel demanded a telescope and focused on the boats. He swore loudly. He'd been tricked — they were all wearing red coats, but the 'marines' were nothing more than ship's boys and older seamen. And at the battery on the opposite side of the harbour the real marines were storming ashore, their landing covered by the rolling cannonade of the two frigates.

Bellowing in anger, the colonel raised his sabre and led his cavalry in a furious charge back along the road and out of sight.

But Cochrane had carefully watched their futile first gallop and seen where the road emerged from between a defile and ran for a space along the side of a gorge. He'd anchored and, with all seamen at loaded guns, waited for his chance.

The mad dash came into view and was met by a tempest of grape-shot that tore into men and horses in a torment of blood and gore, the impetus of those behind sending them into the tangle of writhing bodies.

The charge was broken. Those who could do so fled out of sight of the merciless guns.

And the marines at the southern side got to work. Attacking from above, the landward side, their assault was irresistible. Caught between them and the smashing balls of the warships, there was no choice for the French soldiers but to flee, leaving their weapons.

Tyger's gunner's party moved in. With smashing hits, a tapered spike was hammered into the vent of the first gun and filed flat. Without long labour with a drill and worm, the weapon was now useless. It took time but, with the cavalry threat removed, they continued until the whole battery was out of action.

Port-Vendres now lay open.

Chapter 17

Aboard HMS Tyger

'A fine piece of work,' agreed Cochrane, sipping a cordial later that day, as the pair of frigates made their way out to sea. 'Yet I'd reckon it unfinished, wouldn't you, old fellow?'

Kydd considered for a moment, gratified that Cochrane was seeking his opinion. 'That there are so many batteries left to shelter under?'

'I was rather thinking the larger picture. Who warns our prey to turn aside and seek shelter under their guns, that there's a British cruiser at large on the coast?'

This was something to which Kydd hadn't really given much thought. 'Is there such?'

'There is. In this country the French can't use couriers for fear of their assassination so they've established communications for their army by means of semaphore stations, much like our own telegraph chain. These run down the coast from France well to the south. They've taken to using them for other purposes – if one of our marauding frigates is sighted the word is passed instantly and our prey vanishes from the seas.'

'So to destroy the posts will not only rob 'em of their warnings but serve to cut off their military communications.'

'With all that means in terms of intelligence lost, orders not passed, confusion on all sides.'

It wasn't a major battle or a glorious sea action but the consequences were highly desirable. 'We'll do it, m' friend,' Kydd said, then saw a slow smile spread.

The smile stayed.

'From Collioure south they're in line of sight, one with the other. I'll take one end, you the opposite?'

The signal posts were not hard to spot: on the skyline, skeletal arms industriously at work.

Tyger eased in to the craggy land, provoking another flurry of signals. This one was on a levelled area atop a ridge. A telegraph house supported the mast; behind and lower there was another structure. Kydd concentrated with his glass – it was a barracks of some kind. These stations were defended against just what Kydd was intending. And whatever was now being strenuously signalled was not by way of welcome.

As *Tyger* moved slowly along, he continued his examination. The post was new – wooden and flung up in haste. It was small but built for purpose with what looked like homely living quarters to one side. His gaze came back to the barracks. He guessed it could accommodate about a hundred, several times *Tyger*'s complement of Royal Marines.

Bombard it from the sea? Probably by deliberate plan most of the complex was beyond the ridge, out of sight and therefore untouchable.

Simply stand off and reduce the semaphore tower by cannon fire? Not so easy: its height above the sea would require guns to be at an impossible elevation and accuracy would suffer greatly. It would be a long and expensive process to achieve anything by this means.

Damn it, there had to be a way . . .

To avoid giving the impression of undue interest in the station he gave orders that saw *Tyger* get under way again, as though satisfied there was nothing of importance, and apparently continue her cruise. But Kydd's mind was racing. If it was not possible to destroy the post by gunfire, the only remaining alternative was to land a force and raze it. But he was outnumbered considerably and couldn't look to a successful assault landing.

He had only one conceivable ally: surprise. That and bluff.

And then it came to him: a night attack, from a direction they wouldn't suspect.

'Ask Captain Clinton to wait on me.'

Kydd got straight to the point. 'I'm going to ask you something in the professional line to which I trust you'll give me an unprofessional answer.'

'Sir?'

'I want you to say if you think what I propose will fadge – will it work at all. Not whether you're prepared to do it, for you're a Royal Marine and will.'

'Very well, sir.'

'I want to reduce our signal post by way of guile. You've seen the country – what I ask is if you and your marines can make privy landing down the coast and head inland. Then a sweep around and come at them from that quarter.'

'Ah. Broken scrub country with gullies and good cover – slow going but tolerably possible. But to storm the position after—'

'No assault. To keep 'em under fire in the belief they're under attack by the local *guerilleros* is all.'

'Er, it could be difficult to—'

'At night.'

'Easier – but it depends on what picquets they have out.'

'Good fellow. Shall we say tomorrow night – moonrise after midnight? I have a landing place in mind.'

The other half of the plan was trickier.

As soon as the enfolding dark had established itself, the boats went in with the marines. Every man in the detachment was under arms – a mere thirty in all but disciplined and well led. They were mustered on the beach in a secluded cove and, with a pair of scouts ahead and a rearguard, headed out into the night.

The boats returned ready for their next duty.

Seamen, their faces blackened with galley soot, took their places and, oars muffled in their rowlocks with rags, three boats made their way into the cliffs of the foreshore. Not directly at the signal post but beyond a twist of rock to one side where, once under the overhanging crags, they could move unseen to the base of the ridge. It was unlikely that sentries were posted atop a sheer cliff-face.

The seamen jumped ashore and began their ascent. Lines secured to outcrops by agile topmen going ahead gave good purchase to those coming behind, encumbered with arms and equipment, and were a means for hauling up their main burden: the deadly load that would cause the post's destruction.

Kydd was with them: he couldn't know what awaited them and, if decisions had to be made, he must be there. By him was Halgren, his coxswain, but Lieutenant Bowden and a dozen seamen, including the gunner's party under Stirk and his picked men, were leading the assault.

There was plenty of time to scale the eighty-foot heights, to bring up the gear and make ready for the decisive moment.

Carefully, inch by inch in the sepulchral darkness, the Tygers moved up to their positions.

The sign Kydd was waiting for would be clear and unequivocal: the sudden burst of firing from inland, timed to take place when the moon rose and gave a sight picture for the muskets. With just thirty men it would be a thin volley but, intelligently spaced and separated, it would do its job of taking attention fully to the front.

And there it was! Surprisingly, it sounded like many more, and to the defenders, no doubt, was a shocking breach of the night stillness.

Consternation and confusion took hold, with ragged trumpet calls, hoarse shouts and figures bursting out of the barracks.

'Go!' hissed Kydd. Scrabbling over the edge of the cliff, the first party ran ahead to the semaphore tower, a light just visible in its single window. Above, the black silhouette of the mast and vanes loomed, still and silent, immense close to.

They kept out of sight on the seaward side, blades out and tensely waiting, while the others dragged their load up to the tower – a fat, ordinary-looking cask.

A muffled shout came from inside. Stirk motioned quickly to a petty officer, who took his three men at a run into the tower. The noise ceased.

A hatchet was smashed into the head of the cask and the pungent odour of pitch filled the night air. Rolled along, the contents spilled about the base of the tower, ready to take flame in its mission of destruction.

Kydd motioned to Bowden: he had decided to take a quick look inside first.

Around the walls there were clips of paper, homely articles, shelves of stationery and a portrait of the Emperor. A single lantern stood on the table, two bodies crumpled on the floor nearby. And lying open on the table was a pad and booklet. Bowden snatched it up, eyes alight. 'The signal codes!'

It was a priceless catch. With it, telegraph traffic on the coast could be intercepted and read, giving warning of enemy troop movements, timely knowledge that a British cruiser had indeed been sighted, and intelligence of all kinds gleaned.

Stirk's urgent shout penetrated. They were ready to set off the blaze.

'Bring it with you!' Kydd told Bowden, and they hurried out as a flicker of orange flame darted up. They had to move fast – as soon as the conflagration in their rear was noticed there would be hell to pay. 'To the boats,' he ordered.

A sudden thought crossed his mind. The value of the code-book would be lost if the French suspected they had it: they'd change the code immediately.

'Give me the book,' he demanded. He tore off the front cover and the first page or two, then leaned into the crackling flames to catch the edges, stamping them out when half burned. Carefully, he threw them clear of the door of the tower, now well alight, and raced after his men. The returning French would find the bodies of the two gallant defenders who'd spent their lives destroying the secret codes.

Chapter 18

'A good night's work,' Kydd agreed with Bowden, back on board *Tyger* and looking over to the flaming carcase of the signal tower on the ridge, proclaiming to the world the power of the Royal Navy to strike wherever it chose.

Clinton and his marines had returned before them. 'We fell in with your *guerilleros* very early and left them to it, they proving singularly eager to engage with the French.' It explained the unexpected swell in the amount of musketry Kydd had heard.

Satisfied, *Tyger* spread her wings and disappeared into the night.

At the rendezvous, a broad cove to the north of Cape Creux, Kydd brought *Tyger* in to a workman-like moor in the lee of a craggy promontory. After his service in this part of the Mediterranean in the last war, he was always conscious of the lurking danger of the tramontana, a cruel northerly gale that could strike out of a blue sky without warning.

Imperieuse was not there at anchor. Why wasn't Kydd surprised?

Two days later the frigate sailed in to a faultless anchoring. Hurriedly boarding, Kydd was received by a blank-faced first lieutenant who led him down to the great cabin.

Cochrane looked up in surprise from an incongruous work-bench set near the stern-lights. He was dressed in an old labourer's smock, and appeared to be filing an awkward metal device clamped in a vice. 'Oh, hello, old fellow. We're here already?'

He tapped the file on the vice, sending a small shower of bright particles to the deck. 'This? Why, you're clapping your peepers on an ingenious solution to convoy station-keeping. With this lamp perfected, your merchant jack will think nothing of sailing in company at night, and in formation. See – this mounted on the stern of his next-ahead will give a white light when he follows true and casts a red or green light to tell him to up or down helm to fall back into line if he strays.'

'Hmm,' Kydd murmured. 'I can see how, er . . . Well, it's a very interesting device. How does—'

'Easy. The lights are encased in tubes set at the correct angle. None but those meant to see them are able to. So, right from the column leader to the end of the convoy, all in line, all together, no one knows how!'

Kydd settled into an easy-chair after first removing some odd objects lying there, feeling somewhat overdressed. 'Did you meet with good fortune with your signal stations?'

'Oh, er, we agreed to punish the French for their temerity, didn't we?' Cochrane said absently, sighting along the axis of one of the tubes.

'We put down four in all,' Kydd responded. 'Once we thought to rope in the Patriots.'

'Did you?' Cochrane said flatly, looking about for a tool and frowning.

'And you?'

'We? Six.'

Kydd took in that this was not an 'I': he was including his ship's company in the achievement. 'Bravo, old fellow. Well done.'

Cochrane smiled and put down his file. 'I'm missing my manners, Kydd. Refreshment?'

An insipid white wine arrived, but Kydd knew that the man seldom indulged for some reason and could be forgiven his lack of taste. 'So how are we to prosecute our little war?' he mused. 'The last semaphore was guarded by a full three hundred. We can't expect to do much more along that line.'

Cochrane chuckled. 'If that's so, then we're occupying the efforts of some thousands to stand watch over the dozens of stations along the coast, they not knowing where we'll punch 'em next. Maybe five, ten thousands – the same as a regular-going fortress that would take an army to tame.'

'It would please me to know what's the state o' things in Spain at all,' Kydd ruminated.

'You're in the right of it. While we cruise about we may be missing a chance to put in our oar where it'll do the most good. I've a fancy to find out.'

'How?'

'Go and ask. I know Collingwood sees the Catalonians as key to stopping the French push south, and while we can't give 'em troops and so forth, he's detached a couple of battleships to lay off Rosas itself to give the Dons heart. They'll know the griff.'

Kydd gave warm agreement to the plan. Only weeks ago Cochrane had been supercilious, cutting and lofty. Now he was treating him not only as an equal but more and more as a friend.

Chapter 19

The Gulf of Rosas consisted of the wide, sweeping curve of the Rosas plain, with its abrupt finish in the north at the Pyrenees. The town itself nestled up against the rugged, near perpendicular hills and mountains through which the coastal road descended on its way south to Gerona and then Barcelona.

It was an admirable haven against the tramontana, and its snug harbour could shelter a fleet, but there were few sail except the majestic bulk of a single 74 in the deeper water in the middle of the bay and two bomb-vessels off the town. Ominously, smoke was rising and levelling to the left at the approaches to Rosas, grey and louring, the colour of war.

Tyger and *Imperieuse* anchored in a wide berth at either side of the 74, and Cochrane and Kydd shortly stepped aboard. Her captain, Bennet, an elderly officer, met them on her quarterdeck. He was at pains to let it be known that he wasn't to be impressed by a visit from the two most famous frigate captains of the age.

'Lord Cochrane, Sir Thomas, welcome aboard *Fame*, and I'll know what brings you to these waters,' he said, leading them to his great cabin, where he took the head of the table. 'Well?'

'As we're on a joint cruise to aid the Spanish wherever we can,' Cochrane opened easily. 'Seems they've a need, that hullabaloo in Rosas.'

'I've landed marines, all manner of arms. What more do you think you can do with a frigate, sir?'

Cochrane's expression hardened. 'Perhaps I'll land and find out for myself, sir.'

Bennet gave a look of dark satisfaction. 'I'll save you the trouble. Here we have Bonaparte trying to pack his troops into Spain. He's given the job to one of his best, General Saint-Cyr, with twenty-five thousands. Either he crosses the central Pyrenees in months or gets across the narrowest in days, here, which leads to the Plain of Rosas, then easy going to Barcelona to rescue Duhesme besieged by the Spanish. This is what he chooses – but in his way is Rosas. He can't go forward without he neutralises this threat to his rear.'

'A worthy cause.'

'But hopeless. I mentioned twenty-five thousands? In the Rosas citadel is a paltry several battalions of Spanish irregulars – that's all, to stand against Boney's many, I say. I landed all the marines I could but they report that the fortification is in ruins, crumbling and quite unfit to defend. I've sent off my other 74 and I'm to pull the rest out and withdraw, I believe.'

'You may, sir. I shall not.'

There was a hiss of indrawn breath. 'What did you say? A town in imminent prospect of falling to the enemy and you'll waste time and lives on it?'

'The stakes are too precious. I'll not abandon hope until I've seen for myself there's none.'

'Do I take it you're advancing your own judgement over

mine?' Bennet snarled. 'If so, I've a cure for that. You'll take my orders and fall back with me as escort to Minorca.'

'No one but a rank shab would let the Spanish see us scuttling away, like beaten curs. I won't,' Cochrane returned tightly.

Kydd cringed.

'You're taken under orders, sir! We sail for Minorca – understood?'

'No.'

Bennet breathed heavily. 'Captain Cochrane, I'll not repeat myself. You'll ready your ship for—'

'I'll do no such thing.'

Red-faced, Bennet lurched to his feet. 'Damn you, sir! You'll take my orders or—'

'My orders originate from the commander-in-chief himself, which I do place before yours, sir,' Cochrane said icily. 'If we are not to co-operate amicably, I find myself obliged to advance on my own.'

Kydd tried to intervene: 'Captain Cochrane desires only to establish in his own mind the situation ashore, sir.'

Bennet swung on him. 'And you, Kydd, will you take my orders or are you of the same mutinous streak?'

With a lurch of inevitability he knew how he would answer. 'Sir, my orders are from Admiral Collingwood as well, and I beg you to reflect that it would go hard on us both should we go against them.'

'Pah! Then get off my ship, and you haven't heard the last of this, I promise you!'

'Oh, and I shall take the bombs under my wing,' Cochrane said loftily. Before the outraged Bennet could speak, he added, 'Being as they shall need protecting.'

Rising to his full fathom and inches height he smiled thinly and left. Kydd could think of nothing intelligent to say in the charged atmosphere and simply followed. After all, Bennet was not a flag officer and owed his position solely to seniority: there would be no repercussions, only avoidable enmity.

'To that citadel, I believe,' Cochrane said crisply. 'They'll have a view, I'm sure. You'll come?'

'You didn't have to rile Captain Bennet.'

'A contemptible fool. I dismiss him out of mind,' Cochrane said airily, as the boat approached a small pier.

'We're fighting the same war.'

It didn't seem to penetrate, and Kydd had other things on his mind – the thud and rumble of siege guns and the occasional fitful swell of musketry. They were blundering into a full-blown action.

There were few people about and they had to find their own way the little distance to the light grey bastions of the citadel close by the sea, overhung with the ragged clouds of gun-smoke and dust.

'Sir.' A short and distracted man in smudged uniform was apparently the commandant, a Colonel Pedro O'Daly, an Irishman in Spanish service. 'You're navy – new come to Rosas, yes?'

'Captain Lord Cochrane and Captain Sir Thomas Kydd. Come to enquire if we can be of any assistance.'

O'Daly looked at him shrewdly. 'You arrive in the final act. I cannot last any longer, sir.'

'Pray what is it that presses?'

'This fortification. Ruinous and decayed. Never repaired since the French took it in the last war – see there, the breach they made. Saint-Cyr is sending General Reille and eight battalions to finish us. They'll cackle when they see their breach ready-made.'

'Then who're they?' Cochrane gestured out to the sound of the guns.

'A vanguard sent to entertain us before Reille's regulars arrive. They've to come through the hills, the coast road denied 'em.'

'So it's—'

'It's a race is the long and short of it. We being here stops Saint-Cyr reaching Barcelona and relieving it, but in turn we're holding on, trusting to be relieved by the Spanish in Gerona, if they can get through to us.'

'So if you can stand for a mite longer, Saint-Cyr is delayed, Barcelona falls to the Spanish.'

'Excepting we can't stand, it's too—'

But Cochrane wasn't listening. His eyes took in the lengths of broken, tumbled masonry, the dispirited soldiery, the gaping breach. 'Right,' he said energetically. 'Shall we get to work?'

'I don't . . .' O'Daly said uncertainly.

'I'm sending for my marines. Yours, Kydd? Need 'em to hold off the Frenchies while we do something about the citadel.'

'Er, yes. Of course.'

The boats put off and Cochrane marched about with nervous energy, his long legs giving rise to a pace that Kydd found hard to match. 'Repair! Repair!' he muttered, darting glances here and there. Then he stopped. 'I have it. Colonel,' he called across to O'Daly, 'if you please, give ear.'

When he came over, his face was expressionless but marked with lines of weariness. 'Captain?'

'The breach. This is how we'll stop it up.'

Demanding every provision bag to be found, Cochrane demonstrated how, stuffed with sand and rocks, they could quickly be filled by a thousand willing hands. Taken to the fallen masonry and thrown into place, one on top of another, it was effectively a wall of stone, proof against cannon-fire, created in minutes.

Cochrane hadn't finished. 'What was that old castle I saw the other side of Rosas?'

'Ah. Castell de la Trinitat. Fort Trinidad to you heathen. And since you'll surely ask, old and decrepit too. We account it worth only eighty men the manning.'

'But it has a fine view to seaward and the harbour both. I think I'll take a sighting.'

From the boat it was impressive. Set high into the precipitous crags that ended near vertically in the sea, it consisted of three mutually supporting towers stepped at different levels with views out to three sides. A relic of the days of Barbary corsairs for defence of the harbour, it was a formidable fortress.

It was a stiff climb over the treeless escarpment to the side entrance and close to they saw it for what it was – an abandoned antique, its stonework faded and crumbling. Inside it had been hollowed out of its fitments, its few casemates decorated with cannon of another time.

'Splendid!' Cochrane declared. 'As will be our fall-back if the citadel can't stand.'

Kydd, however, had noticed something. 'A fine edifice – but if we're obliged to quit it under fire, I can see the defenders hard driven as they scramble to get out by this only path fully in the open.'

'I'll give it thought, old fellow, never fear. Now, where's their commander?'

It didn't take long to discover there was none. 'Then I shall take it in charge. So where does that leave us?'

As if on cue there was a distant surge in the firing around the citadel.

Cochrane turned to Kydd. 'Supposing you take on the bombarding of the French attacking our friends there? I'm thinking the bombs would object to being left out of the sport.'

Kydd agreed it made a lot of sense. The charts had shown sufficient depth of water for the bomb-vessels close in to hurl shells at the enemy positions, and even if *Tyger* could approach only within a quarter-mile or so, the shot from her great guns would create mayhem and confusion in the crowded siege area.

Chapter 20

The two bomb-vessels were anchored well in with the town of Rosas. Kydd chose the larger to board, *Meteor*.

'Commander Collins. A distinct pleasure to make your acquaintance, Sir Thomas.' A slight-built man of years, he was clearly in awe of his visitor.

When they were sitting together in the diminutive state cabin, he politely waited for Kydd to speak.

'I would know your tasking, that you're here in Rosas, Captain.'

'This is our forward position, Sir Thomas. Admiral Collingwood desires we take station here – as good a place as any, being handy to be called for operations north to the border or south to Cartagena.'

'Rather than be distant in Minorca.'

'Just so.'

Cochrane was lucky: these as well were under the commander-in-chief's orders and he was within his rights to take them up. 'Then know that we've work to do, sir,' Kydd said briskly. 'The citadel is being sore pressed by the French, who are expected—'

'I know this, Sir Thomas,' Collins said defensively. 'As no one has seen fit to employ us.'

'And I am. What is your state?'

'Ready for immediate service. Eighty-two thirteen-inch shells, twelve only ten-inch. These including the tender I share with *Lucifer*. The other bomb, Commander Powell, that is.'

'Then shall we calculate your positioning?'

Kydd had had some experience in the bombardment of Granville years before but left it to Collins to supervise the technicalities of siting the pair.

Back aboard *Tyger*, he set Brice to work with a hand lead to verify the depths shown on the chart.

He'd only just sat down to a snatched meal when a messenger from shore arrived with news. It was from O'Daly. 'General Reille's arriving from the hills. He's guns and some eight thousands in these first columns. We must expect to be invested directly.'

First the citadel, then Fort Trinidad with its derisory band. These overcome, the way would be open for Saint-Cyr to flood the plain with his troops to march on Barcelona. Each hour of delay would be of value.

'Tell *Meteor* and *Lucifer* I expect them to be in place to open fire at daybreak,' Kydd ordered, dabbing his mouth with a napkin.

'And ask the gunner to see me.' With hard use of the guns the next day he and his mates would be working well into the night: many cartridges to be filled, flints to be sharpened, firing quills to be prepared.

Kydd's last hours before dark were with O'Daly, spotting the enemy's movements. Over to the left, occupying the near ground by the sea, was the first of the horse artillery detachments. And just visible as black dots winking in and out of view, sappers were throwing up protection, well within range of the big mortars in *Meteor*.

Further around the next point of the citadel opposite the breach was the main thrust – six siege guns behind their own earth ramparts. A single row but to move even these the long way across the treacherous defiles and stony tracks through the mountains must have been an agonising haul. The infantry was concentrated around them: when the breach had been pounded enough for it to be practicable, they would storm the citadel or receive its capitulation.

Maps were drawn up with these features and a signalling arrangement put in place to lay down fire where indicated. It was as much as they could do. To see the enemy, even at a distance, had made Kydd's skin crawl. This deliberate preparation over days for bloodshed and slaughter, with no room for manoeuvre or guile, turned his stomach. Much more to his taste was the intricate ballet of sail and gunnery that was war at sea, where it tended to be the better man and ship that prevailed.

The night passed slowly. He'd sent a note to Cochrane detailing his plans and dispositions and received a courteous answer, explaining the first steps that were being taken to make Fort Trinidad an effective fall-back, leaving unsaid the implication that the citadel was expected to be taken.

With dawn came a brittle tension that neither side seemed to want to break. At ten precisely the French lines erupted into a thunder of guns as they opened up. The drifting smoke nearly hid the outlines of the citadel, but in the favourable breeze the view of the activity in the siege works was clear and the bomb-vessels needed no encouraging.

Already sighted in, the massive *whuump* and sheet of flame of their mortars dominated the bay, and through his telescope Kydd watched as the shells arced high to plunge down and explode in a vivid flash and dirty brown smoke. Army battle-field mortars were playthings compared to these monsters and it must have come as a terrible shock, for the sea-borne beasts were seldom in range of an army.

Lucifer joined in, the two alternately mauling the French positions until their firing died away.

The siege lines were their prime objective for, if the heavy guns pounding at the breach were successful, it would then be close-quarter fighting and, unable to tell friend from foe, their contribution would be at an end.

Through his glass Kydd saw still figures dotting the raw earth of the works, an upturned gun, others scattering under the merciless rain of death.

For all that day, whenever a siege gun fired, the bombs would throw in a shell or two and it would cease. It was turning into a frustrating stalemate for General Reille. He had the men but couldn't take the citadel without a breach to let them in – and he could not secure one while his guns were being neutralised.

It couldn't last.

Recovering, the French moved fast. Along the foreshore they ranged their own mortars and field artillery and put the bombs under fire.

That was what *Tyger* was there for. Sighting between the two anchored ships, springs taken from her anchors to the capstan, she loosed fire at the batteries from her eighteen-pounders, round-shot and grape driving them back in disarray.

The French retired and peace reigned on the field of battle. A forced lull – but the army of unknown thousands needed to be fed, powder replenished, stores restocked. They'd expected to descend to plains ripe for plundering but their supplies had now to be painfully dragged across the mountains. They'd been fought to a standstill by a handful of sailors.

All through the rest of the day and that following there was no visible change in the situation.

Then, on the third day, an innocent line of bushes in a cleft of the sand-dunes facing the anchored ships was whipped away, revealing the muzzle of a heavy gun, one of the siege guns sacrificed to another purpose.

It spoke almost immediately, a flat blast of sound that ended in a great plume of shot-strike close enough to wet the bowsprit of *Meteor*. Under cover of dark the gun had been dragged down to the water's edge and it changed the equation completely.

The bombs, with their loading of powder – many pounds' weight for every thirteen-inch shell – were in no condition to face a trial by artillery. Their boon of a high firing arc that could send shells sailing over lofty walls was a distinct disadvantage against a flat-firing cannon with many times the range.

The obvious move would be to withdraw out of reach but that would be to hand the battlefield to the French – and therefore the citadel and the town shortly after.

'I want a stream and kedge at bow and stern,' Kydd growled.

Bowden looked at him with a serious expression, Bray with a tight smile. Both had worked out what Kydd had in mind. With the two anchors out they were going to warp inshore using the capstan to take advantage of every inch of water over the shoals and engage in a personal duel with the cannon.

Kydd blessed his foresight in having Brice make survey of the inshore waters.

As preparations went ahead the French gun spoke again. It was at least a twenty-four-pounder and well served, although its rate of fire was not impressive. It was concentrating on one target, *Meteor,* making the task of laying and correcting for fall of shot easier than alternating between the two. This last ball had slammed low across midships of the bomb to the dismay of the forward mortar crew.

'Stretch out, y' lubbers!' Kydd bellowed at the launch taking in the stream anchor. He bunched his fists in frustration: it was not in his nature to harass those who were doing their best but the situation was grave.

'If 'n we can get in a ship's length more it would help, sir,' the gunner said, eyeing the range anxiously. *Tyger* had a number of guns but each was intended for close combat and rapid fire, not precision targetry. Their mark was an imaginary square around the enemy muzzle of about two feet or so a side, and at something like three cables range – a quarter of a mile – it was asking a great deal to place a ball in an area half the size of the ship's wheel from a gun with only the crudest of sights.

The third shot from the shore hit home, taking *Meteor* in the fore-deck and sending up a shower of dark splinters, but Collins was intelligently heaving round on his springs to present his bow, a smaller target. *Lucifer* was still gamely throwing out her shells at the siege-works but her turn would come.

At last the launch cut the anchor suspended underneath and bobbed free. Instantly the boatswain had the ready-manned capstan hauling in. *Tyger* inched slowly ahead into shoal waters.

A leadsman in the bows was singing out the depths but already Kydd, looking over the side, could detect the dull gleam of a sandy bottom interspersed with dark blotches of rock and seaweed. At least in the Mediterranean there were no tide movements to allow for.

Another shot struck *Meteor*. This brought down a spar and its canvas. Her crew worked on with the fearful knowledge that a round anywhere near either of the magazines would transform the ship into an erupting volcano.

Tyger was as close as she could get, with the kedge taken out so the ship could be ranged broadside and all her guns brought to bear. Even before the move was completed it was clear the French had seen their danger and they shifted target to *Tyger*.

The first ball was wide, skittering well out to sea in a succession of ever smaller plashes but the implication was clear. *Tyger* had more guns but she had the smaller mark to hit; while the French gun had a slow rate of fire, it had a vastly bigger target.

At last it was *Tyger*'s turn. Her weapons would be fired in turn from forward, letting the gun captains have a chance to see where their shot was striking.

The first smashed out. It was a good try but low in the dune and to the left, a barely visible kicking up of sand, the worst possible substance to take a round-shot. Only a direct hit would make a difference.

The second came soon afterwards: not much better and difficult to see where it struck.

A third. The shore gun fell silent. Were they taking cover?

Then Kydd realised the bombs had ceased activity, presumably in trepidation, waiting for a result to *Tyger*'s defensive firing.

'Signal, "Resume action", pennants of both,' he snapped. He wasn't putting *Tyger* into danger for nothing.

A fourth and fifth lit up the air. But they were not succeeding, the target was far too small and the nearest had been about ten yards to the right.

Then the French resumed their deadly gun-play. They'd seen that, sited well, nestled down in their sandy redoubt, they'd little to fear even from the broadside of a big ship.

Their next shot was high, but fair for line. Kydd winced at the air disturbed by the near miss. This was Bonaparte's famed artillery laying down fire true – and improving.

He toyed with the idea of having the best gun captain aboard go along the guns sighting each in the hope that his eye would tighten on the prize. Toby Stirk? But even as the thought was born it died. Kydd had once served on a gun himself and knew that each was an individual beast with its own ways and flaws, which its gun captain was best placed to know.

Tyger's guns roared again. An overshot, causing a disturbance in the barely glimpsed camp beyond.

Almost at the same time the French gun slammed out with a brutal crunch that Kydd felt through the deck as *Tyger* took her first hit forward. It produced a high, muffled shriek that kept on and on until it stopped suddenly.

Kydd's heart went out to the unknown individual whose blood was the first to stain *Tyger*'s deck in this commission. White faces turned to him but his features were set in the stern calm necessary for a captain under eye.

Meteor and *Lucifer* were still loyally blazing forth but *Tyger* was the sole target now. If she could be put out of action the enemy gun would make short work of the two bomb-vessels. It was a duel to the death and the French were getting the better of it.

Monotonously *Tyger*'s guns smashed out, the balls all striking within yards of their mark. In a sea battle it was a winning display that would have seen their crews cheering madly, but here was received in despairing silence.

Another shot from the French gun hit home. Low across the waist just yards before the main-mast, it was almost certainly aimed at the quarterdeck. Two men were carried groaning below, victims of a demolished plank-sheer.

Kydd began the usual slow pace of officers under fire. It was so frustrating to be anchored and still, unable to manoeuvre or do much to avoid the murderous battering that was affecting them all.

The first hour saw three hits, two trivial and one low down forward, punching through the bow timbers and into the lower deck – the mess deck, where sailors had their being. No one was there at the time to be cut down by a lethal spray of splinters.

There was now a sizeable hole in the curve of *Tyger*'s bow that made improbable her survival in anything like a head sea. The swell of her stout bow, where shipwrights had laboured to shape timbers with a steam chest and adze to go through a right-angle to meet the stem, could not readily be repaired with the straight lengths of planking on hand. She'd been gravely wounded.

The exhausted gun crews served their iron beasts until the watered sheepskin rammers sizzled dangerously as they swabbed out – still they fired, on and on.

More deliberate, aimed fire came from the enemy gun. Not at the rigging as was the practice of Frenchmen at sea, for these were army artillerists. They saw before them only the mass of a ship and fired at it with no comprehension of its vulnerabilities.

Kydd guessed the quarter-to-a-third-of-a-mile range was beyond their usual fighting experience but they were making good practice, securing a dismaying proportion of hits. More men were paying the price, and Kydd's face was a mask of enduring as they were carried below to the surgeon's knife. They'd made the French pay, but the delay that the Spanish in Gerona so desperately needed was being purchased with their blood. How much more would be demanded before they could withdraw with honour?

The evening at last drew in and with it the prospect of relief.

The last shots were exchanged in the spreading dusk, over-bright gun-flashes in the gloom, until all at once there was nothing but a deafening silence and the stink of gun-smoke stealing slowly across the anchorage.

Tyger still held the field, but at what cost?

Nearly dropping with fatigue, Kydd made his way forward and down the hatchway to those who had done their duty and suffered.

He stopped suddenly at the foot of the ladder. Starkly lit by three lanthorns before him, he saw rows of men, some writhing and quietly moaning, others ominously still. Holding back a wave of desolation, he became aware that Scrope, the middle-aged surgeon he'd taken aboard for his careful relia-bility, was speaking to him. 'And it's mainly splinters, Sir Thomas, as must be expected. Only one or two's taken hits b' shot.'

'The butcher's bill?'

'One killed, nine wounded, o' which three badly.'

Dully, Kydd granted that for a three-hour pounding it could have been much worse. 'Who was . . .?'

'Killed? Harris, fore-topman.' The bright, laughing youngster, who had come aboard the previous year as a wide-eyed volunteer and already a topman. Kydd's eyes misted in grief.

'Wounded? Berkeley, yeoman of the sheets. Skull stove in, I've my doubts he'll see the dawn. Lashley, fo'c'sleman. Crushed ribs and suffering right grievously. And . . . and the other . . . well, says as how he'd like to see you when you was free, like.'

The man was barely conscious, his eyes rolling in near-unendurable pain, the lower part of his body a dark mass of coagulated blood . . . and the heart-stopping sight of just one leg where there should have been two.

Kydd had seen men maimed and destroyed but what made this different was that the pitiful husk that lay there was, of all men, Joyce, the eternally jovial, vastly experienced old sailing master, his life ebbing out before his eyes. He knelt beside him as Scrope left quietly. 'Mr Joyce. Can you hear me?'

It eventually penetrated and he turned towards him, ashen and cadaverous, his eyes pits of torment. 'S-sir?' he gasped. 'You c-came.'

'Of course, old friend.' Kydd turned away to reach for composure.

'It's – if ye'd h-hear me. I have t' ask a boon of y-you.' The voice was quavering under the intensity of the man's effort.

'Say it, and that's an order.'

'Aye aye, s-sir.' The smile was a ghastly parody and it wrenched at Kydd's control.

'It's j-just that . . . well, if'n ye can find it in ye to let Missus Joyce know I was knocked on the head, not like this'n. S-see, we're close an' all and sh-she wouldn't like t' find out . . .' The voice trailed off, Joyce passing in and out of consciousness.

'You just rest now, m' friend, and you're going to tell her yourself, do you hear me?'

There was no response, and Kydd straightened slowly, staring unseeing into the gloom, then turned and found his cabin. There, in private, the tears fell on his pillow.

Chapter 21

As the promise of day dawned, it brought a sight that
made all thoughts of enduring unthinkable. Kydd told
himself he should have seen it coming. So obvious, so logical
– so inevitable. Before there had been one gun, now on either
side there was another. Three times the threat – three times
the suffering.

The French had won.

'Signal "Retire", both pennants,' Kydd ordered stiffly.

Their retreat was done in a stifled hush, the enemy not
deigning to open fire, no doubt to save precious powder for
what must come.

First *Lucifer*, followed by *Meteor*, stood out to sea on the
morning breeze and then it was *Tyger*, leaving the wide bay
innocent and empty.

Kydd had nothing to be ashamed of in withdrawing, but
the unfortunates in the citadel would know that the retreat
of the ships had doomed them. There was nothing he could
do about it: his duty now was to fall back on Fort Trinidad
and Cochrane.

During the night Berkeley had faded and died without

regaining consciousness, as had Lashley, suddenly retching blood and expiring. The life of Joyce hung on a thread – in mercy Kydd had had him transferred to the coach, with two of the more badly hurt.

The boatswain and his mates were everywhere about the ship. The passage of a single rampaging ball had casually taken with it a large amount of neatly trimmed gear, all of which had to be spliced and re-rove, set up and secured. More extensive repairs would have to wait.

His face drawn with exhaustion, Kydd lost no time in seeking out Cochrane in one of the musty chambers of a tower in the fort.

Cochrane's expression was grave as he heard the cost of Kydd's stand. 'I grieve with you, dear chap,' he said sincerely.

'So?'

'We must expect the Crapauds to move fast, I believe,' Cochrane murmured. 'I've done what I can. Do you want to see?'

He went to the slitted window. 'The sainted Spaniards who built this place did better than they realised. See, we command the approaches over the foreshore, and on the other side,' he went to the opposite window, 'we are guarded by precipitous bluffs. To our rear we have near impossible rocky inclines. None is in easy line of fire from inland and I'm sanguine we'll hold out.'

'And if not?'

'Should they attempt a sally, this is what's waiting for them.' He motioned Kydd to follow him up the stone steps to the next level and pointed to where part of the wall had tumbled to ruin. 'An old breach, and one that they're sure to storm.'

He indicated the interior. A wooden slide, like a coal chute, dropped away to blackness below. It gleamed with what, from the rank smell, had to be cook's slush. 'I had the *Imperieuse* carpenter build 'em, a good job he made of it too. The villains crowd in but straight away losing their grip are shot down to end at the base of the tower in a heap where our men are ready to, er, attend on them.'

Other deadly traps were pointed out, nets, false steps, throat-high trip-wires, fish-hooks. A fiendish collection, and more were under construction.

Then there were the subterranean charges, laid to detonate and bring down parts of the castle.

Cochrane had brought to bear all his lethal creativity in one giant devil's trap.

That night a midnight assault carried the citadel, and soon after, came news that the relief column from Gerona had been ambushed and wiped out on its way to O'Daly, his remaining hope lost. Without pause the French marched into Rosas town, their immediate supply situation now eased by looting.

'Many would say that, the citadel fallen, there's no point in further resistance,' Kydd said, as he and Cochrane took their evening repast.

He'd be glad to go. Joyce was still alive, hanging on to life with a tenacity that was the admiration of all who saw him. If he could be transported to the hospital at Minorca there was an even chance he could live. And *Tyger* was sore wounded and badly needed a dockyard, if ever she was to keep the seas again.

'Are we still delaying Saint-Cyr on his mission to relieve Barcelona?' Cochrane answered quietly. 'We are, for any prudent general cannot abide an active threat in his rear as he moves forward. He has to take this contemptible castle or fail.'

'Then we can expect the brute to come knocking on the door,' Kydd replied dully.

Chapter 22

In the soft morning light, as men were relieved from their dawn stand-to, a trumpet sounded, thin and pure, on a rocky point of the foreshore: the chamade, a summons to parley.

Under the white flag a French lieutenant stumbled forward, met by one of Cochrane's band. After much politeness a letter was handed over.

Cochrane broke the seal. 'I've a notion what it says but I'll grant the beggar a reading.' He gave it the briefest of glances. 'General Reille. Admires our courage and so forth but invites us to discuss terms for a capitulation. He shall get his answer.'

Within the hour the encamped great host of France witnessed two frigates of His Majesty criss-cross slowly across the bay, the *tricolore* of France floating high at the main of each – firmly in subjection beneath the proud colours of England and Spain.

The insult was quickly answered. Kydd and Cochrane watched snaking columns of troops heading into the gorges and rifts between the scrub-covered hills and ridges about them. Before evening the encirclement was complete, including the occupation and manning of the heights above.

By the next morning guns were in place. Not siege pieces but large enough.

Opening up they quickly scored hits on the highest level of Fort Trinidad. To Kydd, this was a much different sensation than it was in a ship under fire. The shot-strikes were not a hollow crunch to the hull or the crack and hissing whirr of splinters but the ear-splitting ring of iron on stone transmitted instantly to the feet. This was followed by the skitter of lethal sharp fragments and sometimes the sudden roar of tumbling masonry.

Gaping holes were battered at the upper levels but none any further down. Kydd realised this was because the guns could not bear, could not depress further below them at a risk of toppling when fired.

The French commander was no doubt under orders speedily to reduce the fortifications. Now there was only one alternative open to him.

There was no real reason for Kydd to be ashore with Cochrane but something made him reluctant to abandon the man for the safety of the impotent *Tyger*. Cheerful and energetic, Cochrane was everywhere with words of encouragement to the fearful, quick to praise, careless of his own safety.

A hail from the sentries brought them both up to the walls. All along their vision were whole battalions of French troops, bayonets fixed, drums thundering the advance, a dreadful sight. A thousand or more on the move – closing on Fort Trinidad.

'The lunatics!' Cochrane gasped.

The lower two levels of Fort Trinidad were untouched and the antique guns in their casemates began their savage reprisal with grape-shot, mercilessly scything down the advancing infantry.

Now on the lower slopes, they were slipping and sliding on the incline, which in parts was near forty-five degrees. Bodies were strewn all around, their musketry futile against the pitiless smash of cannon and mortar.

The assault was over before midday.

'They'll be back – they have to be,' Cochrane conceded. 'I do propose we must think to quit.'

'Now?'

'When it's right to.'

Another day of delay was granted to the unknown Spanish besieger of Barcelona. Were the French at the extremity of their endurance yet? Would they then be forced to surrender in humiliating circumstances to the Spanish Patriots?

It was Kydd's practice to be with Cochrane when he took his pre-dawn stroll about the ramparts, together seeing the night retreat as daybreak stole over the hostile landscape and the malice of the enemy was revealed once more.

This new morning, as the black eased to grey and the delicate light took on colour, they stood at the edge of one bastion, Cochrane idly looking down its length as though sighting. 'It does cross the mind that if ever our ordnance fellows get it into their heads to screw a species of rifling into our cannon, as they do to turn a musket into a rifle, then we stand to turn gunnery on its head.' He pointed to an odd row of boulders on the opposite slope. 'Should we wish to bring down a mark there, the practice of triangulation from two points will fix it laterally, and a similar for—'

'Damn it – I saw something move!' Kydd hissed, straining to make it out in the soft light of dawn.

'The stone?'

'There!' Kydd was sure of what he'd seen.

Cochrane froze, staring hard. Then he pushed Kydd roughly aside and ran up the nearest turret steps. The next moment the morning was rudely split apart by the unholy concussion of a mortar firing, echoing away into the stillness.

Its shell took the ground not far from where Kydd had seen movement – and the whole width of their vision came alive. As though magicked into existence, soldiers rose and thrust forward into a charge, a wave of grey-coated infantry throwing themselves at the walls.

It was courageous, heroic – and doomed.

It should have worked. Their plain grey coats had allowed them to draw near in the crepuscular light of pre-dawn and, but for Kydd's sea-sharp vision, their numbers would have overwhelmed the defenders. But they were cut to pieces by grape and musketry before they could stumble the last yards to the walls and by mid-morning it was over, the bleak notes of the retreat sounding over the field of battle.

Cochrane stood at an aperture, looking pensive. 'They've drawn back to lick their wounds. Methinks we should choose now to take our leave.'

Out in the Bay of Rosas, not far from the dark shoreline, *Tyger* and *Imperieuse* lay together with the bomb-vessels and smaller craft, a longed-for sight. But first they had to break out of the castle in full view of the enemy, then slither down the treacherous slopes to the water's edge. And the act of ordering in the boats would give the game away, enabling the French to wreak a bitter revenge.

But this in no way dismayed Cochrane. Decision made, he flung himself into the task, spiking guns under cover, preparing magazines for blowing and even assembling valuables for evacuation.

Once all was readied he signalled for the boats.

His solution for overcoming the slow stumble down the

rocks was as simple as it was ingenious. Dozens of lengths of rope were let fly down the slopes – forming perfectly acceptable man-ropes as might be found by anyone coming aboard a man-o'-war.

The first defenders emerged, clutched a rope and lowered themselves backwards as fast as they could.

Kydd flinched, expecting a holocaust of shot, but none came. He glanced at Cochrane, standing cool and imperturbable by the sally-port as men poured through.

'No firing?'

'I would have thought not.'

'Why so?'

'The French. A logical race, don't you think? They know if they attack us leaving we're as likely to turn back, pull up the drawbridge and stay. They're desperate above all things to take possession so . . .'

As the last men made their way out, *Imperieuse*'s gunner reported.

'Do your duty, if you please,' Cochrane said calmly, and waited for the man to return.

Then the three wasted no time in boarding their boat and putting off. From a distance of some hundreds of yards in a muffled *crrrump* and rising dustcloud the first of the charges went off.

'And now we can get on with the rest of our war,' Cochrane said, with satisfaction.

Chapter 23

The Cabinet Room, No. 10 Downing Street

'Stay – do stay, old fellow,' wheezed the prime minister of Great Britain.

Spencer Perceval, chancellor of the exchequer, nodded, shuffling papers until the last of the ministers had filed out of the room.

Portland was slumped, a diminished figure yet formally attired, as always, in his full-bottomed wig and formal regalia.

It had been a bruising interchange. The usual sparring between Canning and Castlereagh had cast a pall on the proceedings making creative concentration difficult in the unusually fraught combination of circumstances. Perceval had wearily played honest broker between them, but the secretary of state for foreign affairs and the secretary of state for war were obsessed with the stand against Bonaparte and could not be brought to see that the most perilous state of affairs was at home.

'Your Grace?'

At first Portland didn't speak. His wasting sickness lay

heavily on him and it took time to bring his thoughts to order. It threw all the more responsibility on those who, like Perceval, were working tirelessly for their country, free of bias by reason of ambition or party.

'Spencer, I'm exercised by the Austrian problem. Not so much as whether we must intervene but whether we can. You understand me?'

'I do, Prime Minister.'

With Europe from end to end in thrall to Napoleon Bonaparte, only the capable and resourceful Archduke Charles of Austria was showing any signs of defiance, willing to join Great Britain in a Fifth Coalition against the tyrant.

'Chancellor, how might we act in this?'

'Sir. It is on the figures alone that I can offer opinion. Shall I . . .?'

'Please do. It will make more sense than the barnyard bickering we've been hearing these last two hours.'

'Then I shall review the success, or otherwise, of our fiscal survival. Each year our navy costs us some fifteen millions, the army eighteen. Subsidy to Continental powers is never less than that sum, and administration of the realm as much as eleven millions. If we include interest on the national debt – which we must – then this will add an obligation of some twenty millions on a net indebtedness in excess of seven hundred millions.'

'Yes, yes, this I'm aware of. Pray tell me the state of our revenues to set against this monstrous succubus.'

'Our financial resources are well defined, sir. Taxes or loans. The one is a net gain to the Treasury, the other a liability incurred for short-term gain. In taxes we might include all arisings from imposts on hair powder to windows, salt to dogs. This is, of course, derisory compared to Mr Pitt's child, the income tax.'

'I know all this too, Spencer, but how much is it yielding?'

'At a rate of two shillings in the pound which it were politically impossible to exceed, then it will be this year in the amount of fourteen millions.'

'I need to know—'

'I will omit the details then. Suffice it to say that our gross uptake of revenue from direct and indirect taxation is of the order of seventy-eight millions.'

'A spending deficit.'

'As must be funded, Your Grace. This is the cost of mere survival. Add to this any extraordinary expenditures, and we edge further into grave debt at peril of our standing in the world. There is our presence in Lisbon—'

'Which we have sworn to retain, our only foothold on the Continent of Europe.'

'—and the Spanish subventions, and prudence dictates a considerable sum in provision for the Continental project being considered in aid of the Fifth Coalition.'

Portland coughed weakly. 'Do allow that all this is known to me, Spencer. What I'm in mortal need of is answer to this question. Do we march with the Austrians?'

'Sir. Granted the need is extraordinary but so are the times. Loans by means of bonds, Treasury bills and similar weaken our credit position and are not to be relied upon. To support the Austrians in this coalition will require a most significant charge to be borne by the taxpaying public of the nation. The archduke is already in possession of bills on us in the sum of two millions, which, unhappily, he is discounting in large amounts to our embarrassment. The most to be desired is for our subventions to any foreign power to be made in specie instead, the price of which is fixed and is then never an instrument of debt.'

'Then why do we not?'

'The burden of remitting them. A frigate has to be found to freight them, insurance cover negotiated, a reliable and defended means of inland transport arranged and, of course, in the first place the specie has to be sourced. Better it is by far to make purchase on the Continent and disburse at source, but here we find no privileged situation – we needs must compete on the open market as with any other bidder, be it merchant or state.'

'The costs compared?'

'For smaller amounts, say up to a hundred thousand, the frigate is more to be seen, for larger the bulk becomes too cumbersome and vulnerable to handle. We must find another way.'

'Purchase.'

'We are not equipped to do so. We must approach a City of London merchant banker who will conduct the business with a correspondent bank of their arranging on the continent. For a suitable commission, of course.'

'Which will closely match the costs of our own remitting.'

'Sir.'

'The raising of a Fifth Coalition is of grave importance, I'll have you in no doubt of that. You shall approach the City and—'

'I have not told you all, Prime Minister.'

'Yes?'

'The cost of maintaining General Wellesley in Lisbon is at some considerable expense. So far he is in receipt of the order of two and a half millions in specie and, further, is in possession of one and a half millions in Treasury bills. If your intention is to advance the same to the Austrians, I do not readily conceive how it will be possible within our current revenue uptake.'

'I cannot accept this!' Portland burst out, provoking a

piteous bout of coughing. Recovering, he whispered, 'Even supposing we impose savage economies of a sort?'

'Sir, it is not a practical hope. When I tell you that of the navy's tens of millions only four per centum goes to a ship's arming and ammunition, the rest to those on shore standing behind the fleet as it goes about its several occasions, then any distortion of this balance will most certainly result in a parlous diminution of its force. Recollect Earl St Vincent with his economies before Trafalgar – a ruinous outcome saved only by his dismissal from post.'

'Ah, yes. You are a good servant to the Crown, Spencer, and I know you would exert any effort to bring about a satisfactory conclusion. I am at my wits' end to know how to proceed – Canning and Castlereagh both are insistent that the coalition be made for any number of cogent reasons. Now you are telling me it is not within our power.'

Perceval looked away in despair. He shouldn't have had to talk at such an elementary level to the leader of the nation, and it was becoming clear that much had slipped Portland's mind. Was this any basis for decision-making at the highest? 'Your Grace, there is a hope that in this matter a way forward may be found. I will set my most promising junior secretary to the Treasury, William Huskisson, the sole task of procuring specie in the sum you desire for disbursement in the Austrian cause. If he's able by some means to secure an arrangement considerably below the usual in the article of charges, there is no question that we might proceed in faith with the coalition.'

'Bless you, Spencer. I shall leave the affair with you. Go now. Above all things, I desire rest but I shall happily see you when there's news for me.'

Chapter 24

Perceval returned to his private office in No. 11, minions retreating in dismay at his expression. He closed the door firmly before sinking into his padded desk-chair with a ragged sigh.

He was aware he was considered a chancellor of the first rank, the best England had experienced since the younger Pitt. This came at a price, however: he was widely credited with miraculous powers but these were not from any supernatural gifts, rather the assiduous study of the financial veins and arteries of the *orbis terrarum parsimoniae* in all its imperfections and caprices. In the past he'd seen and forestalled economic tides and disasters, given careful stewardship to the nation's assets and reserves of treasure, and steered the ship of state clear of the treacherous shoals of unsecured debt.

But, as he'd protested to the prime minister, these were extraordinary times. With a tyrant astride virtually the entire civilised world, his usual powers of fiscal management were limited only to where England's writ ran, and that had shrunk to nothing much more than these islands.

In the larger picture, Bonaparte's Continental System had

now swallowed all of Europe, and if the kingdom of England was going to survive it would be only as a result of its financial fitness. This had been secured until now by a sound attitude to trade, which had encouraged enterprises of all kinds to adapt to the oppressive regime. And as taxation was a direct function of trade volume, those monies laid out on the navy were well spent.

But tax, loans, bonds, ingenious schemes, he'd tried them all and, with a national debt of staggering dimensions, he'd reached the limits of his ability to furnish the pecuniary muscle to Britannia's sword arm by any honourable means.

Yet this all-devouring fiscal maelstrom had an even wider player, overarching Napoleon Bonaparte and Great Britain both, and one that neither might control nor seek to dominate by force of arms: the shadowy web of labyrinthine alliances, obligations and power that was international banking.

This was not the commonplace extending of facilities to merchants, manufacturers or estates, still less the competitive and grubby business of mercantile loan-broking. It was a world dominated by a very few houses that had accrued such capital from astute merchant exchange that they were in a position to talk to governments, to deal in amounts that took the breath away. Names like Baring, Coutts and the coming Rothschild were spoken in hushed tones in the City of London.

Led by tight-knit families, whose heads could bind their house to daring acceptances with risks unthinkable by lesser men, their margins were equally breath-taking. Their reach and power had increased beyond measure in the wars for it was their practice carefully to place family members in selected capital cities of the Continent. The trust and obedience they represented allowed bills of exchange to be uttered in Rotterdam that would be honoured in London and the reverse, to the immense benefit of merchants in countries otherwise understood to be at war with each other. It even extended to Paris: because of Bonaparte's pressing need for liquidity, through these houses a paper written in Paris would be honoured in London – for a fee.

Their success was due in most part to a cold-blooded attitude to risk and profit. Loans to sovereign powers were possible in enormous sums to fight wars, fund conquests and survive ruin – at a commensurate rate in fees, commissions and charges. Agents negotiating such moved in a world of utmost secrecy and delicacy, being equipped by the house with the best intelligence obtainable. They were privy to mysteries and secrets at the very highest.

Perceval knew few of the details. England's secret service was ill-equipped to penetrate these great international houses, but then again, for what purpose? They were outside the polity of any nation, and to offend by intruding risked losing their good offices when it counted, a disastrous consequence.

He had himself made use of them on occasion to raise an emergency borrowing and found them correct, courteous and meticulous in the accounting. The loan would not come cheap but if accepted would be certain and to the letter of the financial instrument employed.

No doubt in this matter of the Austrian subvention they could cover the amount, three to six millions realisable within six weeks, but the charges levied on the risk of an Austrian defeat would be punitive. And if secured as usual on British revenue, when exports to the Continent had fallen sickeningly in the wake of Bonaparte's Berlin Decree, they didn't bear thinking about.

Yet what else was there?

At the very least he'd stand by what he'd promised Portland and set Huskisson to work. The young man was a brilliant asset to the Treasury, hard-working, lucid and exact in his dealings, a very model of probity and rectitude. It was said that any department of state begging a budgetary advance would as likely receive by return a five-page lecture on thrift.

He would be set the task of securing two-thirds the amount in specie, sourced on the Continent by any able to supply it, but with the usual proviso: that the contractor be examined in open court by the Bank of England. Privately owned, the bank had every reason to ensure the integrity of the trans-action by reason of its stewardship of the credit-worthiness of the City. Practised since the time of the elder Pitt, this open examination was seen as a prudent measure against the temptation to peculation by any government.

Huskisson didn't stand a chance, of course. He would work himself to the bone, trying every possible contrivance but in the end be defeated, both by his own lofty ethics in the face of a world with an ethos not his own but at base the sheer impossibility of extracting a significantly reduced charge on such a colossal amount. Nevertheless, to keep faith with Portland it would be done.

Perceval rang for cordial and a cold plate. It deserved the last shred of his concentration before he admitted to the prime minister that the Fifth Coalition was a practical impos-sibility.

He caught himself, frowning, as he began to ponder.

If – and just supposing – he were able to best these moguls of finance by some clever but not altogether honourable stratagem, where did the sin lie? To put the desperate need of the country ahead of one's personal honour, was that not to be contemplated?

But it opened a line of scheming that, while distasteful to him personally, might yet provide an answer.

And the advantage at the moment was his. Under Pitt, and

then himself, the City of London had gained a reputation for honesty and straight dealing that was unmatched in the world. Its trustworthiness had attracted an immense amount of business and at a rate the French could only dream of. Merchants had streamed out of Europe to London to conduct their affairs, bringing with them their connections and prospects. All had profited.

Therefore he and the government he represented were trusted. If he could think of some scheme based on this there was every prospect it could come off and the Fifth Coalition be saved.

The complication – the grave disadvantage if looked at from the personal point of view – was that it might well succeed but after the event it would inevitably be exposed, to the shame and dishonour of the British nation. That, of course, was intolerable and could only be avoided if a sacrifice were found to heap all blame upon . . . Himself. Could he bear it? Could dear Jane bear it?

Into the night he plotted and schemed, and some time in the early hours he came up with a plan. It was one that met all the criteria for what was needed and – with a modicum of luck – might even allow him to get away with it.

But it was one he himself could not carry through. This would be the affair of one gifted individual of the utmost integrity and sworn to the most extreme secrecy, one who was not daunted by personal danger and, like himself, could not be tempted by earthly treasures.

He had not the slightest idea who this might be or how he could be found – but he knew someone who did.

'My dear sir – and so early in the morning!' George Hammond, permanent under-secretary of state for foreign affairs, shook his hand warmly. 'Do come in, take a pew.'

Perceval had never visited Carlton Gardens, more the territory of the Foreign Office, and was somewhat guarded. Hammond, however, was effusive and welcoming. 'Methinks you're here for reasons other than leaving your card.'

Hammond was the discreet but knowledgeable gatekeeper to the covert, even sinister world of the secret service, the loose and informal aggregate of all clandestine activity of the state. Perceval knew him as the funnel into which he was occasionally asked to pour large amounts of money for darkly shrouded reasons.

'I have a problem that I fancy will yield only to one with gifts of discretion and judgement, able to penetrate abroad without he is noticed.'

'I see. Sir, you will understand I must ask it of you but – public business or private?'

'The affair is of the greatest importance to the state, sir. In the utmost confidence it is—'

'Sir, I do not need to know this. You shall have your man. Leave it with me – and a very good day to you, Chancellor.'

Hammond waited until he heard the outer door close. Then he lifted a silver bell and rang softly. From an inner office came a discreet functionary.

'James, do desire Mr Congalton to step along, there's a good chap.'

Chapter 25

Mayfair

'My dear, a gentleman visitor to see you,' Cecilia announced to her husband.

Their town house had been busy this season and there had been quantities of callers.

'Dear soul,' Renzi sighed, 'if you wish me to finish wording these invitations this forenoon . . . Who is it?' Although now titled Lord Farndon, he'd grown attached to the name he'd used for so many years at sea, Nicholas Renzi.

'Oh, a Mr Congalton. He says it's on a matter of business and you'd understand,' she finished.

Renzi paused, then slowly put down his pen. 'I'll see him now,' he said quietly, 'in the drawing room.' He had met Congalton before as his contact point in the Foreign Office when engaged on high business of state, such as his involvement with the Ottomans. But it was unusual to the point of incredible that this spare, abstemious man of indeterminate years and pallid complexion should venture out from his Whitehall fastness. The affair he was going to be sounded out about must be of crucial importance, that he was approaching Renzi personally.

'My lord,' Congalton said, rising with a bow, as Cecilia ushered him in.

'Pray do be seated, sir,' Renzi said, adding, 'My dear, please allow us our privacy.'

Knowing the man, he didn't trouble with social preliminaries. 'You have something for me, Mr Congalton? We shall not be disturbed.'

'A matter more than usually pressing and of an elevation at a particular *sensibilité.*'

'Ah.'

'Involving directly as it does the chancellor of the exchequer of this government.'

'Please go on.'

'It is the will of the government in council that a Fifth Coalition be raised against Napoleon Bonaparte, our primary ally being Austria in the person of Archduke Charles. However, in the chancellor's estimation, this country will be unable to secure the necessary subventions in our present economic state, the amount required in the short term being of the order of millions.'

'Yes?'

'The principal bar is that, employing the usual banking arrangements, the charges associated with the securing of specie to that sum on the Continent will be ruinous to the country and cannot possibly be entertained.'

'Understood.' What the devil . . . ?

'However, the prime minister has privately allowed to Mr Perceval that the matter is of such moment to the country that he leaves it in the hands of the chancellor to effect a solution by any means. Mr Perceval has chosen to take this at its broadest signification and has formulated a scheme of the greatest delicacy that he believes will answer.'

'Sir, this is hardly—'

'I would not trespass on your time, my lord, were I not to believe you to be particularly well suited to the mission. I will be brief. The task at hand is the acquiring of specie in the sum of some millions within the Continent of Europe for immediate disbursement. The normal channel is to approach a banking house known to us in the City and negotiate an arrangement that sees them instruct their correspondent bank to source and release the specie *in loco* against securities furnished by the Treasury.

'I have to tell you that the risks attendant upon the transaction – an Austrian defeat with a consequential run on the Bank of England, or conceivably an unwise military intervention by us, mayhap a contraction of trade and therefore our revenues – imply a scale of charges that this country cannot bear and therefore a coalition is unhappily impossible.'

Renzi kept silent. His role must surely soon become apparent.

'Mr Perceval has been good enough to outline to me a plan to bring these charges back within the capability of the Treasury to meet them. Now, sir, what I'm about to tell you is of the greatest possible secrecy for what he has revealed might well in lesser hands result in high-level legal actions of both a criminal and civil nature. He acts out of motives of the purest patriotism and places his own honour and reputation in our hands.'

'I understand, Mr Congalton,' Renzi said gravely.

'Then this is the essence of the plan. The house of Beyer will be asked to make tender on the matter and will return with a comprehensive figure for the acceptance that will include all charges and commissions. This will necessarily involve their correspondent house, Haart of Antwerp. In the meantime a lesser third party will be privately approached with a business proposition they will be unable to refuse – a chance to bid for the specie contract in return for a marked reduction in their charges.'

'A very reasonable commercial motion, surely.'

'The content of the offer will be privily communicated to Beyer with the advice that unless they do match it this very considerable business will pass out of their hands, if not in perpetuity.'

'Again, a not unknown situation I would imagine.'

'You would not think it if I were to tell you that the bearer of the invitation to tender does so with a very considerable incentive: he will be prepared to back the reduced bid with his own capital in the trust that further business will be forthcoming. In truth, the capital is secretly provided by the state in the name of this individual for the purpose of instilling the necessary confidence in his standing.'

'Mr Congalton. I take it you are considering myself as prime instigator of this . . . this fraud, sir. If so, I cannot be a party to it.'

'My lord, your scruples do you credit and would warm Mr Perceval's heart were he to have heard your words. You are right in the particulars. It is a fraud. Yet consider that it is in your country's gravest interest and at no time will it to be thought proper to act upon the bid, merely to flourish its existence before Beyer to secure a lower charge schedule from them. There is no question of a loss of monies to that house that would benefit the Crown, and the state's capital will be withdrawn at the earliest possible time.'

'It is still a deception.'

'You will be weighing your qualms against the nation's need and as well the subsequent benefits accruing to the Crown in the future of a more . . . considered attitude by Beyer to government loans.'

Renzi stood up, turned on his heel and paced the room. 'Very well, this I do appreciate, sir. However, I can conceive of a condition that makes the entire scheme worthless.'

'Do tell, my lord.'

'My knowledge and thus credibility in the practice of high finance is non-existent. To negotiate at such a level would be transparently risible.'

Congalton gave a thin smile. 'Do I understand you to accept in principle, my lord?'

'In principle, yes.'

'Then I'm able to disclose the details. You shall proceed in your own name as usual, being in possession of both a recent bequest and a realisation on your Caribbean holdings.'

'I haven't any. The estate is my brother's and—'

'And as a wealthy nobleman you will be accompanied by your man of business. As it is your intention to conduct affairs at the highest level you will have engaged for this an agent of a well-known merchant banking house to act under your direction, a not unknown procedure, and you need not fear to be shamed for lack of the technical knowledge of international finance.'

'He would be of value only if he is knowledgeable of the scheme in its entirety,' Renzi said carefully.

'In this affair there will be but three in possession of its secrets in full: myself, you, and the agent, who will be selected and hired for the purpose by myself personally. You may be assured that appropriate steps will be taken to ensure his discretion in the matter.'

'Then . . .'

'Then with your agreement, we shall proceed. Before you leave for Antwerp—'

'Antwerp?'

'Just so. There will be time before you embark to get to know your man and learn something of the milieu you will be entering. A final word from myself with specifics, and you'll be sailing. Expect your man at noon the day following tomorrow. Good day, and all fortune attend you, my lord.'

Chapter 26

Punctually to the hour a footman bore in a card on silver tray: 'Cornelius Meyrick, Financier, Sacher-Wilms'. It was expensively engraved and had an elusive whiff of fragrance.

'My study, if you will,' Renzi told the servant.

The room was small, lined with books and but two padded chairs – and was sacrosanct to Lord Farndon while in his town house. They would not be disturbed.

'My lord?' The man stood politely in the doorway, cradling a slim document case.

'Ah, Mr Meyrick – or should that be "Herr"? Do come in and take a chair. Your coat?'

The man sat elegantly. With elaborately curled hair in abundance, extending to sculpted side-whiskers, his snowy silk cravat and opulent fur-trimmed coat, he was of another breed of humanity. 'You are observant, my lord, but "Mijnheer" would be more appropriate, perhaps.'

Dutch, not Swiss therefore, and almost without the trace of an accent. 'It seems we shall be working much together, sir. I would know more of you in order that my trust will not appear misplaced.'

There was a faint smile.

'You are a financier?'

'In the broadest sense,' Meyrick replied smoothly. 'My chief occupation is as Continental agent for the house of Sacher-Wilms in the acceptance of financial instruments bearing varying degrees of risk. I am therefore well acquainted with the current fiscal climate and practices thereto in the chief cities — Zürich, Amsterdam, Berlin and the like, you may believe.'

Renzi could only admire his aplomb and faultless delivery, the expression of polite interest as reassuring as it was impenetrable. 'I'm sure Mr Congalton would have chosen you before most, sir. Yet it intrigues me that the essence of our affair is surely in competition with your house.'

'Not so, my lord. My services have been leased from Sacher-Wilms, true, but for the term of this engagement my loyalty most assuredly lies with you, the client, sir.'

'Do pardon if I offend, but how might I trust this statement?'

For the first time the smile held warmth. 'Sir, Mr Perceval has been good enough to agree pecuniary terms with me of a substantial nature. It is very much in my interest to achieve a good result.'

Renzi gave a brief nod. 'As speaks a true financier.'

The smile stayed as Meyrick answered, 'An agent labours from one commission to the next and would starve were he to pass up presenting opportunities. Your requirement is well suited to my proficiencies and inclinations and I'm sanguine the conclusion will be a happy one.'

'I do believe we shall get on, sir,' Renzi said, and held out his hand.

The smile faded and the handshake was brief. 'As will become evident,' Meyrick said, with a chilling seriousness.

'My lord, it is now for me to assure myself that you yourself are fitted for the role you've been asked to perform.'

Renzi held his gaze but said nothing.

'We shall be entering in upon a situation that is at the same time one that will be alien to your sensibilities and, more importantly, not necessarily what it appears to be on the outside. We shall be conducting our affair in circumstances of considerable peril to ourselves and our cause, where the immense stakes will excite cupidity and envy on a scale beyond your believing. If we are to succeed, I must have your undertaking that my advice will in all probability be superior to your views and will therefore be taken. Execution of financial papers will be under my advice and to your responsibility. Do I have your concurrence in this, my lord?'

'You do.'

The smile came back. 'Then with this *modus operandi* we shall go forth and, I have no doubt, conquer.'

Chapter 27

The following morning they met in the park and strolled together, a chance for Renzi to ask questions.

'Tell me, it seems fantastical in the extreme that financial houses handling vast wealth should exist in the heart of Bonaparte's empire untroubled by his exactions and control, their chief object to run smooth the mercantile desires of the City of London.'

Meyrick's silver-topped cane swung out, decapitating a daisy neatly and precisely. 'Not so. Recollect that the Emperor has many requirements not met by his plundering, foremost among them the financing of his exports, now sadly curbed by your cruisers. Accordingly, he must woo those who have ways to cross artificial borders, to make capital transfers invisibly and provide financing in anticipation of his conquests. Should he move against them, they'll flee his dominions, like so many merchant houses before. He needs them as much as you do, my lord.'

'Ah. Then does this tolerance extend to the principals that they might enter and leave at will?'

'To the principals and their clients both. That is to say,

within limits of conduct to be observed by both sides, these entirely devoted to the concealing of such from mortal eyes.'

'Might I ask specifics?'

'For instance, you will be brought into Antwerp by a device you will not enquire about too closely and shall reside in such a manner as will prescribe your daily movements. I can affirm to you that this will not in any way impede the provision of your comfort.'

'I see.'

'As a further illustration, it may surprise you to know that an appreciable number of Englishmen even now wander free upon the sacred soil of France, guests of the Emperor.'

'It would.'

'At Dunkirk, Wimereux and Gravelines. Visitors are ushered into extensive, discreetly guarded compounds and are shown the greatest courtesies and entertainment for the period of their stay. Provided they remain within the social bounds recognised, they are free to come and go as they desire.'

'These are scions of high finance, I presume?'

'Hardly. These, my lord, are smugglers.'

'They're . . .?'

'Who are highly valued gentlemen. They pour gold and specie into Bonaparte's pocket in return for a portion of the brandy and silks that are in abundance in France. He therefore decrees they must be protected and encouraged at all costs.'

'Tell me more of the higher sort. Do your merchant banking houses live in a state of amicable benevolence or in violent competition one with another?'

'They are in contention, but it is in the interest of all to acquit oneself in a manner of unreserved courtesy and civility. This serves further as a sovereign mask to conceal one's inner feelings in the course of negotiations – which is the reason for my caution that all is not as it seems. As to rivalry, all may be said to live or die by their skill in the capital market, and with the risks and gargantuan sums involved, there are few indeed occupying the heights and these not inclined to yield their position.'

A child burst free from its mother and ran into their path, chasing a ball. Both stopped and looked at the happy soul. Ball caught, the youngster lifted his eyes to the two grave men standing there. His face crumpled and, with a sob, he ran to his mother, who looked back fearfully at them.

Meyrick's calm recounting was far from reassuring. It hinted at a ruthless, veiled world outside the ken of mortals, where unimaginable mountains of wealth changed hands in an atmosphere of the most unimpeachable social graces. Could he think to enter it and be taken for one of them?

'You will not need to concern yourself with this, my lord,' he said, as if reading Renzi's thoughts. 'You are a wealthy noble who desires to give worthy employment to your considerable holdings. In essence, a client only.'

A goose to be plucked, Renzi mused.

'It is essential you should present as a man of very considerable capital for me to be justified in bringing you forward.'

'I haven't—'

'My lord, at this very moment steps are being taken to make you so.' A ghost of a smile passed. 'Fortune has looked upon you favourably – you have just been made the subject of an ancestral bequest that will enable you to enter in upon the stock market in a large way, the funds of course being a temporary placement of the Treasury until this business is concluded. They will have selected a poorly performing company, which, on receipt of your capital, will excite speculation among the lesser breeds of capitalist, as to what it is you perceive in the industry represented. This will drive up the value of your holding to a remarkable degree for the short period we require. You will be contacted by letter when all is in hand.'

'I see.'

'In addition I would beg you will execute some form of lien on your Caribbean property that—'

'It is not mine, sir! As I told—'

'You are the elder. Do prevail upon your brother to do so for your own sake. A matter of weeks at the most, and no risk to either of you.'

'Very well – but I cannot promise Richard will see how he should do this for me.'

'Splendid! Now we will talk of how we shall proceed. Beyer is being approached in the usual way by the government to produce a form of tender for the provision of the specie. Their corresponding bank is the house of Haart in Antwerp, who will provide the figures upon which Beyer will bid. We, on the other hand, will approach another, smaller, house – that of Goldstein. They will have declined to enter the round, for their resources cannot yield up the sum of specie required.

'Your ingenious offer is as follows. You are prepared to invest a sum sufficient to swell their working capital to the point where they can in fact make a bid. The proviso is that their charges and fee schedule is so much less that they will be very sure to take the business from Beyer and Haart. This you say you are doing with a view to your joint future in dealings with the British government. The prospect will much interest them you may believe.'

'Sufficient to accept?'

'Naturally you will be under discreet investigation by their agents in England, who will subsequently confirm your standing in securities as I have outlined.'

'What will happen when Mr Perceval receives their offer?'

'The Treasury would prefer to stay with Beyer as a known

entity and therefore will, *sub rosa*, let them know the contents of the Goldstein tender, giving them a chance to revise their own before the bids go before the Bank of England.'

'My position therefore is as a man of privilege and wealth desiring only to make increase on my capital, deferring as I will to my adviser and agent, yourself.'

'You may even admit to having engaged me from Sacher-Wilms, I being not unknown in Antwerp.'

'Just so.'

'Your demeanour is that to be expected of one of Fortune's darlings, not to be troubled by vexing questions of Mammon and pelf.'

'I believe that possible, Mijnheer Meyrick. Er, would my wife the countess be accounted welcome, do you think?'

'A woman in a man's world would be a singular thing and I could not recommend it. Besides, this enterprise on what must be accounted for you enemy territory has its uncertainties and perils that I'm sanguine you would not wish her to endure.'

They walked on in thoughtful silence.

'Then we shall meet again when I have your note that your financial arrangements are in hand. Good day to you, my lord.'

With an elegant doffing of his hat, Meyrick strode away.

Chapter 28

'My dear, in this instance it is just not possible,' Renzi told Cecilia.

Her curiosity had been piqued by their visitor and, agreeable to their pact never to have secrets from one another, Renzi had told her of his mission. She had claimed a right to be by his side as she had been in Denmark, but saw that this time it wasn't to be and subsided. He would be back soon enough, Renzi promised – Antwerp was barely a day's sail away with a fair wind and the business would not take long.

She had been the soul of discretion when his surprised brother Richard, also in town for the Season, had called in response to Renzi's hurried invitation. Leaving them alone together, she had smiled sweetly when he left, baffled but respectful.

'Bless him,' Renzi said, in wondering tones, holding a paper. 'I have here indisputable evidence of his quite ridiculous debt to me secured by his three Caribbean estates in the sum of some hundreds of thousands. It shall give me much pleasure when the affair is over to burn it before his eyes.'

He hesitated, struck by the enormity of what was happening. 'My dearest, would you kindly find me a small chest with a lock. It shall contain all papers connected with this proceeding to be quite separate from all else of my business or I will surely go lunatic. Only myself and you shall have a key.'

A second document shortly was added: a statement of account from his bank, with the infinitely polite and deferential tidings that he was now the richer by an appallingly large margin.

The third followed the same day. A furiously scribbled note from Congalton: *Put all you have in Consolidated Sicilian Sulphur.*

Renzi dashed off an order to his broker. It was complete. He was being trusted, as few could have been, with not much less than the future of his country.

His note to Meyrick went off immediately and the man appeared with impressive celerity.

'So, we leave on the morning tide from Gravesend tomorrow. I take it you have a manservant of some discretion? No other, if you please. Lesser servants will be engaged as required by my own factotum, who will smooth the way for us.'

'No regalia?'

'Your appearance will be rich, but restrained, preferring to keep to the company of your peers who would not be impressed by mere baubles of state. I am in haste, much to do. My carriage will call for you at four tomorrow. Until then, my lord.'

135

Chapter 29

Port Mahon

Cochrane had sympathised and stood by Kydd as the injured *Tyger* had fallen back on Port Mahon. In the dockyard the master shipwright had shaken his head – this was beyond their repairing. The same stout oaken timbers that gave *Tyger* her bulldog strength were not available in the Mediterranean or the great steam chests for their bending and shaping. It was not an extensive repair, but local material and tools were not up to the job.

Kydd eyed the wound in the bow with dismay. Their temporary repair of planks and canvas thrown off to expose it to the naked sunlight, the damage was worse than he'd feared. Not a neat hole punched into her hull timbers but an angled blow on the turn of her bluff bows that had entered and left at different points, shivering the timber strakes between. *Tyger* was no longer fit to take on Mediterranean tramontanas or Atlantic gales, which made her a liability to Collingwood.

Gibraltar didn't boast a dry dock, which left no choice

other than to return to England, the place of *Tyger's* birth, to receive her healing.

The crew heard the news with satisfaction, and he was overcome with secret joy at the chance of seeing Persephone. But it was tempered by the knowledge that in sailing he would be leaving *Tyger's* loyal sailing master, Joyce, in Minorca. He'd visited the gravely wounded man, assuring him that his place in *Tyger* would be kept for him, but knowing that it was a promise it was unlikely he could honour.

Life aboard had to go on, however, and there was now the serious matter of taking a wounded *Tyger* through a Biscay passage without a sailing master.

In the face of chilly rain squalls *Tyger* slipped out to sea to make her way south out of the Mediterranean. However, sailing large in the peevish south-westerly in Biscay enabled her to keep her bow downwind, and there was little to inconvenience beyond continual work at the pumps.

They made Plymouth in good time and the legendary name of their captain ensured every attention was given them. Estimates of the repair were put at some three weeks and, with a light heart, Kydd set out for Knowle Manor and home. The word was still a thing of warmth and unreality.

He'd set down roots, but not in Guildford where he'd grown up. It was where he and his true love had chosen to combine their lives into a single thread of time, one with the other.

Chapter 30

Hearing the trap grind over the driveway, Persephone threw open the door in delight. Still wearing her painting smock she ran to him.

Later that evening, they walked hand in hand up the ridge behind Knowle Manor, the last of the light filtering through the forest in a delicate tracery of silhouetted branch and twig. Persephone stopped, gazing up at the sight in rapt contemplation. 'I never tire of it, my love. The countryside here I vow is the loveliest there is to find in the kingdom.'

For Kydd, anything that pleased Persephone commanded his attention and he agreed whole-heartedly. The warmth and plentiful rainfall in this part of the world yielded a warm beauty, a rich, deep verdancy. 'And in all the world as I've seen it, Seph,' he replied sincerely.

They walked on to where the woods thinned and gave way to the bare moor, rolling and mysterious. This was the boundary of their estate, where the beauty of Devon woodland met the wildness of the outside world – a magic place.

She paused, then took both his hands and said softly, 'As will be lost to us soon, my darling.'

He jerked away, astonished. 'What did you say?'

'That land belongs to Martin Riggs. You haven't met him. He lives on his farm the other side of Bere Grimstock, dear old soul. He ran sheep but only a few now he's getting on. He's been approached by a projector crew from Truro who're talking down his moorland property with a view to buying it.'

'You'll be telling me why?'

'The worst of reasons, my love.'

'Which is?'

'You may not know it but Cornwall and Devon are known around the world for their china clay mines. I've seen them! Out of the ground is dug white clay to be used by our potteries for making porcelain of the purest white. There are not so many places in the world apart from China where this is found, and there are those who will pay a lot to get their hands on deposits not yet touched.'

'Is it then a bad thing for your Mr Riggs that in his old age he realises a pretty penny to ease his years?'

'I cannot begrudge him that. It's rather the manner of its getting. China clay is snatched from the ground in so many pits with an over-plus of water you must see to believe.'

Kydd was appalled. 'The ridges here torn up and left for dead?'

'It's more the arisings, which are deathly pale and stream down from lagoons dug above. We'll be continually receiving tricklings of this directly down the hill.'

'We'll speak to him about it, offer him something to stay tight on his land.'

'It's not so much Martin but his family, an odious parcel of money-grubbing detestables, who see only the guineas and not the ruin to our little Arcady. They are determined upon it whatever he says.'

Kydd could feel her unhappiness – an unexpected blight on her romantic soul, this intrusion of the gross and worldly into her own perfection of being. It must have weighed on her, with no one to share it while he was away, and he resolved to find a way, no matter what.

It was time to bring out the Kydd books of account. The purchase of Knowle Manor had taken the bulk of the prize money he'd invested over the years in consols, along with the Russian fur-salvage money. That left gun money and head money from various actions, income from estate tenants, and seven hundred pounds, a belated dowry from Persephone's parents, plus a scattering of revenue from some other sources.

It was a respectable amount, but repairs and improvements to Knowle Manor had made inroads into it and, Kydd being inexperienced in the arts of estate management, he had felt it prudent to leave the balance intact against running costs and any unforeseen expenses.

'Perhaps we could borrow . . .' Persephone began, but he quickly intervened.

'Against what? I cannot risk our home.'

'But prize money. Those three brigs you told me about?'

'Very slight pickings and nothing to count on. Every officer in the service will attest that delays in years are not unusual. With Spain no longer good prey and the French being generally shy of a mill, I cannot expect the same good fortune with prize money as in the past, my sweetling.'

Chapter 31

The matter was still unresolved when Kydd announced he had business at the Admiralty and a trip to London was necessary. In truth, the excuse was weak: what he really wanted was to take his eye-catching wife back to London, now at the height of the Season.

As usual they would stay with his great friend Nicholas Renzi, now Lord Farndon, married to Kydd's sister.

Cecilia fussed over them and apologised, 'Oh dear, Nicholas is not here. Away on his business,' adding, 'I think you know what I mean, Thomas.

'Persephone, my dear, you and I will plan our days. Thomas will want to go to his club and I need help with a musical entertainment I promised.'

It was indeed pleasant to enter Brooks's and be welcomed like an absent friend. Kydd sat contentedly by the fire, a whisky at his side along with the *Morning Post* and its news of Town.

Before long the stout figure of Peregrine Fookes MP

appeared, with a beaming smile. 'Tiger, you old villain! They said you were here.'

'Ahoy there, Prinker. How goes it for you?'

'Fair, tolerably fair. And the life matrimonial for you, dear boy?'

'Very acceptable, the maid being so hard-won, as you must say.'

Fookes looked at him closely. 'Then there's naught to trouble this son of Neptune?'

'You know me too much, old chap. Just a mite of concern over a deficiency of lucre, nothing to worry of.'

'Oh dear. Baize or turf, can I ask it?'

Kydd laughed. 'Not gambling, Prinker. Against my religion. Just want to buy some land touching on ours and not enough in the pot.'

Relieved, Fookes joined in the laughter. 'So the prince of prizes is at a stand till he sights another.'

'Not so many about, these days.'

'Then you'll have to gain an honest fortune on dry land like all other.'

'An old sea-dog learning new tricks? I wouldn't think it imaginable, Prinker.'

Fookes stroked his chin. 'There's one line o' business that has your name all over it, Tiger.'

'Oh? What's that, then?'

'One that's seen more'n a few sit fat and easiful in these times of war and pestilence. Oh, and perfectly honourable for all that,' he hastened to add, seeing Kydd's expression.

'Tell me, Prinker.'

'You know your ships and sailoring, not to say corsairs and their ilk.'

'Some would say.'

'Then there you are – and only needs you to stir from here

once in a while, totter down to Pope's Head Alley and show yourself.'

'I don't follow,' Kydd murmured.

'Why, nothing more than set yourself up as underwriter at Lloyd's Coffee House. For those who know their ships and voyaging, premiums at five per cent on an Atlantic voyage, eight to the Baltic I'm told. Money for old rope, as sailors do say.'

Eight per cent on the value of ship and cargo to the value of some he'd seen with his own eyes was something like thirty thousand pounds! And with Saumarez and his battle fleet long since established in the Baltic that was pure profit, of course, on a three-week voyage.

'I can't just—'

'Oh, but you can. Sign up as a subscriber and anyone can do business.'

'How do you know all this, Prinker?'

'A friend.' Fookes shrugged. 'Does well out of it. Henry Massie. If you be interested I'll introduce you, Tiger.'

Kydd was soon outside a chop-house near the Merchant Taylor's Hall. This was not familiar territory to him, the crushing busyness of the commercial heart of the City of London in all its contrasts – bow-fronted shops opposite massive colonnaded frontages, cobbled roads a-clatter with carts and coaches, passers-by strolling among darting messenger boys, and everywhere the stink of horses.

'Hold on, old fellow!' Prinker hailed a jostling, somewhat portly man in a rumpled brown coat and spectacles.

He wheeled round with a worried look, then eased. 'As I've a hill of work, Prinker,' he grumbled. 'Who's your friend?' he went on, eyeing Kydd doubtfully. It was difficult to hear his words against the dense Cornhill traffic.

'You've heard of him, Henry. This is your Sir Thomas Kydd, hero of the seas.'

Massie gave a short bow. 'Y'r servant, sir.'

'Who is desirous of venturing a little of his prize-money in the underwriting line. It would oblige me much, dear chap, should you entertain him for a space on the sport to be had.'

'An hour! All refreshment on Sir T, o' course.'

'Done! I bid you farewell, sir.'

Kydd caught a flash of appraising eyes and heard a gruff 'Forward!' as Massie launched himself at the crowd.

It was not far: at the end of Cornhill where it converged with Threadneedle Street Kydd recognised the portico of the Royal Exchange and, beyond some grubby buildings, the frontage of the Bank of England.

Without pause Massie entered the Royal Exchange and immediately the din of the street fell away to an agreeable hum. Turning to the left, he nodded to a beadle in scarlet and black and found a seat in a well-patronised coffee shop.

'Ha! I can now hear myself think. How do ye do, Captain, and did I hear it right that you wanted to know the lay in these parts?'

'It would gratify me above all things, sir. But first is it permitted to call for a dish of coffee at all?'

Massie signalled a waiter. 'Now did I hear aright you're interested in hazarding your own hard-gotten on an adventure?'

'If such is possible.'

'Estates have been lost, bankruptcy never far.'

'Fortunes have been made also, Mr Massie.'

'For those only who understand their business.'

'How is this conducted, pray?'

'Simple enough in the telling. Pay your fee as a subscriber and you will be given access to the Great Room. In it there are brokers who have received instructions to draw up a policy for a voyage by their client. The object then is to hawk it about to find the best premium to which an underwriter will clap his scratch. That is all, my friend.'

'Umm. The policy—'

'Our standard Lloyd's printed form, which we all know and love, its clauses and provisions hoary with time, well known and trusted by all.'

'Then where is the hard work, pray?'

Massie gave a cynical smile. 'You can't smoke it? It's playing the risk, and few can do it. Will this ship, on passage from, say, Newcastle to Gothenburg and sailing in October meet with fog and collision or will the evil buggers of oared privateers out of the Skaggerak somewhere think to molest her? If there's a chance of either or any, then what's to be the premium?'

'I see.'

'The broker wants it low, the underwriter wants it high. And we come to an agreement.'

Kydd was beginning to see some of the difficulties. 'If the ship meets with misfortune?'

'The underwriter forfeits the entire amount he has signed for.'

'And a successful passage?'

'The underwriter receives the full amount of the premium if not shared with other names.'

'You've been very frank with me, Mr Massie. I thank you for your courtesy.'

The man gave a friendly smile. 'Let me show you something of our emporium,' he said, getting to his feet. 'We've long since abandoned Pope's Head Alley yonder and now share this grand edifice with others at an eminence. I should say "we" as being the Society of Lloyd's, once the patrons of Lloyd's Coffee House now removed to here both as proprietors and inhabitants at once.'

A large room to the right was pointed out as the Captain's Room. 'Where your salty gentlemen are wont to come to take their brew and exchange talk on venture and enterprise upon the briny in every ocean. Many a yarn here has saved a ship casting away on some foreign shore.'

They reached a wider, high-domed lobby.

'The public may only pass here, the Outer Room. Should you be elevated to the condition of subscriber then much more commodious facilities will be open to you. Is this in your contemplating?'

'I believe it is, Mr Massie.'

'Then I shall speak to the master. Shall we meet again at two?'

It was as easy as Fookes had said. The master cast an astute glance at who was being put forward and accepted Kydd without a word. The Trustee Deed was brought and Kydd duly signed. For his fifteen pounds he was given an ivory 'ticket', his pass into the inner sanctum, and was introduced to the head-waiter, the important individual who, since the Coffee House days, had ensured smooth running for the subscribers.

Kydd was now a subscriber to the Society of Lloyd's and could set up as underwriter in his own right.

Massie clapped him on the shoulder. 'Forward, sir – into the meeting-house of Neptune and Boreas!'

The subscribers' room was even loftier than the other and boasted three spreading chandeliers over an atrium that contained rows of high-backed old-style coffee-house booths down each side. On the walls were notices, some with men clustered anxiously around and a number of rousing pictures of ships at sea.

'There is our arena. The boxes are for brokers and underwriters to meet and discuss their business and over there you may see the pulpit – it's where remarkable or singular news is announced.'

They moved further into the room. At the base of a central pillar was a lectern on which an individual was consulting a massive book.

'Where it all ends. The Book, by which we mean the Loss and Arrival Book. An entry there is final. A vessel arrives safely in port – the underwriter is glad and relieves the broker of the premium. Or it is a loss, captured as prize or cast away. The assured is then free to demand his insurance monies. The fate of so many is there for all to see.'

To the left a long desk was scattered with newspapers and bound books. 'For our perusing. Shipping news and intelligence from all the high seas.'

They moved over and Kydd saw *Lloyd's List Daily*. He picked up the latest issue: it was just as he'd remembered it from years before. The front half-page with its Stock Exchange quotations, the price of gold in Mexico and Portugal, cochineal in Surinam and so forth, but the main interest was further down: the Marine List.

In modest type, '*Tanner's Delight*, Charleston to Gravesend, lost at Fazenda, greater part of cargo saved'.

The Azores, in a howling gale a quick-thinking captain of a sinking ship driving the vessel ashore to preserve its freighting.

'*Commerce of Bristol*, Nevis to Cork, is taken at Tobago, French privateer.'

On such a passage, what the devil was the ship doing there? Picking up a private cargo?

But by far the majority of the entries, covering the back of the page as well, were good news: '*Nancy*, Hambro, Liverpool arr from Smyrna.'

A tricky voyage across the worst of the eastern Mediterranean. Then on her own through the straits, rounding Iberia to face the menace of Brittany privateers in the Channel in the last days on passage but then safely arriving. Hambro was presumably the shipping agent.

'*Friends of Barnstaple*, Cundie, Bristol arr from S. Seas.'

A six-month voyage in who knew what cargo from the unimaginably distant South Seas. Danger every morning, every night, at last reaching the barely remembered green and settled land of England to pick up a pilot and tie up in Bristol, voyage over. And only this single-line entry to tell the world of their adventuring.

It was all here, how Britannia was ruling the seas, and the reality of what he was achieving at sea for them in *Tyger*. It meant so much more now.

'Tell me, many's a time in my dispatches I've handed on intelligence of a mercantile nature to the Admiralty,' Kydd began, recalling his time in the Baltic, forging trade links in the face of a hostile Continent. 'How does this reach you – or, should I say now, us?'

'Ah. We greatly prize our good relations, not to say friendship, with their lordships. It's the job of the master to keep this going. A lot is sensitive – don't want the French discovering sailing times of the Baltic convoys and similar – so it's limited to the eyes only of those in the Great Room who have a need. On the other hand, we like to be alerted to which ships are convoy runners as we know what to do with the beggars.'

'I'm gratified to hear it,' Kydd responded. Probably they'd be black-listed in the future to the detriment of their premiums. The bane of an escort – to find that, nearing port, during the night a ship had clapped on sail in an attempt to make harbour and be first to market. The escort then had to guess whether the vessel had been seized by a privateer, forcing him to take action to protect his remaining charges, or if he should give up to look after the honest ones.

'I'd be obliged for a copy of a Lloyd's printed form,' Kydd said. He had a lot of reading to do before he would hazard any money.

Massie passed one over, with a weighty and well-thumbed tome: John Weskett's *Complete Digest of the Theory, Laws and Practice of Insurance*.

'One last question.'

'Say it.'

'I've seen in ship's papers its Lloyd's Register classification. Does this mean—'

'Useful for assessing premiums. Subject to survey a vessel is classed – the letter is the hull and the number its rigging and fittings. "A1 at Lloyd's" is the best of both. All the rest of the details of the ship are kept in the Green Book, only seen by those who're on the Register, and you're not.'

'Then what I was after was a steer on what an underwriter looks for, if there's some sort of roguery – as a young 'un I was caught up in a coffin-ship plot as was the insuring of a ship that wasn't meant to make port.'

'We rely on a case of fifty years ago. It settled in law that to seek insurance on a voyage it's taken as a working fact that the ship is in seaworthy enough condition to make the voyage. If the ship is lost due to flawed or absent gear, then the claim fails.'

'What if—'

'Shall we call it a day? You've enough to get through there, and if you feel the need, I dare to say a broker wouldn't take it amiss if you stand behind me for a few sessions.'

Chapter 32

Persephone listened attentively as Kydd told her of his day, but when he brought out a Lloyd's printed form she smiled sweetly and left him to it.

He sat back as he took in the preamble, *In the Name of God, Amen*, and ending . . . *to the Charges whereof we, the Assurers, will contribute each one according to the Rate and Quantity of his Sum herein assured.*

It went on:

> *Assurance is made upon any kind of Goods and Merchandises and also upon the Body, Tackle, Apparel, Ordnance, Munition, Artillery, Boat and Other Furniture of and in the good ship and vessel . . . whereof is Master, under God, for this present voyage . . . beginning the Adventure upon the said Goods and Merchandise from the Loading thereof aboard the said ship . . .*

What was covered by the policy? And against what hazards?

> *Touching the Adventures and Perils which we the Assurers are contented to bear and do take upon us in this Voyage, and they*

are of the Seas, Men of War, Fire, Enemies, Pirates, Rovers, Thieves, Jettizons, Letters of Mart and Counter Mart, Surprizals, Takings at Sea, Arrests, Restraints and Detainments of all Kings, Princes and Peoples of what Nation, Condition and or Quality whatever; Barratry of the Master and Mariners, and of all other Perils, Losses and Misfortunes they have or shall come to the Hurt, Detriment, or Damage of the said Goods and Merchandises and Ship or any part thereof . . .

It was a bewildering litany of all the adversities and calamities that were the lot of the mariner, whom Kydd was now proposing to outlay his own capital to compensate.

He read it once again and then, with a sigh, turned to Weskett on marine insurance. The book was turgid, opinionated and detailed to a fault, but in the end Kydd had his bearings.

The whole business was risk – at base the ship, her owner and cargo charter parties all wanted the same thing: a safe arrival. To be recompensed for a loss was one thing, but what was needed was a fast, incident-free and safe delivery of her freighting, to the heightened reputation of ship, master and owner. The risk, therefore, was in the nature of the passage and likely perils to be encountered: the master and his ship could be relied on to do their utmost to make good landfall and safe arrival.

It cleared up much of the mystery. And Kydd had had the unusual distinction of taking a merchant ship out to New Holland in the peace, learning much about the gambles and ploys necessary of a master.

The next morning he met Massie at the chop-house. 'What ho, the mariner turned scribbler,' Massie greeted him, wiping his mouth of the remnants of a sustaining breakfast of kippers.

'Shall we at the business?' Kydd asked, with a grin.

'It awaits!'

Kydd showed his ivory ticket to the beadle-waiter and they found a booth to sit in. Before long a figure in an old-fashioned tricorne approached, frowning at Kydd's presence.

'Oh, Frederick, this is Sir Thomas Kydd of *Tyger* frigate. Kydd, this is Frederick Ashley, our most respected broker.' Wary nods of acknowledgement were exchanged. 'Our sailor friend is come to see how we conduct ourselves in maritime insurance.'

'Hmph. He'll keep his peace, I trust, while we get on with it?'

'Certainly. Now what's to do?'

Another quick frown was flashed at Kydd but then he gruffly opened, '*Fair Penitent*, barque of four hundred tons, Leith to Barbados in whisky and iron-work. Stephens o' Newcastle master, sails a week Monday. Care to write a line on eight thousand?'

Massie turned to Kydd and looked at him enquiringly. He was being asked an opinion!

'North about or . . .?' he asked politely. Was the passage to be around the north of Scotland, then across the Atlantic or down the east coast of England, the Channel and away? The first was longer, but safer from the privateers of the North Sea and Channel.

'South.'

'Ah, well . . .'

'In convoy.'

'To Falmouth or all the way?'

'To Falmouth only.'

Not so good, but the days of swarming St Malo corsairs lurking off Britain's Channel ports were largely gone. The master would have the sense to depart Falmouth in the dark and so forth. The cargo was not perishable and Barbados was encountered before the Windward Islands and therefore before the main Caribbean hazards.

'A good risk, I'd say.'

It was Massie's turn to frown and Kydd remembered too late that it was part of the bargaining to talk up the risk and therefore the premium.

'I'll take five.'

Ashley produced a slip of paper and slapped it down in front of Massie, who with a cursory glance, wrote, '£500. Henry Massie, five hundred pounds,' and added the date.

Without a word Ashley took it up and, with a last sharp glance at Kydd, left.

'Gone to raise the rest. Then stamp duty at Sea Policy Office on the assurance document and it's done. Clear?'

To hazard more than two years' pay with a single line of writing on only his own experience was a sobering prospect, but he could see how his first-hand exposure to the reality was going to be a considerable advantage.

Another broker arrived, plainly an old friend. 'Your thoughts on this'n, Henry,' he said, smoothing a slip. He read it out: '*Three Friends*, ship of six hundred tons, Swansea to Barcelona and return, in slate for Spanish wine.'

Massie was thoughtful. 'A reasonable voyage with a good return. Usual privateer risks off Cork and the Lizard but—'

'Should I put my oar in at all?' Kydd said.

'Your valued comments would be better received after—'

'I'd decline. To accept, that is.'

They both looked at him in surprise.

'Only weeks past I was in action a ways north of Barcelona to stop Johnny Crapaud flooding in over the Pyrenees. In the end we lost. I'm supposing they're in Barcelona by now, making the voyage nonsense.'

'We've not heard this,' Massie said doubtfully.

'I don't know how fast armies march but the numbers I saw are telling me the Dons won't be able to stop them. You'll hear soon, I'd wager.'

'Well, there you are, old boy. Have to decline, I'm afraid.'

Before lunch there was another approach, a sizeable full-rigged vessel, with a cargo of textiles from Liverpool to Maldonado in South America.

Kydd could see it all in his mind's eye – the beat out into the Irish Sea, this time of the year, almost guaranteed a fair north-easterly kicking up a brisk chop, then past southern Ireland in a direct lunge south-south-west to pick up the trade winds. After that, easy sailing until the doldrums, sinking them astern to sight Brazil and then with the north-east trade winds a fast passage south to the River Plate.

Risks? An Atlantic blow in this season was not unlikely but every hour south from the Irish Sea made it less so. Privateers in soundings, the entrance to the English Channel: the ship was cutting directly across this area but would be spending very little time there. And since Spain had made peace there was far less threat from cruisers and gunboats on the South American seaboard. If the master was known on the coast he'd be aware of the treacherous mud and reefs extending far out and . . .

He was getting the hang of it.

In the afternoon Kydd allowed himself the thrill of writing his first line, solemnly declaring, '£100. Thos. Kydd, one hundred pounds', writing under Massie's florid hand. It was a quick North Sea voyage, Gravesend to Tonningen.

Castor, of Hull. What did she look like? he mused.

Sea-kindly, bluff and tall-sparred or low and broad, there to do a job, to carry heavy cargo across hundreds of sea miles? Whatever, his money was with the ship now, her fate lying with her master's decisions.

He knew as well as any sea captain the other risks and hazards, the difference between general and particular average and, indeed, petty average, and hazily the more arcane terms – bottomry, when the ship herself was staked on a voyage, primage and the like – but for this voyage these, he could see, didn't concern him. As Massie had been so emphatic, it was all in playing the risk.

It would be a week or two before there would be definitive news of the voyage and, in the meantime, he'd immerse himself further in this world within a world.

Massie was now pleased to have him at hand, giving insight and opinion on a variety of elements of risk, but Kydd was feeling ready for a serious investment. After all, he was there to make sufficient to be able to close the china-clay project.

At one point he couldn't help questioning his own growing success. If what to him was standard practical application of seamanship gave him the edge over even the most seasoned broker, why weren't there perhaps retired merchant captains as underwriters? He put it to Massie, who told him they had no capital to hazard. And retired captains and admirals of the Royal Navy would not desire to be seen in any trade or profession, however distinguished. At the moment, therefore, he had it largely to himself.

As the days passed he found he was sauntering up to flick through the pages of the Loss and Arrival Book.

And on the tenth day he saw it. '*Castor*, Hendricks, Tonningen arr from Gravesend.' Just that, and he'd made his first fistful of guineas! And it would appear in the next day's Lloyd's List for all to know.

His heart lifting, he set about preparing for his big one. It had got about the floor that the famous frigate captain Kydd of *Tyger* was taking an interest in maritime insurance and there were more than a few curious to know why. He fobbed them off with the implication that, as a future admiral, he wanted a first-hand grounding in the art and was then respectfully left alone.

He would know it when it came: a broker with a challenging risk that the underwriters were reluctant to accept. The premium would rise. He would notice something that others had not – that the risks were much less than they appeared. He would say nothing but accept a large cover to the relief of the broker at the high premium expected. The voyage would succeed and, his bank account swollen considerably, he would return to an adoring Persephone.

The something? Well, that would have to be first spotted, then exploited. He would be ready.

'Kydd, is it?' Tayler, a broker with an irritating ingratiating manner, slid into the booth next to Kydd instead of the customary opposite side.

'Yes?'

'A thorny one, here. Wondered if you could give me a few thoughts on it.'

'You're looking for an acceptance no one will touch.'

Tayler looked hurt. 'Your brethren have been a mite squarmish, it's true, but I take that to mean they're not familiar with the waters.'

'Which waters?'

'The Arctic. I've just been told you're no stranger to those parts.'

'I've sailed there twice, the latter time to lay waste to it.'

'Oh. Well, this concerns a simple voyage, Hull to Archangel.'

'Yes?'

'Ah, some would say with an unusual twist to the venture.' Better and better!

'Tell me,' Kydd encouraged.

'The charterers have a freighting of the very finest porcelain as is intended to purvey to the court of the Tsar. The usual Baltic ports being closed to them, it's thought that a landing at Archangel and overland to Moscow would answer.'

'I see,' Kydd replied noncommittally.

'I'd be obliged to know your views of the risks, sir.'

'The High North is not to be scouted, Mr Tayler. A polar hurricanoe once experienced is never forgotten and the ice-mountains there have to be seen to be believed. The winds at the top of the world—'

'I've heard that in the past it was a regular-going thing for our merchantmen to make voyage there for furs.'

'In well-found ships calculated for Arctic conditions, sir. Your barky, can you tell me of her – or, better still, give me a sighting of her entry in the Green Book?'

'It would be irregular, but if you must . . .'

'Thank you.'

The book was produced, other entries discreetly hidden with a sheet of paper.

Maryport Packet, Hull registry. The rest was an incomprehensible mass of abbreviations.

'Pray tell me what all this means, Mr Tayler.'

At 700 tons and a four-year-old vessel only, in the common barque rig of a merchantman, her net register tonnage for cargo less than to be expected as a proportion of her overall gross register tonnage, almost certainly indicating extensive ice-strengthening for the late-year Baltic trade. She would have little difficulty with the conditions he had seen.

'Her master?'

'Ah, this is Captain Marley, a gentleman of many years in the Halifax and Labrador trade. Most respected for his—'

'But not the Russian Arctic?'

'I understand not but, as I was saying, a most respected mariner.' Kydd remembered his time off Nova Scotia, the freezing fogs, ice-floes, calms. If this captain knew his polar seamanship, he was more than qualified for the run to the White Sea and Archangel.

'As you say,' Kydd said, with a theatrical sigh. 'And I'm as well remembering that we're at war with Russia, of course.' Apart from his own brief incursion, it would be extremely unlikely that the war was making any kind of difference to the sleepy, now deserted port. Only a fevered welcome would await any visitor from the outside world.

'Yes. There is that difficulty, but I'm told that no objection would be made to trade under any flag.'

Kydd gave a cynical smile. 'Your informant did tell you that it is the Dutch who rule commerce in this part of the world? No? Historical, from the time of Barents. And they are our enemies too. This is not looking so well for your client, Mr Tayler.'

'I see. In confidence I have to tell you I've not had interest shown from any other underwriters and now you've been so kind as to point out why. I thank you, sir.'

He rose to go, but Kydd stopped him. 'Stay, sir. This is an interesting case, a fine shipment of porcelain to the Tsar at a pretty penny to England's account.'

'Very fine – the best Staffordshire can produce and, as you say, a very valuable freighting.'

'At eight per centum, a not inconsiderable premium, but with a potential for future trade of this kind . . . This leaves me in a quandary, sir. I would very much like to assist Britain to seize this opportunity to enrich herself at the enemy's expense but there are difficulties. Allow that if I can see my way past them, I shall write a line. Until this afternoon, sir?'

Kydd took a stroll to consider the situation. All the conditions he'd set himself had been met. It was not surprising that Tayler knew very little of the High North: few did, for trade had not been carried on there for some years and knowledge had faded. If he took advantage of this, it was only in reward for his own expertise as in any profession. And if he made an acceptance it was to the advantage of both parties.

Go ahead and put down a substantial amount or let it pass?

There could be only one answer. What was he doing here if not to make a considerable return? The likelihood that another like it would come along soon was remote, and his time while *Tyger* was repaired was slipping by.

He'd take it, but how much to hazard? The more he laid out, the bigger the return. In reality the risks were not much more than any North Sea crossing: the master would be canny enough to take advantage of the fjords along the Norwegian coastline if it came on to blow. And being far from waters where battles were being waged, there was less war-risk than usual.

He'd take a plunge, Knowle Manor and the estate not to be hazarded. The sum he had in mind would be covered by his savings. He didn't have to touch it: only in the event of a catastrophic disaster to the ship would it be claimed, and the great majority of vessels arrived safely and uneventfully in port.

* * *

'Mr Tayler. I've given this some thought and have decided to write.'

A flash of relief couldn't be concealed and Kydd knew why. Whatever he committed would tempt others to join, knowing that the naval captain who had actually been there had seen fit to write to the risk.

He couldn't make it too easy or there might well be bargaining downward. 'On certain conditions that I do insist upon, sir.'

'Oh?'

'That the ship be fitted with bow-graces.' If she'd been built for the late Baltic trade it was a certainty that she had them already.

'Er . . .?'

'Guards at the bow against the ice,' Kydd said impatiently. 'And, more importantly, that she bears simulated papers.'

'I beg your pardon?'

'Mr Tayler. This ship is about to set out on a voyage around the entire coastline of Norway, the north of Sweden and Russia, all of which are in arms against us. Do you expect a British-flagged vessel to survive for long in those seas? You will inform me in writing that these conditions are met.'

'They will be, sir, you have my word on it!' the broker said fervently.

'I have been fortunate in prize money, sir. At eight per cent, I will write a line.'

The slip of paper was produced and Kydd wrote carefully the amount, then underneath, 'To conditions agreed', and a separate signature, which he demanded Tayler counter-sign.

It was done.

The passage would take two to three weeks at best, a month

or more if winds were foul. Another couple of weeks for word to return and he would then be able to realise on his daring outlay. And Persephone would be on the way to securing her land!

Chapter 33

Off the coast of Holland

'Shall we step below, gentlemen?' the captain offered pleasantly. The *Grutskens von Mecklenburg*, private yacht of the Antwerpen League of Merchant Corporations, had raised the low, undistinguished coastline of Bonaparte's puppet kingdom, and their entry into these waters had to be discreet.

'Of course,' Meyrick said, ushering Renzi down to the softly lit saloon.

Remembering the financier's words, he followed without comment into the spacious, dark-panelled cabin where chilled champagne and caviar awaited. The vessel was intended to carry a dozen or so but, as the only passengers on this voyage, they commanded the complete attention of staff and crew.

'Not so long to wait, my lord,' said Meyrick, easily, with the air of one for whom this was by no means a new experience.

The journey had been remarkably seamless: a fast packet to Heligoland, the curious and tiny possession of the British that had recently been taken from the Danes. Positioned handily hours off the German coast, it was now an importing haven on a large scale, an entrepôt for the goods that were flooding into the Continent in brazen contempt for all Bonaparte could do.

After transferring to the yacht it had been a sumptuous overnight passage, with Renzi's man, Jago, and their baggage following on a different route by humble Dutch *schuyt*.

It was a wondering marvel for Renzi to think that this evening he would be laying his head in the greatest comfort at the centre of one of Napoleon's most important possessions.

The almost imperceptible heel of the vessel lessened and he realised they must be easing speed, possibly heaving to. The forward scend, the pitch of the wave crests likewise diminished. They were coming to a stop, which almost certainly meant an interception.

Pulse quickening, his senses took in the sequence, his time at sea informing the situation.

After a short delay there was a slight thump forward – a boat was coming alongside. The yacht remained still, gently heaving in the short swell. They must have been boarded – was it a party of soldiers armed to arrest, or a band of Bonaparte's notorious *douaniers* bent on enforcing the corrupt but all-pervading Continental System?

Meyrick was remarkably composed, idly sipping his champagne.

There was a quiet knock at the door and it opened to reveal a hard-faced officer in green-frogged uniform with gold ornamentation. He said nothing, scanning the cabin carefully, then, with an obsequious bow, which Meyrick returned with a nod, closed the door and left.

* * *

If anything, landing at Antwerp was an anticlimax. They remained below until the last moment. Waiting at the grey rain-swept dock was a plain carriage that they boarded quickly, pulling down the blinds. Softly sprung, with a perfumed shot-silk interior, it set off with alacrity, arriving at its destination after twenty minutes.

It was now dark so Renzi could not make out much of his surroundings beyond an impression of an anonymous building in the Dutch style and an ornate entrance from which footmen advanced to assist them. Inside he was aware of a richly furnished hall, highly polished wood marquetry and several valuable Dutch masters. They climbed a sweeping marble staircase to the next floor and proceeded down a passageway decorated in the French style. Renzi took in the careful elegance – sculpted curlicues and ornamentation finely adorned with gold leaf and crystal of the greatest delicacy.

Meyrick stopped at a door with an elaborately costumed footman standing stiffly outside. 'This is your guest apartment. Please understand that it would not be considered polite to wander the halls on your own. A trusted servant will be on duty day and night, your man will have his quarters opposite and I will be in the adjacent apartment. We will not be disturbed, this I can assure you.'

The footman produced a key and led them inside. The room was large, a conference table in the centre before a crackling fire, a well-appointed secretarial desk opposite. With sumptuous hangings and stylish furniture abounding, the careless display of wealth was almost intimidating and Renzi, no stranger to taste and fashion, knew that no mere aristocrat could command such extravagance.

Meyrick settled in a chair and contemplated for a space. 'We're in one of the halls to fellowship, shall we say, that are run by the big merchant houses for their occasional requirements. You have no need of the details. At the moment you are perceived as an "interesting visitor", introduced by me for purposes that are self-evidently mutually profitable. Nothing so crass as questions concerning your visit will be asked, for you as my guest will rely on me to make introduction as considered most appropriate.'

'When will—'

'Tonight. There will be a reception for the new Norddeutsche agent for Angerstein, a trivial occasion but one that will bring together those with an interest in the London markets. Included will be Beyer's man in Haart and, more importantly, Saul Hübner of Goldstein, both of whom I will point out.

'Your task will be to remain close-mouthed and reticent. On no account should you explain why you are here or engage in any conversation of a revealing nature. You are a newly fortunate man of capital who has all the time in the world to make disposal of it. I shall call for you in an hour, my lord.'

Jago appeared silently, imperturbable and not in the slightest trifle awed. The *schuyt* had apparently taken a more direct inshore route and he had arrived earlier.

Renzi had given some thought to his dress: much was conveyed by appearance and he had no intention of being taken either as a sharp-eyed financial vulture or a feckless mark ripe for the plucking. It was to be the doeskin pantaloons, tight glossy kidskin patent-leather shoes and a cream waistcoat overtopped by a deeply unfashionable black silk cravat with a single diamond clasp, while his sweeping dark frock-coat had the equally unfashionable horn buttons worked into the faces of gargoyles. With his hair massed at the front but in a minuscule old-fashioned queue and a dab of pale face-powder he was the very image of one who, in possession of a fortune, cared not a whit for fashion or the world's ways.

Meyrick called for him promptly, only the flicker of an eyebrow any recognition of the character of his dress. 'Are you ready, my lord?' he asked deferentially. The conceit of a man of fortune with his agent was clearly about to begin. Meyrick was a faultless study in black, his hair slickly coiffured into the latest romantic look, and on his fingers three diamond-encrusted rings of remarkable beauty. He carried himself with an impeccable bearing of modest pride and affability that evoked an instinctive feeling of trust.

The reception was a glittering affair in a splendid hall on the ground floor, with antique tapestries and ornamental furniture of a startling perfection. The room was dominated by the most ornate fireplace Renzi had ever seen, and lit by five chandeliers bearing scented beeswax candles, whose brightness would have made even the most modest adornments shimmer.

They entered without announcement and barely a flicker of interest from the elegantly groomed men talking together. Renzi adopted a languid, bored expression as he sauntered in behind Meyrick. They approached a group, dominated by a slim, dapper individual holding forth in what sounded like the Flemish dialect.

Meyrick waited politely for the man to finish, his audience thoughtful and appreciative of some insight or other.

'If I might interrupt, M'sieur le Loup Noir,' he said in French, obviously for Renzi's sake.

The black wolf – what did that imply?

The man turned to Meyrick but his gaze was on Renzi, who met startling deep set, beady dark eyes.

'This is the Lord Farndon from England, my friend, on a visit to Antwerp. My lord, do meet Friedrich, Markgraf of Skalvia, a most respected individual of the House of Haart.'

Ah – so this was the enemy: he who must be comprehensively fooled into accepting Renzi's standing and outrageous move into his financial domain.

With the antique title, the man must be a stateless Prussian, one of the many dispossessed by the cold-blooded dismembering of his country at Tilsit, since finding his riches in the cauldron of risk and audacity that was international banking. And therefore a most formidable foe.

'How do you find this country, sir? A trifle different from what you'd be accustomed to?' He had answered in faultless English with a polite expression of concern.

Renzi regarded him coolly. 'Having arrived only this afternoon, my impressions are as yet unformed, sir.'

'Are you intending to stay for long, may I ask?'

'As long as I care to, this being my first crossing to the Continent since coming into my fortune.'

'How singular. Antwerp is not known for its sightseeing you may believe, rather its unparalleled access to the bourses and chancelleries of the Continental polities. Will you—'

'Mijnheer Meyrick being good enough to act my host, I leave it in his hands to conduct me to the places and people he deems will interest me. A good evening to you, sir.'

Renzi returned the wordless bow with a slightly less deep one and turned away with Meyrick, who gave a barely perceptible nod. He had passed the first hurdle.

They strolled together, Renzi finding his look of studied languor hard to sustain, the atmosphere so charged with the exotic mystery, even odour, of untold wealth and the presence of individuals with greater puissance than mere princes and kings.

As if by chance they found themselves approaching a large man, in an astrakhan-trimmed coat. He wore a fierce black beard, and was volubly addressing his listeners in some eastern European tongue. He concluded by facing Renzi with a piercing glance.

'Ah, Úr Hübner. This is the Lord Farndon of England come a-visiting and he has desired me to introduce him to the more interesting inhabitants, and where more so than at the house of Goldstein's most worthy standard-bearer?'

The man was clearly ill at ease with English, and Renzi tentatively answered in the Hochdeutsch of Goethe. 'My honour to meet you, sir.'

'I am no German, sir!' the man answered gruffly, but in the same language. 'Rather of the illustrious race of Magyars.'

The first Hungarian he had ever met.

'Indeed? The home of the sainted Corvinus, destroyer of Wallachians and Ottomans, and founder of his inestimable Bibliotheca Corviniana?' Renzi couldn't help responding, his assumed look of boredom dropping away, forgotten.

Meyrick's forehead creased into a frown and he caught himself, quickly reverting to a cool attention.

Hübner beamed. 'Would that we had the Black Army still. Well, my English lord, whatever it is brings you to these benighted shores I wish you well of it. Take care of him, Cornelius.'

Would that he had anything other than betrayal to bring to the black-bearded giant.

For some reason the hum of talk dwindled to nothing and Renzi followed Meyrick's gaze. At the massive walnut figured doors at the end of the room a frail man was dressed in a sapphire gown faced with gold and crimson. His headgear was a neat round circlet confining a silver-threaded cloth, his hands concealed in capacious sleeves.

'That's Aram Pambouki, the Armenian,' whispered Meyrick. 'The grand old man of us all. We're greatly honoured.'

In the stillness the man looked this way and that until he saw Renzi, then moved forward purposefully, the silent groups making way for him.

He had been noticed.

Chapter 34

The note came next morning.

'You've done better than I thought, my lord,' said Meyrick, after reading it. 'We shall go, of course.'

It was from Hübner, an invitation to dine at the Borkonyha, a well-known Hungarian restaurant.

'In Antwerp?' Renzi said, puzzled, then remembered that until a dozen or so years ago it had been the chief city of the Austrian Netherlands. The old Habsburg customs and tastes would be still abroad.

With Renzi in nankeen breeches and long-tailed coat, Meyrick similarly attired, they made the restaurant in good time to see Hübner waiting for them, his bear-like frame advancing towards them with delight. '*Kiváló*, you came, my friend!' he roared.

They entered the brightly lit richly appointed space, a faint hint of spices and garlic on the air. Renzi saw that there were no guests, only the maître d'hôtel at attention before a line of staff, each in colourful dress. The entire place had apparently been reserved for them.

'Sit, sit! We're all to be Magyars and Gypsy tonight.' Over his shoulder Hübner shouted an order.

A waiter bore in a tray of tulip glasses filled with an oily transparent liquid.

'We drink together – a toast. *Egészségedre*!'

Renzi sipped carefully. It was a delicious species of brandy, with fruit notes of apricot but a hint of menace in its strength.

'Carpathian Pálinka!' crowed Hübner. 'Fit only for the brave!'

Behind Renzi a dulcimer began a soft plinking, its cascade of notes like a waterfall, its sibilant tones of arresting beauty. He twisted in his seat to see a horizontal stringed instrument played by striking with miniature hammers. Told it was a cimbalom, he raised his glass to the musician and was rewarded with a shy smile.

'You will leave the order to me, gentlemen.' A torrent of Hungarian sent the maître scurrying away and Hübner turned, beaming. 'The wine also? The kingdom is justly famous for its tipples – and the name of this restaurant, Borkonyha, means "the wine kitchen"!' He roared with infectious laughter.

Renzi pulled himself up with a start. He could see how the evening might develop and it was not in his plans to let his cards show.

Through the enticing appetisers of delicate stuffed pancakes, goose liver and many varieties of smoked sausage, he kept his countenance but then the cimbalom was replaced by four extravagantly dressed gypsies who bounded to a stop before the table. A violinist to one side began a complex, soulful air, and in slow time the four executed an elaborate dance with much posing and clicking of heels. Then in an instant the tempo turned wild and, with a breathless twirling and shouting, the dance came to a climax. At its end the troupe stood motionless, holding a dramatic pose.

It was passionate, exciting and enchanting, and it took all of Renzi's will to remain detached.

A bevy of smiling girls emerged with a variety of steaming dishes, which were placed in the centre of the table. A rich paprika and cream catfish stew with dumplings, apparently the host's favourite. Breaded calf's foot with a special sauce. Roasted pork knuckle with horseradish and lemon. Stuffed cabbage. More . . . They did not leave – instead each guest found a girl sliding in next to him delicately serving the delicacies on offer, Hübner with one on both sides.

'Bikavér!' he bellowed. 'The Bull's Blood!'

Into Renzi's glass tumbled a gush of deep red, a wine more full-bodied than any he knew, complex and lingering. 'A truly fine wine!' he exclaimed. 'Where does it come from, pray?'

'The Eger mountains, not so far from Transylvania. It has an ancient history,' rumbled Hübner, lifting his glass to Renzi. 'You like it – good!'

Through the haze of wine and excellent food, Renzi thought he detected a speculative gleam in the man's eyes, or was it merely defensive, a rustic from central Europe hoping to impress an English lord? He was inclined to think not – no mere Gypsy could rise to commanding such a position within a leading merchant banking house like Goldstein.

The meal progressed agreeably with more traditional dancing and a succession of remarkable wines. He glanced at Meyrick: the man had a faint smile and was perfectly in control, his conversation with Hübner and the girls light and affable.

'Tokaj!' summoned Hübner. Recognising the tan brown of a Spätlese, Renzi was prepared for the sweetness, which was truly delightful, not cloying.

The evening must be costing a considerable sum: what was its object?

The Gypsies were replaced by the cimbalom and a lute, and over a sublime chestnut purée dessert, Renzi felt his guard slipping and settled back. If he couldn't enjoy an evening such as this when it presented, he was a sad looby. With a stab of guilt he thought of Cecilia. How she would be drawn to this robust merriment!

Suddenly he was aware that Hübner had pulled up a chair to sit with him. 'M' lord, you are enjoying our little feast?'

'Most pleasurable, Mr Hübner.'

'Saul, please.'

'As has me exercised why you are so . . . amiable to me.'

The big man chortled. 'Curiosity! Only unforgivable curiosity, *lieber Freund*. An Englishman in the heart of Bonaparte's dominions? It cannot be for the health!'

'This is no business of yours, Mr Hübner,' Renzi answered evenly, toying with his glass. He sensed a crossroads in their relationship approaching.

'Of course not, m' lord. None at all!' he said heartily. His voice lowered. 'On the other hand you are in a foreign land with your man of business, whom I know to be a staunch friend to honesty and straight dealing. It simply occurred to me that you may wish to meet one, as we'd say, with more creative methods. A substantial loan, investments – or a safe haven for capital where England is no longer the secure and stable home it was,' he ended meaningfully.

Renzi's mind cleared in an instant. The man was fishing, of course. If he was rebuffed now, there was no harm done – but at some point in the future he would have to renew the acquaintance so why not start the business now? He shot a glance at Meyrick, in easy conversation with the attentive girl on his left – but he didn't miss the sudden flash of a warning look his way.

'Saul, *mein Gefährte*,' he began expansively, his speech slurring

174

just a little. 'Allow that I've no need for loans and my portfolio has been unusually kind to me these last months. And my capital is quite safe, I'm told.' He drained his glass ostentatiously. It was refilled instantly.

'Safe? Capital? Those are not the words to use together in the same sentence, I observe. A venture, equity in an enterprise of boldness, this is how the merely rich rise to wealth and power! Put it to work and—'

'I already have my plans,' Renzi said haughtily, 'as are far beyond your conceiving, I believe.'

Hübner stared at him, then rallied. 'I thought so, you rascal. Big plans, with a grand vision, I'm bound to guess.'

'Not less than millions attend on these plans.' Renzi sniffed.

After a breathless silence Hübner asked diffidently, 'Another Tokaj, or will it be an Eszencia, the nectar that the fourteenth King Louis said was *vinum regum, rex vinorum* – wine of kings, king of wines! They will send out for it if I demand so!'

Renzi raised a languid eyebrow. 'I would not put you to trouble, Saul. It's been a splendid evening.'

'No trouble for a friend!' A waiter was quickly dispatched. 'You do tease, if I may say it, m' lord. In all modesty I can claim certain knowledge of all the great matters of finance afoot at this time and none of the scale of millions . . .'

Frowning, Renzi considered, then leaned forward and confided, 'It is in my power to relieve Beyer and Haart of the burden of dealing with the British government in affairs of the placing of subventions on the Continent. Does that explain your scale?'

'Beyer? No one can do this.' He peered into Renzi's face. 'And you're going to try?'

With an expression of satisfied superiority he replied, 'I have . . . information that makes it certain, my large Hungarian friend.'

Baffled, Hübner slumped back, his control slipping. Across the table Meyrick was staring at them, ignoring the girl completely. Renzi didn't care – it was working.

'To dish Beyer and Haart both – to be a part of this I would give much, I tell you.'

Renzi looked at him pityingly. 'Dear Saul, I rather think this is beyond your capital resources. Listen. In the strictest of confidence I can tell you that, in a short while, a Fifth Coalition will be formed with Austria, requiring an immediate settlement on the Archduke Charles of some several millions in specie, sourced here. I fear within the time this will be beyond your competence, *alter Bursche*.'

'M' lord Farndon. Please give me a chance – the amount, tell me!'

'Oh? Then the Treasury are looking to three millions within six weeks and more when Austrian troops take the field. You see?'

'Ah,' muttered Hübner. 'I cannot readily . . . It must be found. The opportunity is too great. Not so much this one on its own but the chance to continue with England, sovereign loans, bond brokering . . . I will think about it and we'll talk again, *hein*?'

Chapter 35

Meyrick was coldly angry when they returned. 'You were entirely out of order, my lord. It was agreed that, for obvious reasons, I should make any approach or offer and you have chosen to flout the agreement. This is ethically intolerable, sir!'

'The approach was not mine, Mijnheer,' Renzi snapped. 'And the results speak for themselves. Do I ignore the way made smooth before me? I think not!'

'This is the early stage only. Any misunderstanding now will most certainly lead to a loss of the entire project later. Sir, I require at this point to be assured of your withdrawal from any initiative that—'

'Mr Meyrick. By our own agreement all financial instruments and documents will be to your advice and my responsibility. How can this be possible unless you are in the lead on negotiations? Your position is in no way different, but grant that I have an intelligent understanding of the elements and may be trusted to know when to defer to you.'

'Very well,' Meyrick said stiffly. 'My journal of proceedings to Mr Perceval will not spare details if any ill-considered act by you brings a close to the affair.'

'Sir. I'm accounted a fair judge of men and what I saw of Hübner leads me to expect an advance by him before very long. We'll see what he brings.'

Within forty-eight hours they had a visit.

'Why, Mr Hübner. How good to see you! Please come in.'

Renzi's rooms were lavishly equipped for receiving guests and the big Hungarian was offered a comfortable chair that he occupied with disarming elegance.

'M' lord, I've given much thought to how we might assist in your project. Without prejudice to future discussion, I'm authorised by my principals to offer an immediate tranche of one third of the capital sum in specie within two weeks and—'

'One moment, if you please, sir. I desire that my agent be present, as you'll understand that his comprehension of the mechanics of high finance is superior in every way to mine.'

With Meyrick settled, Hübner began again but Renzi cut him off. 'Sir, this will not do. I'm desolated to point out that, after some salutary experiences, the Bank of England will deal with only the one Continental house, it being of sufficient standing to make acceptance of the whole – which is why it must tolerate the insupportable charges of Beyer. A partial interest will not do, sir.'

A hunted look appeared. 'The Goldstein fee structure, I can assure you, will reflect our earnest desire to conduct business with so eminent a client.'

'I'm truly sorry not to allow you to continue, sir. It has always been in my thinking to deal with a house of worth, one that, with my privileged information, is able to cut across the Beyer-Haart bid with one of its own that achieves a totality of the requirement.'

'Is there . . . anything that might be . . .?'

'I cannot think it, sir.'

Meyrick stirred politely. 'There does occur to me one possibility, gentlemen.'

'How so?' demanded Renzi.

'My lord. You have considerable resources of capital. If in some way this was placed with the Goldstein assets it would allow them to move on sourcing the specie and thusly bid.'

'Go on.'

'We are constrained by London's insistence on dealing with a single house. Therefore it must be that the Goldstein name alone appears on the tender. Your capital in some form at the back of it will undoubtedly allow them to bid for the whole, appearing as a house with assets quite capable of servicing such a requirement.'

Hübner, his features carefully composed, said, 'Forgive me for blunt speaking . . . There cannot but be a fee levied upon us in this arrangement, the magnitude of which has to be known.'

Renzi broke in with visible enthusiasm: 'I see what you are proposing, Mr Meyrick, and I like the idea. My intent is to dish Beyer, not make profit on my friends. Besides which, if we are going to succeed, it's only by cutting our bid to the bone that will shift the British Treasury from their old ways. I therefore ask you to draw up a scheme as will enable Goldstein to tender.'

A memorandum of association was drafted by the end of the day, its provisions bringing general satisfaction.

'So. The entirety of our combined holdings will be more than enough to achieve our objective,' Hübner allowed. 'I will go to my principals and set a formal agreement in train.'

'Splendid!'

'Just one matter to be cleared up. They will want to be certain about the, er, actuality of Lord Farndon's assets and afterwards the precise nature of any subsequent instrument of alignment.'

'The good earl has no need to flaunt his fortune. Here . . .' Meyrick fumbled in his document case and withdrew a paper, holding it folded. 'With your permission, my lord?'

'If you must.'

It was the debt acknowledged and secured on his brother's Caribbean properties, which Hübner examined carefully.

'That alone would satisfy most,' Meyrick said. 'Yet it has to be pointed out that the great majority of his lordship's wealth at present resides in a rapidly rising investment of stock, which he's had the sagacity to secure in its first blooming. If you require—'

'Thank you. That will not be necessary.'

Renzi's pulse accelerated. Was this all it needed to conclude the business?

'We have our agents in the City of London only a day's sail distant. You can be sure they will discover for us the true extent of his lordship's prosperity.'

Cold reality set in. The bait had been taken but the fish had by no means been hooked. If these canny and experienced men detected even a whiff of collusion it would all be over. And there was every fear that he would then be taken for a spy and suffer rapid elimination.

The game had just turned deadly.

Chapter 36

Aboard the French flagship Océan, *Brest harbour*

Admiral Jean-Baptiste Philibert Willaumez, in command of the operational squadron in Brest, was nearly the most senior admiral of the French fleet and with experience to match. His would necessarily be any command that sought to grapple with the stubborn British, who refused to recognise the supreme dominance of the French Empire in the affairs of Europe.

Impatiently, he set down the newly delivered packet. 'Get out,' he ordered his aide and others working in the great cabin of the immense 120-gun ship-of-the-line.

He slit the outer covering, its seal of a golden bee leaving no doubt of its origin. These were orders written for his eyes only by Emperor Bonaparte himself.

The package was thickly stuffed with papers, diagrams, lists, the typical product of the fertile and meticulous brain of the Emperor. Nothing left to chance, the details painstakingly worked out to their ultimate ends in a tight web of events and directives.

While Bonaparte had enjoyed spectacular successes on land, naval warfare was a different matter. There were too many variables: on the one hand, wind and sea, which could not be commanded, and on the other, the fierce initiatives of Nelson's sea-children.

Willaumez spread out the papers on his desk. It was to be a major enterprise, no less than a break-out from Brest, sailing south to force aside the blockading British before Lorient and Rochefort to allow the ships bottled up in those ports to join him. Then, a dash across the Atlantic to fall on the Caribbean to relieve the hard-pressed Martinique and Guadeloupe, the last two sugar islands of significance, and afterwards in vengeance to take Jamaica as a prelude to destruction of the poorly defended British possessions.

Would it work? Possibly — but he was veteran of break-outs at Trafalgar, the following year and the year after, none of which had resulted in anything much more than a rapid scuttling back to lie safely under the fortresses of a French harbour.

Nevertheless it was a chance, and a wave of glory would break over the admiral who could pull it off. Even more, if this was him, he would win the Emperor's favour and silence the critics within the navy who plagued him.

It was worth a determined effort.

Notes and summaries quickly appeared under his elegant hand, the material for his fleet orders. He worked rapidly and surely for he'd been expecting something like this for some time. The setbacks in Iberia were almost begging for a diversion while Napoleon flooded Spain with his best troops to confront the upstart Wellesley.

He must not fail: Bonaparte had a way with generals and admirals who were unlucky enough to lose battles. The fate of Villeneuve after Trafalgar was reason enough to energise him and the orders had been insistent that the sortie take place soon, before Martinique was lost to them.

He worked on and finished a little before midnight. Now it was the turn of other hands: his staff would turn his intentions into hard prose, signals, the minutiae of fleet supply and communication, to the smallest detail. Each ship would know precisely what was expected of it and, in his Fighting Instructions, how to do it in the face of the enemy.

Satisfied, he laid down his pen.

In the days that followed, the treacherous Brittany weather changed. It began to chill and bluster, the winds veering wildly until they steadied from the west – dead foul for leaving. It was what Willaumez had been waiting for.

For the English blockaders it was a truly dangerous situation. The westerlies hammering against the countless rocks and granite crags of the hostile French coast turned it into a lee shore of formidable menace. And as usual, believing the wind was at the same time preventing any French battle group from putting to sea, they took the opportunity of moving safely another dozen miles and more offshore.

Willaumez knew that if he succeeded in beating out in these conditions he should achieve what he so greatly desired: a break-out with not a soul to see him leave, free to strike out where he would.

The signals to begin the process of getting under weigh were thrown out, emphasised by a gun. He'd planned for this hour and, *merde*, it would go his way. If necessary he'd take the entire day to assemble his fleet of eight battleships in the Goulet, the rock-girt entrance to Brest.

There was a good reason for caution. The southern side of the entrance ended with the extraordinary Chaussée de Sein, a fifteen-mile rampart of half-concealed bilge-slitting reefs that in any kind of blow kept ships well away from its white-torn length.

But for those who were aware of it, there was a break in the fearsome reef, Raz de Sein, a passage through gouged by tides running at six, eight knots. Too narrow to work a ship through by tacking, if the wind was in the right quadrant it had tide-scoured water depth sufficient on the ebb to pass even the deepest-draught ship, thereby saving the thirty-mile trip to sea and back to round the outer extremity.

Only when his fleet was in a ragged line and making for the Raz de Sein did Willaumez's fears ease. Emboldened, he signalled for more sail – and at that precise moment he saw, more as a shadow in the white mists of spume and mizzle, the very thing he dreaded: the looming bulk of a ship-of-the-line.

His mind flared with resentment. What the devil was a British ship doing so close inshore in this? Any sensible seaman would keep such a wall-sided vessel well out to sea for all the leeway it must be making, here among some of the deadliest rock shoals in the world. Now the secret of his break-out was known and, for all he knew, the blockading fleet was about to crowd in to give battle.

Hastily he dispatched a frigate, which returned with word that there was no lurking fleet – just one supreme seaman left to keep watch in fearful danger.

There was nothing for it but to press on.

As if blessing his resolve a single shaft of sunlight beamed down and illuminated the tiny but deceitful Tévennec island, turning its dark crags bleached-bone pale. One by one the great ships rounded it, and with winds hard a-beam and on the strong ebb tide, they thrashed their way to the south, leaving the British 74 to disappear as it put about for the beat out to round the Chaussée de Sein.

The gloom of night set in as they formed up for the passage south but it would only be an overnight sail to raise Lorient at first light. There they would brush away the blockade and welcome out Commodore Troude's battle squadron to swell their numbers to invincibility.

As dawn stole over a much calmer sea there were simultaneous cries from the masthead. Unbelievably, the 74 that had sighted them in the gale had not only made it out to seaward and around the Chaussée but during the night had overhauled them and now lay squarely across their course, along with the local blockading squadron, which had been alerted.

The three sail-of-the-line ahead between them and Lorient were clearly offering battle to his eight, soon to be made eleven.

Odds of two or three to one against them – he could do it. Willaumez stopped his slow pacing and fixed his gaze on the nearer, calmly under topsails, no signal abroad. Those veterans knew what they had to do but his own fleet had never acted as a body together.

What would his strategy be? One column to double the end of the enemy line and engage from leeward while the other pounded them from their superior windward side?

Then cooler counsel prevailed. His orders from the Emperor were to one end: to take overwhelming force to the Caribbean and recover the situation there, not to risk losses and battle damage before he'd even started.

The British commander was playing it well. He couldn't know their ultimate destination but it seemed he'd already suspected that Willaumez's intention was to combine with the Lorient squadron and had placed himself directly across the port approaches. There could be only one interpretation: that he was prepared to fight to a finish to delay the conjoining until the Channel Fleet could reach them, undoubtedly alerted by the 74 that had sighted them.

While Willaumez pondered, the two fleets passed each other warily at a mile range, and as he watched, the British executed a smart 'tack in succession' that took them about, tracking his course.

Something had to be done. He glanced up at the sky: lowering scud, grey overcast and the westerly veering more northerly. Evening was not far off. Given that the object was to arrive at Rochefort with an intact and enlarged squadron ready to augment with the ships there before making off across the Atlantic, there was one course of action that would meet this.

It was all in the timing. As if baffled, he led his squadron to the south-east until the wary English ceased following, returning to their station off Lorient. It would appear to them that his attempt to lure them away from their watch over the port had failed. Especially as he then hauled his wind and in a wide circle returned to just north of Lorient.

In the fading light of evening the English saw him lie to in the shelter of the island of Groix and take in all sail, furling industriously with the obvious aim to snug down at anchor for the night, before bringing the business to a conclusion in the light of day.

Just as soon as the darkness descended Willaumez made his move. Loosing canvas once again he put to sea under all plain sail, setting course direct for Rochefort, having sent in a schooner to Lorient to order Troude to follow when he could, for the Channel Fleet would be down in full cry when they heard of his break-out and he had no intention of lingering to meet them. The Lorient watchers would be swept up with them, allowing Troude to escape and join him.

When morning broke it was with a beautiful clear horizon. No pursuing sail to distract in the clean line of sea and sky – his ruse had succeeded!

Now there was only the English Rochefort squadron of two or three ships-of-the-line to sweep aside and he was well on the way to completing his mission.

The welcome sight of the battlemented round tower of Baleine on the Île de Ré rose above the horizon. The outer anchorage of Rochefort, Basque Roads, was only twenty miles ahead.

But suddenly, way over on the starboard bow, a rocket soared up and detonated with a low thud high overhead. It was a frigate, an English scout, and she'd signalled their presence to an unknown force somewhere out of sight. Instinctively he brought his fleet together in two columns and awaited what had to come.

From the direction of the island at the other side of the bay came first one then three sail, English colours and ships-of-the-line. The blockading squadron.

His eight ships would prevail and the unknown junior admiral whose flag flew in the first would know it, but that was not his concern: it was to let them pass, then hammer in the stopper.

With the Lorient additions and the five he expected in Rochefort, Willaumez had nothing to fear. Just as soon as he was ready he'd sail and crush the English, if they showed fight. For now, the comfort and good holding of the Basque Roads anchorage ahead beckoned.

The wind shifted to a sulky south-westerly as they approached. Then, oddly, the sail-of-the-line left off the chase and retired, leaving only a pair of frigates to follow them. Perplexed, Willlaumez dispatched a frigate of his own to investigate while he anchored in five-fathom water.

It headed back for the English squadron and very soon saw what it was about.

From the north, three of Troude's Lorient squadron were coming.

The wind now in the south was foul for their joining Willaumez. Faced with the English battleships, their commander made the decision to decline battle and retreat. This was not so simple for the English gave chase. The French fled for the protection of the formidable gun batteries of the Sables d'Olonne, where they anchored with the precaution of seizing springs on their cables to place their broadsides outward-facing.

That did not deter the English ships. Closing inexorably, they opened fire at close range, ignoring the thunder of the shore batteries' massive thirty-six pounders: the fort guns on the low, sandy island were too low to carry over the sheltering ships, which masked their aim.

They fell silent one by one as the gunnery duel rose to a crescendo, the slam of sound and roiling smoke bringing spectators to the shore to gape at the spectacle. The English closed so near that in one French ship the flaming wads from her cannon set fire to it. And so fierce was the onslaught on the others that cables were cut and very soon all three were grounded wrecks.

Satisfied, the English admiral broke off the action and went back to his station.

The French watching frigate lost no time in returning to Willaumez to tell him of the horrific events.

The lesson was not lost on him. If this was what just three English ships could do, and the Channel Fleet chose to come, it would be a very hard-fought affair.

He would leave nothing to chance. He would shift moorings. There was an inner anchorage, protected by the Île d'Aix and its fortress to the north, a tangle of sand shoals and the Île d'Oléron to the west, mud shallows to the east and the formidable rocks of the Plateau des Pailles to the south, a near impregnable situation. The entire French squadron weighed and came to anchor there.

In the morning the Channel Fleet of the Royal Navy arrived, issuing into Basque Roads in an unstoppable tide, a majestic 120-gun flagship in the van and rounding to, coming to rest on the far side of the Île d'Aix, with every sign of desiring an encounter.

Chapter 37

London

'How did it go?' First Lord of the Admiralty Mulgrave asked solicitously of the bent figure that entered Bellamy's, the grubby rooms that were the House of Commons' nearest article to that of a dining hall.

Castlereagh flopped into the high-backed bench opposite, his eyes closed in weariness. Mulgrave signalled to a waiter, and a veal pie and cheese appeared in front of the secretary of state for war.

'Wretched.' Castlereagh sighed, picking at the pie. 'Avoided a censure only by half the Irish members absent for some papist festival.'

The news of the irruption of a powerful French squadron from Brest had shocked the country. This was generally the prelude to some disastrous descent on the colonies, or worse, and what was the government of the day going to do about it?

'At least we know where they are,' Mulgrave confided, looking about the near-empty tables. 'A telegraph from *Naiad*, detached from the Channel Fleet to Plymouth with the news. Seems Monsieur Willaumez has every intention of going on a cruise but is at the moment detained by Gambier in Basque Roads – that's the Rochefort anchoring.'

There was no need to dwell on that monumental relief when the clattering telegraph apparatus on the Admiralty roof spelled out that the Willaumez squadron was not in fact loose at sea on a voyage of depredation, but in a place known to them.

'Thank God for that,' Castlereagh said, with feeling. 'You'll let the public know?'

'Of course. Something like our brave tars have cornered the brute, who is now cowering in his lair. It'll not answer for ever, dear fellow. In his own good time he'll sail from La Rochelle and Rochefort with augmentation sufficient to give us pause.'

'Meanwhile you'll keep 'em safely bottled up?'

'Even that's not assured. At that distance our full-scale victual and supply becomes problematical and there's always wood and water to find. They can't lie in idleness for ever, therefore. No, this is a hard nut to crack.'

Castlereagh finished his pie. 'Why not send in the fleet? A species of cutting-out expedition writ large crosses the mind.'

Mulgrave gave a thin smile. 'I rather think not. The enemy are snug and tight in their own heavily defended harbour, which is all set about with reefs, shoals and mud that sailors do abhor. This is not the Nile or anything like it.'

'And I fancy your man on the spot is not a Nelson.'

'Gambier? Not really. One of the canting tribe, he sees fit to ply his tars with improving tracts rather than valiant signals. I dare to say if ordered he'd do his duty but in my thinking any kind of failure in putting down Willaumez will go ill with the people.'

'So?'

'No easy answer. Without question the French when ready will sail on whatever mischief is planned and then we'll probably lose them, so something has to be done while they're still at anchor.'

'A fighting captain to take the war to the enemy while Gambier keeps watch?'

'Hmm. Possibilities. We'd need to find something for him to wield to give reason for his warrant.'

'How about . . . fireships?'

'My dear fellow. They've not been used this age anywhere to my recollection. But an idea, I'll grant.' Mulgrave reflected. 'More than a little chancy, however – not to mention dangerous.'

'If it doesn't work we'll be pilloried.'

'We'll get someone who'll make it work, for God's sake.'

'You mean someone lunatic enough to ride 'em in,' Castlereagh said flatly.

'I do, and I think I know who might well be so qualified.'

'Pray tell.'

'The good Lord Cochrane.' Mulgrave smiled beatifically.

'Hmm. I see your point. The people's hero and if it fails he can't be blamed and it follows neither can we for sending him in.'

'It may serve, too, to keep his Radical ranting within check for a space.'

'Have we still fireships in number sufficient?'

'Probably. They've never been used. Else they'll make do with what they have in the way of old ships set self-immolating.'

'Splendid. So we have a way forward, I believe. Send for the gentleman of the hour forthwith, if you please. If you think it needs must, I'll see him before he goes.'

Chapter 38

The Admiralty

'My lord?' Cochrane strode in, his shock of red hair and height giving him a compelling presence in Mulgrave's neat office.

'Do sit, my lord,' Mulgrave said mildly. 'My apologies for taking you away from your illustrious field of battle but the matter presses.'

'As it must, the Spanish coast lying unharried all the while.'

'Then, sir, consider this. The French under Willaumez have lately sallied from Brest and now lie in Rochefort in numbers that cause us to take fright of our colonies. They must be destroyed, and remembering your celebrated exploits there in *Pallas*, I thought to take counsel with you as knowing the ground better than any man.'

'I do. And I'd wager that Willaumez is not to be found in Basque Roads but in the inner harbour, Aix Roads.'

'You are correct, of course.'

'Where they may lie in perfect safety.'

'Sir, this cannot be suffered to continue. Their destruction is our first duty, and your advice to this end will be most valuable.'

'Aix Island and to its south is girt about with hazards. I will not be party to an action of significance in those waters, sir.'

'You will not?'

'Do I resemble a fool, sir, a looby? I repeat, this is not—'

'With fireships?'

'I beg your pardon?'

'Were a commander to be granted a flotilla of fireships in the right quarter for the wind to then bear them down on the anchored ships would not this answer?'

Cochrane sat back contemplating, a smile playing. 'If you are offering me a command such as this, be aware, sir, that there will be conditions attached.'

The first lord of the Admiralty raised his eyebrows. 'Oh? I'd be interested to hear them, sir.'

Leaning forward, Cochrane rapped, 'Explosion vessels. I will have two, three vessels preceding the fireships that are in their nature but laden with powder carcasses to my specifying, intended to explode among the enemy.'

'I see. I should think that quite possible.'

'And the other, I am not unaware that my appointment to such a post will excite a *frisson*, not so much a jealousy among my brother officers over whom I shall have been placed. I desire that a way may be found whereby my position is regularised beyond repine.'

'Ah. Well, I suppose it can. In view of your superior qualifications for the position, Lord Gambier will be, er, directed to make you responsible for the actions of the fireships and thereby unable to vary the appointment. Will that answer, pray?'

'Shall I have forces sufficient for the task?'

'I have identified and caused to be manned eight fireships for your enterprise. They, with store-ships and transports, are being prepared in the Downs at this hour while two bomb-vessels will sail shortly. In addition, I'm able to offer you the services of any captain and his ship you deem a suitable associate in the endeavour.'

'Very well, I accept the post. And Captain Sir Thomas Kydd will suit most handsomely.'

'I understand his ship is under repair in Plymouth. Should it be in a fit state for sea, and Sir Thomas is agreeable, he will receive orders to join you. I see no reason for delay so I'll bid you good fortune, sir, in this great venture.'

Chapter 39

'S till dry 'n' all!' The carpenter's muffled voice echoed up from deep within *Tyger*'s hold, right forward where the orlop platform had been taken up to expose the footwaling and limber holes at the very lowest inside part of the ship's hull. Finally in the water after her repair, it had been a time of anxiety. Would the complex of cant frames and sharply incurved strakes at her bow take to the new-worked timbers in a critically vulnerable part of her fabric?

'A fine job your chippies have made of it, I'm obliged to remark,' Kydd said, in admiration, to the master shipwright. There would be the usual form of appreciation on its way out to the King's dockyard that afternoon – a large hamper of pies and beer in earnest of the good-hearted efforts that had seen her shot-torn side made as good as new in so short a time. They were now ready to resume their commission off the coast of Spain.

Kydd was pleased he'd made his big move into marine underwriting when he had: *Tyger* would be about her true calling

196

now and he could no longer attend at Lloyd's. There was no question that he'd been fortunate to find a good prospect for his first foray and that he had particular competence above all others in the Great Room. It was looking as if Persephone's land would be hers, and when he was at idleness between voyages again he would make hazard on another voyage.

'We'll take the list off her now, Mr Bray. I believe a re-stow of the hold in order, don't you?'

The boatswain would then want to tighten in the shrouds, perhaps set about rattling them down so the foot-ropes ran perfectly parallel to the deck, something that was both seaman-like and appreciated by bare-footed seamen swarming aloft. Then the gunner would want to see to his iron beasts, that they'd not suffered overmuch in the furious cannonading they'd kept up for so long.

'Captain Kydd, ahoy there!'

Startled, Kydd looked over the side to the stone quay. A single figure stood there, giving a friendly wave: tall, red-haired, even in plain clothes, he was quite recognisable as Lord Cochrane. 'Come aboard, brother!' he bawled back, surprised to see him there instead of wreaking havoc along the Catalonian coast.

Kydd's cabin was in something of a state, Tysoe taking the opportunity of rousing out his cabin stores before any projected foreign cruise, but Cochrane politely ignored it.

'You've heard of the alarums about the sally from Brest?'

'I did. Haven't we got the entire Channel Fleet keeping 'em under eye at Rochefort?'

'Just so. It can't be tolerated, in course. We're outnumbered and if they choose to sail together as a squadron we'd be hard put to discourage them going where they feel inclined. No, the rats have to be destroyed in their nest is their lordships' firm opinion.'

'I hope you're not saying we're going to—'

'Yes, I am.' He suddenly grinned – a wolfish, elated expression that animated him. 'And, what's more, they've seen fit to trust charge of the thrusting blade to your friend, forsooth!'

Kydd returned his grin, but with a hesitation. 'So the fleet's given over to you?'

'Not the Channel Fleet. It stays in Basque Roads. We've those that draw less water to go in beyond Aix Island, where Willaumez is lying in what he thinks is perfect tranquillity, and flush 'em out.'

'Then it's frigates against sail-o'-the-line? What madness are they asking you to—'

'Hold hard, dear fellow. I said they'd given it all over to me and I've more than a notion of how it's to be done. What I'm here for is to beg you'll come in with me and join the diversion. We've worked well afore now and there's none I'd trust as I would you, Kydd. Say you will!'

It all seemed most improbable, but Kydd trusted Cochrane's seamanship. He had real knowledge of the area, was always intelligent, resourceful, cool in action and, above all, careful with his men's lives. If the Wolf of the Seas thought there was a way, he'd willingly be part of it.

'You in command of the assaulting force, no senior to interfere?'

'As was my demand when offered the situation,' Cochrane said loftily.

'Then you'll see me alongside,' Kydd replied. 'If I've the orders that say I might.'

'You'll have them! When will you be ready to sail? We have to get at 'em before they take it in their minds to make a run for it.'

'I'd say small days.'

'We're to leave then when you're stored. On the way I'm sharpening my scheme and will have it ready for us by the time you arrive. And I'm to think it not impossible as we'll make history shortly, m' friend!'

Chapter 40

HMS *Tyger* put to sea three days later to join *Imperieuse* at anchor in the Sound. The dockside and Plymouth Hoe were crowded with family and well-wishers frantically waving, hoping to be noticed by the men going to war. Knowing he could not wave or make unseemly display on the quarterdeck, Kydd had made a secret arrangement with Persephone. As they swept around Devil's Point caught by the tide, there was a figure to be seen not on the immediate foreshore but halfway up the bank by a walkers' bench. As the gallant frigate passed not a hundred yards offshore the lady, for it was assuredly a she, waved and blew a kiss.

As if by chance, the captain of the noble ship whipped off his cocked hat and bowed as if to the assembled crowds, who roared their appreciation, but his eyes were on the lady, who curtsied demurely and blew another kiss.

He held the scene long after they'd rounded Drake's Island and laid course for the open sea, his eyes prickling. From now on, wherever naval service took him, there was someone who cared, whose thoughts were with him wherever he was on the high seas, who was longing for his return as he was to her.

Eddystone Light laid safely to larboard, the two frigates stretched out south under all plain sail and in a bare three days had sighted the low, featureless sprawl of the Île de Ré, one of the several islands lying guard over the outer anchorage.

It was there not so very long ago that *Tyger* had been on her shameful mission to repatriate the French general Junot, of the army of Lisbon, back to France with his colours of war, arms and loot. Now she was there for a very different purpose and it would be a sweet revenge on those bitter memories.

They were met by frigate sentinels and sailed on into the wide waters of the bay. Ahead in a defensive cluster was Admiral Gambier's Channel Fleet.

Kydd boarded the giant *Caledonia* just behind Cochrane, standing beside him on the quarterdeck as the commander-in-chief was informed of their arrival. To their surprise a succession of captains appeared from the cabin spaces and stood about uncomfortably. Had they interrupted some form of meeting?

The flag captain appeared, inviting Cochrane to step into the great cabin.

Left with the others, Kydd tried to make conversation but he knew none of these captains and there was a peculiar tension in the air.

Mercifully it was less than half an hour before they were invited below. Kydd felt it proper to enter last and found a seat towards the end of the polished table, noting that Cochrane was sitting next to Gambier, ahead of all the senior captains.

This was the admiral who had commanded at Copenhagen when the entire Danish fleet had been captured after a cruel bombardment of the city, and Kydd remembered his ponderous, deliberate manner.

'Gentlemen, I'm gratified to find that our numbers are now complete for the task we've been asked to perform. Their lordships have seen fit to approve my initiative and are providing the necessary materials and support for its execution to take place in the very near future.'

There was a stony silence, eyes flickering towards Cochrane, who sat back, fiddling with a pencil, a genial smile playing.

'In addition they have provided me with one who has both knowledge of these waters and a record for bold conduct in operations of an unusual nature.'

At the opposite end of the table sat a rear-admiral, presumably one of the Channel Fleet subordinate commanders. Grey-haired, with a grim and unforgiving expression, he remained bolt upright as Gambier continued.

'Therefore for the benefit of those not acquainted with the officer, might I introduce the leader of the assault squadron, Captain the Lord Cochrane?'

The rear-admiral slapped a palm down hard on the table, a thunderclap in the confines of the cabin. 'Good God, sir! What are you about?'

Gambier's face was almost comical in its shock and astonishment. 'Wh-what did you say, sir?'

'What did I say? You're to tell us why in Hell's name a junior frigate captain is given command in this dangerous and crucial affair over myself, in rank and experience far above he!'

'Admiral Harvey, calm yourself, I beg. Captain Cochrane is certainly well fitted for—'

'That is a preposterous and foolish position, sir, and reflects badly upon myself and you, sir – yes, you!'

Kydd had never heard such language used to a commander-in-chief. And this must be the legendary Eliab Harvey, whose fabled interceding in his *Temeraire* at Trafalgar had saved *Victory*. He had gone on to confront two other French battleships simultaneously.

Gambier looked confused, bewildered by Harvey's anger. 'I do ask that you remember who you are addressing, sir.' His voice was weak and uncertain. 'I am not accustomed to—'

'Neither am I accustomed to being passed over by a junior officer! Such is injurious to my pride, my honour and, be damned to it, my reputation at large.' His features were now red with rage.

'Admiral Harvey. It is out of my hands, sir. The Admiralty has ordered me to take this officer under my direction to conduct the operation. What else might I do?'

'If I'm to be passed over and the appointment given a junior so far below me in rank and office then I vow I'll strike my flag and resign my commission!'

'Sir, your words are intemperate and unfitting an officer of rank. I ask you to—'

'Me! Who'd take any old and rotten 74 to board and seize the biggest three-decked Frenchman in Aix Roads and bring her out!'

'Sir! This is insupportable!'

'I've yet to begin!'

Gambier turned white. 'This council is over,' he said, in a tight voice. 'Clear the cabin!'

In an appalled silence the officers got to their feet, stumbling against each other in their efforts to reach the open deck. With shocked faces, they turned to Harvey.

'He knows he's to loo'ard of the truth!' the old admiral spat. 'Well off course! I'm not to be treated like a common blackamoor just to feed his interest. He's not heard the last of me, God damn the rascal! If I had my way he's to be impeached for tainted management. Too much the canting Methody, the psalm-singer instead of . . .'

He tailed off resentfully taking in the ring of faces, pale and affronted, then saw at the cabin door the still form of Gambier, gripping the handle so hard his knuckles showed white. 'Admiral Harvey. You'll quit this ship for your own and hold yourself ready to take my dispatch to their lordships, where you'll make explanation for your conduct. I will no longer have you under my command. The meeting will resume this afternoon at three. Carry on, please.'

Kydd's spirits fell. That things were turning out so ill at the outset of the action did not bode well for the essential comradeship and dependence on one another that was at the heart of the Royal Navy's success in this war. And, of course, Gambier was now less one precious ship-of-the-line, *Tonnant*, a powerful eighty-gun of the breed.

Was it the Cochrane genius for making enemies or something else?

Kydd accompanied Cochrane to *Imperieuse* for a noon meal before the afternoon meeting.

'A rum do, as any of my honest tars might remark it,' Kydd said, as they sat together.

'Not as who's to say,' Cochrane said, without any particular malice. 'The fellow is an unthinking choleric and must face the consequences of his behaviour. Given what we have to do, a satisfactory outcome.'

'The meeting. Have you considered your course?'

'You mean have I my plans? I do, old fellow, I do. And you figure in them centrally, I'm bound to say.'

Kydd smiled. 'I await my fate with some interest.' This was something like the old vitality returning.

Chapter 41

Gambier sat in the centre of the table, Cochrane opposite. 'I would have this council move on with expedition,' he said, without any further preliminaries. 'Our intelligence has discovered that Admiral Willaumez has this day been removed from post for being indolent and lacking in aggressive spirit. He's replaced by the more active Zachary Allemand and we can expect a far different treatment.'

It was sobering news.

'Therefore I give the floor to Captain Cochrane, leader of the assault, who will outline to us his plans.'

With a wintry smile, Cochrane began, 'In a word, gentlemen – fireships.'

There was an immediate ripple of dismay about the table. In all of recent history there had never been a successful fireship attack by the fleet. As well, service in such fearful sea vehicles was considered dangerous in the extreme and in the event volunteers only would be called. And on every side such moral outrage was conjured by their use that captured crews could expect rough handling, if not summary execution.

In dawning horror, Kydd realised that, as he was being held central to the action, he could count on a front rank role – with the fireships. All his life he'd held a preternatural, deep-seated fear of fire that had nearly unmanned him on the two occasions he'd been brought close to one. And now he was being expected to take part in a deliberate mass burning. Why hadn't Cochrane mentioned this?

Cochrane continued, 'Yes, with explosion vessels and copious numbers of Colonel Congreve's war rockets. I'm sanguine that this will be enough to stir even the laziest of Bonaparte's captains.'

Kydd felt dread in the pit of his stomach.

'Our intent is to come in by the Boyart shoals passage until wind and tide serve. The frigates and sloops designated will anchor, at which point the fireships will be let go downwind into the heart of the enemy anchorage. Crews will be recovered after igniting their charges by this detachment's boats.'

'Who shall lead the assault?' Kydd found himself asking.

Cochrane smiled happily. 'Why, in the first instance myself in the explosion vessels, in the second your own good self, sir, at the head of the fireships.'

Kydd held himself in. It had to be faced: his place in the action was now publicly declared and he could not withdraw without good reason.

'Just what are your forces, sir?' asked one of the battleship captains idly.

'I'm now promised twelve fireships on their way to us, and additionally I've been given eight store-ships here to be prepared as fireships, with the frigate *Mediator*, which will be Captain Kydd's flagship.'

Kydd did not join in the titter of amusement at his sally.

'Two bomb-vessels have been found, which will keep the fort on Île d'Aix entertained while the sport lasts.'

'And what shall we be at while you are possessed of the field?' another captain asked.

'That, sir, is a question for your senior, who shall dispose of his vessels as the situation demands and he sees fit. I will have done my duty.'

There was quiet while the implications sank in. If the fireships were taking central stage, was Cochrane stealing all the action, excluding the battleships from distinction on the field of battle? That wasn't the real reason: the wild tumult of the night, with its flaring terrors careering out of control, was no place for a disciplined line of battle.

The meeting broke up.

Chapter 42

'Shall we get to work?' Cochrane called breezily to Kydd. 'I've a feeling we'll be without all our promised fire-chariots and we'll have to make shift to find others.'

In his great cabin in *Imperieuse* he outlined what he was expecting. 'Simple enough, dear fellow. I go first with my fireworks and you lead the fireships in with *Mediator*. This being your concern, you'll want to take charge of the fitting out yourself. That's fine – I've enough to do.'

Mesmerised by the thought of the flames to come, Kydd could think of nothing to contribute and sat mute.

'I say, old fellow, you look a little under the weather. Care to get your head down for an hour or two first?'

'N-no, thank you. Just talk of fires makes me a trifle queasy.'

'Oh, quite,' Cochrane said, looking at Kydd curiously. 'We spend all our professional day guarding against a blaze, and here we are, doing our damnedest to start one.' He hesitated, then went on, 'So you'll want to see about your flock? I notice we've the first two new arrived with a quantity of store-ships at their tail.'

Kydd pulled himself together. 'Ah, how many in sum shall we be putting in?'

'Um, for every one that embraces a Frenchy there'll be three that miss, so we'd be wise to provision for, say, twenty-five, thirty?'

'I see your reasoning, but we've only the two fresh come and another six expected. Does this mean we're to find another several dozen for ourselves?'

'Quite. Well, your part-of-ship, I'll leave that to you, dear fellow. I've a mort of bother to attend to. Adieu!'

Leave it to him? Kydd hadn't the slightest idea how a cargo of fiery death was to be conjured – to him it was an arcane and deadly art. As far as he was aware, there were no publications on the subject and he knew no one who'd ever had experience in one.

But he had two specimens of the pedigree just arrived, lying well clear of Gambier's fleet. And on board presumably a crew of fire-raisers who knew what they were about.

It was the first time Kydd had ever seen a proper fireship. From the outside, *Furnace* was like any other full-rigged ship – three-masted, gun-ports, of a size with any ship-sloop and little to point her out as the lethal carrier of a fiery doom. He boarded aft by a rope-ladder, immediately struck by the plain, utilitarian appearance of the vessel. No ornamental work about the stern windows, the figurehead replaced by dowdy scrowl work and no carved wood to be seen anywhere.

'Sir Thomas, be welcome on board. Captain Elijah Moorsom.' The man had an unfortunate pomposity about him: whether the result of being under the eye of a publicly famed hero or his nature, it made for awkward conversation. An older man with carefully set grey hair, he bowed stiffly, straightening to meet Kydd's eye almost defiantly. 'You came to visit, sir?'

'I did, Captain. As leading the fireships into action, I came to learn what I can of the craft from you, sir, if you will instruct me.'

'If that is what you desire, sir.'

'And to fit out a further dozen or so transports as fireships to augment our numbers.'

An uncomfortable pause followed, before Moorsom muttered, 'This will not be easy by any means.'

'Why so, sir?'

'Many might believe it a simple task to fill a ship with combustibles and set it adrift, but it is more than that, sir, much more.'

'Oh?'

He paused. 'I think it right you should make tour of *Furnace*, the better to understand the art and science involved.'

'Very well.'

Moorsom stood aside, ushering forward a mature man in something that resembled a warrant officer's jacket. 'Mr Jones, the firemaster. With him his fire workers. These are the gentlemen who on any fire vessel will be responsible for its meet and proper expenditure.'

So, 'expenditure' was the term given to the final fiery ride to Valhalla and these would be the men who would make it so.

'As will train the volunteers in the new fireships,' Kydd added.

'I would think so.'

Kydd wanted to get on with it – time was precious. 'Shall we begin the tour?'

'Sir. You must first understand that there are three stages in the preparation of a ship for her expenditure. The first, to fit her out for the purpose below. This in no way hinders her operation as any other ship of war and, indeed, *Furnace* has most recently been an escort in the North Sea coal trade.'

That took Kydd aback, but then, on reflection, it was eminently reasonable. The vessel was pierced for eighteen guns, presumably six-pounders, and would perfectly suit the role, her lines modest and with a fine run aft. The gun-ports were empty now, the guns landed: their carrying into action without crews would be a waste. 'I see.'

'The second stage precedes the day selected and is when the fire-stores are brought aboard and distributed. The third is in the hours preparatory to the assault when the crew are reduced to a minimum and the priming is set.'

Kydd suppressed a shudder. There was no avoiding it: he would be in the lead and presumably the one to touch off the holocaust. 'So *Furnace* is fitted out but not stored?'

'That is so. No precautions beyond the ordinary are therefore required against accidental fire. A different matter when the fire-stores are brought alongside. This way, Sir Thomas.'

They went down the after companionway into a mess-deck. Jones proceeded ahead, lifted a hatch grating and stood back. 'The fire-room, sir.'

Kydd peered into the dimness. As far as the eye could see, continuous long troughs ran the full length of the vessel, cross-pieces dividing them into sea-chest-sized compart-ments, for the moment empty. Jones swung down and waited for Kydd to follow. In the darkness he could see the troughs and partitions but also other structures.

'Them there is fire-trunks,' Jones said. 'Sits above the barrels and funnels the flames up. We've fire-scuttles there 'n' there as will play along the deckhead, and ye'll notice in the ship's side we has fire-ports. These are plugged an' caulked now, but when we gets going, they suck in air to get the whole thing roaring.'

Kydd looked about him in growing discomfort. It was dark and cool down there at the moment, but what would it be like as an uncontrollable inferno?

'Where does the crew go?' he asked, conscious his voice was tight.

'Why, way aft,' Jones answered, and, keeping his head down, made his way to a sudden break in the lines of troughs, a bulkhead in the shape of a truncated V, behind which was an empty space. 'The sally-port is yonder,' he said, pointing to the ship's side. Kydd made out a door just sufficient for a single man bent double to get through. This would be the escape route for the last man – after he'd touched off the hellish blaze. Himself.

He gulped, making his way unsteadily back to the square of light that was the hatchway, scrambling back into the life-giving air and to a concerned Moorsom.

'Ah, yes,' Kydd said, breathing deeply. 'I see.'

'A lot more to know about. Shall we go to my cabin?'

It was a good deal humbler than *Tyger*'s, and Kydd sat on a collapsible chair at Moorsom's single cabin table.

'The science of the fireship is well-known and practised, sir. I will tell you of it.'

Over a welcome glass of equally humble wine it was revealed to Kydd.

'The object is not to conduct a long-drawn-out trail of fire, rather a short and fierce conflagration. This is not easy, for a devastating explosion is not to be desired, nor a sickly squib. Rather a consuming pyre, which owes its vehemence to the updraught of flame being fed but constrained by arti-fice. For this we have scuttles, ports, trunkings and other devices that artfully direct and hold in check.'

'The fitting out of our transports must be well done, I suspect.'

'Just so.'

'Tell me about the, er, fire-stores.'

'The chief ingredient for a satisfactory result. We have first our fire-barrels filled by parts, Swedish pitch, tallow, saltpetre and corned powder. This mixture we brew in an iron pot until melted. This is the chief instigator. Next in importance are our bavins, these being bundles of birch brushwood tightly bound and laid in the troughs you saw. Over these we lay profuse amounts of dried reeds, well dipped in a composition of rosin, sulphur and tallow. The same is applied to the fire-curtains, which are nailed to the deck beams and employed to bear flame on the underside of the decks. Then—'

'And then we get to the priming stage.'

'Only in the final hour. Then we lay out our fuzees and—'

'A skilled job, and I'm sure I'll learn more of it on the day. This has been very enlightening, sir, and I'm obliged to you. It's clear to me that we should commence, without a moment's delay, the fitting out of the transports offered for our use as fireships. How do we stand in the article of fire-stores?'

'There were five hired transports accompanying us with materials. I will do a reckoning on your figures. Another dozen?'

'At least.'

Kydd left as soon as he decently could. The atmosphere of pent-up wrath had been insidious and deeply menacing, and he was glad to make sanctuary of his cabin.

He immediately sent out two requests. The first was to Gambier, asking that every carpenter and his mates be lent to him for the purpose of converting the transports under supervision of Moorsom and the other captain. No doubt the remaining fireships would turn up and the pace of work would then quicken.

The other, to Cochrane, asked if he might begin the process of calling for volunteers. There was a very real possibility that they would fall short of numbers for, while courage was not lacking, there was among sailors a deep-rooted loathing of infernal machines, and in this kind of warfare there was no prize money or any other incentive, apart from loyalty to ship and country.

From all over the fleet, boats started arriving at the fireship anchorage, now designated as the lee side of the Rock of Antioche near the entrance of Basque Roads. Without the ability to land anywhere, the work had to be done in place, timbers cut and shaped in the crowded spaces of the ships, their decks torn up to allow access, exposing their innermost parts.

Chapter 43

It was time for Kydd to take up his post in his 'flagship'.
'Lieutenant Bowden, I'd be obliged if you'd shift out of *Tyger* for a berth in *Mediator* for the time being. That's not to say you'll be part of the fire crew,' he hastened to add. 'And if you'd detail a sailing party who'll not be so employed either.'

From this point on, his place of duty and rest would be aboard the doomed ship.

Mediator was a frigate, her appointments at quite a superior level to *Furnace*. Previously an Indiaman, her captain's quarters were larger than *Tyger*'s and she did not lack carved work, even if everything removable had been taken away.

At the same time there was a defiant, sad air about her. Still handsome, her prow obstinately high and proud, as though ready to take to the seas back to the Orient, as she had so often done, she was condemned to an unworthy fate.

Like the others, she had been set upon by the shipwrights but, having one more deck level, she was easier to work on. In his cabin aft, however, the din of sawing and thud of mauls was distracting to a degree. There was a stupefying amount of work to do in forging this spear to be launched into the vitals of the French squadron. Who would lead? What formation was best suited to, in effect, an aimless drift under sail? And there was the distribution of limited fire-stores against the list per ship Moorsom had provided.

Bowden had taken the burden of day-to-day command from Kydd and he worked hard at his task until he had all his resources deployed.

Kydd found Cochrane in the bowels of a brig, *Perroquet*, a coaster captured two weeks earlier and in the throes of conversion. But this was nothing like the alterations Kydd's craft were undergoing. Gazing down from the deck-edge, he could see that the lower deck was being strengthened by a close wedging of cross-timbers but there were no signs of a fire-room with its troughs.

'Ahoy there!' he called down.

'Oh, do come and join us,' Cochrane replied, waving what looked to be a carpenter's adze.

Kydd made his way down. At least a dozen men stood about, idly watching them.

'How do you like her?' Cochrane grinned.

'What . . .?'

'My own design. For an infernal machine. An exploding vessel that will put the fear of Satan and all of Hell into the French.'

'How are you going to . . .?'

'There – look. When I'm done, this will be crowded with casks and leaguers that will contain more than a thousand and a half barrels of gunpowder. All set on end and bound up to increase the force of its detonation. This framework serves to direct the explosion where I desire and in any space left I will wedge combustibles – your Valenciennes composition attracts me, with its sulphur and antimony spurting unquenchable flame wherever the blast showers it.'

'Good God above,' was all Kydd could manage.

'And overtopping all, hundreds of bomb shells, thousands of grenadoes, anything with a native violence, held down for maximum explosive effect with wooden wedges and two layers of sandbags. I shall personally sail this argosy of death in the van of our blazing lance of destruction!'

Kydd realised what was happening. Just as he'd come upon him days late at a rendezvous in thrall to his invention of the hour, the kite for moving ships, now Cochrane was engrossed in the wonder and trickery of exploding ships. He would not get much help or direction from him until he tired of it. 'Yes, I can see this, old fellow,' he said, trying to sound enthusiastic. 'It's just that I'm wondering how we're progressing on the operation plan. Column or broad-front approach. Support from cutters and sloops, this kind of thing.'

'Oh, yes. Well, this is your call, of course. You're chief of fireships. I shall be busy enough with *Perroquet*, and I'm having three infernals in all, I'll have you know. Hmm – I wonder if they should be renamed before they go in? *Parrot* doesn't seem quite the thing for the magnificence of their fate, does it?'

'I'll be about my business, then,' Kydd said heavily. 'Have we anywhere some reliable charts of the inner harbour? It would be a sorry end to our enterprise should we ground on a reef or similar before we've chance to close with 'em.'

'Oh, er, probably. Ask my sailing master. He'll know.'

Kydd suppressed a rising irritation.

Within a short while he found his worst fears confirmed. All the masters had the 1757 Jeffrey's chart, their soundings taken at the time of the British attempt on Rochefort in the Seven Years' War, but this was small scale and not of a professional standard. Some also had copied French coastal charts but the inner harbour was naval waters, and as no merchantman had business there, details were not shown.

This was a grave worry. With the whole business only days away, something had to be done.

Kydd returned to his ship and sought out Leech, *Tyger*'s replacement sailing master. A younger, more retiring individual, he seemed to be aware that he was succeeding a far more experienced, mature man and seldom put himself forward.

He and Kydd ransacked the chart drawers where Joyce's private charts were tucked away, but they had no luck. While Basque Roads was well covered, the inner harbour south was not.

The ancient seaward island of Oléron funnelled the waters down to a tight V between itself and the mainland, the southern ending constricted in impassable rivulets. Halfway up and halfway across was the island of Aix that lay just north of the entrance to Rochefort to the east, a well-placed sentinel to the big dockyard and naval base.

The French were anchored in disciplined lines just south of the island. The channel past the east of the island was narrow and rock-strewn – all vessels of size would enter by the west channel where Basque Roads transformed into Aix Roads.

Here, the most effective defences were those that were hidden. Reefs, rocks, sandbars, shoals – known to the locals but deadly to the intruder. The worst lay parallel offshore from Oléron, the Boyart shoals. Long and sinuous, its reach and outline were unknown, and it lay as an invisible barrier across the inner harbour, the channel barely a mile across, allegedly to eastward of it.

Kydd pondered. Fireships could only attack downwind.

Once set on their course they were essentially helpless; therefore positioning was all. The prevailing wind was westerly, as it was at the moment, and it was unlikely to shift in the next few days. Therefore the fireships had first to progress down the channel to a position where the winds pointed directly at the anchored French.

There was only one solution. He would have to survey the waters himself.

Chapter 44

'The pinnace, five men with Mr Gilpin and his sextant,' Kydd ordered, naming the senior midshipman. 'With a hand lead and a boat's compass.'

Tyger moved down to a position closer to the Boyart shoals and hove to. The boat was launched and made fast progress under sail, the cutting winds of spring surprisingly raw, and Kydd was grateful for his old grego, which he clutched about him. The seamen sat awkwardly, discomfited by the wet and cold of the brisk sail.

Kydd took in the vista: the board-flat island of Oléron to windward; in the distance the equally low-lying Aix. And the sea-surface between quite innocent of anything that lay beneath. A bracing sight came into view: the distant vision of the mass of ships of Allemand's fleet in three straight lines south of Aix Island. His pocket telescope told him the canny Frenchman had realised that if there was to be an attack it must come from exactly where Kydd had planned: he had moored in alternating zigzags so the full broadside of each ship could fire between ships in the next column.

It was a dismaying discovery. The drifting fireships would

be subjected to the broadsides of the entire fleet at anchor with leisure to fire with care and accuracy. No one commented, the seamen stolid and unspeaking. Gilpin, at the tiller, flicked his gaze occasionally to Kydd, more concerned at doing well under the eye of his captain than the proximity of such a massing of the enemy.

Kydd was under pressure of a kind he'd seldom had to face before. On his word that the operation was impossible without grievous loss of life it would be called off. But with this would be the end of any chance of settling with the French fleet as it lay, a fearful menace for the future, and a decision he would have strongly to defend before the commander-in-chief. Or did he cravenly allow it to go ahead and live with the consequences to the common seamen?

To give himself time to think, he started his survey towards the island of Aix at the point where the fireships would assemble to begin their death ride. The tide was low, and ugly grey-brown humps of muddy sand had emerged, their long north-west south-east orientation giving clear indication of the direction of the tidal currents.

'Oars.' The seamen obediently ceased rowing, lifting them clear of the water.

'Lecky.' The seaman with the hand lead let it plunge down over the side and, jolting it lightly on the sea-bed, sang out, 'By the deep four.'

They approached a little nearer, and every fifty feet Kydd took soundings until he knew where the maximum fifteen-foot draught of the fireships was endangered. He had his first point.

'Bearings, Mr Gilpin – the lighthouse on Chassiron.' Kydd turned and took a bearing of the Chauveau light on the opposite shore, both conspicuous aids to navigation maintained by the French in these dangerous waters and now vital for establishing their destruction. 'The angle between them,' Kydd ordered. No harm in having a cross-check of the position.

Gilpin got his sextant and, laying it flat while sighting, opened out the angle and called the reading. Kydd jotted it down, then brought the boat around to face Oléron and the northern end of the Boyart shoals. The same procedure, conveniently the same sea-marks for bearings. Already he could see that the channel for the fireships was going to be much less than a mile, allowing for only two or three of them abreast to get through.

Eyeing the crowded mass of French warships at anchor he brought the boat down closer and established a vital point: if the wind was still in the westerly quadrant as this raw breeze seemed settled into, it would be from here that their lonely last ride would begin.

They moved over to the Boyart side. The tide was out as far as it would go so dreary sea-bed hillocks and the odd kelp-covered rock were visible up and down that side of the channel. By eye he estimated the location for a second point and headed for it. Soon the tide would be on the make and it would be a hard stretch back to *Tyger*, nearly a mile off at the edge of the shoal.

A final look about and, with the position sounded and chosen, bearings and angles taken, it was time to return.

'Well done, you men,' Kydd told them. Already he had a germ of an idea that would greatly increase their chances of survival. 'Out oars. Give way—'

The sudden crump of a gun was startling against the busy sough and rustle of the wind, the far-away keening of a sea-gull. Eyes swivelled, trying to place it.

'Sir!' One of the seamen pointed to the largest islet on the mud-bank. On it there was some sort of low, rickety structure but above it, undeniably, dissipating gun-smoke. As they watched another gun opened up, the leaping flash telling of a heavy-calibre weapon. Not one but several!

The French had woken up to what they were doing. Yet in the process of trying to stop them, they had revealed the ambush they were setting up to take on any ships threatening an assault on their fleet – a hastily mounted battery of artillery opposite the one in the fort on Aix Island.

Not far from the pinnace the shot-strike in the sea plumed up twenty feet or more. These could only be some of the dreaded thirty-six-pounder coast guns of Napoleon's sea-defence fortresses and together could easily smash slowly advancing fireships to flinders. And they were in a mere boat.

It knocked Kydd's idea askew – and to return to *Tyger* he had to retrace their route, which would mean passing the guns at point-blank range. By crossing back to Aix he could probably slip past in shallower water but at that proximity the military on the island would make short work of them.

'Boats putting off, sir.' Gilpin had been watching the French fleet and a dismaying number of boats under oars were emerging from between the ships.

They couldn't stay where they were, they couldn't make off past the Boyart guns, and everywhere to the south was increasingly constricted enemy waters.

And on the other side there was *Tyger*, so near and yet so far.

In despair Kydd found his pocket telescope and brought her into view. Something was going on under her bowsprit. He concentrated, at first unable to make it out.

Sail dropped from the yards and was sheeted home as the frigate took the wind. The motions had been a sharp-eyed officer-of-the-watch buoying and slipping the anchor to get under way as rapidly as possible – and there she was, a bone in her teeth, heading straight into the channel for them.

In a sudden eruption of sound, cannon on her starboard side opened up, one after the other, sending ruin and death into the gun-post in a flail of dark wreckage.

As she drew abreast, *Tyger* rounded to with backed sails, and as the enemy took to their boats at a run, so *Tyger*'s own boats put off.

Stroking hard they reached the abandoned, smoking works and Kydd could see them set about it with crowbars, hammers and spikes. By the time they had finished, there would be no more threat to the fireships from that side of the channel.

On the Aix side the dozens of enemy boats had come to a stop at the sight of the frigate, some backing about to retreat from the scene. It was sobering, so many boats on hand that Allemand could call on to throw into a fight of any kind.

But Kydd's idea was restored. 'Well done,' he told the officer-of-the-watch, as soon as he stepped back aboard. His quick thinking had saved Kydd, his boat's crew and, as like as not, the fireship assault itself.

Chapter 45

It was something of an anticlimax to return to *Mediator* but there had been quite a deal achieved. The fire-room was ready – trunkings emerging through the deck, ports now unsightly maws and the decking in the process of being replaced.

All was hanging on completing the fitting-out of every fireship, making it ready for the final stage of taking in combustibles and explosives. It was now nearer hours than days and Kydd's heart beat faster as he took boat to *Perroquet* and Cochrane.

'At half a day's notice,' he reported. The final fireships had arrived and, with them, all remaining fire-stores and the second bomb-vessel, *Ætna*, armed with her ten-inch mortar, and bringing the famed Colonel Congreve to supervise the deployment of his war-rockets.

'And I'm prepared and ready this hour,' Cochrane said, his breezy enthusiasm calming Kydd's apprehension. 'Three charming explosion vessels now loading of their fury. I've the liveliest expectations of our adventure, don't you?'

'I do,' Kydd said, finding himself swept along in the

moment. 'I'm supposing we go by night, the better to discommode the enemy.'

'Certainly. It hasn't escaped my notice that we have a new moon these nights, an entirely and completely dark stage on which to steal upon them.'

'It occurs to me that the gods are favouring us with the weather, too,' Kydd replied. 'As the westerly is strengthening, and with the tide directly towards the enemy, we couldn't ask for better.'

His idea now came out. 'It being black as pitch, we've a problem with the Boyart shoals. Any fireships in the dark taking the ground will be a sad pother to the others. To prevent this I've made survey of the inner harbour and fixed two points of departure direct into the heart of the enemy. Before we start out we position a pair of vessels moored at these points with lights aloft who'll be the fireship guides. Steer down on 'em then between, and you're lined up for the enemy.'

'Ha! Well done, dear fellow. I do declare we're ready to go full-cock on the enterprise. Tonight?'

'Tonight?' Kydd's fear clamped back in.

'Before Allemand takes it in his head to sail, yes.'

'Sea's getting up.'

'Yes. If we have a good stiff breeze in our sails, and with a tide on the flow of three, four knots, we'll be galloping in. Tonight!'

Word spread quickly.

For Kydd it was an immediate move, dressed in his oldest sea-worn rig, back to *Mediator,* now fireship flag. The next time he set foot on *Tyger*'s deck would be when it was all over – after he'd been recovered from the inferno he'd set off.

Loading fire-stores began: an immediate prohibition of any

flame was piped as the deadly process was carried out. Lighters came alongside with the fire-barrels – large, stout and filled with a waxy substance no one seemed inclined to investigate. Smaller kegs of 'composition' were opened on deck and the contents melted over stoves. This was used to soak tight bundles of reeds, which were taken below to stow in the troughs above the bavins, the birchwood kindling. Some was coated in the trunks and about the connecting channels, the fire-master supervising all with the utmost care.

The smell of the ship was now different, alien. Stinks of sulphur, turpentine and saltpetre, vying with the honest reek of caulking pitch, wafted through, especially after the tightly sealed and caulked side-ports were knocked out. A hush descended, not unlike entering a cathedral. The men, in awe of the horrifying machine they had brought into being, talked in whispers, and tools were carefully laid down instead of thrown carelessly aside.

It was now not a ship of the seas but a lethal weapon of destruction. All non-essential crew were dismissed. Kydd could do little to assist and took to his bare cabin, left with his thoughts.

There was no question he had to see it through, be the one to lead in the fireships, the first to touch off his pyre. It went against his feral dread of fire, but he would do his duty whatever it took.

Hearing the last *thunk*s and blows as wedges were driven home, his mind wandered and Persephone floated into focus. Hurriedly he put her firmly out of his vision – this was no place for her dear presence. Instead the utterly contrasting world he'd left not so long ago returned to him. Marine insurance was the last thing he would have guessed he had talents in. Lloyd's and its labyrinthine world blending far voyaging and high finance, with its millions from underwriter backers like himself, were making it possible for British trade to ply the globe. And he had his own personal stake in this drama, one that looked set to make him a pretty penny.

How was the vessel progressing at this moment? Clearance outward bound from Hull with full insurance on her papers, shaping north around Cape Wrath, her experienced captain making a sound westerly offing before shaping course for northern Norway then—

'Sir?' It was Midshipman Rowan, who'd volunteered to act as messenger. Kydd had agreed reluctantly. No doubt the lad would have a yarn or two to share later.

'Oh, yes, what is it, younker?'

'Mr Bowden's respects and desires to tell you that enemy boats are massing.'

Kydd didn't waste time, clambering up on deck immediately. In a broad front before the French fleet a tide of armed launches, gunboats and galleys were advancing in menacing array. Surely they didn't think to stop fireships in this way.

Then, as though brought to an invisible point, they stopped in a line the best part of a mile long.

Was it that they were manned by volunteers ready to leap aboard blazing and abandoned ships to deflect their course, to do some death-defying manoeuvre of towing or lashing the wheel? It would not affect their assault, that would go ahead, but it raised the sceptre of bloody hand-to-hand fighting in boats as the accompanying recovery craft battled them.

The odds were lengthening but Cochrane showed no signs of being disheartened, seeing to last-minute adjustments of his cargo of detonation, now to be increased by the addition of hundreds of fused bomb-vessel shells.

Kydd took to pacing the decks in the keen wind, watching the stationary line of boats and, beyond, the vast expanse of the French battle fleet. Could what they were going to do really end in anything like a victory? He tried to shrug off the feeling – if others smelt his despair it would spread.

Fire-storing was completed in all fireships by early afternoon. There was nothing to be done now until the last hour of daylight when the priming would be laid.

The breeze across the deck was increasing, now a stiff westerly bringing with it a fair chop as it confronted the last of the flowing tide. In a way it was reassuring – the worst scene would be seeing a calm steal over the water, leaving the fireships drifting and burning impotently.

Kydd paced on, keeping his thoughts at bay. The stakes were high: anything was worth trying if it dealt a mortal blow to this mighty threat to Britain's sea lanes.

The wind freshened – and one by one, then in a body, the French boats left their line, driven downwind by the now respectable gusts to take shelter behind the battleships.

Bowden came up to pace beside him but his captain's conversation was stilted, halting. Sensing Kydd's mood, he made his excuses and left.

Rowan quietly made his report: 'Time, sir.' The preparative flew at the mizzen peak of *Imperieuse*. Prepare!

Kydd ordered it to be repeated at his own signal halliards and saw sudden activity on the decks of the fireships. What had been so long planned for was now happening.

While it was still light enough to take precise bearings, the tiny sloops *Redpole* and *Lyra* got under weigh in a smother of spray, their vital task to take position at the two points Kydd had established and raise a guiding light for the fireships.

Another signal jerked up in *Imperieuse*. Negative, and number fourteen. This meant that Cochrane believed weather conditions too lively to attempt linking the fireships as planned

– chaining them together in divisions of four so one snagging an enemy would wrap in others. They would now proceed independently.

'Clear the ship of all but the sailing party and fire-master's crew!'

Anyone not involved in the final ride must leave now.

Bowden came up to make his farewell to those departing. His stuttered wishes for good fortune did little to hide his anxiety.

Chapter 46

'Lay the priming, sir?' the fire-master requested formally. 'If you please,' Kydd answered. The ship would now go to the condition of a loaded pistol to full cock . . . and he would pull the trigger.

He followed the man below to the space at the after end of the fire-room reserved for the final act. Kegs of priming match were carefully broken open and coils of pale, sewn-canvas hose were taken out. In the light coming from the fire-scuttles above, these were painstakingly laid out in a double line starting from forward and visiting each trough on its way aft.

The snaking lines were taken to each fire-barrel and looped three times around them, gobs of priming composition smeared liberally everywhere in dark streaks of reeking unpleasantness, the whole brought to one in the form of a final trough athwartship that finished in a flurry of knots hidden in the composition. There, on signal, Kydd would plunge his fire to transform this whole into a hellish inferno.

'Nothin' more you can do here, Cap'n,' the fire-master said

gently. 'We opens the ports when we gets under way an', well, then we gets ready to leave quick, like.'

'Thank you,' Kydd said distantly, unable to indulge in any black banter.

He regained the deck in indecent haste. To occupy himself, he traced by eye in the fading light the course their fateful charge must take. First, in a slant south-east comfortably on the starboard tack past the wreckage of the Boyart fortifications until they reached the two moored sloops whose lights would be there for all to see. Then helm up, ease out the braces and sheets and head direct for the French fleet, tying off for the final run to immolation.

The final run. Daylight was now low and near gone, in that condition of luminosity sailors called a 'darkling sea', when even small waves cast long black shadows. And there, across almost his whole width of vision facing the French fleet, he could swear there was a definite wave-pattern revealed by the phenomenon. Not a cross-sea or an adverse current but something more sinister – a regular line, black ripples thrown into relief that owed nothing to nature.

It was roughly where the French boats had held their line before they put back. He stared until his eyes watered and then was sure.

'Mr Rowan!' he roared.

'Sir.' The young man was behind him, clearly put out that Kydd had felt the need to raise his voice.

'Take the boat, go to *Perroquet* and tell Captain Cochrane that I believe there's a boom athwart our course!'

It was a potential disaster of the first magnitude. Over there, strung out between massive anchors was a floating barrier of some kind, from what he could see of the indications fully a mile or more across and certain to be made heavy enough to bring anything short of a ship-of-the-line to a full stop. He was torn between relief to be released from his trial by fire and sorrow at the end of their cause. Cochrane must now investigate and, in the short time left, decide whether or not to call off the entire mission, an agonising decision.

Rowan was back after an excruciating delay and breathlessly raced up to Kydd. 'Captain Cochrane tenders his thanks and finds it is a boom.' He paused for breath. 'And I'm to tell you that you and your flotilla should hold yourself ready to proceed at the original time.'

A terrible vision gripped Kydd of a mass of fiery ships locked in a hopeless embrace at the boom when—

'Sir, he's going to sacrifice his explosion vessel against it,' Rowan finished.

So quick-witted and ingenious! Kydd's heart warmed to the man, cool and effective where he himself had been dithering in the throes of his dread.

'The signal that the boom is broken and it be safe to move forward is a white rocket. That it is not, and to abandon the enterprise, a red rocket.'

'Well done, Mr Rowan. You've just earned yourself an evening on the water.'

'Let all the fireships know, sir?'

'Stout lad.' There was a good hour or two before the tide turned; he'd have enough time. Kydd returned to his pacing as the night drew in.

It was going to be a dark night, a truly black one, in fact. With the invigorating wind and strong spring tide in their favour, their mission could not be more blessed. *If* Cochrane was successful in blowing apart the boom . . .

Time passed slowly in the smothering blackness.

The wind didn't slacken, still a commanding stiff breeze, and Kydd unconsciously took in the chuckle and gurgle of water as it passed down the side of the anchored ship on the ebb tide. As eight bells approached he heard the sound diminish, then fade altogether.

Slack water between tides.

'Stand to, the sailing party,' he ordered, but they were already at their lines.

A tiny pinprick of light over to the south-east was *Perroquet* and very shortly she'd begin the operation by sailing to destruction against the boom. Then all would know their fate.

He watched tensely. And then he was aware that the dot of light was still there but moving. Cochrane was on his way. Glancing out to the east, he was heartened by the twin guiding lights of the sloops on station, beaming bravely into the night. He watched as one was obscured by the bulk of *Perroquet*, reappearing as the vessel passed.

Her light grew more indistinct as she made her way into the distance. Then he saw the progression come to an abrupt stop. She had reached the boom.

Heart in his mouth, Kydd waited. The next thing he would see was the gigantic explosion that would occur at any time.

Still black, impenetrable darkness. He could hear the fretful slap of lines aloft, as the hard breeze continued, and a babble of water past their side – the tide was making in the opposite direction, towards the invisible anchored fleet. In only—

The night was torn away with a soundless flash that froze the entire scene into silhouette. It was instantly replaced by an orange-red flare, and the cataclysmic thunderclap of the explosion, half a ton of gunpowder, reached them in an appalling peal that split the night.

The light died into drifting red embers that fell slowly until there was blackness once more.

Kydd rubbed his eyes – white rocket or red?

For long minutes he waited, fists clenched in the terrible suspense.

Nothing.

Longer – was Cochrane inspecting the length of the boom or was he—

A second eruption of sound and flash caught him unprepared and he flinched. A second explosion vessel sacrificed? The boom must be of enormous size.

Or was it? Memories came from years past of experiments he'd witnessed when working with Fulton, the eccentric American inventor – his torpedoes against a hapless ship that had taken colossal amounts of powder to sink. The trouble had turned out to be simple: in the sea, explosions vented their wrath always upwards, never down. Had *Perroquet* been thrown away in vain, never a chance of destroying a barrier that lay under water?

As if in confirmation a red rocket soared skyward in a lazy arc.

What it must have cost Cochrane to throw in his hand! With their way barred so completely it was all over and nothing more was possible.

Taking him by surprise, a boiling rage swept over Kydd. To have success snatched away right at the beginning when they had done everything right was galling and infuriating and he wouldn't have it!

The boom. A lightly built fireship would have no chance against it . . . but *Mediator* was an ex-Indiaman, teak-built and heavy in her scantlings. If he trusted his conclusion that an explosion was useless against it, should he try another solution – clap on all sail and in a mad charge go for the boom in an attempt to break it?

Yes! Damn it to Hell, he would!

His orders cracked out: men raced for the shrouds, sail

spreading in ghostly pale towers while the straining anchor cable was hacked through until they were free.

Gathering way Kydd conned the old ship towards the guide lights, then gave orders to throw the helm over to head for the boom a half-mile or so ahead.

The last sail was sheeted in and, under a crazy press of canvas, *Mediator* made better speed than she had in her life before, the washing roar of her wake sounding like a mill-race. It was lunatic, dangerous, exhilarating, this ride to Valhalla.

'Down! All hands, stand by for ramming,' Kydd bellowed. When it happened it would send every man skittering along the deck unless they held fast to something.

At the wheel the helmsman stood braced but resolute and—

'Poulden! What— Why are you aboard?' he shouted at the man. There was no reply and Kydd guessed there had been last-minute arrangements that saw the old quartermaster take the wheel for his captain's great trial.

Holding a line from aloft, his hands in a death grip, Kydd kept his eyes on the darkness ahead, willing *Mediator* to fly to her destiny. Once he caught a glimpse of boats pulling frantically to get out of her path. Then they were thumping aside wreckage in the water. Any moment now . . .

The impact was stupendous – the shock of the blow followed by the instant wild rearing up and merciless descent of her bluff bows, as if she was a wild beast falling on a prey. The ship barely slowed, crunching down in a prodigious wallow, the inertia of her half-a-thousand tons driving her on and over in a shriek of tortured timber cut off like a knife when they were through.

It was done!

Minutes later, with a shuddering sigh, Kydd saw another

rocket rush up from the boats. A white rocket! They had snatched success from disaster!

The fireships got under way, the single lanthorn at their main showing them crowding for the same guide lights. It was on, and *Mediator* was far out in the lead.

'Ease sheets!' he bawled. If anything carried away now it would be a sad end to lie helplessly dismasted; in any case, it was better the fireships arrived together in an unstoppable wave of fury.

'Mr Bowden, a hand below to see if we're making water.' Only a serious leak had significance – *Mediator* would meet her demise well before they had to worry about pumping ship.

Kydd's elation fell away when he realised that he must now carry out his task to the end.

He went to the helm and stood by Poulden for a few minutes. The man had her bowsprit directed firmly towards the middle of the spread of lights that was the French fleet at anchor. He grinned mirthlessly – the lights were those of crews roused out to defend against what could only be the onslaught of the most terrible strike of all, and they made a glorious aiming point.

It was time.

'Hands to your stations!' he ordered, with a lurch of the heart.

His post was below in the fire-room and he should go to it but the sea breeze and clean night air tugged at him until the sailing party, tying off lines at their final position, darted curious looks his way.

Instinctively he looked back over the stern-rail, trying to pierce the darkness. Somewhere there should be the recovery boat from *Tyger*, whose job it was to take off the final party, but he knew that *Mediator*'s reckless bolt ahead must have left them far behind. Would they end having to throw themselves into the sea when the ship took fire?

Reluctantly he took a deep breath and ducked down the hatchway.

The fire-master was waiting and touched his forehead. 'A mite shook up but the wedges held,' he reported. 'Ready t' go, sir.'

'Sailing party?'

'Nearly done, sir.'

At that moment Bowden came down. 'All square on deck, sir,' he said diffidently. 'One hand on the wheel, one to stand by.'

It meant that the ship was to all intents and purposes sailing herself, no more to tack about or haul her wind, the helmsman there for any last-minute course correction with a messenger between deck and fire-room.

'Thank you. Well, I don't believe you're needed any more, Mr Bowden. Take your party off, if you please.'

'Aye aye, sir.' He hesitated and held out his hand. 'If I m-might wish y-you all the l-luck in the w-world,' he said awkwardly, in a soft voice, the stutter of his youth returning after all these years.

Kydd took it, touched and in some way strengthened by the gesture. 'Away you go,' he said gruffly.

The ports were now open to the outside, and over to larboard, by the light of the dark-lanthorn held by the fire-master, the sally-port showed white water rushing past, its speed exaggerated by their closeness to the waterline. Into view the prow of their ship's boat bobbed, its jib taut and straining, the bowman ready with a coil of line.

In an effortless swing the line was hurled and caught at the port and the boat hauled in, sails flapping and snapping as it was towed along.

The sailing party were heaved aboard, Bowden turning to give a last wave, and it was Kydd who had to cast off the line to watch it curve away out of sight.

They were alone for the final act. Poulden on the wheel with his messenger, who would give the word when they were within six cables or if there was any emergency. The fire-master with his mate . . . and Kydd.

There was nothing to do but wait for word, and they stood together in a difficult silence.

The messenger clattered down. 'Fleet ahead, five cables, sir.'

It was Rowan. 'What happened to Lecky?' Kydd rasped, aghast that Poulden's messenger was not who he should have been. The young midshipman had no business being involved in these last scenes.

'Taken with the quambles, sir,' the lad said and, without a pause, turned on his heel and raced back on deck.

'Port-fire, sir?' the fire-master prompted.

'Yes, please.'

Kydd went to the sally-port and gingerly eased himself out to look away astern. There was no sign of *Tyger*'s recovery pinnace. 'No boat,' he said brusquely. 'So we needs must cast ourselves in the sea when . . . when I order it. When you're in, stay together, sing out, and when the boat comes they'll pull us in as one. Clear?'

There were silent nods and he could see the improbability of it all was not lost on them.

Distance was running out.

The mate came down, carrying the port-fire with extreme care, and held it out for Kydd to take. This was the reality, the finale – this dark and chilly place, stinking of sulphur and other fumes, was, with this device and by his hand, about to be turned into an insane fury of flame.

It was innocent enough: an iron rod two feet long with a curl at the end to hold a length of slow-match coiled about its length. The far end glowed gently in the gloom.

Kydd took it, its weight surprising him. As if in a dream, he paced over to near the sally-port where the fatal knot, the start of the train of fire, was nestling in its trough.

His heart began thudding as he took in the small black twisted lump at the finality of the snakes of match radiating out, then the quietly glowing port-fire. He had been told that when it happened it would happen fast and he should be prepared. But what could prepare him for that which must come?

On deck when they saw the distance had closed the helmsmen would becket the wheel to hold it on course and the two would join them quickly and . . .

'Sir?' The fire-master pointed excitedly at the sally-port. *Tyger*'s pinnace was hauling slowly into view. So concentrated on his deadly task was Kydd, however, that it didn't make much impression and his gaze returned to the mesmerising scene of his drama.

There was a sudden clatter at the steps. Poulden and Rowan burst into the space.

Now it had to be done.

'Signal *Tyger*'s boat,' he croaked, gripping the port-fire tightly.

Poulden went to the port. 'Alongside, sir,' he reported formally.

'Get out!' Kydd blurted thickly, knowing he was now trembling.

The tip glowed on serenely, waiting patiently to do its work.

Behind him he heard the four scramble out, thudding into the bows of the pinnace. A muffled shout came from outside

– they were all away and he was on his own, the last in the ship.

Sweat threatened to blind him. He held out the instrument. It wavered and shook uncontrollably as he extended it towards the place appointed – and in that second he knew he couldn't do it. He couldn't turn the world into a crazed, fiery Hell. Nothing could make him—

A stray spark detached and fell, directly on the composition-soaked twist. It flared instantly, a savage orange and violet-hearted blaze, which leaped to the deck-head and beat at Kydd with its deadly heat, racing outwards along the lines of match to lick at the fire-barrels, the trunking, the scuttles in a berserk onslaught that nothing could resist – nothing!

It reached into his vitals, the core of his being in its madness and he fell to his knees, his mind and brain paralysed.

Dimly he was aware of noise, shouting, thumps that meant nothing in the extremity of his condition, the heat increasing to an unbearable pitch, his clothing now beginning to smoulder.

He felt something on his sleeve, his shoulder and he fell to one side, incapable of any last effort to save himself.

'Come on, cuffin, ye're a right lump but ye've done yer job right handsome an' we're getting ye out o' here.'

The words were from another world, and Kydd tried to turn and see what it was, but he was being roughly bundled across the deck.

'Scruff 'im, Ned,' he heard, and felt the indescribably sweet coolness of the night. He did not protest as he was seized by his collar and manhandled out, his lower body taking the instant cold of the sea as he draped for an instant over the gunwale of a boat before he was heaved in.

Aware only of the bulk of the *Mediator*, now ablaze from

end to end, he barely saw Doud beating madly at the mainsail of the boat where it had burst into flame, or Stirk squirming out of the sally-port and plunging into the sea to reach for the pinnace.

The boat fell away from the ghastly pyre into the anonymous blackness of night and Kydd finally found peace.

Chapter 47

'Mr Bowden's respects, an' light is breaking, sir.'

Kydd sat up groggily, peering at the figure with the lanthorn. Gilpin, acting mate-of-the-watch, stood stolidly by his cot, waiting. 'Ah, yes. I'll be up presently,' he said, the last warmth of the sleep that had finally come falling away abruptly.

Gilpin left and Kydd swung out, landing with a thump, pulling on his sea-rig without thinking.

The desperate lunacy of the previous night came back in all its immediacy, tugging at his reason and forcing him to struggle with it once more. The shocking drama of flying into oblivion, other fireships close by beginning the process of flaming destruction, Congreve's war rockets tied to their shrouds randomly shooting out in blazing arcs to the hazard of friend and foe, desperate and frenzied gunfire from the menaced fleet and then . . . *Mediator*'s gallant end at his hands.

It was a personal victory of sorts over his own feral dread but in the end it was only an accidental spark that had completed it for him. After that point he could remember nothing except, from a far distant place, the voice of Toby

Stirk before the indescribable relief of the open air. Now in the cold of the morning he realised that his old shipmate had spotted him in trouble through the port. Then in a feat of cold courage and seamanship he'd clawed his way on board from the boat into the conflagration and manhandled him back into the world of life.

And now he must go up on deck and face them all.

It had lightened to the extent that the frigate anchorage where they'd started from was now nearly all revealed, the ships closer by darker greys against the lighter morning mists obscuring those further out.

'Good morning, Mr Bowden,' Kydd said, touching his hat in response to Bowden's removing his.

'Sir. And might I say on behalf of the entire watch-on-deck how happy and relieved we are to see you back aboard.' His smile was shy but sincere.

Kydd took in the others. They all looked back at him, respectful, grave. 'As cannot match my own delight at a happy return.' The navy didn't make a fuss about such things and he'd leave it at that.

More important now, was dawn revealing the extent of their success – or failure?

As the light strengthened, one by one men made their way up on deck to peer into the receding mist. If Allemand's fleet was still there in all its menace it would have to be dealt with by other means – the prospect of a combined fleet descent of this scale upon the colonies or trade routes was too chilling to contemplate.

'Nothing yet,' Bray rumbled. 'You'd think some would be razed.'

Kydd kept his silence for he was thinking the same thing. There should be many burned carcasses littering the sea if they'd succeeded.

'There's one!' Brice exclaimed, pointing to a shadowy bulk, even in this light plainly canted over, probably hard aground.

The boatswain swore he could see another further off and then, quickly, the dawn threw off its veil and all was made gloriously plain. Not one of the French battleships was left at its mooring. Just two frigates on the far side were all of the entire fleet still afloat.

Every one – without exception – was scattered and aground, from the massive 120-gun flagship *Océan* to the humblest sail-of-the-line, hard up and helpless on mud, sandbank or bilged by rock.

Allemand's battle squadron was no more.

Excitedly they discussed what they were seeing. All the beached hulks were downwind from their original defensive positions. For some reason, like the Spaniards under the threat of Drake's fireships, they'd taken fright and cut their anchor cables, drifting with the tide and winds in the night vaguely to the south-east, desperately seeking the Charentes river and entry to Rochefort.

In the night a maze of shoals had taken them one by one, the most deadly being the Pailles reef on the opposite side of the river. Through his telescope Kydd could make out *Océan* and others levering guns over the side, jettisoning water and provisions, all in a vain attempt to float off.

The night could not have ended in a more complete victory. Cheers resounded in *Tyger*, relief showing in every face.

Kydd hid his elation as he ordered away his gig to take him to *Imperieuse* and Cochrane. There was absolutely no question that the action of the fireships had won the day without a single shot fired from any ship-of-the-line. It was their very own triumph!

He was cheered as he was piped aboard *Imperieuse*, a very improper thing but heartfelt. Cochrane, however, was not in the same mood, and quickly brushed aside Kydd's congratulations.

'I grant you, they're all scattered, aground, ruined. But did you notice? Not a one shows so much as a scorch mark. If it wasn't the fireships that did for them, what did?'

Was this jealousy, that his cherished explosion vessels had been expended against the boom and played no part while Kydd's fireships had won the day?

'Your infernal machines that went in first. They were what achieved our victory, dear fellow.'

'What do you mean?' Cochrane asked.

'The Frenchies cut their cables and ran surely enough, but they did this because they thought all those fireships were more explosion vessels come to blow them to Hades. After your monstrous detonations, can you blame them?'

'Hmph. Well, we've not finished the job.'

'What? They're destroyed as a squadron, not a threat to the meanest soul.'

'Gambier should be bringing down his heavy guns and bombarding the wrecks. What if the French can refloat some of the less damaged?'

'He might still do it.'

'He'd better signal soon. High water coming, and then what's left of them will try to get away.'

Kydd returned to *Tyger* feeling dispirited. The emotional cost of the struggle with his demons and the surging feeling of triumph afterwards had been held cheap by Cochrane's attitude. No doubt if Gambier felt the same, a few 74s would be employed to do what Cochrane wanted. But sending in heavy ships right to the very threshold of the Rochefort naval base in these light winds but strong tides would be a risky thing. He could send lighter craft, frigates and lesser, but against ships-of-the-line with their armament still intact? And at a chancy range by having to stand off the shallows, the effect of their pop-guns would be feeble.

Most likely the next signal would be a recall, they having completed their task. And then it would be a return to England and the greater war.

The tide returned to the flow, and as the morning progressed, the mud-flats and blotched rocky ledges disappeared under the flooding waters.

No signal came.

Gambier and his fleet were anchored well to the north of Aix Island in Basque Roads and could only be made out from the fighting tops, where Kydd had posted a roster of midshipmen to keep watch on *Caledonia*. Still no signal.

He climbed to the main-top with a telescope and carefully quartered the south-east where the forlornly scattered hulks of French ships lay, with the few remaining burned-out wrecks of fireships.

There was a large amount of activity on nearly all of them, large splashes overside from guns toppled in with valuable stores and powder. But no sign of a general abandoning of ships. If they could be floated off they were, to all intents and purposes, undamaged and a nearby dockyard was available for refit.

Kydd now had to admit that Cochrane had a point. If it were in any way possible, some ships of heavy metal should be sent to destroy them while they were helpless.

A half-hour before high water there was still no communication from the flagship. Now was the time to strike, in the few hours at the top of the tide, then retreat on the ebb.

To his surprise Kydd saw the telegraphic code flag and Gambier's pennant soar into *Imperieuse*'s rigging. Cochrane was going to signal something directly to the flagship.

The signal master's mate read the transmission. It was direct and unequivocal, not in the language of a scouting frigate with intelligence, but like a message coming from a fellow admiral with a criticism.

'Half the fleet can destroy the enemy.'

How Gambier would take such impudence before the eyes of his entire fleet was going to be interesting. Cochrane had clearly lost his temper and was doing things that were very unwise. Kydd debated whether he should go across and reason with the man.

An hour later and there'd been no response.

Another signal was made from *Imperieuse*: 'Eleven on shore.'

In a further hour another: 'Only two afloat.'

This time from Gambier's *Caledonia* a general signal from flag to his fleet was made. 'Prepare sheet and spare anchors out of stern ports with springs ready.'

It made no sense – it was not preceded by a 'prepare for battle', indicating an intention to close in on the helpless enemy or any kind of explanation. Not long afterwards all captains of sail-of-the-line were called to a quick conference. Kydd saw them return to their ships and finally the mass of battleships got under way – for the enemy!

The two French remaining afloat, the frigates, cut their cables to make a run for the Charentes river and both in their panic piled up on the mud. Every French flag vessel was now at the mercy of the oncoming armada. Cochrane could not complain now.

Kydd called *Tyger* to quarters. Anything could happen at this point and he had men in the tops ready to loose sail and fo'c'slemen standing by to buoy and slip the anchor. There was nothing more he could do as he watched the battle fleet approach.

But then, completely unexpectedly, it all changed.

When only three miles off Aix Island, which had only to be rounded to reach the grounded enemy, Gambier brought his fleet to a stop and anchored.

Kydd's mind raced. It had no meaning: all that had been achieved was that the fleet was now just a few miles closer.

There was no further movement that he could detect in the anchored fleet.

'Sir — *Imperieuse*.'

Kydd saw that Cochrane was getting under weigh and, knowing him, was steering for the enemy.

It was madness. His assigned task completed, he was no longer an independent squadron commander. He was now sailing without orders, a near criminal act when part of a fleet.

But be damned to it! It was a glorious, wonderful act, so in the Nelson mould.

A cutter started to move, a brig-sloop with it, falling in astern of *Imperieuse*, then joined by a gun-brig.

Every eye on *Tyger*'s deck was on Kydd and he made up his mind. 'Headsails and driver. Forward there — slip!'

Their own anchor ready buoyed was let go and they followed with the tide towards the fatal shoals.

Imperieuse soon found a victim, one of three together on the Pailles shoal itself, and by means of a kedge anchor with a spring attached oriented the ship to begin a bombardment. Kydd soon found one of his own, a dismasted 74 that showed fight as soon as he lay off it.

Tyger's long eighteens had spoken in frigate battles of desperate renown but never had entered a duel with a battle-ship. With guns twice the size and half as many again, the Frenchman was not about to strike her colours, and the heavy rolling thunder of her guns began.

This was not going to be in any way possible, Kydd realised. Their gun size and numbers were too unequal.

In despair he looked for the brigs and cutters, who must be suffering cruelly. Some were, but others were making the most of their shallow draught and manoeuvrability to come in on the quarter of the enemy where its guns could not bear. However, all they mounted were close-range carronades, whose weight might well give pause to a privateer but were ludicrous to pit against a battleship.

Then, in a flash of realisation, Kydd saw what Cochrane was up to. He was trying to shame Gambier into coming to their support and thereby bring the British heavyweights into the action.

This could not happen too quickly. It was now approaching high tide once more and the French had won the time needed to lighten ship and lay out anchors ready to haul themselves off.

The first to move was the great 120-gun *Océan*, slowly coming upright with the tide and then, with all of five anchors ahead, hauling herself off to make for Rochefort and safety. Closely following were two more, substantial 74s, which crept after the flagship and out of danger.

It was too much for Cochrane. There was a lull in firing as *Imperieuse* threw out an urgent signal: 'The enemy ships are getting under sail.' If that didn't stir Gambier, nothing would.

There was no reply.

Ten minutes later just before resuming the fight there was another: 'The enemy is superior to the chasing ship.' Usually given in the open ocean in a fleet engagement, nonetheless the meaning was obvious.

Another two Frenchmen managed to slip away and Cochrane sent his final signal: 'The ship is in distress and requires to be assisted immediately.' Plain, unequivocal, unanswerable except by action from Gambier.

And this time it brought results. *Indefatigable* frigate, cutters and brigs, even ship's launches with Congreve rockets were ordered in – with *Revenge* and *Valiant*, veteran 74s. But by now the tide was on the ebb and the wind had dropped. Even with stunsails abroad, the ships were slow and in considerable risk of being carried into the shallows.

Cochrane had managed to work his way into a position where he was engaging all three of the enemy simultaneously. That he was at some distance was why he and *Imperieuse* were surviving but Kydd saw shot-strike and damage in his ship as their relief worked their way towards the firing.

At last there was action from Gambier.

The two big ships rounded Aix Island and held for the east where Cochrane was in a fury thundering away at his three opponents. They joined in a menacing semi-circle around the luckless French and opened up, their heavy guns the death-knell for the immovable hulks. Pounded to a ruin, first one, then another of the courageous French took fire. One blew up with a sullen thump and a volcano of debris, while two more struck their colours under the relentless fire.

But time had run out. The ebbing tide was threatening to do the same to the British. If the two battleships didn't round Aix Island within the hour they would themselves be left hard aground right outside an enemy naval base. And, as Kydd had seen, the wind was shifting foul from the west.

Imperieuse was first to move, her sails fluttering precariously as she clawed around the island, but the battleships were not so fortunate. With their ponderous bulk, they were both headed by the fluky light winds and fell away deeper into the wider bay.

Kydd was occupied with escaping the closing trap as *Tyger* clung to the breeze and followed *Imperieuse* around Aix to the safety of their anchorage. From there he watched as *Revenge* and *Valiant* fought clear. Only by masterful seamanship in going about to fetch the channel on the inside of the Boyart were they able to haul themselves north and back to the sanctuary of the fleet.

For the next hours the two frigates lay at anchor, waiting for the tide to turn again. The two ships-of-the-line had proved decisive against the three they'd tackled and Gambier must manifestly send in more. Over the fifty yards that separated their ships at their moorings, Kydd could almost feel Cochrane's fiery impatience.

Soon it was becoming clear that the flood was near peaking and there would be more attempts by the French to warp off.

In the distance another 74 won clear and limped towards the Charentes river. Where were Gambier's heavyweight settlers?

Kydd eyed *Imperieuse*. No urgent signals were being thrown out. Was Cochrane trusting that ships-of-the-line would be sent soon? On the other hand neither was he weighing to get back to the Pailles reef where another four were still held fast with two in the mud opposite.

Puzzled, he hesitated. If he made sail for the enemy alone it could be taken as an implied rebuke for Cochrane's idleness.

What was going on? Then it began to dawn on him. For all Cochrane's cool courage in taking on so many of the foe with his relatively light frigate guns he'd not been able to achieve much at all. Only when *Revenge* and *Valiant* of equal metal had come up were the enemy seriously faced with destruction.

He'd achieved his object, to draw them in and to demonstrate without question their effectiveness. Now it was Gambier's responsibility to finish the job and Cochrane was not going to suffer damage to his ship and the loss of men's lives to do what was demonstrably the task of others. His own inaction was a calculated reproof of his commander-in-chief's inactivity.

In the light of this, Kydd most certainly was not going to weigh either.

But even though the wind picked up and backed a little there were no more sailings from Gambier's fleet.

Time passed – and two more French lifted from the mud and spread sail for the river. Another, slewing about, eventually freed itself from the mud-bank and followed.

That left only the two on the far side of the river, now safe while the tide ebbed during the night.

In the morning they were still there. And so was Cochrane. He wasn't about to leave while an enemy remained in the field, and Kydd took boat to go to him.

In the great cabin of *Imperieuse* Cochrane remained seated at his desk with his back to Kydd when the lieutenant of the watch announced him.

Without waiting to be asked, Kydd pulled up a chair next to Cochrane, who looked up as he sat.

'Good morning, old fellow. Come to pass the time? Shouldn't be long now, I wouldn't have thought.'

'I came to—'

'Read this.' Cochrane held a letter at arm's length, as though in disgust.

Kydd scanned it quickly. It was from Gambier, in his own hand.

My dear Lord Cochrane
You have done your part so admirably, that I will not suffer you to tarnish it by attempting impossibilities, which I think, as well as those captains who have come from you, any further attempts to destroy those ships would be. You must therefore join as soon as you can.

'You're ordered to break off the action.'

'Ha!' Cochrane said, with a bleak smile. 'This is a private letter, you'll perceive.'

Kydd was handed another, in Gambier's hand as well.

'The public one.'

This was entirely different and went into detail, directing an attack on the remaining French vessels with rockets and *Ætna*, the single bomb-vessel. It concluded ludicrously with Gambier's strong doubts even so about its success.

'I'm not at all sure what is meant by this,' Kydd said, scratching his head in perplexity. 'What will you do?'

'Nothing.'

'But you're ordered—'

'Time and tide wait for no man, 'tis said. They'll not wait for Dismal Jimmy either.'

Through *Imperieuse*'s broad stern-windows they observed the tide on the flood slowly submerging the desolate flats and ledges – and lifting the last of the stranded vessels to sanctuary. In forlorn sight were no more than a dozen or so wrecks dotted about, blackened ruins, all that was left of their adventure.

'Thus being the end of the matter,' Cochrane said drily. 'Nothing more swims that we might burn powder at. Shall we rejoin Flag, do you think?'

Chapter 48

The evening was not far off as Kydd watched *Imperieuse* spread her wings and gracefully set course north away from the anchored fleet, hours only after rejoining. No one knew what had passed between Cochrane and Gambier.

Imperieuse was on her way to England, carrying the commander-in-chief's dispatches, the traditional honour given to the captain and ship that had most distinguished themselves in a victorious action, consequently to be the first to taste the inevitable burst of public joy.

Kydd didn't begrudge him this for it was Cochrane's command, the fireships and infernals that had brought about the scattering and ruination of the French battle-fleet, not Gambier's battleships. Kydd's own role had been that of subordinate, and any inner claim to heroism had to be balanced against the stark terror and near undoing he'd suffered.

He and his ship had been taken up by Gambier and were being sent to relieve an outer frigate on patrol, a humane gesture for, in its daily tedium, *Tyger*'s people would find rest after the fires of combat until it was decided that Allemand had no further interest in any confrontation with the Channel Fleet. Gambier and his valuable ships would return to their rightful place – in the English Channel. A measure of peace would then descend on Basque Roads when the original Rochefort blockade squadron would resume its unblinking watch and guard a few miles to seaward.

'You will honour us, then, Sir Thomas?' Dillon broke into his thoughts.

'Oh, er . . .?'

'The gunroom dinner tonight,' his secretary answered patiently. 'At which we celebrate our late victory and desire you to tip us some warm words at our triumph.'

'Of course, dear fellow. I hadn't forgotten.' He always valued these invitations as a not-to-be-commanded expression of the bond between captain and quarterdeck, the vital spark uniting them into like-minded brothers-in-arms.

Besides, wasn't it the only opportunity a captain got to descend from his lonely splendour and meet his friends?

Now under easy sail far out of sight of land and admiral, a master's mate stood on lonely watch at the conn and *Tyger* gently heaved in a north-westerly swell.

With a quarter-moon about to dapple the waves with luminous silver, below, her officers took pleasure in each other's company.

'Wine with ye, Mr Leech,' Darby called, across the table. The gunner was reticent, a listener always, never with a yarn of his own, and seemed to have taken to the reserved sailing master.

'They sprang you from a ship-of-the-line, I hear, Mr Leech,' Kydd offered.

'Aye, sir. Naught but a 64, *Malplaquet*. Sent into ordinary at Medway only,' he added awkwardly, and Kydd hid a smile.

It would be a considerable change, the staid company of five or six lieutenants in an older ship set to long-distance escort or far-colony guardship now exchanged for the edgy tenseness of a crack frigate always in the news and where action against the enemy was never far distant.

The roast pork disappeared fast, well appreciated, and the warmth of the evening increased as the wine flowed.

'I don't think much of Frenchy naval waters,' Brice ventured. 'All shoals and bilging reefs. In a tide—'

'Not a bit of it,' Boatswain Herne returned. 'Take the Nore. For flats and swatchways, currents and banks it can't be beat. Why, your safe channels change with the moon near enough, and do recollect, Mr Brice, the mutineers o' 1797 were dished in the end by Trinity House taking up their buoys as they couldn't then move for fear of striking ground.'

Kydd knew that for a fact, but he was never going to reveal to this table the part he had played in those desperate days.

'As has been our sure shield since the Dutch,' rumbled Bray. 'No one's ever made it past Black Deep since to try conclusions with us.'

'Could it be the French thought their situation the same, that we'd never dare enter?' Bowden threw in.

'They'd be sad loobies to think that.' Herne chuckled. 'In the last age, wasn't it Hawke who took Aix Island and nearly Rochefort itself?'

'Ha! And our fireships did for 'em now.' Bray chortled happily. 'As demands we raise a glass to it!'

Kydd obliged, his words as the cloth was drawn suitably bloodthirsty in keeping with the sentiment of the evening. He also made a point of acknowledging the cold-blooded bravery of the volunteers who had gone in with the fireships.

'A fine job, to be sure,' the first lieutenant muttered, a shadow passing over his features.

'You've reservations, Mr Bray?' Kydd asked quietly.

Hesitating, the bluff senior lieutenant glanced once at him, then said shortly, 'The whole affair mismanaged, is all.'

The table ceased its conversations in surprise. This was the fiercely loyal Bray criticising his superiors.

'You think so?' It was better out now when whatever was troubling could be dealt with in the open.

'Aye,' interrupted Herne. 'Should have sent in the fireships in the daytime. That way they sees which course t' steer. As it was, all on 'em wasted, not a one reached a Frenchy to burn.'

'That's not so,' the gunner said. 'Night-time, that's when ye wants a clinking great fire comin' down on ye, spewing nasty great flames and looking like it's come from Hell itself.'

'And, of course, if they cut their cables in fright in the dark,' Bowden grinned, 'they'll not see their seamarks to get around their precious shoals – didn't that happen to each and every one?'

Bray was going to say his piece. 'Why didn't Dismal Jimmy send in the fleet to finish off the buggers? Every loon knows fireships are there to raise merry hell an' all, not to act as finishers themselves. Why hang back?'

It was a question to which Kydd himself wanted answers.

'Charts,' came Leech, who hurriedly put down his glass at finding himself suddenly under eye.

Bray frowned. 'Charts?'

'I'd think so, sir. Our own were poor enough things, wrong scale an' didn't even have the Boyart on 'em straight. If'n I was an admiral I'd be a mort reluctant t' risk my heavies wi' those charts he has.'

'As I says, all mismanaged,' Bray rumbled. 'If he saw that, he should have asked in the first place for bomb-vessels as could stand off and mortar the bastards.'

'That's right,' Darby nodded. 'Sending in all our small fry with shallow draught didn't fadge a whit – they's all mounting carronades and couldn't ever reach the beggars, let alone do any damage worth a spit.'

Brice twirled his glass. 'I tend to side with Mr Bray. Mismanagement. In detail as well as in the round. Did anyone notice, the two sail-o'-the-line that he did send had the deepest draught in the fleet? Why not *Bellona* and *Resolution*, with the lightest?'

He went on, 'And why, *pace* our Mr Leech, did he not call for ships and captains knowing the coast, with masters having sound experience of these waters?'

'Well, Cochrane took us in. He knows Basque Roads well enough from his time in *Pallas*.'

Before Kydd could intervene, Bray snapped, 'Two things. The first – then why didn't Gambier take notice of what the man was saying? Second, not just my view, but the fellow's a trouble-maker, fine enough fighter but doesn't know how to lead. Should have found someone else.'

Bowden blinked, sighting Bray through his glass. 'Needed a right fiery mad kind of chap to take this on. Who else would there be?'

Without hesitating Bray shot back, 'One who any would follow – Sir Thomas, o' course!'

The good-hearted laughter that this brought did much to dissipate the uncharacteristic growing resentment at the handling of the engagement, and it wasn't long before the gunroom was echoing to their favourite songs and well-loved yarns.

Afterwards Kydd knew he should have intervened. Criticism of a senior officer albeit in the warm comradeship of a gunroom dinner was never to be encouraged, even if it did allow the frustrated high spirits of a crack frigate's officers free rein for a space. He couldn't help sympathising with their sentiments but he hoped it didn't show. That two-thirds of Allemand's sail were licking their wounds in Rochefort was not something they could be proud of: the enemy had escaped and there was no denying the fact.

As he climbed into his cot he wondered how Cochrane and his news were being received in England. Would the public account it a victory or blame them for not turning it into a rout?

Chapter 49

When they returned from their patrol eight days later Gambier hoisted the Blue Peter. At long last they would be leaving the scene of whatever they had achieved. Kydd could feel *Tyger* joyously leap forward to take the windward outer scout position even if she had to curb her impatience to keep with the fleet.

Without incident they reached soundings and, with a favourable westerly, made Portsmouth in one board and came to rest at Spithead.

The bum-boats and hoys flooding out to greet them left no doubt it was a victory the public wanted at this time, and they had one. All hail to the heroes! The spectacle of mass jubilation that Kydd remembered from fevered days past was seen once more with seething crowds from Portsmouth Point along to Southsea. And the faint sounds of marching soldiers with military bands could be heard out at the anchorage. It would be a rare time for all hands that night!

Word came that liberty would be granted and the Tygers quickly flooded ashore to join in the rollicking, leaving Kydd in peace. There would be no mail for a while, their movements not known, but he'd penned a quick note to Persephone to join him. He sent for newspapers and settled down to find out what Britain made of their action.

As was by now traditional, the victory dispatch of the admiral commanding at the time was printed in full in *The Times* and there it was: a fulsome and remarkably admiring account that did more than justice to Cochrane's daring and initiative.

The Almighty's favour to His Majesty and the nation has been strongly marked in this success. He has been pleased to give the operations of His Majesty's Fleet under my command . . .

It went on to praise Cochrane to extravagant lengths that made Kydd blink in surprise.

I cannot speak in sufficient terms of admiration and applause of the vigorous and gallant attack made by Lord Cochrane upon the French line-of-battleships which were on shore, as well as his judicious manner of approaching them and placing his ship in the position most advantageous to annoy the enemy, and preserve his own ship; which could not be exceeded by any feat of valour hitherto achieved by the British Navy . . .

He smiled wryly. This should go far in soothing the man's ire but something else caught his eye that would please him far more: he'd been elevated at last to the honour of Knight of the Bath, the King himself insisting on its early awarding.

The minor sheets were lyrical, sparing no flowery or turgid prose to express their adulation of their hero, with Kydd himself mentioned in most of them as his brave lieutenant at the head of the fireships, the two riding to glory together.

It was embarrassing but it would blow over. By all means

if he cared to he could go to London for what remained of the Season and wallow in the public eye once more – but he'd found that in its invading of privacy it was not really to his taste.

Persephone arrived the next day, noticeably affected by her welcome as Lady Kydd, wife of Sir Thomas, hero of Basque Roads, and on boarding *Tyger* she blushed prettily as Kydd kissed her hand.

And then the mail came and with it an imposing letter from Lloyd's. He hadn't wanted to tell her of his venture into underwriting at this stage and tried to slip it away but, curious, she wanted to know what was inside.

It was nothing to do with marine insurance but, rather, an extravagantly worded invitation to a ceremonial dinner to be held very shortly at which the guest of honour was to be Sir Thomas Kydd who, in recognition of his intrepid deed at Basque Roads, breaking the boom in *Mediator* and leading in the fireships, was to be awarded a sword from Lloyd's Patriotic Fund to the value of one hundred pounds.

For Kydd this expression of regard from those in a position to understand and respect valiant striving was in a far different class from the noisy but unthinking yellow press and he reddened with pleasure.

'Touch the bell, my dear. It's London Town for us!'

Cecilia greeted them warmly again. 'How could you have notice of such an event and not let me know? It's my honour indeed, you both!'

'Is Nicholas in, sis?' Kydd asked.

'I'm sorry, he's not in Town.'

'Oh, away on . . .'

'Yes.'

Persephone turned to her sister-in-law. 'Dear Cecilia, my

ostrich feathers never travel well. Do you know of a shop nearby as will part with a pair? I'm so wanting to look the lady when our hero is presented at dinner.'

'My darling – I'll treasure this moment,' Persephone whispered, as they prepared to enter the banqueting hall.

Kydd, feeling the loving clasp of her arm on his, looked on the woman of his heart. Their eyes met and he melted.

The doors swung wide and, in the blaze of candlelight on gold lace and silver plate, the master of ceremonies boomed effortlessly, 'Captain Sir Thomas and Lady Kydd.'

In the sudden hush they processed in and Kydd felt the deepest happiness.

Chapter 50

'Here he is again.' Cecilia was reading from the *Morning Herald*. '"Gambryad", a classical poem in twelve stanzas, touching upon laurels denied and laurels won in the late action at B_ R_. Respectfully dedicated to the right noble Lord C_ who . . ." That's your Cochrane, is it not, Thomas?'

'I expect so, Cec.'

'It's really disgraceful,' she said crossly. 'All this fawning after the man when all the world knows it was your breaking of the boom that gave us the victory.'

Persephone gave an unladylike growl. 'That's only a Whig rag, Cecilia, to be expected of the Prince of Wales's shabby crew. When it's run in *The Times*, read by gentlemen, it's really too much. Here – "Lord Cochrane's Victory. The Lord Cochrane's recent triumph stands beside that of the Glorious First of June in numbers of enemy ships taken and destroyed, all at his own hand and none other. Of which leads this newspaper to conclude that if equal justice is to be served then nothing short of a barony might suffice in due recognition."'

Kydd found it hard to be annoyed. The presentation sword,

now in its splendid mahogany case, was a magnificent weapon. With its pronounced artistic curve, it was not a fighting sword but of eye-catching beauty, complete with a blue and gold bullion sword knot and, in its gilded foliage and Royal Arms, the figure of Britannia and an etched legend, something to be deeply proud of.

A parchment certificate was included, detailing his actions that night in command of *Mediator* in exquisite calligraphy, and he'd been touched to be told that it was the work of the boys of Christ's Hospital. They and the engravers had no doubt worked double tides to complete this work of art.

'And fancy that!' Persephone chuckled, reading from an article in the last part of the newspaper. 'They think there's a run afoot on Exchange to corner the gunpowder trade.'

Kydd took the paper and found the article. 'A cove calling himself Percy Profit, what does he know of it?'

He read on.

All of Change Alley is in a fluster I've to tell my loyal readers this morning. With my ravens out and panting with urgency they've brought me back informations that startles even your world-weary scribbler.

Consolidated Sulphur it is that's setting its counting-house clerks to double time to take in the caskets of lucre pressed on them by those hearing of the Great Purchase of their shares and desiring more of the same.

Your dutiful scribe saw it his duty to look closer into this and confides to his gallant readers that herein lurks a Great Mystery that he now offers to them in the form of Clues that they may trace for themselves.

Clue the First: that one of the prime constituents of gunpowder without which it will never be heard to shout its defiance is Sulphur.

Clue the Second: that the world's main source of the purest and best is Sicily, on the slopes of the volcanoe where it is generously deposited by same.

Clue the Third: that supposing, and one noble and disinterested soul must find it in him to arise and point it out — supposing it were that a single commercial concern gained a monopoly over its supply, it would stand to dictate terms to the world in the manufacture of gunpowder with incalculable consequences . . .

Kydd laid down the paper. 'The fellow's right, but it's sulphur he's talking about, Seph. I dare to say we find it in other places, like Iceland and such, but, come to think of it, not with the same purity. You'd have to spend a heap more on refining it from there and the powder barons might not care for the expense.'

'Gunpowder being so dear, you'll have to call off some of your battles,' she teased.

Kydd laughed with her.

Later in the day he found occasion to call in at the Great Room at Lloyd's where he was touched and embarrassed when the whole room stopped to applaud him. He bowed left and right until they resumed their usual din. Then, as inconspicuously as he could manage, he went to the Loss and Arrivals Book. It would cap a resounding few days if he could return to Persephone with a substantial contribution to securing their land.

Gingerly he opened it to the right page and his eyes found the entry.

Not yet! The ship was well on her way: she'd been spoken off North Cape and again past Kola Inlet and therefore her voyage was nearly over. With the seasonal weather in her favour it wouldn't be long now. But then again, he chided himself, he had to allow time for the news of safe arrival in Archangel to be formally forwarded before he could claim his reward.

In a warm glow of anticipation he stepped out into the bustling street.

There was a print shop down the road and his eye was drawn to an etching of an unmistakably naval cast. With those stern-lights it was patently a great cabin, with a seated admiral sternly reading, a ship's chaplain standing behind him. Bursting in through the door was a Jack Tar and an officer with a drawn sword. There was no indication of who they were but the speech bubbles of each left no doubt.

'Moab my wash pot is, my shoe, o'er Edom I will throw,' the admiral was solemnly intoning while the sailor exclaimed, 'Your shoe won't do for the French Fleet. I think we had better throw some shells your Honor!' As if this were not pointed enough, the officer was impatiently demanding, 'Why Admiral? D—m their Eyes, they'll escape if we don't make haste!'

Kydd was troubled. If the unease of the fleet was spreading into the general public, there were going to be disagreeable repercussions of the sort he remembered from the very public altercations around Commodore Popham of some years before, and he didn't want to be drawn in.

Two days later, in *The Times*, broad hints were dropped that Cochrane's successes had been won in the face of the obstructing and jealousy of his 'helpless seniority'. There was now no question: the mob was going for Gambier and his perceived reluctance to engage.

To be expected, Cobbett and the Radicals crowed with glee at one of theirs shown to be a gallant hero mortified by the servants of the state, but then it grew worse.

To his astonishment and disappointment, Kydd saw that Cochrane would be addressing the crowd in a protest meeting on the subject near Westminster, which, as he recalled, was his seat as a Member of Parliament. If he wasn't careful he'd find it more and more difficult to disentangle his allegiances.

The next day, the meeting was reported in dismaying detail. Huge crowds, riotous scenes, the watch turned out. What the devil was Cochrane about? If he carried on like this it would be disastrous for his career, which would be a lamentable loss to the country.

'I'm going to see the looby,' Kydd told Persephone, when she returned from an afternoon's shopping.

'My dear,' Persephone came back tartly, 'the man's a Radical, past redemption. He's taken by the fantasy and can't be reached by reason. Thomas, if you go you'll be seen in his company and be tarred by the same brush. Please don't!'

'He's not so bad, Seph, believe me – and a fearless fighter. It's just that . . . he's fallen back into his old ways, blaming those in power for all the world's imperfections, seeing 'em as personal enemies. I'll talk to him. It's the least I can do.'

A quick scan of a newspaper had revealed that he'd be speaking at the Crown and Anchor tavern in the Strand that night and, having thrown on inconspicuous plain clothes, Kydd took a hackney cab to get there in good time to hear what was said.

The street was seething with excitement and the podium was simply a chair perched on a table. Tankards of beer were being passed about gleeful spectators.

Kydd was elbowed to the rear but saw Cochrane clearly as he stepped out of the tavern to a roar of welcome. He mounted his improvised stage, with as much presence and natural confidence as when he'd addressed his men from the quarterdeck, Kydd thought with an odd twinge.

The drift was as he'd feared. In loud, cutting phrases, Cochrane railed against the aristocracy, the established civil government and the system of taxation, a vitriolic diatribe that left few untouched. At each pause the crowd, obviously thoroughly enjoying the spectacle, cheered him on lustily, and even at a distance Kydd could see a swelling satisfaction in Cochrane's face. His heart sank.

It came to an end when, in a husky voice, he pleaded for release from talking. Kydd tried to reach him but it was quite impossible in the crush so he cupped his hands and, in a voice that had sounded above Arctic gales, bellowed, 'Cochrane, ahoy!'

Cochrane hesitated and looked about him. Kydd repeated the hail and, lifting his hand in acknowledgement, Cochrane demanded way be made for his good friend and fellow fighting seaman, Sir Thomas Kydd.

A renewed roar of approval went up and Kydd was propelled forward in a rush.

It was not as he wanted it.

Cochrane was clearly delighted by his presence. 'Dear fellow! Come to royster with the good folk who desire to hear how it is in the world of men?'

'Not as who would say,' Kydd found himself replying. 'I was hoping for a word or two – in a quieter place.'

'And so you shall! The snug is granted to be my empire for this night.'

A foaming tankard of stingo was thrust into Kydd's hand. 'To a more peaceable condition than what's been just past for us.'

'Peaceable? How can you say that, dear chap? The country's in a ferment, demanding justice and—'

'M' friend. You're not in oration to me, I hope.'

The fire in Cochrane's eyes died and was replaced by suspicion. 'And you're not here to tell me to temper my ways, I trust!'

'We spoke once.'

'We did.'

The face was hardening. He didn't have much time left. 'As I told you then a mort of how others saw you.'

'How do *you* see me?'

'I see a man foremost in the sea profession, a true fighting seaman, whose deeds will never be forgotten by history but . . .' He struggled for the right words.

'But?' Cochrane prompted, in a brittle tone. 'If it were any other I'd this moment turn my back, but you, Kydd, I'd hoped you'd see what I'm doing for the common weal, the ordinary folk, throwing a light on the old venality and corruption that plague the ruling class, that need rooting out and—'

'Dear fellow.' Kydd heaved a sigh. 'All I'm saying is that England needs her sons of the sea more at this time than any other, and if you wage war on your own kind, it won't be able to count you in their numbers. Do be content with your victory and fame and—'

'Ah. I see what you're saying.' The expression eased, and something of the Cochrane he knew returned. The unaffected, natural and self-confident air, the indulgent, waggish fellow.

Kydd loosened. 'Then you'll agree—'

'And I forgive you for the error.'

'Error?'

'You are seeing me as one person only. I am two.'

'I beg your—'

'I am two. And you are mistaking them. One is my character as a naval officer as I do assume when I step aboard

Imperieuse. The other is as a man of the people, which role I do fearlessly embrace when ashore. The one, dear Kydd, is not responsible for the other. Do you understand me?'

'No, I do not. How can you—'

Cochrane rose in his chair. 'Then there's not a lot more to be said, you'll agree?' he snapped.

Sorrowfully, Kydd briefly held his eyes then left.

Chapter 51

It was very agreeable to be seen around town with a beautiful woman on his arm and Kydd made the most of it. At Vauxhall Gardens they were noticed by his old friends, whose open admiration for Persephone was most gratifying. At the races, Prinker went out of his way to act the introducer, and Kydd found himself chatting amiably with ministers of state, industrialists, and city folk of every description.

There was no question, he was at an eminence in society. The most satisfying part was that his lady was there by his side. As the daughter of a relatively undistinguished retired rear-admiral it was generally agreed that she had married well. What a difference from the time when they'd first encountered each other: her mother had thought him a penniless and common sailor, even if a newly promoted commander.

Kydd knew his orders would be coming through shortly and that this couldn't last, but while it did he would enjoy it. Perhaps he would invite his old friend Bazely to a rout where quantities of ladies might be expected. He would be in his element.

* * *

The next few days brought some extraordinary developments.

It was reported that the Honourable Member for Westminster had stood up in the House to deliver a comprehensive and stinging attack on the government in its handling of naval matters leading up to the action of Basque Roads – and demanded an inquiry. That the Member was none other than Lord Cochrane, the naval hero of that hour, lent venom to the assault and set everyone talking.

'He's damning himself for ever in the eyes of the Admiralty,' Persephone observed, reading the closely written columns in the newspaper. 'You'll not be seen with him any more, will you, my love?'

She had grown up in the shadow of the rulers of the navy, with their eccentric and inscrutable ways.

'I do not think so,' Kydd agreed heavily. The man was unreachable now and he had no intention of getting involved in his philippic crusade. There couldn't be much more Cochrane could do to foul his own hawse more thoroughly.

The situation became embarrassing for Kydd. With flimsy excuses, he was stopped as one who had fought by Cochrane's side and interrogated as to what it all meant, why a genuine warrior hero was throwing it all aside instead of basking in his due public adulation. Kydd had no ready answer.

It was Bazely who broke the latest news at the rout while he and Kydd were refreshing their glasses. 'Have ye heard?' he confided, one eyebrow lifting. 'His Nobs has mounted his charger and, wi' lance in hand and a merry whoop, is a-going for your Dismal Jimmy.' He took a sip of the punch, watching for Kydd's reaction.

'I'd believe anything of that benighted fool,' Kydd answered bleakly, then asked, 'So what's this, then?'

'Ha! Every catchpenny rag will have it b' now. He's allowed

to the first lord directly as he won't vote with the government when they goes for a vote o' thanks to Gambier for his success at Basque Roads. Even says as how he's to oppose it, the wight having held back from close action.'

'The lunatic! He's done for now. They'll never forgive the red-headed idiot.' Something must have shown in his face for a beaming hostess making her way to him, like a ship under full sail, suddenly halted in consternation, her hand to her mouth.

'Their lordships'll find it hard to come back on this'n.' Bazely chuckled grimly. 'Send him back t' sea at the run, I would dare t' say.'

Kydd agreed that it had gone too far. There had to be a reckoning, either one or the other to blame for what all the papers now were saying was a shameful episode, requiring some form of explanation. It was a measure of the standards the navy was held to, these days, after more than a decade and a half of struggle against a gargantuan foe.

To put their demands into perspective he wanted to shout to the world, asking what they would have called it if the French had audaciously penetrated the anchorage to fall on the fleet at Spithead, driving every single battleship in sight on to the mud or fleeing in panic up the Solent, to the utter destruction of the Channel Fleet.

This was unimaginable to the British, of course, and through his own efforts Cochrane had managed to turn victory into a surly questioning of events.

The inevitable response was not long in coming. Not from the Admiralty or Parliament or any official. James, Lord Gambier, Admiral of the Blue, made petition to be tried by court-martial to answer for his conduct upon any charge a court might see fit to bring.

With a sinking heart, Kydd remembered being called as a junior captain to the trial of Commodore Popham; as the closest to Cochrane he could not avoid a forward role, no matter how it played out.

It brought back the deadly drama of the packed courtroom – the great cabin of *Gladiator* – and his desperate dilemma as to whether to side with Popham, with whose action he did in fact sympathise, or damn him with the literal truth. And now it was going to repeat uncannily but with himself a figure upon whose every word the public would hang.

How would he appear? Who would call him as witness? More to the point, what would he say in evidence?

The thoughts rushed past until Bazely came into focus again, looking at him with a slight smile over a meal at Kydd's club.

'Oh, sorry, old fellow, I was just . . . thinking.'

'I've a small notion what about.' Bazely emptied his glass. 'Of course, Cochrane won't be calling witnesses. He's not the prosecutor, he can't.'

'He's a witness himself.'

'A smart move on the part o' their lordships. The whole direction o' the trial is theirs.'

'And as the aggrieved defender Gambier can call or disbar who he likes. So I might not—'

'Don't count on it, Kydd. Ye'll be there. One way or the other ye'll be standing afore the court to say your piece. Have ye plotted a course t' steer yet?' Bazely asked.

Chapter 52

A note arrived in the early afternoon of the next day. Kydd took it into the study and firmly closed the door.

It was short, in a scribble and phrased with the barest attempt at politeness. From Cochrane, it stated that a court-martial on the conduct of Admiral Gambier was to be held and he was to be a principal witness. He desired Kydd to know that he would esteem it the act of a friend were he to assist in the matter.

Under, in a more reasoned tone, it was pointed out that there would be no other opportunity to oblige Gambier to account for his disinclination to close with a helpless enemy to finish him. It would be a service for which future subordinates would fervently thank them, and which therefore was a moral duty.

This was asking Kydd to stand next to Cochrane in destroying the career of the officer he'd personally served under at Basque Roads and earlier at Copenhagen. And be identified as such for ever after. It would mean as well that he would be publicly aligning himself with a Radical whose views were not only opposed to his but threatened public order.

Could he do it?

On the other hand, Kydd's sympathies were with the man in his condemnation of the hesitations that had let the French slip away. A Nelson would have gloried in the priceless opportunity to crush and extirpate the whole, but Gambier hadn't even tried. Why not demand the reason? Hadn't Admiral Byng been shot on his own quarterdeck for exactly that, hanging back in the face of the enemy?

A reply was expected in haste but Kydd was not to be rushed. He would sleep on it, giving it until noon the next day before he made his decision.

In the cold light of day he came to his determination. If the facts of the matter were to be tried, all the accustomed logs, journals and so forth arrayed before the court, then let these speak for themselves. Gambier's actions – and inaction – would be laid bare and the verdict would be arrived at without needing recourse to witnesses with no more to add.

He would decline, and be spared unnecessary conflict. In any case Cochrane had really brought it on himself, and no degree of friendship could justify his own sacrifice. Nevertheless, he'd promised himself that he would give it until noon and that he would stand by.

'*The Times*, my dear?' Persephone asked sweetly, offering Kydd the paper. He'd explained his dilemma, and when he'd revealed the course he would take, she was much reassured.

The court-martial took prime position in the paper and its details were laid out exhaustively. It was to be aboard that same *Gladiator* in Portsmouth harbour, before a panel of full admirals as listed to answer the charge that 'Admiral the Right Honourable Lord Gambier, on the 12th day of the said month of April, the enemy's ships being then on shore, and the signal having been made that they could be destroyed, did, for a considerable time, neglect or delay taking effectual measures for destroying them.'

Kydd noted the report with satisfaction. It was quite a fair and specific expression of what he, Cochrane and the fleet expected to be examined, and by the end of the trial it must all come out.

He read on.

The Admiralty prosecutor had indicated that there would be no restrictions placed on the number and quality of witnesses called by Admiral Gambier in his defence while for the prosecution the same indulgence of witnesses, with the entirety of the fleet's logs and journals, would be thrown open to them without any form of hindrance offered. A thorough and revealing court-martial that must satisfy Cochrane completely.

He was still reading when Persephone interrupted him. 'We have a visitor, Thomas.'

It was Bazely, politely waiting to be shown in but with a stiff, defensive air about him.

'Come in, old trout. Anything I can do for you?'

'Ye've hoisted in details o' Dismal Jimmy's trial.'

'Yes, I have. Do sit, dear fellow. What do you think of it at all?'

'It stinks.'

'Wha'?'

'You can't see it? The scrovy villains are laying for Cochrane, setting the gullion up for a fall at the first fence.'

'What are you talking about? The charge couldn't be fairer and—'

'Cast y' eyes down the list o' the great an' good sitting on the bench. Notice anything?'

'Um, they're all pretty senior and, er . . .'

'Every one on 'em without fail Gambier's drinking matey

or one who's crossed blades wi' Cochrane at one time or t'other. Billy Young, Ned Dickson, Duckworth, Sutton, Dalling, a drabtail crew to chalk up in any man's log. How fair a trial is that, cuffin?'

'They'll have the facts as they can't deny,' Kydd answered stoutly, but inwardly disturbed by what Bazely was saying.

'It gets worse. I've a good friend been asked by the provosts t' help sort the evidence. He says as how they're casting out documents an' charts an' such as don't fit the tale.'

'Gambier's tale.'

'He's been asked t' redraft his dispatch, like. And this includes y'r own notes o' soundings, cully.'

Kydd fell silent. That Gambier had friends he knew. That he could command the subverting of a court-martial at the expense of an infinitely more worthy fighting seaman was another matter entirely, and he felt anger rise. If they had control of the facts and their apportioning they stood a very good chance of winning the day.

Not if he could help it.

'I'm going to witness,' he rasped. 'Cochrane is a strange character, peculiar in his opinions, but I'll not see him overborne by that crew of skulkers.'

'Your decision, o' course, m' friend, and I can see why, but to go up against their high an' mighty lordships at this time is not t' be thought of, is my believing.'

'They can't stop me, and being something in the nature of a public hero I'll be listened to, damn it!'

'*No!*' Persephone's harsh cry broke through, shocking him with its intensity. She was standing in the doorway and had obviously heard all that had been said. 'You can't! The knave's not worth it!'

'My love,' Kydd said gently, 'it's only as a witness that I'll be going. They can't hold that against me.'

'You don't know them. They'll never forget – never forgive that you stood against them in the interest of some . . . some Radical scapegallows! Don't you see? It'll damn you and—'

Kydd's face set. 'My dear, you can't ask it of me. He may be a wild fool but he's a priceless seaman. If—'

'Don't do it! For my sake, Thomas, I beg you!'

'Persephone. You're forgetting one thing. Not so long ago that man and I went through the fires of Hell together. We faced the worst the enemy could do to us – together. If we stood side by side then, who am I to abandon him now?'

It was unanswerable and, with a broken sob, Persephone fled from the room.

'If there's anything I can . . .'

Kydd quickly scribbled a few words. 'Send on this note to our villainous Cochrane, if you will, Bazely. I've a barrelful of explaining to do now, I believe.'

Chapter 53

Before evening a reply came from Cochrane, effusive, grateful, in quite a different tone from before. Kydd guessed what was going on: suspicious and defensive, he hadn't thought that Kydd would come forward on his behalf, that he could be counted as a friend, and it must have cost him to pen the first note.

Here he was something like the old Cochrane, making quick and incisive plans yet revealing little of his overarching motives. There was as well a suggestion that they meet privately before the trial. Although this could be regarded as conspiracy by some if they were discovered, Cochrane felt it to be desirable in formulating a counter to Gambier's scheming.

Kydd wondered if he knew something of what Bazely had found out. Probably – Cochrane had friends of his own. As to a meeting, Kydd didn't think it advisable: it would assuredly work against him if it came out.

There was no point in worrying any more about it. By now it would be known that his name had been mentioned as a witness and essentially his fate was sealed.

Early the next day he returned to *Tyger*, ostensibly to tidy up paperwork but really to avoid the public and await developments in a more martial environment.

Brice, officer-of-the-day and the only one of the officers left aboard, had little conversation in the face of what was looming. The trial of a full admiral for his behaviour in battle – no one could remember the last time it had happened, but with the captain of his ship so closely involved he was more than a little overawed.

Developments came sooner than Kydd had expected.

At a little before midday the dockyard signal tower hoisted *Tyger*'s pennants and 'captain to repair aboard the flagship', the naval way of requiring Kydd to make his way to the port admiral's residence. He knew the elderly but affable Montagu and wondered what lay in wait for him.

'Dear fellow, my apologies for breaking in on your leave like this but something rather urgent has come up, and we have need of you.'

'Sir.'

'Oh, forgetting my manners. Sherry?' He picked up the decanter but, for some reason, seemed rattled and avoided Kydd's eye.

'Not now, thank you, sir.'

'Well. We've just taken receipt of some intelligence, and I've orders to act on it without delay. A French armament of unknown force has been reported at sea on its way north-about on the Irish coast. No doubt to do us a mischief there, or is it to be closer to?'

While Kydd digested this, Montagu returned to his desk, in the process knocking over his silver stick leaning against it. Politely Kydd picked it up for him and waited.

'Er, I want you to take charge of a parcel of sloops for a sweep up the coast of Ireland. If you find 'em, trail them in the usual way and send word back. Clear?'

It was. He was being packed off safely to sea on a pretext during the time of the court-martial.

Kydd felt for the honourable old man at being used in this way. He wouldn't make it difficult for him. 'Aye aye, sir. When do I proceed?'

'As soon as you may, dear chap. And . . . and thank you for your consideration at this time.' The relief in his voice was clear. 'Flags will have your orders and so forth ready in a brace of shakes.'

The next morning, officers recalled and liberty-men back on board, *Tyger* put to sea and, within a short while, was bowling through a stiff south-westerly breeze, three sloops bucketing in her wake.

Kydd kept to himself his views of why they'd been sent to sea at such short notice but Bowden was sharp enough to make a shrewd guess, which he tried quietly to bring up, only to be met with a stony stare.

Across the Celtic Sea, Kydd ordered an extended line of search. With the much-reduced masthead height of the sloops, this was nothing like the twenty miles even a pair of frigates was capable of in good weather, but it didn't signify in the circumstances.

Days later they wheeled about the south-west reaches of Ireland and, on the crest of a deeply surging swell and winds astern, they surged north after the phantom squadron, while Kydd wondered sourly how the drama was unfolding in *Gladiator*. In a way he was grateful to be spared the ordeal but he felt demeaned at knowing he was safely out on the pristine ocean.

No French sighted by Malin Head, the squadron gave up and put about for the long haul south into the teeth of the same south-westerly.

The weather grew overcast and sullen, and it wasn't long before Atlantic rain squalls were coming in endless succession on the beam as they made their long tacks south. Hard, spiteful, driving. There was no reason for Kydd to stay on deck but he did, some primitive impulse keeping him there to be punished for his sins.

Still rain-swept and blustered, *Tyger* finally put down her helm for the Channel, riding the waves once more until the mongrel splotch of Portsmouth emerged out of the murk and they were able to take up the moorings they'd left from.

The trip ashore was wet and boisterous, and by the time Kydd finally mounted the steps in the ceaseless rain to the port admiral's office he was wrung through.

'Dear fellow, let me take that cloak. Goodness me, you're soaking! Flags – fetch me my sea rig as will fit this officer. No, I won't hear of it!' he replied, to Kydd's protestations. 'The least I can do after your Irish voyaging.'

Towelled down in the signal office and in warm gear, Kydd presented himself. 'Nothing sighted, sir,' he reported formally. Then, on impulse, he asked, 'The court-martial, sir. How did it . . .?'

'Lord Gambier? Er, acquitted on all charges, honourably discharged,' Montagu said, in a flat tone.

Kydd took the news with dull resignation. Could it have been any other? In charge of proceedings had been the secretary to the Admiralty, no longer the capable and far-seeing Marsden but the ambitious arch-political Wellesley-Pole. Brother of the sepoy general, now beleaguered in Lisbon, he had little knowledge of the Royal Navy.

'I wish that there was aught I could do for you,' the admiral continued, the warmth in his voice obvious. 'You'll be getting orders soon, I'd expect.'

'Thank you, sir. I'd be glad only of a rest at moorings, I'll confess.'

When he'd left, Persephone had made her way back to Devon and Kydd decided to remain aboard *Tyger* until his future was known. In the meantime he heard of Cochrane's shabby treatment. False charts, controversial evidence, witnesses brow-beaten, others not questioned.

Gambier's defence was in essence one main point: that while it was all very well for frigates and lesser to venture beyond Aix Island, it was asking too much to expect him to order his fleet of irreplaceable sail-of-the-line into the same shallows. In his judgement, and given the poor quality of charts at hand, it was not to be countenanced.

Kydd's lip curled in contempt. In the last analysis the fact remained that below Aix Island there had been a significant number of French battleships. If they could enter there then so could the British, particularly with Cochrane showing them the way.

Should he go to Cochrane in brotherly sympathy? Knowing the man, he thought not.

Instead there was one cheering thing he could find to do. By now the voyage he'd underwritten must be over and the formal arrival reported. It was time to collect his due.

The minute he stepped into the Great Room at Lloyd's he felt suspicious. He was greeted, but with a grave glance and formality instead of an amiable wave. If this was something to do with . . . But it couldn't be: his assessment of the maritime elements had been impeccable. Yet . . . He hastily made for the big central pillar and the Loss and Arrivals Book.

He leafed hurriedly to the right place and, with thudding heart, found there was an entry.

Maryport Packet, Hull to Archangel. Then, in calmly inscribed words that he couldn't at first take in. *Cast away, White Sea. Constructive total loss, cargo not recovered.*

Reeling with shock he fell back. With effort, he pulled himself together and babbled huskily at a passing waiter, 'Where do I . . . That is, how do you . . .?'

'Mr Juppe, chief clerk. All Lloyd's intelligence goes t' him,' the man said kindly, eyeing Kydd.

It was easily enough told. On the last stretch of the voyage, as the ship left the stormy Barents Sea to enter the calmer White Sea before Archangel, the worthy Captain Marley had suffered an apoplexy in his cabin. The mate, unfamiliar with those waters, had sailed too close to the sheltering land and been taken aback by one of those sudden fierce blows Kydd remembered hurtling without warning down icy slopes. Dismasted, the ship had been carried on to the desolate rocks of some island where she'd broken up with the loss of seven of her crew and the entirety of her freighting.

Kydd stepped slowly out into the uncaring daylight.

His estimate of the marine risk had been completely correct, but what were the chances of a captain being struck down like that?

It didn't matter now, for at this moment he had to face that he'd lost his entire savings. Knowle Manor was safe, but for how long? No reserves to pay for repairs, improvements and so forth, the likely sale of their silver and furniture, even the rights of tenantry in the village to pay for expenses.

And, of course, the shame of being pointed out as a failed

insurance gambler. With the unbearable task ahead of telling Persephone that she faced nothing much more than existence as an impoverished goodwife.

Tears pricked.

Chapter 54

Antwerp

The room was smaller than Renzi had expected, dark, intimate. It was dominated by a large polished table. A single chandelier illuminated the features of each who sat around it, the shadowed lineaments betraying every flicker of emotion. He took his place in the centre with a cool detachment, knowing that even a hint of unease or nervousness would be his undoing.

'Herr Richard Köhler, the general secretary of Goldstein,' a subdued Hübner said, with a gesture, indicating the motionless individual who sat at the head of the table, his gaze steadily on Renzi, 'and to his right Herr Erich Schäuble, financial director. To his left Ton van Witteveen . . .' It went on until all seven had been named.

This was in effect the House of Goldstein gathered together to hear him.

Meyrick nodded pleasantly this way and that, then introduced him: 'The Lord Farndon of Eskdale Hall in Wiltshire, of a noble lineage of centuries as by now you must know.'

'We have made discreet discovery of the high-born gentleman and are satisfied in his particulars,' Köhler said quietly, 'and welcome him to our convening.' He dressed in the old-fashioned way, but with taste and quiet extravagance.

Renzi smiled tightly. He was the seller, these were the buyers, and he wasn't about to be impressed with anything less than hard profit.

'And this day we meet to discuss a proposal by Mijnheer Meyrick that promises to be of interest to all about this table.' Schäuble had a high, reedy voice but the others paid him serious attention.

'Nothing less than an accession to the highest level of financial affairs that the British Treasury does allow,' Meyrick said importantly.

'Just so. At the expense of other houses grown fat and complacent over the years,' Köhler noted, his expression neutral.

'Only if this present company does move with some haste,' Renzi said immediately. 'An opportunity such as this comes once and then is gone. I do allow that if there is no substantive agreement concluded this day then my offer will be withdrawn for transfer to a more accommodating party.'

Meyrick stiffened but said nothing.

'Then perhaps we will open the business,' Köhler said, with flawless control. 'I understand the substance of the situation to be as follows: in a very short time His Majesty's government will enter into a Fifth Coalition, principally with the Austrians. There will be the usual subventions but to accelerate the process of mobilisation of the Austrian forces a very considerable sum in specie will be required *in loco* at short notice. Bids will be called in the usual way but it is intended that of Goldstein will be included. This will be on sacrificial terms in order to secure the contract with a view to detaching the present incumbent from future business with the British Crown.'

'A fair summary,' Renzi said impatiently. 'And my role will—'

'This house believes you to be desirous of a converging of interests, following our successful discharge of the contract. In this regard you are prepared to furnish the collateral necessary for Goldstein to tender.'

'Contingent upon agreement on fee levels and percentage draw-down schedules,' Meyrick murmured.

'Naturally,' Köhler came back smoothly. 'We would first desire to be assured of the precise nature of the assets Lord Farndon is bringing to this arrangement.'

'In this regard I will—' Renzi began, but was instantly overborne by Meyrick.

'My principal does not wish to realise on his fixed assets until this is necessary – the Bank of England being satisfied with his standing in respect to the tender, this will probably not be required and his long-term yields preserved. I propose in the first instance the furnishing of a draft for the amount at a nominal ninety days' sight, secured against his majority holdings in Consolidated Sicilian Sulphur, which, your London agents will have told you, when taken with his note-in-hand for six hundred thousands, far exceeds your requirement.'

'I see,' said Köhler, blank-faced. 'Then shall we discuss the fee structure? Supposing Herr Schäuble to be satisfied with a draft then . . .'

The negotiations continued through the morning but Renzi was satisfied. No one believed that the project was not worth pursuing to its full logical conclusion and while Meyrick continued to press for a more advantageous position it was clear that Goldstein was gratified at progress.

By the middle of the afternoon there was an agreement,

and by evening both sides retired on a promise to reconvene later for the formalities.

'Well accomplished, my lord,' purred Meyrick, in the privacy of Renzi's apartment.

'Their enquiries in London did satisfy to the full. This is pleasing. It implies that our qualification for the invitation to tender will be rapid.'

He smiled indulgently. 'It may allow me time to bid for an even more impressive contract. Here – let me see what you make of this.' He handed Renzi a faultlessly written document in a flowing hand that could only have been the product of much skill and patience.

It was in French and was a courteous invitation to be present at Leghorn to inspect, value and bid upon the freight there assembled, the ninth day of the following month, which Renzi was pleased to remember was Cecilia's birthday. As to its meaning he had no idea whatsoever. Or why a simple cargo should need bids from financiers as eminent as Meyrick.

'I wish you joy on its securing, sir. Whatever it may be.'

Clearly in an expansive mood, Meyrick was happy to explain. 'This is nothing but the Emperor of the French engorging himself with riches at the expense of his conquests, which we merchant bankers cannot be seen to scorn.'

'Do you mean to say—'

'The freight is plunder, sir. Booty, lucre, treasure as wrested from the unwise countries that see fit to oppose his will. In this instance I dare to say it is Spain.'

'Why the bidding?' Renzi asked, although he was beginning to have an inkling of where it was leading.

'The spoils are concentrated somewhere, then shipped to Leghorn, there to be transformed by the successful bidder to commodities far more useful to Bonaparte – currency, negotiable bonds, credit in distant capitals, hard bullion, diamonds and other baubles.'

'Concentrated somewhere?'

'As he doesn't trust his own countrymen. I'm not to be troubled by details but I understand it to be an island offshore to Spain. This is no concern to me as it's the responsibility of the client to present the goods at Leghorn.'

'How will the bidder find the bonds, currency and so forth?'

'You'll pardon me when I say that this is not of concern to yourself, my lord.'

'Of course not. More to the point is how our current project is in your view proceeding,' Renzi said, with an edge to his voice.

Meyrick drew himself up. 'I rather fancy with a marked degree of success. Ours is an unusual arrangement but in view of the impressive advancement open to Goldstein they have concurred.'

'Unusual?'

'Their business is normally with another merchant bank, an institution, government or similar, not an individual. These usually place their capital to different locations to spread the risk.'

'And I have concentrated my capital in one.' Renzi smiled broadly.

'My lord, might I say at this point that you should be more than a trifle concerned.'

'Oh?' Something about Meyrick's attitude sobered Renzi. Perhaps things had been going rather too well.

'Yes. Within hours Haart and therefore Beyer will learn that Goldstein will be active in this contract. It will not be hard for them to uncover sooner or later that the origin of the threat to their dominance is your capital placement. I speak entirely theoretically but point out that, you being a single individual and not a company, their fears may be comprehensively lifted if your good self is in some way . . . eliminated from these negotiations.'

A chill wave invaded Renzi's vitals. It was no longer a chess game – he was in very real peril of his life.

Chapter 55

Word came. Goldstein were ready to sign.

'My lord, I have to ask it, you are prepared to sign, given what I warned you of?'

'I am.' In all the talk of high finance in England there had been no thought for provision of agents for his security and protection. He was most decidedly alone.

'It could be possible to delay and desire the signing to be enacted by agent proxies in London,' Meyrick murmured, his features uncharacteristically furrowed.

'I think not,' Renzi found himself answering. Any delay could be dire in the larger picture.

'Very well. The signing will be this evening at the château in the presence of the principals. You will not be expected to negotiate on any further point, the matter descending the scale into my hands and that of the Goldstein nominee. You will then be free for the time being.'

'To return to England?'

'Most certainly not. The aim of the whole is to present Beyer and Haart in London with the proof that if their own tender is not very significantly reduced then their business relationship with the Treasury is terminated. Until that goal is achieved, we must remain to attend to any last-minute details which will see that object concluded.'

'I see.' Renzi was hoping that he could leave Antwerp before the issue was decided. Now it would be necessary to brave the accusing looks and sorrowfully presume that the Goldstein bid had been matched by Beyer, and the Treasury had decided to go with a known house.

Only then could he get back to dear Cecilia.

The carriage provided was princely, and in the early evening, in his muted finery, he joined Meyrick in the plush interior, all green velvet and gold fittings.

The door was noiselessly closed and they swayed off.

'When do you expect completion?' Renzi asked neutrally.

'We have excellent communications with London. I expect, with Mr Perceval's urging, the Old Lady will move with an acceptable celerity as will see the invitation to tender issued in some three days or so.'

'Old Lady?'

'Of Threadneedle Street. The Bank of England.'

'Oh.'

'And then we may expect an even more rapid response from an affronted Beyer, say within the week. At that you may consider your part in all this at an end.'

Renzi eased down into the soft cushions. No more than a week and he'd be back talking about the stables with Cecilia. His person, as an inoffensive nobleman, was intact, even if it was one with an absurd over-plus of monies. His character as a fop was known to the French but he'd acted the boorish self-opinionated new-money capitalist, leaving the details to his man of business. All in all, a satisfactory result.

He moodily exchanged small-talk with Meyrick until, unexpectedly, the coach jerked to a stop.

Meyrick frowned, then let up the window blind and leaned out. He was met with a babble of Flemish from the driver and, after irritably making reply, pulled back in.

'A collision of vehicles ahead, blocking the road,' he said crossly. 'I've told him we're in a hurry and to go the long way round.'

The carriage turned about awkwardly and set off back where they'd come from.

Almost immediately it lurched to a stop.

Meyrick met Renzi's eyes with instant suspicion and alarm. His hand went inside his coat and came out with a small pistol, which he cocked and held at the ready.

After a polite knock at the carriage door it was opened, revealing a hard-faced man dressed as a footman, who drew down the steps and moved aside.

Another, a major-domo of some kind, came forward, bowed and regarded them both, only a flicker betraying his sight of the pistol. Meyrick barked a question and at the answer put it away.

'A transparent subterfuge,' he muttered. 'We've been bailed up by a confected accident and these are Haart's men, inviting us in to join them while it is sorted out.'

They walked forward towards an imposing mansion, the major-domo falling in behind them, others waiting in the shadows nearby.

'I cannot believe anything will happen to us. Yet it proves how extreme a situation Haart views any trespass on their territory by Goldstein or other. The course you must take—'

At the top of the steps an individual appeared, whom Renzi recognised instantly. Le Loup Noir – Friedrich of Skalvia.

'Good evening, gentlemen,' he said unctuously, his deep-set eyes clamped on Renzi's. 'They told me you had met with a mishap on the road. It is deplorable. I've complained of these so many times – but do come in off the street, take refreshment while it is dealt with.'

Meyrick bowed politely and Renzi followed suit. But what had he started to say – the course to follow?

They entered a reception room arrayed in medieval accoutrements with a fire roaring and a pair of easy chairs close together. Meyrick was ushered to a separate chair a little distance away.

'Cognac?'

The warmth of a most superior vintage slipped down gratefully.

'It's a happy coincidence that you're here this night.' Friedrich chuckled. 'I've been meaning to make your further acquaintance, my lord Farndon.'

'Indeed?' Renzi responded coldly.

'You're finding Antwerp an interesting, not to say profitable, visit?'

'My business is not your concern, sir,' Renzi said, with a lofty disdain. The fire cast shadows across Meyrick's face and he could make out nothing.

'Not even in the matter of the Fifth Coalition with the Austrians?'

The silky tone threw Renzi to an icy alert, his thoughts racing. It could go anywhere, depending on Friedrich's objective, but at the top of his concerns was the overriding need to secure the signing of the Goldstein commitment. He'd do whatever was necessary to ensure time for this to happen and the final process complete.

He leaned back luxuriously. 'I haven't any idea what you're talking about, sir. It's all nonsense to me.'

Friedrich gave a smug smile. 'We have our sources and they tell of—'

'Herr Markgraf, I'm not here to waste my time and capital on some kind of passing political fancy. A more enduring investment is much to be preferred.'

'Forgive me for the intrusion, my lord, but you intrigue me. What can possibly be more interesting than a grand coalition?'

The fire crackled robustly and Meyrick shifted uncomfortably. His expression could now be made out, and it was one of shock, dismay and frank disbelief. All to the good.

'Don't worry, Meyrick, old fellow. The affair is all but completed. No harm in letting the Markgraf know.'

He turned languidly to Friedrich and briskly continued, 'Russia. The canal of Peter the Great between the Volga and Don.'

'But . . . but that's been lying fallow this age.'

'Quite. And in the meanwhile Great Britain has led the world with its daring canal building, its competence and proficiency in this field unmatchable. Can you credit how much Alexander would advance to any who could let him succeed where his ancestors failed?'

Stunned, Friedrich fell back, staring at Renzi. 'Good God,' he said faintly. 'I've not heard a whisper of this.'

Meyrick recovered himself and added urbanely, 'Not for your common financier, of course, my dear Friedrich.'

'No, no, I understand. What I cannot is why you are wasting your time with a two-pfennig house like Goldstein when—'

'Thank you, Friedrich. Your interest is noted, and as the affair progresses, I've no doubt Haart will become involved. Now, we do have an appointment and, if you'll pardon, we must resume our journey. Come, my lord.'

* * *

The carriage swayed off, the Markgraf outside on the steps to bid them farewell.

Meyrick sat back, mopping his forehead in relief. 'A colourful conceit, my lord, and well delivered. It will hold them until the Goldstein project is complete. Might I remark that you possess a ready wit and uncommon ability to deliver? Should you desire it, the profession of high finance in its upper reaches would be open to you, I believe.'

The château, set within a grove of tall trees and high walls was ablaze with light, and no fewer than twenty footmen descended the steps to attend on them. Passing through an elaborate entrance hall in the Continental style, they mounted the grand staircase to a richly appointed upper chamber adorned with portraits and silverware.

A central table was set about with documents and ink-stands. Around it men stood, smiling gravely.

Köhler offered Renzi a quill. It was soon done.

The papers would be packaged together and sent that night to London. It was all but over.

Köhler smiled and solicitously ushered Renzi forward. 'The banquet, my lord.'

One by one they went into an adjacent room to a grand dinner.

Chapter 56

London

As he stepped out on to the busy street, Kydd's mind worked furiously. In a short while he would be back at sea and his power to act in his own salvation would then be past. He had only until then to restore his fortune.

Should he continue at the underwriting? It had been the worst of bad luck that his first substantial foray into the field had failed. He'd seen for himself that the odds were considerably on the side of voyages ending in safe arrival. If that wasn't the case, the merchant marine would be in a hopeless extremity and, most patently, it was not, which was why the British were winning the sea war, not the French. Another try would almost certainly succeed – but where was the risk capital going to come from?

No, that was not the answer. Even if he started again in a small way it would take years to build up the necessary substantial assets to lay out again.

Then prize money – where it all came from originally!

He'd been lucky before but there was no guarantee that

he would be in the future. It was a different world now. The Spanish were no longer in the war, removing in one stroke a rich source of prizes, from coastals to the legendary Manila galleons. He remembered the mercury frigate he'd recently captured, then had to destroy. It would easily have settled the land problem. He swore aloud, causing a passing walker to recoil in consternation.

Nearing a tavern Kydd was tempted to sink one or two pints but remembered that he could not – for the first time since those far-away days as a sloop commander with the Channel Island squadron he must mind every penny. In a single hour he'd gone from a highly respected member of Brooks's club to one who rued the price of a beer in a common alehouse.

Why not find a way out as he'd done then? Set up as a privateer captain again, knowing the trade as well as he had done to land the prizes that had been the basis for his personal wealth!

The answer came as quickly: for exactly the same reason as a frigate was no longer the high road to riches – lack of opportunity. No enterprising investor would see fit to arm and equip an ocean-going privateer with the lean pickings to be had, these days, however famous a captain in command.

And the very thought of giving up his beautiful and deadly *Tyger* for the racy assassin of a privateering schooner was too much to contemplate.

It didn't leave much else.

Much as he hated the idea, should he go to Renzi, lay it all before him, talk about the calamity, see what could be done? His friend was much more a man of the world than himself, with his own straight-figured perspective on things and might well have ideas that would never occur to him.

The more he thought about it, the better it appeared. He

felt a calm beginning to settle at last. It might even be possible to keep Persephone out of it, unaware of events.

He'd taken a room at a modest inn, having come to Town only to look things up in Lloyd's. It was a stiff walk all the way to Mayfair, but it was what he had determined to do.

'Why, Thomas. You're in London again!' cried Cecilia. 'Do come in. Will you be staying long?'

Too late he remembered that Renzi might not yet have returned. 'Er, Nicholas – is he come back at all?'

'Not yet, the wicked man. I suspect he's enjoying the sights in . . . where he is,' she finished lamely.

This was a severe setback. He'd not thought about what he'd do if Renzi were not at home to consult. 'Oh, yes, of course.'

'Are you feeling well, Thomas? You look decidedly peaky,' Cecilia said, in concern. 'I shall ring for a roborant.'

'No – please don't bother. I need to think.' He went haltingly to an armchair.

'If I didn't know you better, my dear,' she teased, 'I'd suspect you to be flustered in drink.' Then she sat next to him. 'It's something serious, though, isn't it?'

'I – I have to think, is all.'

'I thought so. Well, tonight you shall sleep here, and over dinner, you will tell me all about what can ail my sea hero.'

He knew his sister cared for him deeply. In the past she'd steered him through more than a few life crises and the tenderness in her voice reached out to him. 'Thank you, Cec, but this really is man-to-man, you understand.'

'Nonsense, Thomas. Every time you say that, there's always something a woman can see that you can't. A great pity Persephone is not here to help us.'

'Ah. It's her, really, that I don't want to know about things.'

Cecilia paused, a frown settling. 'Thomas, you're not . . . This does not concern a – a lady, does it?'

Kydd gave a wan smile. 'I wish it were that simple, sis.'

'So, dear brother, what is it that's causing you trouble?'

'I should really be talking to Nicholas, Cec, believe me.'

'Man problems are the same as lady problems, but different,' she pronounced unarguably. 'Now do get on.'

He couldn't help it. He had to share the burden, and she would keep it quiet from Persephone. 'It all started when this cove wanted the land above our manor for a china clay pit,' he began, and after suitable explanation went on to his venture at Lloyd's. 'It would have been all plain sailing if that careless master hadn't decided to have an apoplexy and leave the ship to a useless mate, Cec. Truly.'

'And now you have to pay for the insurance.'

'We all, not just me, but the most by far.'

She sat back, concentrating. 'Then it's a matter of money. Restoring your means and then Persephone will not even have to know.'

'In one, sis.'

'Dear Thomas. I keep a sharp eye on the steward's books at Eskdale. I know our situation. You won't need Nicholas to tell you that even with what we've put by for the new stables I don't think we've anything like enough to help you out.'

'Cec, don't think on it!' Kydd cried in anguish. 'It's my problem, God help me, and I've to find a way out. I came for . . . well, advice only. Please believe it!'

'I do, poor lamb. If there was only something I could think of that might help you. How I wish Nicholas was here. He's so good at this. Calm and logical, he always finds a way through things.'

'Never mind, sis. He's not and that's an end to it.'

She looked away in despair. 'I so hate to see you like this, my dear brother,' she said, in a low voice. 'After all you've done for your country and you're thrust down like this, as if you were a—' A sob escaped her. 'If only . . .'

'Dear sis, don't take on so. If I can—'

He broke off as he saw her face lighten. 'Thomas. There could be a way.'

'Cec?'

'But would I be breaking my word to Nicholas?' She stared at him as though he had the answer. He shrugged wordlessly.

'I'll do it! He'd understand and it wouldn't be as if I was betraying him.'

'Dear soul, you've lost me completely.'

She fumbled in her bodice and produced a small key. 'He sometimes does things for the government, you know, secret things. You must have suspected.'

'I've seen him in one or two strange scenes as I've been able to assist with.'

'Then you'll appreciate he doesn't want to muddle these things with his real life and keeps that kind of thing separate. Before he left he got a quick note from someone very trustworthy that had him posting up to London with all haste to purchase a huge parcel of shares or stocks or whatever it was. I've still got the note. Thomas, if you invest in the same as he did you'll get your money back!'

She didn't wait for a reply, hurrying out and bringing back a small chest. With a triumphant flourish she opened it and extracted the note.

In a scrawl it simply said, *Put all you have in Consolidated Sicilian Sulphur*, and it was signed by one *Congalton*.

'Put all you have?' Kydd said in awe. 'This Congalton must be very sure of it.'

'Just between the two of us, Thomas, I can tell you he's

the gentleman in London who Nicholas sees and, goodness me, what he doesn't know of things would be very little, I'm thinking.'

'I've just remembered – wasn't it that crew I read about in *The Times* who are cornering sulphur so the gunpowder makers have to go to them?'

'Really? Then Mr Congalton was right,' Cecilia said, breathless. 'Do you think we're too late to get some? Shares or stocks, whatever they are.'

'If they can do what it said there's no time to be lost, sis. I'm going to move quickly on this.'

'Thomas – you've got no money to buy them!'

'I'll find some, whatever it takes. A chance like this doesn't come every day. Tomorrow, to make sure, I'm going to lay it all by the tail, get my bearings right, then clap on all sail to get back my coin!'

'How exciting!' she exclaimed delightedly, and hugged him tightly.

That night Kydd stared up into the darkness and let his thoughts go over the situation. It had to be said that he'd chanced upon a sovereign opportunity to mend his fortune. This Congalton had strongly advised putting not just a little but Renzi's entire means into these shares. Cecilia had told him he'd done so, and *The Times* had confirmed the soundness of that advice.

So the opening was there – it was galling that Cecilia was right: he had no money to buy them.

Was that strictly true? He was squire, lord of Knowle Manor and the tenantries of Combe Tavy. Improved, it must be worth a not inconsiderable sum and as security of some kind against . . . No, he couldn't do it! If anything happened to their home he could never forgive himself.

So let the chance slip by for ever, resign himself – and Persephone – to a humble life as . . .

Torn, sleep was impossible until in the early hours a thought came that was so obvious. Renzi was not available so find someone knowledgeable in the dark arts of stocks and shares to verify his conclusions sufficiently that he could feel safe in hazarding Knowle Manor.

It didn't take long to come up with a name. Cochrane. He recalled hearing that he was no stranger to the City and, if he remembered rightly, even had a relation who was a professional in the field. At the very least he would be advised fairly and squarely.

Sleep came at last.

Finding Cochrane was not easy. After the court-martial he'd continued to be loud in his condemnation of Gambier and, at the restored vote of thanks in Parliament, had spoken against it in a rousing speech from the benches. The vote had passed but with many opposed. He'd gone on to be conspicuous at public meetings with his Radical friends and to be a thorn in the side of the government.

And, as an ominous portent for his future in the navy, *Imperieuse* had gone to sea – with a temporary captain in command.

Unexpectedly in the late afternoon a visitor was announced. It was none other than Cochrane.

'You've been asking about me, Kydd.' Cochrane was tousled, unkempt, and his coat had seen better days, but the tall redhead was as full of fire as he'd ever been. He settled in an armchair without being asked, twitching his feet as though having walked a distance.

'Dear fellow, can I get you something? You look, um, well used.'

'A full and busy life is all. Now?'

'Well, a small thing, really, but it would be of much service to me. I'm in need of advice, of a financial colour as it were, and this world with its wicked ways being as it is, I desired to speak with one I've the greatest trust in.'

'I'm flattered, old chap, but my own experiences some might say are of the more quixotic. I rather fancy I'm not to be your counsellor. What is it that you desire me to give you a course to steer?'

'I've recently been alerted to the existence of a company with a very interesting objective that's made 'Change sit up. From a quite separate source I've learned that its future course is, who's to say, golden, and I beg to know if I should hazard my means upon it.'

'Ah. A chancy thing, your share trading. Many's the one who's laid out his savings in full on some wild scheme and seen it disappear in a night.'

'This I know.' Kydd hesitated then went on, 'However, I would be much loath to see this opportunity go by, my personal finances being in want of replenishing at this time.'

'I see, and you have my condolences, believe me.' He reflected for a moment, then added, 'If it's advice you're needing, I've an uncle who's more than a little fly in these matters. Done well in the Caribbean and now here. I'll give you an introduction.'

The Honourable Andrew Cochrane-Johnstone welcomed him, intrigued that his nephew was so warmly recommending. A slight, rather dumpy individual, his well-pomaded hair and ornamented waistcoat smacked more of the eighteenth century than the nineteenth, but Kydd cared not a jot if the man spoke any kind of sense.

'So what can I do for you, Captain?'

'Only advice, sir. You are noted for your business acumen. Are you familiar with the current situation on the Stock Exchange?'

'Ha! If I were not, I should not last long in business.'

'I have received notice that should I invest well in a certain company it would be of much profit to me.'

'Oh? Pray which one, that I might give an opinion.'

'Consolidated Sicilian Sulphur. They are reputed to be in the process of cornering the market in sulphur and therefore gunpowder.'

'Indeed so. A fine fancy in a world of war on all sides. Yes, I've heard of this.'

'Do you think it true? If it is, then I should strongly consider the investing.'

'This is the wrong question to ask, is then my advice to you, sir.'

'Pardon?'

'The question should rather be, does the world believe it to be true? If they do, then the shares will rise in value. If not, then the converse. True or not, this is the reality and your actions will conform to your observation.'

'What is your view?'

'Again, you should not make enquiry of me. Rather you should ask the world for their conclusion, which you will easily determine by examining the asking price of these stocks.'

'And what does this tell you, may I ask?'

'One moment.' He fetched a newspaper and consulted its inner pages. 'Ah, here we are. Yes, up again this morning. From this you may deduce that the world is indeed interested and finds the stocks desirable.'

Kydd held his breath and let it out again. 'A substantial

purchase of shares now, how much would you estimate their yielding over, say, six months?'

'If they continue to increase at this rate I would expect to see above a hundred, a hundred and sixty per centum on capital.'

'And three months?'

'Proportionally.'

'Then I do believe I will hazard my money.'

'Very well, if that is your decision. But you will find matters not so easily ordered.'

'Pray, why so?'

'At the first, the Stock Exchange is not open to members of the public to enter as they please and promiscuously buy and sell what takes their fancy. Second, the procuring of shares is unlike that of groceries or fish. Only gentlemen of some standing intending to place purchase orders in very respectable sums will be entertained by the brokers concerned. And, third, if indeed you desire to purchase in some substantial degree and at once, the delicate equilibrium of the market is disturbed. In short, the price you will have to pay will necessarily increase as demand is seen to have risen.'

'I see. Um, I really do need to make provision in the shorter term. Is there any way . . . ?'

'What scale of purchasing do you have in mind?'

Kydd hesitated, then mentioned a figure that would secure the land for Persephone and replace their savings, plus generate a small over-plus.

'About . . . six hundred shares, at today's prices. You have this sum?'

'Well, not in a bank. My country estate is worth this and will stand as security against a loan.'

'It may not be necessary,' he said easily. 'After all, why pay interest on a formal loan when there are other ways to achieve what you want?'

'I'm very grateful for your advice, Mr Cochrane-Johnstone, taking up so much of your time as it has.'

'Not at all, sir. For one of Nelson's heroes nothing is too much trouble. But I fear that if you wish to proceed there are further complications.'

'Oh?'

'The effect of a sudden purchase in such an amount will create comment with your price consequently raised. To avoid this, the transfers will have to be spread across many, a laborious task requiring much discretion. No broker will welcome such a burden.'

'I see.'

'And to have your estate recognised in a financial instrument in the shorter term as you desire is not going to be easy.'

'This is vexing to a degree,' Kydd said. 'I'd hoped to have matters arranged before I'm sent back to sea.'

'This may yet be possible. Hmm. Yes! Should you wish me to act for you, I do believe my influence and standing in the City will permit me to conduct matters to your advantage.'

'That is most kind in you, sir.'

'Yes, you may leave it with me. There will be a fee of sorts involved but this will be trivial. Now, sir, please to let me know your details as will allow me to advance the business and I trust all may be made ready for this hour tomorrow.'

It was simple, not to say painless, to be made owner of an appreciable portion of an international business and Kydd felt both elated and guilty.

A document bearing Cochrane-Johnstone's impressive seal testified to his acting for him, in token of which a not inconsiderable sum changed hands. Another document authorised his agent to complete the transfer of a specified number of shares of Consolidated Sicilian Sulphur stock to Kydd within the span of no more than three days. The instrument of payment was a promissory note whose tenor matched Kydd's requirement for a three-month holding and was secured against his estate, bearing a four per cent interest and in favour of Cochrane-Johnstone.

Without any further delay he dutifully signed in the right places.

As he left, Kydd yet again ran through the sequence of events in his mind. On advice from an unimpeachable source, Renzi had bought into Consolidated Sicilian Sulphur in a big way. Current indications were that he knew something that others had picked up to raise the price. Even if it appreciated at half the current rate he would be at the least restored to fortune in just a few months.

Chapter 57

Antwerp

J ago brought in a tray. 'Post for you, m' lord.'

This was puzzling, for only Whitehall knew to make use of the local British consul as a forwarding address. Was this going to be official release from the increasing tedium of his sumptuous confinement?

The man retired, leaving him alone with the missive.

He took it to the window, looked closely and saw that it had been expertly opened and re-sealed. He returned to his chair and broke the seal. Plainly written, it was from his sister Fanny – he had no such sister – so this was Congalton.

It was brief – and devastating.

My dear Nicholas,
It is with anguish in my heart that I tell you your ailing aunt Maud has not recovered from the operation as expected. Pray do not feel you have to return for some days while you wind up your business affairs but your early attention to Maud's settlement would be appreciated.

He knew instantly what it meant. The whole enterprise had not gone as hoped and the bid Goldstein had tendered seemed not to have affected Beyer's final figure. The Treasury would not be going forward with the Goldstein tender, as intended, and must accept the Beyer-Haart figure at its no doubt ruinous level.

He was being asked to stay on for a few days: they probably intended him to see if Goldstein would drop to an even more ridiculously low sum but this was most unlikely.

The reference to a settlement was transparent: they wanted their capital back with the shortest possible delay and therefore cost to the Treasury purse. At least that could be done: a quick sell note to his broker would liquidate the holding.

What was puzzling was why the project had failed.

His fast-increasing understanding of financials told him that the Goldstein offer would be like a bombshell to the complacent Beyer and only a very rapid response dropping their charges to the same or better would keep them from losing their priceless position. Why had they felt so confident that they'd declined to move on their bid?

The only logical reason wasn't long in suggesting itself: the plot had been betrayed. Beyer had been informed that the Goldstein offer was for show only, however sincere their approach, and they'd therefore felt safe to maintain their pricing. Nothing else fitted.

Who stood to gain by it? No one on the government side, of course, or the Goldstein concern, even if they knew. Meyrick? He was from Sacher-Wilms and therefore outside it all. But what if . . .

It wouldn't make any difference, it was all over now, but at least he'd have the satisfaction of unmasking the villain. He crossed the corridor to Meyrick's apartment.

The man came to the door in an Oriental smoking robe and precious-stone-encrusted velvet slippers.

'Mr Meyrick, a morsel of your time if you would.'

'Why, of course, my lord. What advice can I give you at this hour?'

'I've just this minute had a communication from London conveying the grave information that we've failed. The Goldstein bid has not served its purpose in obliging Beyer-Haart to greatly reduce its fee structure.'

He watched Meyrick intently but not a flicker of emotion surfaced. Instead, with a look of sorrow, he murmured, 'Oh dear. This is a grave disappointment and I'm truly sorry to hear it. I'm not sure there's very much more we can do in the circumstances.'

'I agree there's nothing more we can do, but I doubt you are truly disappointed. Why did you betray us, Mijnheer Meyrick?'

The control was masterful, not even a blink of the eyes. 'Pray to what do you refer? I do not understand you, sir.'

'Wholly as a precautionary act I had you followed,' Renzi lied, softly but menacingly. 'You spoke at length with a covert agent of Haart who passed on your treacherous intelligence to Beyer. My man Jago in the next apartment to yours is prepared to testify to this effect. Shall I call him?'

The same unnerving, total control. Then he spoke:

'It will not be necessary.'

'Then?'

'I confess myself . . . disappointed.'

It was not the response Renzi had expected but he followed along. 'Disappointed?'

'I'd hoped you'd learned more of the financial craft by now, my lord. The reasons for my act are, as always for a financier, in the numbers.'

It then dawned on Renzi. 'You've lifted a fee from our side for going through the motions but with an even bigger fee from Beyer for allowing them to preserve their outrageous margins.'

'Just so.'

Renzi gave a half-smile. The ways of finance were closer to the law of the jungle, it seemed.

'Then it leaves me with only the question of what I will do with you,' Renzi said, in truth perplexed at his next move.

'Oh, do not trouble yourself on my account, I beg,' Meyrick replied easily. 'Like you, I took precautions of a reasonable nature and should anything untoward happen to me then regrettably the world will discover the true nature of the wealthy but harmless Lord Farndon to the undoing of whatever clandestine activity you are conducting for your Mr Congalton.'

He saw something in Renzi's face and a glimmer of a smile appeared. 'Have no fear, my lord. Your secret is safe, it will not be sold. It is no less than my lifelong immunity from any unpleasantness originating from the British government, you see.'

Chapter 58

London

For Kydd it was as if a long-time burden had been shifted. It was just a matter of waiting it out for three months. If the clay-pit projector was pressing, the sympathetic Martin Riggs could be bought off with a loan secured on his shares – whatever it took to preserve their Arcadia. He, the man and head of the family, had taken decisive steps and secured their future, and could take great satisfaction in his bold move.

That night he took a youthful delight in the consternation he caused among the prim and righteous of society by flagrantly escorting a beautiful woman – Cecilia, Countess of Farndon – to the newly opened Theatre Royal in Covent Garden, they little knowing it was brother and sister enjoying each other's company alone together for the first time in many years.

A fine supper followed, at which they caught up on their separate adventures, then returned to her town house at a disgraceful hour.

Kydd slept soundly for the first time in weeks and in the

morning, at Cecilia's suggestion, took a long perfumed bath and did nothing for the rest of the afternoon.

But conscience pricked him: with orders expected at any time he knew he should return aboard his ship. There was a war on and the Admiralty dispositions were likely to be ready for such a known warrior of the sea.

In the morning he took his leave of Cecilia and caught the early coach for Portsmouth, the familiar road south endlessly unwinding as he sleepily contemplated life with its many complications.

At Hindhead Kydd broke his fast, idly leafing through the morning's *Times* left by another passenger. Percy Profit was burbling on about something, but before he could take it in there was a brisk shout. 'All aboard! The Portsmouth mail, leavin' now!'

He took the newspaper with him and settled back in his seat while the others clambered on board and the driver made much of checking his horses and the traces.

What was that scribbler saying now? He found the piece again and read the first few paragraphs about highlights of the London scene.

Then it hit him in a cold wave of shock.

Qui vult decipi decipiatur! *He who desires to be deceived, let him be! The human race is at base venal and ever more will be so, never more exemplified than in the doleful case of Consolidated Sulphur, which my loyal readers might remember your Profit Prophet warning of its foolish and unaccountable rise. That an otherwise intelligent modern investor could be so gulled as to believe any company capable of monopolising the gunpowder trade passes belief. Now the wiser, it is unhappily too late for them. In a giddy fall whose rapidity astonishes even your diligent reporter these shares*

are now trading at a ridiculous figure, which may not be quoted,
as of a surety they will be even less by the time my good reader
lifts his eyes from these pages. True to his calling, your scribe let
loose his ravens to uncover unwelcome truths and he is in a posi-
tion to state positively that the precipitous decline was occasioned
by none other than the mysterious figure whose massive purchase
of a majority interest originally began the charge, and who has
now divested himself of his entire Consolidated Sulphur stock at
one stroke. It doesn't take the wit of a Newton to calculate that
reason finally prevailed with this gentleman but what of those
carried along in his wake and now left with nothing but worthless
paper? In this day and age . . .

Feverishly Kydd fumbled for the list of quotations on another page. He found Consolidated Sicilian Sulphur listed halfway down – at a piteous figure, far less than he'd paid. It meant . . . it meant he was ruined.

A raw slash of betrayal cut into his brain, the need to act nearly choking him in its intensity, but the coach was lurching off, grinding over the cobblestones of the inn for the open road.

'Stop the coach!' he shrieked, suddenly overcome with the implications of the news in the paper. '*Stop it!*'

It jolted and slewed before coming to a halt, and a homely but irritated face appeared at the window. 'What's all this noise, then? This is the Portsmouth Mail! Ye can't hold us up, you silly bugger. What's goin' on?'

His head cleared and Kydd saw that getting out would not solve anything. He must hold off from making any rash move until he'd had a chance to think.

The other passengers were looking at him with the kind of horrified fascination reserved for a madman on the loose but he didn't care. 'Drive on,' he blurted, and fixed his stare out of the window as the driver, grumbling mightily, resumed his way southward.

The roaring in his ears gradually reduced and he had to face the hideous conclusion: if he realised on his Consolidated Sicilian Sulphur scrip now he would get less than pin money. If he didn't, well, it couldn't matter: the result would be the same. And that was comprehensively and completely to ruin him.

When the promissory note was presented for fulfilment on the due date his estate would be forfeit, along with their personal chattels, as he'd included an extra amount over and above the value of the estate. Other avenues of cash raising were not open to him, he had no more assets to call on – he was as destitute at that moment as any beggar on Thames-side.

It was an appalling image, made worse by a vision of Persephone confronting bailiffs coming to take her home and hearth . . . A wrenching sob consumed him, causing the man next to him to shy away in alarm.

He was Sir Thomas Kydd, captain of a crack frigate in His Majesty's Royal Navy! Yet it was no good. There could be no exception made. Before long they would be coming to arrest him, a bankrupt, the debtors' prison doors creaking open for him, a juicy scandal for the mobility to chatter excitedly over for weeks – then incarceration and oblivion for years untold.

In a fog of misery he descended at the Sally Port and took a wherry out to *Tyger*, affronting the waterman by carefully counting out his fourpence in halfpennies and farthings.

Avoiding the cheerful greeting of the officer-of-the-day, he went to his cabin and locked the door.

It was now simply a matter of waiting but a little while and then the sky would fall in on him.

Chapter 59

Antwerp

Renzi gave a wry grimace as he quietly made his way back to his apartment and noiselessly closed the door. That he had bluffed Meyrick into his confession gave him no satisfaction. For whatever reason, the affair was over. They had failed and Perceval was now placed in a perilous financial situation that had no other end conceivable than the Fifth Coalition collapsing.

It was a serious setback for Britain for, without any show of convincing opposition to Bonaparte, wavering alliances and desperate feelers for military partners would lose all credibility. It was something he could do little about now.

He was reduced to nothing much more than casting about for a diversion to fill the remaining few days in this confined but sybaritic luxury.

At four in the afternoon a visitor was announced. Renzi was curious as it would first be necessary to pass the layers of discreet guards on his privacy.

A gentleman was shown in, elderly but exquisitely dressed, his mature features calm. He bowed politely. 'Do forgive my trespass upon your time, my lord.'

The voice was soft but strangely compelling, his French perfect but not that of a native.

'You have the advantage of me, sir.' Renzi had been too intrigued to take note of the name.

'Of course. My card.'

'G. Finkelstein, Finanzdirektor, Thiers Oder, Bankkaufmann, Basel'. A Herr Finkelstein, finance director of the merchant bankers Thiers Oder of Basel, Switzerland. It meant nothing to him.

Renzi caught himself. The man was an unknown and therefore must be treated strictly in accordance with his assumed character, that of a rich fop. 'I'm pleased to make your acquaintance, Herr Finkelstein.' He spoke with the boredom of wealth as he nodded an acknowledgement. 'You've come to tell me something to my advantage, I dare to say. Do please be brief. I've a craving for entertainment of the other sort tonight.'

'I vow I will not unduly delay you, my lord. May I sit?'

'Oh, I suppose so.'

'I would first commiserate with you on the untimely failure of your stratagem to achieve a more . . . modest rate in your dealings with Beyer-Haart.'

Renzi swallowed his astonishment and forced himself to calmness. 'Sir, your knowledge of my business is not to be borne. How is it—'

'I do apologise if I seem a trifle abrupt but you did caution me to briefness.'

'I did. What is it you want, pray?'

'It's generally known that the British government need to source an amount of specie to fund their new coalition. Any reasonable financial intelligence may deduce this. That your Treasury should be so willing as to use Goldstein to bring pressure on Beyer-Haart is remarkable indeed. They are a stiff-necked legion and are not inclined to surrender their position lightly.'

It was alarming. Just what did he know of the scheme? And now, when he was most needed, where was Meyrick, with his inside knowledge and expertise? Renzi was on his own.

'I have no idea what you are talking of, sir. My purpose here was to deploy my capital under advice, the reasons for which I've not particularly concerned myself. Kindly get to the point.'

'The point, my lord, is this. Rather than submit to Beyer's rather extraordinary imposts, I offer the services of my house. If you are not familiar with it you are to be forgiven for it's more a consortium of Swiss interests with powerful and, should I say, discreet methods, and not inconsiderable resource backing. It would be very much in our interests as a relative newcomer to make entry into the City of London sovereign funding market by this means – with an offer to meet your requirements at the same level as Goldstein but directly and securely, no artifice or devices necessary.'

Stunned, Renzi tried to tease it out. This was an entirely new player in the game, prepared to bid very low to secure access to lucrative government contracts and restore back to Perceval the means to achieve his coalition.

But if he negotiated, he would be revealing that he was an agent of the British government. His future would be irrevocably compromised and his worth to Congalton – to his country – would then be over, finished.

Frowning in annoyance, he said sharply, 'Sir, I've told you before that what you're saying has no meaning for me. I was asked to make my capital available for some wild scheme that would see me make solid gains. It fell through but my capital is safe. You're talking to the wrong man. Do you understand me?'

Finkelstein regarded him steadily. 'You're not connected in any way to your government?'

'Good heavens, no! How can I put it plainer? If you—'

'I see, my lord. Then I shall not waste any more of your time.' The man had clearly hoped that Renzi would be his direct route into contact with the financial powers in government.

'I tell you what I'll do,' Renzi relented. 'My man of business may have some ideas. Do stay here awhile and I'll consult him.'

'My lord?' Meyrick stepped back in astonishment at Renzi's appearance at the door once again.

'Mijnheer. I've been reflecting on your words. And am grateful for the lessons you have taught me.'

'I'm glad they were of assistance to you.' The man was guarded, watchful.

'The chief of which has been that numbers rule above all.'

'Yes?'

'So I'm here to make you a proposition, should you be interested in a transaction on a scale as before.'

'Do go on, my lord.'

'Awaiting my pleasure in the apartment is a species of Swiss banker. In some way he knows of our former scheme and offers to source the specie directly and at the same rate as Goldstein. I put it to you that, if you find them sound and dependable and can negotiate a form of contract then, sir, the fee for the whole is yours.'

The brief flash of satisfaction was all Renzi needed to know he'd succeeded.

'The fee, of course, contingent upon due delivery.'

'We understand each other, my lord.'

'Just so.' A smile appeared. Meyrick went over to his desk and noted down carefully what Renzi told him of the interchange, then looked up.

'You should be aware that the Helvetic Republic is no more.' This was the artificial state created after Switzerland's conquest by the French revolutionaries. 'To all intents and purposes, Bonaparte has restored the confederation, which now consists again of the old cantons and is to a large degree independent. This is chiefly for his own convenience. Their national desire for privacy and discretion plays well into his own need for the concealment of financial and other operations even from his own ministers.'

'Quite. But do I need to know this, Mijnheer?'

'You do, my lord. For the contract you conjecture will undoubtedly be sourced and funded from French assets and holdings, which have at their root the lust for profit.'

'They would fund their own opponents?' Renzi said in astonishment.

Meyrick merely shrugged.

For Renzi, though, the world had changed. Out of despair, triumph. From nothing gained, everything achieved. If Perceval had difficulties about taking advantage of French finance it was his dilemma. All that he was conscious of was that, when Meyrick had secured an understanding, he could leave at last for England.

Chapter 60

Aboard HMS Tyger

'I tell you, I saw his face – stricken, it was,' Brice told a hushed gunroom. 'Like he's been told by the sawbones there's nothing more could be done for him.'

'He must have said something, dammit!' Bray blustered. 'You were officer-of-the-day, he's the cap'n coming back on board and – and—'

'Not a thing. Went to his cabin, locked it. Haven't seen him since.'

It was an unreadable conundrum and deeply unsettling. Soon the ship's company would be asking awkward questions, getting restless and losing cohesion with the absence of their figurehead, their leader.

'Has to come out some time,' Brice muttered darkly. 'Has to – we'll get orders very shortly, need to victual the barky and so forth.'

Bowden came in. 'It could be he's lost someone dear, and needs to get over it.'

In horror they looked at each other. 'Not . . . not . . .'

'Whatever it is, we're to sit tight and in his own good time he'll tell us,' Bowden continued firmly. 'Not conjecture behind his back, like a lot of old women.'

'Hear, hear,' agreed Dillon, whose worried expression was quite untypical of him.

'Haven't you talked with him?' Brice asked curiously.

'No. The door's locked to me as well.'

At breakfast there was no change and the officers began discussing how the ship's routine would shape in the absence of orders or direction.

Then, quite unexpectedly, a figure appeared at the door. Kydd.

In bewilderment they scrambled to their feet.

'Sit, gentlemen, I beg.' The voice was soft, gentle – and distant. 'I – I've come to talk to you all.'

His features were deathly pale, composed and the gaze fixed on no one in particular.

'That is to say you deserve an explanation of what has happened that is going to take me from you.'

There were unbelieving gasps.

'There is no use my hiding it from you for much longer. The world will learn of it in due time and I'd rather you hear it from me.'

'Sir, we do—'

'Thank you, Mr Dillon, but it must be told. Gentlemen, I've been unfortunate enough to have suffered a double blow to my fortunes, the totality of which has left me in a ruinous state.'

There was a stunned silence.

'To a degree that leaves me unable to continue upon a gentleman's life. In short . . . I am ruined.'

'But, sir, you—'

'The over-plus of my debt ensures that it will be the debtors' prison and disgrace, precedence dictating that my commission in the navy will be terminated.' In the appalled hush he finished simply, 'I'm not certain at what point all this will take place but expect it to be . . . shortly.'

A sudden babble of comment erupted but Kydd held up his hands for quiet. 'The ship will go to usual harbour routine. Mr Bray will take charge and command in readiness for handover to your new captain.'

A spasm of grief distorted Kydd's face. 'Pray keep this from the hands for now,' he choked. 'There are few who know my fate. One of those in ignorance I may say is m-my w-wife.'

The tears were open as he turned away, stumbling off in the utmost misery.

For a long minute the gunroom was held in thrall to shock and anguish, then everyone spoke at once. But soon the discussion came to an end – for their level-headed captain, with prize money in consols, Russian fur salvage and an estate in Devon, it must have been a titanic series of blows that had laid him low, and they knew for a certainty that, among other things, he would never accept any collection of monies they could contrive between them.

In mute helplessness they could only stare at each other.

Chapter 61

'I tell ye, he's not wrong,' hissed Doud. 'Got it from the steward who heard 'em talking a-tween 'emselves, all flummoxed like.'

'I can't believe it! Not Tom Cutlass, mate, he's too fly b' half to be flammed by those shite-hawks in the city.' Stirk shook his head in utter disbelief. 'No, mate, they's fouled their hawse with what they heard.'

'I don't reckon it, Toby. Bo'sun, he's in a foul takin' as he's to muster his stores when the new captain comes aboard.'

Pinto's face grew long and soulful. 'For a man as that, it's a hard thing t' bear. God an' all his angels help him.'

'Aye, an' what we goin' to do, then?' Halgren rumbled, his honest Swedish face wrinkled in bafflement.

'What do y' mean – what *we* going t' do?' Doud parroted. 'What's anyone goin' to do when a man's suffered such a lacing? He's got t' take it and that's an end to it.'

'Be buggered to it!' Stirk swore, his fist crashing down on the mess table. 'You're sayin' as we sits here while he gets hisself skinned? I won't 'ave it!'

'Oh, yeah? An' what does you aim t' do, m' brave fightin' cock?' Doud snarled.

'Well, then.' Stirk morosely gazed down at his grog. Then he looked up and said, 'I know one who wouldn't let it go, not he. A right headpiece, seen him clew up an answer in a twinklin', him.'

'Who's that, then?' Doud spat.

'Why, yez remembers him – quartermaster's mate o' the starb'd watch in the flyin' *Artemis*. Name o' Renzi. As was.'

'Ha! Who's now bin rated lord and away off out of it,' jeered Doud.

Stirk glared at him. 'If'n the beggar knew what a moil his old shipmate's in, he'd not let it go, like I said.' He seemed struck by the thought. 'Could be an idea, at that.' He brightened. 'We could do it. Anybody knows where he lives?'

'In a bloody castle,' muttered Doud.

'In Wiltshire somewheres,' Pinto said, with a withering glance. 'Remember when 'e got spliced in Guildford? I yarned with the carriage hands as was waiting t' take 'em off.'

'That's easy, then,' Doud came back. 'We ships ourselves down t' Wiltshire an' enquires o' the people where a nob called Renzi lives in a castle.'

'Don't be a loon. His tally's now Lord Farndon. All we got t' do when we get there is ask where his castle bears.'

It suddenly became very possible.

'We're not goin' t' get leave out o' watch if we say we're off t' rouse out a lord an' all.'

'An' a hund'd miles isn't just straggling – we'd get taken up.'

'Don't be a ninny! Y' holds out y'r liberty ticket t' them interested with y'r thumb over where it says th' port.'

'Cost'll be more'n a few cobbs.'

'I has a bit put by,' Stirk said. The others pledged their savings, too.

Chapter 62

It was a most extraordinary sight for the villagers and farmhands of the rural lands to the north as the Salisbury stage clattered through their bucolic calm. While the men perched on the outside of the coach were undeniably sailors, they appeared stone-cold sober, their expressions more to be seen in men on a deadly mission than that of jolly roystering.

At a stop called Noakes Poyle they did indeed hear of a Lord Farndon but this one definitely had no castle. Confused, they were rescued by a yokel in the tavern who for half-a-crown offered to take them there in an empty hay cart.

'A gallows sight shameful f'r a parcel o' right taut-rigged sailormen t' be seen navigating a farmyard gig,' swore Pinto, hugging his knees. In their best step-ashore rig, the men couldn't have been more exotic in the deep countryside, attracting more than their fair share of stares.

'So y' wants t' walk, then, cully?' sneered Stirk.

They suffered at slow speed along the rough track the yokel knew but at last he stopped and gestured over a slight valley to an imposing white edifice with sweeping gardens and orchards. 'Eskdale Hall,' he said respectfully, keeping to himself the question of why four hardy seamen were bent on visiting an earl.

'So steer us a course as gets us there,' Stirk ordered.

They joined a better road and stopped outside the ornate iron gates. A semi-circular gravel road curved a quarter-mile towards a flight of marble steps leading up to a grand entrance.

'Well, clap on more sail, get us in. We paid ye enough.'

The hay cart lurched into motion and passed into the grounds, its cargo of sailors looking about in respectful admiration.

'Blast m' eyes if this isn't fit for an admiral,' Stirk pronounced. 'Renzi, m' old shipmate, ye've done well for y'self.'

As they came nearer to the stately residence gardeners looked up, horrified. One ran back behind the bushes.

A figure emerged at the top of the steps in satin costume. He took one look and shouted, making frantic shooing gestures.

The cart ground to a halt and the yokel looked back at the sailors helplessly.

'Why've ye stopped? That's the front door, and we've come a-visiting. Go, we're on course, y' codshead.'

The footman ran back inside and came out with half a dozen others. They advanced purposefully but stopped when they were close enough to take in the mettle of the visitors who had dropped lightly from the cart.

'You men! Get back, clear off, you can't come here!' The portly butler was clearly outraged. 'This is the Earl of Farndon's residence. Go, or I'll – I'll call the bailiff!'

'Earl o' Farndon. That'll do us, cuffin. Give 'im a hail that there's some here who'd be right happy t' see him.'

'Be off with you, you villains. His lordship is not in the habit of consorting with sailors!' the man spluttered.

More footmen and gardeners spilled out, joined by a growing crowd of other servants drawn to the spectacle.

'We're at a stand, Toby,' Halgren said, flexing his huge biceps and, in the process, drawing gasps of admiration from the maids.

Well outnumbered now, it didn't seem there was much more that could be done – but then Doud stepped out in front and muttered, 'He liked this'n, lads.'

Hands on his hips he burst into song:

'I sail'd in the good ship Kitty, *with a smart blowing gale and rough, tough seas;*
Left my Polly, the lads call so pretty, safe here at anchor — yo, yo, yea!
She blubber'd salt tears when we parted and cried, "Now be constant to me!"
"Do not be downhearted, my dear," I said, so up went the anchor — yo, yo, yea!'

Soon the full-hearted chorus was being joined in not just by the sailors but by many others, leaving the butler spluttering.

'And yet, m' boys, believe ye me? I returned with no rhino from off of the sea;
Mistress Polly turns her back and no more I sees her, so again I heav'd anchor — yo, yo, yea!'

'He's not heard ye,' Stirk said. 'Britannia?'

Doud threw back his head and roared out the old favourite:

'Ye free-born sons, Britannia's boast,
Firm as your rock-surrounded coast;
*   Ye sov'reigns of the sea!*

On ev'ry shore where salt tides roll,
From east to west, from pole to pole,
Fair conquest do ye make—'

'He's there, lads!'

At the top of the steps an unmistakable figure, wearing fine breeches and silk cravat, was staring down at them as though he'd seen a ghost.

'My lord! I do apologise – these men came unannounced in a haywain, the villains! Demanded to see your person and—'

Renzi descended slowly as if the vision would disappear before he reached it. And then he advanced, hands outstretched. 'Why, Toby – Ned, Pinto! Well met, shipmates,' he said, without thinking, the years rolling back. 'Can I bear a hand with anything?'

'What is it, Nicholas?' came a faint call from a window. It took Cecilia just a moment to recognise Stirk before she flew down to join them.

'Miss Cecilia,' he said, touching his forehead. 'Oh, beggin' yours – y'r ladyship.' He bowed awkwardly.

She melted. 'Oh, do come in, all of you! No, not the kitchen, Purvis, the blue drawing room,' she told the butler, 'and do, er, rouse out some refreshments for these bold mariners.'

Inside, nothing could tempt Stirk to sit in an ornate chair or on a chaise longue. Instead, like the others who clustered protectively around him, he stood and composed what he had to say.

'I thank ye, y'r honour, for receivin' us but we're come as we remembers the good steer y' gave us always when ye was afore the mast with us.'

Renzi shot a glance at Cecilia, who smiled and told Stirk,

'Do bear away, my hearty, and tell us what it is you wish a steer upon at this time.'

'It's like this'n,' Stirk said awkwardly, his evident worry reaching out to her. 'It's not us who needs it, it's our cap'n, who you'll know is Tom Kydd as was.'

All lightness and gaiety fell away.

'Is there a difficulty of sorts?'

'It's right grievous. He's on to a lee shore an' no bower or sheet anchor left t' haul him off.'

'You'd better tell me everything, Toby,' Renzi said.

'He got taken aback b' something ing'surance, wanted t' mend his fortune, and I heard he put all he had on a scurvy crew who then went down with all hands, takin' all his money an' estate with 'em.'

'You're saying he made an investment in stocks that failed?'

'Somethin' gave him copper-bottomed confidence it couldn't lose, which he trusted, and made him lay out all his rhino on it.'

A sudden shriek came from Cecilia followed by the crash of a tea-cup as it fell to the floor. 'No! No! It can't be! I've – I've ruined poor Thomas. It was me!'

She ran sobbing from the room, followed hastily by a shocked and bewildered Renzi.

They returned after some minutes, she chalk-white and trembling, Renzi with lines of worry deep in his face. 'Thank you for telling me this. You were right to do so. It seems that I . . . I was unwittingly the cause of this and I must find some means of redress.'

Stirk looked at him unblinkingly.

'Which is not so easily done, I do confess.'

No one moved, all regarding Renzi gravely, trustingly.

After a little while he said, 'In course I shall see him. *Tyger*

335

is in Portsmouth? Then I will go there.' The sailors still stood awkwardly. 'As we will all together. My carriage – quickly!'

As it flew down the country lanes Renzi had time to give it thought but the situation grew murkier and more hopeless the more he pondered.

If Kydd's Knowle Manor and other assets were lost, it implied a monstrous debt, far more than he himself could possibly cover. Going guarantor for a rescue loan would not serve because he knew Kydd would never allow him to be involved.

Time and again he went over the possibilities but they always came to nothing, while beside him the four sailors sat bolt upright in the plush seats.

They swept through the Landport gate into Portsmouth proper, the stately carriage emblazoned with arms an exotic sight.

But even by this time Renzi had no plan or even words of condolence he could offer his closest friend in his trial. It wasn't right. He couldn't see Kydd in his broken state with no hope to offer him. And he couldn't leave these men, who'd trusted him, to go back to their ship with nothing to show for their remarkable journey.

Uncertain, the Tygers got out of the carriage.

And then Renzi saw there was at least one thing he could do. 'Toby, I've a plan as will give me time to think of something, but it needs you to help. Will you?'

Chapter 63

Tucked down under reefed topsails *Tyger* clawed her way southward. Her position off the head of the leading weather column of the Lisbon convoy was the most uncomfortable of all, but best placed to respond to any predatory lunge from the vermin that lurked in wait for stragglers in the myriad craggy bays and islands of Brittany.

Orders had come: brief and to the point. His Majesty's Frigate *Tyger* was to resume her duties with Admiral Collingwood's Mediterranean Fleet, reporting to his base at Port Mahon in Minorca.

Hope had died in Kydd as he read the words. Any prizes to be had in those parts were few and paltry now, ironically because of the fine job he and Cochrane had done in spreading fear and dread up and down the coast. But had he any right to expect more? And how long would he be pacing the quarterdeck of his own ship?

Miserably he took in the lines of sea-tossed ships, eighty-three of them, token of the slow but steady build-up of men and stores, victuals and munitions that Wellesley was patiently amassing in the Portuguese capital. A magnificent sight, but one that he himself was probably seeing for the last time.

The bell forward tolled away in business-like tones: *clang-clang, clang-clang*. The watch half finished, the helm would be relieved, as would the lookouts, gratefully descending from their blustery perches to the warmth of the mess-deck. Kydd resumed his slow pace, both officers and men avoiding him, not out of fear or respect, he knew, but out of pity.

Their departure from Portsmouth had been eased a little for him by the small drama that had taken place as they lay along the lines, ready to proceed. A boat had come alongside, one of many at the time. Kydd, having told off the first lieutenant to take the ship to sea, was able to observe a face under a jammed-on cocked hat of the old sort appear above the gunwale, red and puffing. A sailor went to ease him over but his helping hand was thrown aside as the man finally touched the deck inboard.

He glanced around as though he knew what he was looking for, and then, spotting Kydd, lurched towards him, a hinged wooden leg swinging and thumping as he made his way over. It was his old sailing master, whom he'd last seen groaning pitifully under a blood-spattered tarpaulin with little hope of life.

'Mr Joyce!' Kydd cried, in genuine pleasure. 'So good to see you up and about on your pins! We're under orders to sail or I would—'

'That's why I'm here, in course,' Joyce responded, getting his breath. There were still lines of pain in his face and his balance was none too steady but clearly he had turned a corner.

'To say farewell? That's thoughtful of you,' Kydd said warmly. The sight of the jolly face was the most cheering he'd had since . . .

'Aye, sir. Can't have th' barky cutting a feather without you have one aboard who knows her ways, like.'

'You mean—'

'Mr Joyce, sailin' master, joinin' ship, sir!' The look of great satisfaction creasing the man's features tore at Kydd.

'I – I'm grieved to say it but we have one, Mr Joyce.' As if on cue the man came over. 'Here he is, our Mr Leech. Do you know him at all?'

'Any trouble, Sir Thomas?' he said, eyeing Joyce with suspicion.

'A little misunderstanding only,' Kydd replied. 'Naught to worry on.'

'True 'nough,' Joyce declared. 'I'm returned on board, as y' sees, therefore we thank ye for y'r services and ask ye to quit the barky.'

'Hold hard, Mr Joyce. You can't—'

'Here's m' warrant. Standing warrant f'r *Tyger* frigate. Not struck off, still faithful an' correct. Now, I'm bound t' say that as yours is naught but a temp'rary scrap, I'm *Tyger*'s o-fficial and true master.'

'Is this so, Mr Leech?' Kydd couldn't remember if the slow-moving Navy Board had got around to confirming Leech's appointment.

'Might be, but at least I'm trim an' sound in all m' limbs as can stand service in a frigate!'

Kydd stiffened. It was the wrong thing to say. 'Mr Leech, I'm sorry to say that any man knows a temporary warrant may never trump a permanent, and I'll have to ask you to give up your berth. You'll have a certificate as to your fine conduct aboard *Tyger* but no King's ship has two sailing masters.'

* * *

Joyce had been heartily welcomed back into the gunroom, raising roars as he'd described in detail how he'd had to make himself a right royal pest until his wife had driven him back to sea in despair. He could be seen on deck serenely clanking about with his new patent 'clapper' leg, provided at the naval hospital, Haslar, which he swore to any who would listen should be replaced by a stout oaken leg of the old sort at French expense, just as soon as their next opponent lay athwart their guns.

Kydd had not had the heart or courage to give the dreadful news to Persephone yet. He had until their next port to compose a letter, breaking the news as gently as it could be contrived – although how he could even begin to put it into words was more than he could conceive for now.

After that he would begin one to Renzi and Cecilia and it would be done. The news would then break on the public at large and he would see through the final humiliations alone.

Chapter 64

Kydd stayed on deck as the ritual of handover took place with the Lisbon squadron frigates, the captain of one taking his time in the customary side by side hailing of news to be exchanged. Kydd was short with his replies and hoped that it would be put down to haste to leave to take up station.

They got under way, this time alone, and sail was shaken out to let *Tyger* run. She took up in fine style, the north-easter a perfect quarterly, and Kydd stayed up clear of the conn for as long as he could before going below with pricking eyes.

He hadn't been fifteen minutes at his desk when there was a soft knock and Brice appeared, apologetic. 'Sorry to intrude, sir, but I have to report, well, a stowaway.'

This was unusual but not unknown. He had to deal with it himself for it could be anything from a desperate attempt to escape the law to a cunning move to smuggle a French agent on board.

'Very well. Send him in.'

A ragged man with an eye-patch was pushed forward. Lean, drooping and lacking sun-touched skin or the well-developed upper-body definition of a seaman, this was not a sailor trying for a berth in a legendary ship.

'I'll handle it, Mr Brice, thank you.'

'What's your name, fellow?' Kydd asked, without particular feeling, as Brice returned on deck.

The man took a step forward, then wheeled about to turn his back on Kydd. Taken by surprise Kydd could only stare at him as he adjusted something and whirled back to face him.

'N-Nicholas! What the devil?'

Renzi put the eye-patch away. 'May I sit, old chap? *Tyger*'s forepeak is never to be recommended for its voluptuary comforts.'

'Do, but what does this mean?' Kydd said, in a faint voice, struggling with what he was seeing before him.

'Your ship's company, and I give you no guesses whatsoever which rogues were responsible, thought it necessary to journey down to Wiltshire to acquaint me of your dolorous situation.'

'How dare they?' Kydd said, in rising anger. 'I—'

'Forgive them, brother, for they did what answered before when we sailed together in *Artemis* frigate and similar.'

'They called on you to give them a steer?'

'In one, yes.'

'There's nothing can be done – by anyone,' Kydd said bitterly. 'So it's all a foolery. Now you've taken it on yourself to come aboard to—'

'I knew in mortification you would not welcome me aboard at Spithead and, dear fellow, by this little stratagem I've granted us time to devise a saving design before you must face the wrath of the world.'

'You're pixie-led if you think there's anything to be done.'

'Is this the seaman bold I see before me that stood on into

the midst of the enemy to prevail? And on more than a few occasions? Who now shrinks from preserving himself and those he holds dear from perdition?'

'Clew up the jawing tackle, Nicholas, I'm not in the mood,' he said, in growing resentment. 'This isn't your honest sea fight, see who you're going for, cast loose your guns, crowd on sail. I'm to be crucified and that's an end to it.'

'So it has to be blackmail.'

'What?' Kydd's head jerked up in astonishment.

'Blackmail. Either you sit with me, now, and give it the right Tartar of a go to haul off your lee shore, or I'm going to Persephone and telling her that her cowardly husband couldn't find it in him to try.'

'You bastard!'

'That's the spirit! Only until Minorca, where I will desert. Where do we begin, pray?'

It took a little time before Kydd could be mollified and Renzi could address the question of how he was to remain on board.

'Either you needs must explain to your inestimable commander-in-chief you have embarked a noble lord to his embarrassment or you have press-ganged him. Far better for me here and now to offer myself under a purser's name as volunteer in the good ship *Tyger*, perhaps as able seaman should I so satisfy? This way I may appear quite legitimately and humbly on the ship's books. I shall endeavour not to disgrace you.'

Under his eye-patch and the other judicious disguises he'd used in far more lethal circumstances, Renzi could be passed off as an absconder from justice of some sort, who could be employed usefully until there was an opportunity to be rid of him. Only the four of the lower deck who'd brought him in knew who he really was. The officers would think it beneath them to notice a wharf rat, and for the rest of the seamen, he could keep out of their way if he was rated captain's steward, with the additional benefit of being close to Kydd.

Only Tysoe would need to know and he was the very soul of discretion. And Renzi insisted, if only for the sake of old times, that he could be trusted to sling his hammock in the coach and be diligent in his duties.

Chapter 65

The conceit worked well: no one questioned the right of the captain to retain the services of a steward and consequently Renzi got his time together with his old friend. They worked over the options carefully, one by one, as the Iberian coast slipped by. By the Strait of Gibraltar they were running out of ideas, and by the time they were shaping course northeast to the Balearics, it was unhappily looking very much a lost cause.

Until, out of nothing in particular, something came to Renzi's mind: Meyrick's next interest, the invitation to tender he'd waved in his face. This had been about Leghorn – to bid on a shipment of Bonaparte's Spanish plunder to be transformed into negotiable financial instruments by the high banking houses of Europe. And the date – Cecilia's birthday, he remembered.

And other details: it was being conveyed from the interior to be amassed on some kind of offshore hideaway, an island from which it would be taken by the French to Leghorn. How impossible would it be to imagine that Kydd could divert and intercept it?

'Old fellow, I've just recollected something I've lately heard. Care to know it?'

Kydd was careful not to enquire the circumstances but immediately saw its logic. 'The French are not about to take out their loot along the roads I've seen. Makes all the sense in the world to heap it somewhere, then ship it out. And on an island – easy to hide, easy to defend. I think your friend knows what he's talking about, Nicholas!'

'I believe he has his sources, which are unusually reliable,' Renzi agreed smoothly.

There was a sickening lurch in Kydd's stomach when he realised its significance. A golden highway out of ruin to the brightness of hope and salvation!

'And if we take it prize, as we're on passage, not yet reported under command, then all shares go to us,' he breathed, his eyes glistening.

'Do steer small, old fellow,' Renzi couldn't help cautioning. 'The chances are not good, no matter what our hopes.'

But Kydd wasn't about to be cast down so easily and thrust into the coach to retrieve a cluster of charts. 'Here's Spain and there's Madrid, right in the middle. Take a road out from there to the coast and . . . and . . .'

But there were many roads, many islands.

No matter how he pored over the small-scale, large-scale and passage charts, no answer leaped out, no sudden revelation.

'I'm sorry I raised this hope in you,' Renzi said, as it was becoming clear that it was like a dead-end in a maze, no way forward possible.

Kydd, however, was going like a madman, flinging down charts and papers in a feverish search for a way through. At length he straightened, breathing hard. 'Sentry, pass the word, all my officers lay aft to my cabin this minute!'

They came, bewildered but attentive.

'I've an intelligence just come to my notice,' he snapped, his decisive tone and hard face causing them to look at each other incredulously. This was something like the old Captain Kydd!

'The French have the problem of getting the mass of their plunder back to home territory. I've had word they take it overland to a defensible island. From there they've to freight it back. I want that ship!'

A clanking outside heralded Joyce, who puffed in and leaned against the bulkhead.

Brice leaned across and whispered to him what was going on.

'Right,' Kydd continued. 'Here we have our situation.' He threw down a first chart, the North Catalonian large scale. 'I want suggestions as to an island suitable for what they intend. I'm supposing it near inshore, off a small port, and has a fort or similar to guard the cargo.' He shifted his gaze from one to another, his eyes glowing. 'I don't have to tell you that the stakes on this are priceless and I mean to take it!'

The tension radiating out from him was making some uncomfortable but they bent to the task. After some minutes they straightened from the desk with the same conclusion, warily apologetic.

Kydd took another chart and slapped it down. 'Central Catalonia.'

They dutifully bent down again and Joyce spoke from the rear. 'I was here in the last war, no, the one before – the American war, that is. The year 'eighty-one anyways.'

'Go on,' Kydd told him.

He shuffled to the front and proceeded with his tale. 'In *Porcupine* sloop, with *Raven* on a cruise against the Dons' coastals. We had a bright young lad, knew the Spanish, an' we let him skip ashore an' keep his ear open, like. Sadly he was lost overside off Mallorca only a year later, and he a right promising topman as I've ever—'

'Your point, Mr Joyce?'

'As I was just to say, we gets word by him of what the Spanish are up to.' He paused for effect, then went on doggedly, 'See, in them days the Dons still had to pay tribute t' the Moors on the African side. Dey of Algiers, he was a damned old thief. Well, the way they does it is by taking the coin to the coast and sailing it across. The lad hears that there's this secret island they piles it up on before loading and we takes a fancy to have a slice o' that'n.'

He had their attention now and continued, 'We sees the island. It has an old-fashioned fort atop so the treasure must be in there. That night we sends in the boats with every man we have an' has at it.'

'And?'

'Well, that's the pity on it. It were empty, no one there. See, they stopped payin' the tribute two year before.'

'A looby yarn!' Bray snapped. 'That's how it was then, not now!'

'No, he's given us a steer,' Bowden said thoughtfully. 'If they thought it the best place to store and ship treasure then, there'll be some who bring to mind the old days and suggest they use it again.'

'So we knock on the door and demand they hand it over?' Brice said, in a flat voice. 'There's those who'd see it our clear duty to inform the admiral as he can then mount a full-fig descent on the beggars.'

Kydd's eyes flared dangerously. 'Are you suggesting we give it all away for want of boldness?' he grated.

Brice stubbornly held his gaze. 'Sir, all I'm saying is what some others might – that you're throwing men's lives aside only for your own . . .' He tailed off at Kydd's icy anger.

'You're out of soundings, Mr Brice!' he snarled. 'You've forgotten the prime detail!'

'Sir?'

'The freighting has to be at Leghorn on the third of next month. We haven't time to warn off Port Mahon. We do it ourselves or not at all.'

By now it was beginning to penetrate what the capture of a mountain of treasure could mean and smiles were surfacing on all sides. Every man had seen the results of Junot's sacking of Portugal, and there was no doubt that this must be of even greater proportions.

'Sir. Can I submit that it were best to intercept at sea rather than make an assault against a fortress?' Bowden asked.

'How the devil can we ensure that?' Bray rumbled irritably.

Joyce came in again: 'We can,' he said confidently. 'We've a date of arrival at Leghorn. We prick off a course th' Frenchy must take between the island and there. We c'n then work arsy-versy to find when he has t' sail. See?'

'He'll not want to stray far from a direct route,' Bowden mused. 'We should be able to calculate it.'

'How do we know his speed made good without we know his rig, the weather, that sort of thing?' Brice asked evenly.

Openly grinning now, Joyce answered him: 'Don't need to, do we, sir? On y'r calculated date o' sailing we'se at Leghorn, we sails back down his track, bound to meet him halfway.'

Kydd leaned back in satisfaction as an excited buzz grew. They had a quarry, they had a plan – and he had hope.

'Two things make me a mite doubtful.'

'Mr Brice?'

'First. How reliable is your intelligence? I must ask it, sir.'

'Completely reliable.'

'Second. How can we be sure it's Mr Joyce's island and none other? All our eggs in one basket, else.'

Renzi's intelligence had not specified the island, only a destination and date. Did a dusty recollection count as proof? 'We can't be sure but we give it a clinking good try!' Kydd replied, with passion.

'We can be sure,' Bowden came back quietly.

'Say on, sir.'

'This island with such a hoard will be accounted a tight secret by the Frenchies. We send ashore at the nearest village and enquire of the fishermen or similar if there's any island close by that it's forbidden to visit on pain of death or suchlike. That'll tell us they've something big to hide.'

'And we can call by on passage to Leghorn,' observed Bowden. 'Do tell us more about your island, Mr Joyce.'

Chapter 66

'Ahoy!'

The faint hail came out of the cool of the night, somewhere off the larboard bow of *Tyger* as she ghosted along, her ship's company keyed up for any betraying sound.

'Thank the Lord!' breathed Bowden and, like the others, crowded to the side of the ship.

It had been a long twenty-four hours. Joyce's island lay at an equal distance between Valencia and Tarragona, a half-mile offshore from the tiny fishing haven of Torquena. To land the two unseen in a nakedly moonlit night had been nerve-fraying and this picking up equally so – but it had been done.

'Well?' demanded Kydd, before even they'd had chance to mount the side.

'Unless they have two islands, this is the place!' called Dillon, as Pinto respectfully gave way for him to climb up first.

'You're sure?'

The young man swung lithely over the bulwarks and faced his captain, knowing his answer would commit the ship. 'The locals have no love for their conquerors and were free with their opinions – and information. The island is off-limits under the strictest penalties and none has ever returned from there. And on it is a strong fort of the olden times manned by a whole French *régiment*.'

'Did you spy any ships at moorings?'

'None, sir. But the village market has been told off to stand by for a victualling exercise of size in the near future.'

'Aha!' crowed Bray. 'And do we not know what that means?'

Kydd's eyes glowed. The chances were starting to fall in his direction – and he wasn't about to let them go. 'We're not going to take the beggar on here – he's got too many friends. At sea, that's where we'll have him. Mr Joyce has the right idea. We kindly let him come here and load, then go down his track from Leghorn and fall on him as he approaches.'

There was little time to spare. *Tyger* got under way and was in position to the north of Corsica within two days of the estimated time of departure from Torquena. In this time Kydd worked her crew unmercifully, gun practice and sail handling, often both together, for the likelihood was that, as the British did for their bullion, it would be carried in the hold of a fast frigate. They would have to fight for their treasure.

At daybreak on the calculated day her bowsprit was set resolutely to the south. From this time forward, any sail rising above the horizon could very well be their prize, and just what they'd find on boarding grew with every telling.

On the morning of the fourth day *Tyger* went to a full alert.

Slightly to larboard of their course a pinprick of sail interrupted the flat, hard line where sea met sky. Illuminated by the slowly rising sun behind them, it stood out clear and distinct. Watched by men at the masthead and then the fighting tops, it lifted until the topgallants were in view.

Then from the main-masthead lookout came: '*A frigate* – I sees a frigate!'

Kydd's heart beat faster. The man had seen the characteristic cut of sail peculiar to a warship with its big crew and had cast away the possibility that this was a stray merchantman off the usual sea-lanes, in fact anything other than a man-o'-war. This narrowed it down to one of two: a British or French warship.

Kydd knew that the business of most frigates in these waters was more on the other side of Italy in the Adriatic, and Collingwood would not waste the good cruising time of his frigates so far past Toulon. The odds were strong that this was the Frenchman.

It was now time for the deadly ballet of a meeting in the open ocean of two frigates to begin.

He sniffed the wind carefully. 'Two points a-larboard,' he ordered.

In this westerly the enemy was bearing down on *Tyger* from upwind and could choose the direction and orientation of the meeting. After that they were equal in the cut and thrust of manoeuvres.

The topgallants rose higher and were joined by topsails. Definitely a frigate. The courses would follow, equally distinctive with their broad and potent driving force.

If the vessel had sighted them it gave no sign, maintaining its course steadily, as he would do if undecided, Kydd reflected. They could only wait.

Quite leisurely *Tyger* cleared for action, the age-old ritual with added meaning: who could tell how the day would end? A bloody boarding, a tangle of wreckage, a dismasting? All had to be prepared for, with the usual stock of equipment and material to deal with shot-holes, broken spars, shattered helm. Kydd did not concern himself with these for they'd done it so often. However, he could be sure of a desperate combat: the French captain would know the stakes and would fight for his life. Kydd eased into a grim smile. The Frenchman had had the misfortune to come athwart *Tyger* at the peak of her fame and lethal effectiveness.

'*Deck there!* Strange sail a point to weather on 'em – no, two!'

This changed everything in a flash. With a lurch of premonition Kydd waited for the situation to resolve. If the two were in any way connected to the first they were in a quite different predicament.

And then, with another shout down, came the blow they had feared. And, worse, the odds had lengthened to an impossible degree. The two were another frigate – and a two-decker battleship.

Kydd bit his lip. They should have considered that the French, conscious of British frigates at sea, would make sure of their passage by conveying the hoard in a ship-of-the-line no less, escorted by two frigates, now revealed as of the heaviest class.

A ship-of-the-line! No frigate could succeed against double the number of guns, weight of metal or strength of timbers, and it was tried only in exceptional circumstances and these were anything but. Add to the equation two superior frigates in escort, and effectively *Tyger* could be thrown aside contemptuously, outclassed in every way. The treasure convoy could forge on to its destination unhindered.

A sickening despair clamped on Kydd. So near to a glorious deliverance from his nightmare, now to see it pass from his ken for ever.

'Sheer away, sir?' asked Bray, stolidly.

'Um, stay with 'em awhile, I think,' Kydd answered, in a low voice. 'When they come up, fall in with them to their larboard.'

He had no idea why he should taunt himself with non-existent possibilities but, who knew, some wild stratagem could spring to mind and it was too cruel to give up now with his salvation literally in sight.

Tyger wore around slowly, the three Frenchmen now protectively close to each other. To Kydd's orders his ship fell in parallel to their progress a mile off, all sailing large, downwind.

'Arrogant bastards,' growled Bray, shielding his eyes with a hand.

'Why?' prompted Bowden, doing likewise.

'Both frigates have run out their guns, that sail-o'-the-line hasn't even bothered.'

In pompous self-confidence, the big ship held a steady course with no sign of even noticing the lone Englishman, her twin lines of chequered gun-ports still closed.

A wave of anger washed over Kydd. It wouldn't have been hard for Dame Fortune to look kindly on him just once. This was the third straight knock in a row he'd suffered and now there were no more chances ahead for him. It was over, and—

'Sir, I might be wrong, but could you take a peek at his fighting tops?' Bowden handed over his telescope diffidently.

Kydd picked out the vessel's maintop, steadying the glass with his elbow in his side and swaying slightly back. An image danced into view and he tried to see what had caught Bowden's attention.

Then he had it. No barricades in the tops – not in itself a surprise for it required that hammocks be swayed up to provide shelter from musket-fire. The ship perhaps hadn't bothered with that, but as the vessel heaved to the seas he could see that the tops themselves were flimsy, curved and open.

Be damned to it! This was no ship-of-the-line – it was a merchant ship in disguise!

In rising hope he took it in. A large one, an Indiaman of sorts, those gun-ports were false, the pennants and so forth meaningless. It solved one small thing that hadn't been clear to him: where would the French have got a ship-of-the-line for the task when they were all blockaded?

It didn't matter now. In a fever of renewed purpose he could think, plan.

So it wasn't a ship-of-the-line and was virtually harmless. But the frigates were very real and to get at his quarry he'd have to take them both on.

His interest shifted to them. One on either side, slightly ahead, disdainful and protective.

The closer had a wide greyish patch running the whole height of its fore-topsail, unusual in a French ship. Staying so long in harbour they could take their pick of new stores. He thought he recognised it: wasn't this *Royan* of the Willaumez squadron they'd chased? If so, it was a forty-gun vessel, which, with eighteen-pounders, was not one to tackle thoughtlessly.

The further ship he didn't recognise: it sat lower in the water, probably stored on the outset of a voyage but was similar in size, as formidable. On both, the sheer numbers of men on deck watching them spoke of a plentiful crew.

As he concentrated on the scene, fluttering signal flags rose. Obediently, the second spilled wind and, easing around the stern of the merchantman, joined the first on *Tyger*'s side in a show of defiance.

Kydd stiffened. How should he begin? With a start he realised that this implied he'd already made the decision to fight, even against these odds. An inner voice asked if this was because he wanted the treasure more than anything he'd wanted in his life and was willing to throw away the lives of his men in a demented falling on a wildly superior enemy. Almost immediately he knew the answer: his men would never forgive him if he slunk away from a king's ransom in prize for fear of the consequences.

He – *they* – would do it!

A gathering warrior's determination rose in him like a tide.

He forced an icy concentration. How would the enemy commander read the scene? He had three pieces on the chessboard. How would he move them?

Weather conditions: brisk, good sailing, *Tyger*'s kind of weather, less so for the lighter-built French.

Relative speeds? Probably favouring the French, but this could easily be offset against the agility of the British topmen in setting and taking in sail.

Manoeuvring? For the same reason decidedly to their advantage, with the additional handicap to the French of having to keep station on a slower-moving merchantman.

In the last essence Kydd knew his tactical goal was to get unfettered access to the merchantman: to swarm aboard and take it. Which meant that not only had he to get past the two frigates but in some way put them in a condition of being unable to interfere.

There was no alternative but to take them on first. Both of them. There could be no elaborate plan – anything might happen.

'Helm up, lay me alongside the closer – that's *Royan*,' he ordered. After some heavy pounding he'd peel away before the other could come up, concentrating on putting one out of the fight, if at all possible.

Surprising him, a monstrous roar of cheering went up from

Tyger's deck as they converged, a fearless, joyous warrior's shout that left no doubt in friend or enemy the spirit of his ship.

They converged surprisingly quickly but, in a move Kydd least expected, the two sailed apart at his lunge, much like a shoal of fish parting before a predator.

He was through to the other side without a shot being fired – but what did it mean?

Of course: their mission was to deliver the Indiaman and its freight safely to Leghorn, not to win a naval battle. *Tyger* was irrelevant to the higher scheme of things and therefore would be ignored unless . . .

'Helm down, lay us aboard the Indiaman!' Kydd bellowed.

Tyger's bowsprit tracked around until it transfixed the lordly merchantman and, thrusting forward, began to overhaul it.

As if in reflex *Royan* paid off, her bows slewing downwind until she had fallen in directly astern, joined half a mile behind by the other frigate. There could be no play at the guns, unarmed bow against unarmed stern. *Tyger* was safe for now as the four took the same westerly directly astern in a barrelling roll.

The only way the French could come up on *Tyger* was by spreading more sail – but stunsails in this brisk weather was risky and would be at the cost of inability to manoeuvre if it came to engaging. And if this captain was any seaman at all, he would know that the Indiaman was safe – only a fool would lay himself alongside while two frigates were in the offing.

So, Kydd would make it interesting for them. 'Our best set o' the sails for running large, short of stuns'ls,' he told Joyce, who could be relied on to wring the best from *Tyger*. In a short time it told, the extra frapping and preventers allowing a flatter profile to the sails, less wind lost, greater speed through the water.

Now the enemy must decide what Kydd meant to do, for why was *Tyger* heading for an intercepting with two frigates doggedly pursuing? It made no sense.

Kydd made his move when the big ship was no more than a quarter-mile ahead, his grim intent to force the frigates into an action.

In a sudden but smooth move *Tyger*'s wheel went over and the ship took up on a slant to starboard. The massive yaw had effect: *Tyger*'s whole larboard broadside could now bear on the Indiaman and, ready for it, the gun-deck erupted with the crash of guns, the war-like roar and stink of powder smoke bringing a savage grin to Kydd's face. How much more satisfying was this, a martial target ahead, a fine man-o'-war under his orders and every reason for a clash of arms?

As quickly as she could, *Tyger* resumed her course, while Kydd peered ahead through the thinning coil of smoke at the Indiaman. He didn't expect much by way of results – apart from a forest of rising shot-strike plumes around the vessel, there was no sign of a hit, but that wasn't the point.

'Hard a-port!'

Again the yaw, again the thunderous smash of a broadside of guns. This time, among the cluster of tall white splashes, the mizzen topgallant sail of the distant ship blew into a frenzy of uncontrolled beating on one side. Probably the clew-block of the sail tack smashed and carried away, not serious as such, but what Kydd wanted. The enemy would come to a conclusion about *Tyger*'s intentions: the crippling of the merchantman for dealing with later either by a victorious *Tyger* or other British warships in the vicinity drawn by the firing.

A wounded, helpless ship far from Leghorn could not be

contemplated and therefore *Tyger* had to be dealt with now.

The yaws had an effect on *Tyger*'s sailing, a checking of her way through the water, with a slowing, as the rudder levered them off course and return, and it showed.

Their pursuers were now close behind, two heavy frigates with pennons streaming and vengeful fury in their aspect.

Kydd had the bare bones of a plan but it was wise to be ready for anything.

Waiting until the gun crews had reloaded, he bellowed, 'Stand by for a double move, Tygers, and don't fail me!' To the conn he ordered, 'Hard to starboard, brace in – haul your wind until we're as close as she'll lie!'

With her broad English rudder, *Tyger* obeyed willingly and, in a sudden wheeling, the frigate came round until her helmsman was anxiously watching her luff, the fluttering at the edge of the sail that indicated she could be caught aback if she went fractionally further.

The following frigates were left floundering and tried to do the same but the speedier *Royan* ran afoul of the other and valuable ground was lost. But Kydd hadn't finished yet. Before they'd sorted themselves out he threw down the helm and gracefully his frigate took the wind, heading once more for the Indiaman.

Left trailing, the French frigates took up again but, wary, they kept well apart. When Kydd did the same as before, they were ready – and did precisely what he needed them to do. *Royan* stayed with their charge while the other went after *Tyger*.

He had forced a separation! Gleefully he eyed off distances, speeds, angles, for at some point he was going to close with this frigate and do his damnedest to bring about enough ruination to put it out of the fight.

They sped over the sea close-hauled, hard to the wind. Kydd had one last advantage that he wasn't going to throw away and duly warned off his gun crews: one side to the guns, the other side to sail-handling. Just as they'd practised.

Royan and the Indiaman were now well over a mile distant and receding.

Now was the time! 'Helm hard a-weather!' he rapped.

Tyger immediately fell off the wind – and across the bows of her pursuer for a perfect raking shot into its bowels.

But it had guessed the move and it too was slewing wildly around and both broadsides smashed out nearly simultaneously.

In the split second before the shot reached *Tyger*, it flashed across Kydd's mind that the French were now ready for any trick or stratagem. The gloves were off.

A splintering crash nearby was the gunwale taking a hit, scattering men nearby, one screaming in pain. The wind of another passing made him stagger and a dull crunch felt under his feet was her hull taking a direct blow.

His mind raced. Was the enemy captain firing for the rigging, as the French seemed to prefer, or was he trying to hammer home killing blows at the hull, as the British liked to do?

It was impossible to tell: the firing on both sides had been instant, no time to point the guns and therefore no conclusion could be made.

But he'd been granted precious time to grapple one to one before the other came up, and he had to take it in both hands.

'Lay us alongside at half-pistol shot!' he threw at the conn. He was going in to a lethal range. His gunners would know as well as the enemy that the first to reload would be doing the killing.

They came together and Kydd took in odd details: the superbly carved nymph figurehead, the extravagantly finished volutes and pilasters around the stern – this was an older vessel still retaining traces of grandeur even if coated now in dull paint. He noted, too, the sea-soldiers hurriedly lining its deck, the demonic activity at the guns, the single still figure on the quarterdeck.

And when fifty yards was reduced to the vision-filling deadly reality of twenty-five, *Tyger*'s guns were the first to speak. One – three together, five, more bellowing guns recoiling in smoke, frantic motion of their crews.

And then dark holes opposite, whole strakes beaten in, sudden swirls among the men on deck, ropes lashing wildly. The flash and roar of guns in return, vicious whirring of splinters, grunts and cries, the sound like an anvil of a gun being struck by a round-shot.

Dillon, beside Kydd, was pale-faced but keeping pace, his notebook clutched in a death grip. And Bray, the other side, his face red and alive with a ferocious animation, bawling at the men, his knuckles white around his sword-hilt.

Firing was general now, an insane bedlam of sound with the stink of powder catching in the throat, fierce cries from the guns below, the random crashes and squeals of battle beating at the senses. But with grim satisfaction Kydd noted that the slam and concussion of their own guns was increasing while that of the enemy was faltering.

It couldn't last – as sailors said, 'The hotter the war, the sooner the peace.' There would be some dramatic incident, an uncontrollable irruption in the striving that would send the unfortunate receiver reeling out of the fight, going down under a merciless succession of hammer blows from the survivor.

And so it happened, so fast as not to be comprehended at once. The battle-decider.

In a fearful crash and howl of splinters and skittering fragments *Tyger*'s wheel took a direct hit. From the forward end of the quarterdeck Kydd swung around in consternation. The wheel and binnacle was an unrecognisable stump. And of the helmsman Halgren and the quartermaster there was no sign.

In sick horror Kydd felt the frigate falter, lurching away from her opponent then, out of control, sliding back the other way. Through the smoke he saw snarling faces closing with death in their eyes, then came a dull crash and shudder as the two hulls touched and rebounded.

Tyger sheered off wildly and the other frigate fell away from the still stubbornly firing British ship. The following wind now became an adversary, catching her along her length and Kydd had no other alternative than to send men aloft to get in sail.

The change in fortunes could not have been more complete. From being near victory at the guns to slowing as a helpless cripple *Tyger* was now at the mercy of her enemies, two frigates who could take their pick of the angle of their crushing final attack. Would this see *Tyger* a mastless ruin in a last glorious blaze of defiance – or would she strike her flag first?

Wrung with emotion Kydd watched the enemy frigate curve away for the final assault – but it continued on, further and further in a meaningless cast away.

Unbelieving, Kydd gazed after the frigate, now half a mile and more on.

Royan had signals of some sort at her mizzen peak.

The implication broke in on him. They'd been spared. The senior commander had realised their helplessness and, object achieved, had summoned the other to continue the escorting of the far more valuable argosy.

'Rig emergency steering!' he barked. 'And clear these decks of this raffle.'

A massive tiller would be slotted into the rudder stock and

tackles ranged each side to take the immense strain, orders being passed from the quarterdeck by a chain of messengers. Crude, but it would bring *Tyger* alive again.

Apart from shot-holes now being plugged, and the boatswain's party in the rigging connecting parted and stranded lines, they had escaped the worst.

'Butcher's bill?' Kydd asked Bray quietly, remembering the absence of Halgren's reassuring bulk at the wheel.

'One killed, three under the knife.'

Kydd nodded sombrely. Everyone aboard had taken their chances equally in this fight and some must lose. That was the law of war – but could he ask more of his men?

'Tiller rigged, sir,' Bowden reported formally, looking closely at him with an odd expression. Others were gazing his way, even more from right forward. What was going on?

Over to starboard, now three or four miles distant, the three Frenchmen were well on their way.

And then he understood. The Tygers did not want to give up.

There was a boat compass where the binnacle had been and he glanced down at it. 'All sail, steer east b' south.'

Towards the enemy!

As the news spread a feral growl at the guns grew into a full-throated roar and in grim determination *Tyger*'s sails were spread one by one.

This time the two French frigates stood close in and protectively, ready for any move.

It was madness to join battle with two apparently undamaged opponents with the handicap of frail steering, but Fortune had two faces and Kydd was going to try.

Royan stood on, exactly between *Tyger* and her quarry, but the other fell back and readied for battle.

There were many more on its deck and he knew why: this

was going to be a finisher – a boarding and whatever the outcome, with another ready to follow. *Tyger* would be fighting for her life.

He kept a straight course for the Indiaman – it was easier on the men below at the tiller and, in any case, the enemy was most certainly going to come to him.

The French frigate clearly had it in mind to head for them close to the wind so it could lay alongside in the opposite direction. It began the rotation and bracing in to take up hard on the larboard tack, taking its time and— Slowly, gracefully, inevitably, its foremast arced down in a scythe of increasing ruin. It had taken a shot from *Tyger* unnoticed and, with the increasing strain of lying close-hauled, it had given way, the mast, spars, stays and shrouds all now a tangled mass on her deck and trailing in the water. The ship was comprehensively wrecked and was demonstrably out of the fight.

An unbelieving roar of cheering erupted from *Tyger* as they swept on past.

'Cease firing, you swabs!' Kydd bellowed at the gun captains unable to resist the target – there would be plenty to shoot at shortly and the odds, incredibly as it seemed, were now even.

Hope leaped again but the half-crippled *Tyger* was in no condition to face a fresh antagonist.

Royan eased back with a touch of helm to bring her unpro-tected stern away so her broadside could bear on the approaching British frigate.

Kydd knew there was no time for subtleties: this would be a brutal, direct smashing match in which courage, skill and raw endurance at the guns would decide the issue.

They came within range. A sinister quiet lay over the battle-field as the nerve of each captain was stretched to inhuman limits. The closer the deadlier, and that precious aimed broadside, the first and only one would tell.

Kydd held off – the French captain did not and, at a hundred yards, the enemy broadside opened up in a chaos of leaping gun-flash and instant roiling of smoke towards them.

The noise of its impact was an indescribable chorus of shattering timbers, mad twanging of severed ropes – and a helpless screaming, which ended in choking.

'Hold your fire!' Kydd bawled. This was now the other side of the coin, the payback for yielding the first volley. In the time it must take to reload their guns *Tyger* would close to half the range and, with her first aimed salvo, do twice the damage.

Tyger swung towards the French frigate, nearer still, and only then did Kydd let her roar. They were close enough that the round-shot strikes could be seen doing their work, each one telling in an avalanche of destruction, leaving wreckage, bodies, dismounted guns, flailing ropes.

Peering through the clearing smoke, he looked for a settler, a stroke of such weight and effect it would affect the outcome. But what he saw on its quarterdeck brought a chill of premonition. Their officers were pointing, gesturing in his direction.

Royan began sheering off, not in fright or retreat but because it had seen something – and that had to be *Tyger*'s smashed wheel, the giveaway stump that told them the British frigate was steering by tiller tackle below, a fearful disadvantage. Before, she could pirouette to take up a winning raking position or slew about to avoid a broadside but now she couldn't – and the Frenchman could.

Already it was pulling away in the first act of circling *Tyger* to lunge at will and the fight now was as good as over.

After all their suffering! A madness seized Kydd, consuming

him until his ears roared with the injustice of it all. Instinctively he bellowed, 'Hard a-larboard! Hard over for your lives!'

The faithful frigate answered her powerful rudder nobly and steadily tracked around. 'Away boarders! Every man who can carry a weapon, follow me!'

A swelling cheer rose, joyous, insane, murderous. A running crowd snatched cutlasses and pistols from the arms chest, pikes from their stands at the mast and seemingly of its own volition Kydd's precious Toledo sword leaped into his hand.

From nowhere Halgren lurched into view swinging a cutlass. A livid bruise covered half his face to disappear below his shirt but his eyes glittered in unholy dedication. And at the last minute Stirk and Doud burst up from below and took position with naked blades.

It happened quickly. *Tyger*'s swinging bowsprit swept around and, like a giant spear, rammed itself across the main deck of *Royan*. It carried away lines in a vicious tangle, timbers crushed and splintered, and by the time the shoulder of her new-strengthened bows had ground to a stop against the Frenchman's lighter side, the two were locked in a hellish embrace.

'*Go – Tygers, with me!*' Kydd yelled, and raced down to heave himself up on to the bowsprit, which led, like a bridge, into the heart of the enemy.

His feet sure, from working aloft those times in swaying darkness, he ran out, the ruin of *Royan*'s boats beneath him, until he reached the far gangway, then dropped lightly to the deck, his sword out and questing.

They could not have achieved a better situation – the spearing bowsprit had effectively cut off the fore part of the ship from the captain and command group on the quarter-deck, leaving them leaderless. He would now speed down to confront them, and Bray, behind him, would have the sense to go down the other gangway forward to deal with the bulk of the crew.

With a ringing war cry, Kydd flung himself towards the darting figures in the dissipating smoke. As it cleared he saw, with a lurch, that they were considerably outnumbered. Nevertheless they spread out across the deck, Halgren to his left and . . . and to the right a crouching figure with a patch flicked up over his eye.

'Nicholas!' he gasped, but the enemy were on them and he was being pressed by a French officer, who thrust and slashed with a maniacal fury. It was his undoing for Kydd's cool parrying tired him and, picking his time, *Tyger*'s captain lunged beneath his guard and pierced his shoulder. The sword, a wicked-looking rapier, clattered down and the man fell to his knees.

Another officer ran forward but Renzi had scooped up the sword and with a muttered 'A trifle more to my taste,' stood to meet him, the rapier in faultless challenge. The officer, too late mistaking his clothing for that of a common seaman, made arrogantly to slash but Renzi, in one movement, effortlessly got inside and transfixed the man's throat, letting him fall in a gurgle of blood.

It was the turn of the tide.

Pace by pace the Tygers advanced together, hewing and gashing, wounding and slitting in a fury until, quite unexpectedly, the last of the enemy threw down their weapons.

'*Je me rends!*'

'It's Jimmy Rounds, then, sir,' Stirk said happily, wiping his bloodied cutlass on a convenient corpse.

Kydd couldn't speak, the moment so overwhelming.

Furtively, Renzi flicked down the eye-patch. 'Not a word to Cecilia, brother,' he muttered.

Chapter 67

With Bray taking possession of the frigate, *Tyger* was extricated from her situation. That the Indiaman was now a fleeing dot on the horizon was not a problem – they knew exactly where it was headed and took their time with jury-rigging *Tyger* for the intercepting.

And at a little before noon the following day the big ship lay sulkily under *Tyger*'s guns.

Kydd himself took away the cutter with picked men and, in short order, had the crew assembled on deck under guard.

There was no point in delaying. It was the work of minutes to enter the hold, stand on the ladder and look down in the musty dimness at the countless rope-tied crates, casks, barrels and coffers. This was the unbearable moment when they stood to learn the reality of what they'd fought for, whether it was treasure or trifles, loot or mere war stores.

For Kydd time stood still: his life could go one way . . . or the other.

'Mr Stirk,' he said huskily. 'Open me that trunk.' He pointed to the nearest.

'Aye aye, sir!' The big man jumped into the hold and, with his cutlass, eagerly sawed through the rope with its officious label carefully attached.

Kydd leaned forward to see. An obliging seaman held a lanthorn out.

Inside was only a floor covering, a carpet. And a fairly ordinary one at that.

Kydd grimaced. This was plunder, certainly, but war loot of the ordinary sort belonging to the common soldiery.

A wave of near desperate disappointment rushed over him. This was nothing more than—

'Sir. It's got summat inside,' Stirk said in surprise, peering in. 'Wait on, sir, I'll heave it out for yez.'

He eased the roll out into the open. It was held closed by neatly hitched string. Plying his knife quickly he then threw back the carpet.

Nestling in a gleaming row were four candlesticks. Gold, each with precious stones set in the base, a display of sumptuous elegance that had no doubt once graced the banquet table of a grandee of Spain.

A gasp of awe went up and the lanthorn light trembled.

'Another!' Kydd ordered, his voice hoarse with tension.

Stirk climbed over to a larger container and got to work. It was a rectangular crate in rough-sawn timbers.

'Don't crowd me, mates,' Stirk grumbled, at the press of spectators who craned over to see.

It was more carpet. And underneath, in tidy, serried rows was an endless succession of gold and silver cutlery packed tightly together.

Kydd held rigid while emotion flooded over him. Others pushed past him to hack at the cords and fastenings of other crates, whoops of joy announcing another fine hoard.

He felt a touch on his arm as someone leaned forward to

whisper in his ear. 'Dear fellow, this is not to be thought prize, merely a restoration to the Spanish Crown.'

'I don't care what it is,' Kydd managed. 'I'm saved, Nicholas.'

'Yes, dear friend. And going on precedent I'd be surprised should you get less than three per centum. That is to say I believe I'm looking at one who can only be described as a moderately rich nabob.'

'Persephone, she—'

'Yes, but, brother, do leave these baubles to others. I've a fancy where there may be something more suited to your elevation.'

Kydd followed Renzi into the deserted captain's cabin, a large and disgracefully well-appointed space. Renzi headed for the after end, where a hatch, flush with the deck, led to the lazarette, a discreet space for cabin stores. It was generally the most intimate and private stowage to be found in a ship.

Pushing aside a table and rolling back the floor covering, Kydd deftly hooked it open and peered into the dark recess, his heart thudding.

'Yes.' He gulped. 'Down there. Bear a hand, Nicholas.'

They squeezed into the lazarette. Using the straps at each end of the large, heavy chest there they levered it up on to the deck and dragged it over to the side. It was not locked, merely secured with a slide catch.

Slowly and reverently Kydd pulled it back and opened the lid.

Gleaming in the light, a fortune in Spanish escudos, *reales* and doubloons lay before them. Wrenched from chancelleries and treasure-houses from Madrid to Aranjuez, the patrimony of Spain that had been on its way to Napoleon Bonaparte.

A sea of gold.

Author's Note

Of all the books so far in the Kydd series this has been the most complex but rewarding to research and write.

Far from being a fading stalemate after Trafalgar, the war in both a maritime and a general sense was intensifying. Beneath the familiar ebb and flow of military fortunes the older and simpler world of the eighteenth century was being inexorably replaced by a different, more ruthless and thrusting scene that today we recognise only too well.

Yet it was the old and tradition-steeped nation of Great Britain that prevailed, not revolutionary France with a dictator at the helm. It was financial acumen that largely achieved this, and continues to the present day with the City of London still pre-eminent among nations.

What astonished me was the titanic achievement of funding the entire war with a tiny income tax and motley assortment of other revenues while dealing with a national debt of a staggering order. Given a multiplier of some one hundred to the pound between then and now, the enlightened war leaders of Britain kept their nerve as the debt mounted to 212 per cent of GDP. This is far higher than at any other time, including the two twentieth-century world wars. At the height of the financial crisis of 2008 the figure was about 70 per cent. Kydd's investment of choice, consols or government-issued consolidated annuities, was a wise one for, as a matter of fact, his three per cent consols were not to be finally redeemed until July 2015, an extraordinary performance since 1757.

Where this realm intersected with the rising power of international banking houses, some extraordinary events were taking place, few of which saw the light of day. Possibly the most notorious was the handling of the Louisiana Purchase by the United States in which payment by American bonds in wartime Paris was realised into gold at Bonaparte's request by Barings of London through Hope, its Dutch subsidiary. The proceeds were at once put by Bonaparte towards the following year's projected invasion of England.

Yet another project saw a substantial part of Spain's last subsidy payable to the French empire secretly loaded aboard the British frigate *Diana* in silver specie, requiring insurance through Lloyd's of London in the amount of £80 million at today's value, the largest single-voyage risk ever insured in those wars but representing the British proceeds of an ultra-clandestine deal with Bonaparte to split the amount in return for safe passage for the remainder.

Lloyd's itself continues as before in its splendid new premises holding to its hallowed traditions. There is still a head-waiter in charge, the wording on policies is much as it always has been, and underwriters meet brokers in their boxes, as Kydd did. Its rise and rise during the Napoleonic wars is a saga in itself, and more than one historian has stated that the war was won in the Great Room of Lloyd's where British ships were sent to sea for a few per cent premium while the French could find no house willing to insure either them or their cargoes.

Before the end of the war Lloyd's was, quite remarkably, accepting French proposals, thereby insuring enemy vessels against war risks from their own side – for a fat premium, of course. A test case was adjudged that, if the policy was drawn up in proper form, the underwriter was liable for any loss, the fact that it was an enemy vessel being neither here nor there. Lloyd's duly paid up.

It was still a time of individuals of colour, excess and originality. From Basque Roads one comes especially to my mind – Admiral Eliab Harvey. I was brought up to revere him in my schooldays at Harvey Grammar School, whose motto to this day remains '*Temeraire, Redoutable et Fougueux*' after Harvey's action at Trafalgar. And it is also noteworthy that the captain of the battleship *Donegal* was the *Bounty* mutineer later sentenced to death and reprieved, Peter Heywood.

But it's difficult to find there one more nonconformist and erratic than Lord Cochrane. Famously later found guilty in a Stock Exchange fraud, his naval genius was undeniable. Less so was his personal judgement. To plumb the depths of his character at this remove is difficult and requires extended explanation, largely associated with his complicated childhood.

Here we have a man who, within months of his legendary successes on the coasts of Spain, was barricading himself in Piccadilly with the most noted Radicals of the day while outside cannon were brought up and Life Guard cavalry gave charge. It was too much even for the fellow extremists inside with him when he began enthusiastically to place barrels of gunpowder about the façade of the building to bring it down on the assaulting forces of the law, as if it were yet another fortress in Catalonia.

His power of invention was unquestioned: at about this

time he submitted a plan to the Prince Regent for a devilish infernal machine, whose main elements were a gigantic mortar and deadly poisonous sulphur gas. In horror the prince hurriedly passed it on to the Admiralty who, terrified by its implications, at once declared it a secret of the highest order and hid it away. Much later Cochrane, as a crusty old admiral, demanded it be dusted off and considered at the time of the Crimean War, but it was too much even for a later generation and it was promptly shelved in perpetuity.

His personal courage was of the highest order. After Basque Roads it went about the fleet that, having lit the fuse and abandoned his explosion vessel to flee in his boat, Cochrane saw that the ship's dog had been left aboard. Without hesitating, he made the boat return, boarded, seized the dog and put off again. Ironically that probably saved their lives for the gigantic detonation threw the wreckage over their heads and into the sea beyond.

The Gambier court-martial has divided historians and the navy ever since. My own take, in line with modern scholarship, is that it seems plain that the trial was indeed rigged: false charts produced, witnesses sent to sea, logs tampered with and interest at work at the highest. Yet it could never have succeeded in its object: it would have been utterly intolerable in war-time to allow junior officers to bring courts-martial against their seniors for their behaviour in any action with which they disagreed.

However, I'm content to let Napoleon Bonaparte have the last word from St Helena: 'If Cochrane had been properly supported he would have destroyed my fleet . . . The French admiral was an *imbécile* but yours was as bad.'

To all those who assisted me in the research for this book I am deeply grateful. My appreciation also goes to my agent, Isobel Dixon, my editor, Oliver Johnson, designer, Larry

Rostant, for another stunning cover, and copy editor, Hazel Orme. And, as always, my heartfelt thanks to my wife and literary partner, Kathy.

Anchors aweigh for Kydd's next voyage!

Glossary

adze	two-handed axe-like tool with broad blade set at right angles; used by shipwright to shape spars, keel, curved timbers
barky	Latin *barca*, ship; pet term for one's own ship
beakhead	carved-work forward, where bowsprit is rooted in the ship
Blue Peter	blue flag with white centre; when hoisted, ship will sail within twenty-four hours
bobbery	a commotion, either joyous as on a spree or in disorder as in a riot
bomb	vessel fitted with mortars instead of guns; intended for bombardment of shore
bum-boat	from bombard, beer provision boat; one trading in small stuff with shore and offering communication
butcher's bill	dark humour of asking for the list of casualties after an action
chamade	drum beat to signal attention that a parley is requested of an enemy
chop house	common fast-food outlet in the eighteenth century, selling, for example, cheap mutton chops and onions
chuckle-headed loon	fool; said to be the result of having a head twisted like a flat-fish
cobbs	cash, coin; from Spanish cob coin
conn, the	around the helm; the responsibility of keeping the ship on its proper course
coxcomb	from the red comb growing from the head of a cock; pretentious fop
cuffin	friendly term for acquaintance

cully	neutral term for acquaintance
cut a feather	a ship going fast enough to raise white water at her forefoot
dandy prat	a foolish one excessively concerned for his appearance
defile	narrow pass or gorge
Drake's Leat	a water supply for ships led from the moors above Plymouth; instigated by Sir Francis Drake after his voyage around the world
drogher	a barge rigged as a schooner or cutter used for low-value bulk freighting
ell	measurement of length a little under four feet
fancy, the	the high-life out for a good time
fettle	from horse handling: to condition, repair
flam	fool, cheat
footwaling	lining of planking over frames in hold floor to ease walking, prevent contents falling between the timbers
fore-peak	the furthest forward in the hold, where the bow comes together to make a triangular space
fret	a sea condition where the waves have not risen so much before a blow but are irritable, fretful
Great Panjandrum	from Samuel Foote; a grand and often self-important official
grego	Latin *graecus*, military cloak; hooded thick fabric coat
griff	what is going on, the general view
grig	a happy-go-lucky and lively soul
gunroom	officers' accommodation and dining place in a frigate, equivalent of the wardroom of a larger rated ship
hookum snivey	on the lookout for a bit of thievery
hoy	from 'hoy' call to stop it; small sloop-rigged vessel plying out to ships
infernal machine	device so terrible as to remind one of the Hadean regions
jobbery	making profit out of public office
knaggy	rough as in knots in a length of rope, poor condition
lading	what cargo a vessel is carrying
leaguer	the ground tier of casks stowed lowest, the biggest at 159-gallon capacity
Levanter	in Gibraltar, a wind from the east, notionally the Levant at the other end of the Mediterranean
lighter	large heavily built flat-bottomed boat to carry goods from shore to a ship
looby	awkward person who is also lazy
Ned Ludd	eighteenth-century mill worker, who incited bands of workers to destroy machines he said were taking their jobs
maul	heavy hammer used for driving treenails, bolts, etc.

merde	French swear word
mole	long stone pier in entrance of harbour or one forming an inner harbour
offing	distance from a danger, land, for example
on the beach	for a seaman, left unable to get a berth in a ship for any reason
orbis terrarum parsimoniae	Latin, the world considered as an economic whole
ostler	stableman at an inn
pelf	derogatory term for money or wealth
picquet	outguard sentinel in a military formation
pinnace	carvel-built ship's boat smaller than a cutter
planksheer	covering of any timber-heads about the outer hull
politesse de coeur	politeness coming from the heart; innate breeding
post-house	an inn or house providing a change of horses for a post-chaise
privateer	private man-o'-war whose commission (a letter of marque) entitles them to take as prize any enemy ship
quambles	ill-defined ailment for skulking purposes
real, reales	silver coins in the Spanish currency: 20 *reales* = 1 peso; 100 *reales* = £1
roborant	restorative drink
rout	disorderly retreat or informal social gathering
sally-port	opening in fortification to allow troops to sortie; scuttle cut in side of fireship to allow crew to escape; man-o'-war steps in Portsmouth
sapper	soldier skilled in advancing a siege by means of excavations
sawbones	pejorative term for surgeon
scabbard	sheath for the sword
scantlings	the dimensions taken off timbers when in place and functional
schuyt	galliot-rigged vessel peculiar to the Dutch
scrowl	decorative but plain carving in place of a figurehead
Season, the	the London social season, roughly January to July
shab	from shabbaroon: drab, ill-favoured person
sheets	those lines from the lower corner of a square sail that lead to leeward, the tack to windward
slivey	tricky, slimy fellow
slush	the fat rising to surface of boiling meat, a cook's prerogative
soundings	where the bottomless depths of the ocean rise to the Continental shelf of Europe, where a sounding line will reach the sea-bed
specie	currency in the form of hard coin as opposed to bills of exchange, etc.
spume	sea froth carried into the air by a gale

stingo	particularly strong and robust beer, as opposed to small beer
tarpaulin	canvas impregnated by tar or paint to make it watertight; said of an officer rising from the ranks because he still smells of it
try-line	lines that may be operated independently of another
vice-president, Mr Vice	in an officer's mess, the youngest member tasked off to propose the loyal toast
watch and watch	watch on, watch off
wherry	from Latin *horia*, oared craft; small oared open boat to carry passengers
wight	old English *wiht*, a human being in the round